Sir Brook Fossbrooke
Volume I

by

Charles James Lever

Sir Brook Fossbrooke
Volume I
by Charles James Lever

ISBN: 978-93-67147-17-7

Published by

DOUBLE 9 BOOKS

2/13-B, Ansari Road
Daryaganj, New Delhi – 110002
info@double9books.com
www.double9books.com
Tel. 011-40042856

ABOUT THE AUTHOR

Charles James Lever (1806-1872) was an Irish novelist and editor. He gained fame with his early novels "Harry Lorrequer" (1839) and "Charles O'Malley" (1841), which were noted for their adventurous plots and humorous style. Lever spent much of his life abroad, particularly in continental Europe, which influenced the settings and themes of his later works. His novels often reflect his Irish heritage and expatriate experiences, providing a unique perspective on the social and political issues of his time. Lever's works often drew on his experiences in Ireland and Europe, blending wit, humor, and a keen observation of social and political issues of his time. Some of his other notable works include "Charles O'Malley, the Irish Dragoon" (1841), "Tom Burke of Ours" (1844), and "The Daltons" (1852). His writing style is characterized by its energetic narrative and engaging, sometimes larger-than-life, characters. Lever spent much of his later life on the continent, particularly in Italy, where he continued to write and edit for various periodicals. Despite the decline in his popularity towards the end of his life, Lever remains an important figure in 19th-century Irish literature. Lever initially pursued a career in medicine but eventually turned to writing, finding success with his first major novel, "The Confessions of Harry Lorrequer" (1839), which was serialized and gained him widespread popularity.

CONTENTS

To PHILIP ROSE, Esq.

My dear Rose,—You have often stopped me when endeavouring to express all the gratitude I felt towards you. You cannot do so now, nor prevent my telling aloud how much I owe-how much I esteem you. These volumes were not without interest for me as I wrote them, but they yielded me no such pleasure as I now feel in dedicating them to you; and, with this assurance, believe me,

Your affectionate Friend,
CHARLES LEVER.
Spezia, October 20. 1866.

CHAPTER I
AFTER MESS

The mess was over, and the officers of H. M.'s —th were grouped in little knots and parties, sipping their coffee, and discussing the arrangements for the evening. Their quarter was that pleasant city of Dublin, which, bating certain exorbitant demands in the matter of field-day and guard-mounting, stands pre-eminently first in military favor.

"Are you going to that great ball in Merrion Square?" asked one., "Not so lucky; not invited."

"I got a card," cried a third; "but I 've just heard it's not to come off. It seems that the lady's husband is a judge. He's Chief something or other; and he has been called away."

"Nothing of the kind, Tomkins; unless you call a summons to the next world being called away. The man is dangerously ill. He was seized with paralysis on the Bench yesterday, and, they say, can't recover."

There now ensued an animated conversation as to whether, on death vacancies, the men went up by seniority at the bar, or whether a subaltern could at once spring up to the top of the regiment.

"Suppose," said one, "we were to ask the Colonel's guest his opinion. The old cove has talked pretty nigh of everything in this world during dinner; what if we were to ask him about Barons of the Exchequer?"

"Who is he? what is he?" asked another.

"The Colonel called him Sir Brook Fossbrooke; that's all I know."

"Colonel Cave told me," whispered the Major, "that he was the fastest man on town some forty years ago."

"I think he must have kept over the wardrobe of that brilliant period," said another. "I never saw a really swallow-tailed coat before."

"His ring amused *me*. It is a small smoothing-iron, with a coat-of-arms on it. Hush! here he comes."

The man who now joined the group was a tall, gaunt figure, with a high narrow head, from which the hair was brushed rigidly back to fall behind in something like an old-fashioned queue. His eyes were black, and surmounted with massive and much-arched eyebrows; a strongly marked mouth, stern, determined, and, except in speaking, almost cruel in expression, and a thin-pointed projecting chin, gave an air of severity and strong will to features which, when he conversed, displayed a look of courteous deference, and that peculiar desire to please that we associate with a bygone school of breeding. He was one of those men, and very distinctive are they, with whom even the least cautious take no liberties, nor venture upon any familiarity. The eccentricities of determined men are very often indications of some deep spirit beneath, and not, as in weaker natures, mere emanations of vanity or offsprings of self-indulgence.

If he was, beyond question, a gentleman, there were also signs about him of narrow fortune: his scrupulously white shirt was not fine, and the seams of his well-brushed coat showed both care and wear.

He had joined the group, who were talking of the coming Derby when the Colonel came up. "I have sent for the man we want, Fossbrooke. I'm not a fisherman myself; but they tell me he knows every lake, river, and rivulet in the island. He has sat down to whist, but we 'll have him here presently."

"On no account; don't disturb his game for me."

"Here he comes. Trafford, I want to present you to a very old friend of mine, Sir Brook Fossbrooke,—as enthusiastic an angler as yourself. He has the ambition to hook an Irish salmon. I don't suppose any one can more readily help him on the road to it."

The young man thus addressed was a large, strongly, almost heavily built young fellow, but with that looseness of limb and freedom that showed activity had not been sacrificed to mere power. He had a fine, frank, handsome face, blue-eyed and bold-looking; and as he stood to receive the Colonel's orders, there was in his air that blending of deference and good-humored carelessness that made up his whole nature.

It was plain to see in him one easy to persuade, impossible to coerce; a fellow with whom the man he liked could do anything, bat one perfectly unmanageable if thrown into the wrong hands. He was the second son of a very rich baronet, but made the mistake of believing he had as much right to extravagance as his elder brother, and, having persisted in this error during two years in the Life Guards, had been sent to do the double penance of an infantry regiment and an Irish station; two inflictions which, it was believed, would have sufficed to calm down the ardor of the most impassioned spendthrift. He looked at Fossbrooke from head to foot. It was not exactly the stamp of man he would have selected for companionship, but he saw at once that he was distinctively a gentleman, and then the prospect of a few days away from regimental duty was not to be despised, and he quickly replied that both he and his tackle were at Sir Brook's disposal. "If we could run down to Killaloe, sir," added he, turning to the Colonel, "we might be almost sure of some sport."

"Which means that you want two days' leave, Trafford."

"No, sir, four. It will take a day at least to get over there; another will be lost in exploring; all these late rains have sent such a fresh into the Shannon there's no knowing where to try."

"You see, Fossbrooke, what a casuistical companion I've given you. I 'll wager you a five-pound note that if you come back without a rise he 'll have an explanation that will perfectly explain it was the best thing could have happened."

"I am charmed to travel in such company," said Sir Brook, bowing. "The gentleman has already established a claim to my respect for him."

Trafford bowed too, and looked not at all displeased at the compliment. "Are you an early riser, sir?" asked he.

"I am anything, sir, the occasion exacts; but when I have an early start before me, I usually sit up all night."

"My own plan too," cried Trafford. "And there's Aubrey quite ready to join us. Are you a whister, Sir Brook?"

"At your service. I play all games."

"Is he a whister?" repeated the Colonel. "Ask Harry Greville, ask Tom Newenham, what they say of him at Grahams? Trafford, my boy, you may possibly give him a hint about gray hackles, but I 'll be shot if you do about the odd trick."

"If you 'll come over to my room, Sir Brook, we 'll have a rubber, and I 'll give orders to have my tax-cart ready for us by daybreak," said Trafford; and, Fossbrooke promising to be with him so soon as he had given his servant his orders, they parted.

"And are you as equal to this sitting up all night as you used to be, Fossbrooke?" asked the Colonel.

"I don't smoke as many cigars as formerly, and I am a little more choice about my tobacco. I avoid mulled port, and take weak brandy-and-water; and I believe in all other respects I 'm pretty much where I was when we met last,—I think it was at Ceylon?"

"I wish I could say as much for myself. You are talking of thirty-four years ago."

"My secret against growing old is to do a little of everything. It keeps the sympathies wider, makes a man more accessible to other men, and keeps him from dwelling too much on himself. But tell me about my young companion; is he one of Sir Hugh's family?"

"His second son; not unlike to be his eldest, for George has gone to Madeira with very little prospect of recovery. This is a fine lad; a little wild, a little careless of money, but the very soul of honor and right-mindedness. They sent him to me as a sort of incurable, but I have nothing but good to say of him."

"There 'a great promise in a fellow when he can be a scamp and a man of honor. When dissipations do not degrade and excesses do not corrupt a man, there is a grand nature ever beneath."

"Don't tell him that, Fossbrooke," said the Colonel, laughing.

"I am not likely to do so," said he, with a grim smile. "I am glad, too, to meet his father's son; we were at Christ Church together; and now I see he has the family good looks. 'Le beau Trafford' was a proverb in Paris once."

"Do you ever forget a man?" asked the Colonel, in some curiosity.

"I believe not. I forget books, places, dates occasionally, but never people. I met an old schoolfellow t'other day at Dover whom I never saw since we were boys. He had gone down in the world, and was acting as one of the 'commissionnaires' they call them, who take your keys to the Custom-house to have your luggage examined; and when he came to ask me to employ him, I said, "'What! ain't you Jemmy Harper?' 'And who the devil are you?' said he. 'Fossbrooke,' said I. 'Not "Wart"?' said he. That was my school nickname, from a wart I once had on my chin. 'Ay, to be sure,' said I, 'Wart.' I wish you saw the delight of the old dog. I made him dine with us. Lord Brackington was with me, and enjoyed it all immensely."

"And what had brought him so low?"

"He was cursed, he said, with a strong constitution; all the other fellows of his set had so timed it that when they had nothing to live on they ceased to live; but Jemmy told us he never had such an appetite as now; that he passed from fourteen to sixteen hours a day on the pier in all weathers; and as to gout he firmly believed it all came of the adulterated wines of the great wine-merchants. British gin he maintained to be the wholesomest liquor in existence."

"I wonder how fellows bear up under such reverses as that," said the Colonel.

"My astonishment is rather," cried Fossbrooke, "how men can live on in a monotony of well-being, getting fatter, older, and more unwieldy, and with only such experiences of life as a well-fed fowl might have in a hencoop."

"I know that's *your* theory," said the other, laughing.

"Well, no man can say that I have not lived up to my convictions; and for myself, I can aver I have thoroughly enjoyed my intercourse with the world, and like it as well to-day as on the first morning I made my bow to it."

"Listen to this, young gentlemen," said the Colonel, turning to his officers, who now gathered around them. "Now and then I hear some of you complaining of being bored or wearied,—sick of this, tired of that; here's my friend, who knows the whole thing better than any of us, and he declares that the world is the best of all possible worlds, and that so far from familiarity with it inspiring disgust with life, his enjoyment of it is as racy as when first he knew it."

"It is rather hard to ask these gentlemen to take me as a guide on trust," said Fossbrooke; "but I have known the fathers of most of those I see around me, and could call many of them as witnesses to character. Major Aylmer, your father and I went up the Nile together, when people talked of it as a journey. Captain Harris, I'm sure I am not wrong in saying you are the son of Godfrey Harris, of Harrisburg. Your father was my friend on the day I wounded Lord Ecclesmore. I see four or five others too,—so like old companions that I find it hard to believe I am not back again in the old days when I was as young as themselves; and yet I'm not very certain if I would like to exchange my present quiet enjoyment as a looker-on for all that active share I once took in life and its pleasures."

Something in the fact that their fathers had lived in his intimacy, something in his manner,—a very courteous manner it was,—and something in the bold, almost defiant bearing of the old man, vouching for great energy and dignity together, won greatly upon the young men, and they gathered around him. He was, however, summoned away by a message from Trafford to say that the whist-party waited for him, and he took his leave with a stately courtesy and withdrew.

"There goes one of the strangest fellows in Christendom," said the Colonel, as the other left the room. "He has already gone through three fortunes; he dissipated the first, speculated and lost the second, and the third he, I might say, gave away in acts of benevolence and kindness,— leaving himself so ill off that I actually heard the other day that some friend had asked for the place of barrack-master at Athlone for him; but on coming over to see the place, he found a poor fellow with a wife and five children a candidate for it; so he retired in his favor, and is content, as you see, to go out on the world, and take his chance with it."

Innumerable questions pressed on the Colonel to tell more of his strange friend; he had, however, little beyond hearsay to give them. Of his own experiences, he could only say that when first he met him it was at Ceylon, where he had come in a yacht like a sloop of war to hunt elephants,—the splendor of his retinue and magnificence of his suite giving him the air of a royal personage,—and indeed the gorgeous profusion of his presents to the King and the chief personages of the court went far to impress this notion. "I never met him since," said the Colonel, "till this morning, when he walked into my room, dusty and travel-stained, to say, 'I just heard your name, and thought I 'd ask you to give me my dinner to-day.' I owe him a great many,—not to say innumerable other attentions; and his last act on leaving Trincomalee was to present me with an Arab charger, the most perfect animal I ever mounted. It is therefore a real pleasure to me to receive him. He is a thoroughly fine-hearted fellow, and, with all his eccentricities, one of the noblest natures I ever met. The only flaw in his frankness is as to his age; nobody has ever been able to get it from him. You heard him talk of your fathers,—he might talk of your grandfathers; and he would, too, if we had only the opportunity to lead him on to it. I know of my own knowledge that he lived in the Carlton House coterie, not a man of which except himself survives, and I have heard him give imitations of Burke, Sheridan, Gavin Hamilton, and Pitt, that none but one who had seen them could have accomplished. And now that I have told you all this, will one of you step over to Trafford's rooms, and whisper him a hint to make his whist-points as low as he can; and, what is even of more importance, to take care lest any strange story Sir Brook may tell—and he is full of them—meet a sign of incredulity, still less provoke any quizzing? The slightest shade of such a provocation would render him like a madman."

The Major volunteered to go on this mission, which indeed any of the others would as willingly have accepted, for the old man had interested them deeply, and they longed to hear more about him.

CHAPTER II
THE SWAN'S NEST

As the Shannon draws near Killaloe, the wild character of the mountain scenery, the dreary wastes and desolate islands which marked Lough Derg, disappear, and give way to gently sloping lawns, dotted over with well-grown timber, well-kept demesnes, spacious country-houses, and a country which, in general, almost recalls the wealth and comfort of England.

About a mile above the town, in a little bend of the river forming a small bay, stands a small but pretty house, with a skirt of rich wood projecting at the back, while the lawn in front descends by an easy slope to the river.

Originally a mere farmhouse, the taste of an ingenious owner had taken every advantage of its irregular outline, and converted it into something Elizabethan in character, a style admirably adapted to the site, where all the features of rich-colored landscape abounded, and where varied foliage, heathy mountain, and eddying river, all lent themselves to make up a scene of fresh and joyous beauty.

In the marvellous fertility of the soil, too, was found an ally to every prospect of embellishment. Sheltered from north and east winds, plants grew here in the open air, which in less favored spots needed the protection of the conservatory; and thus in the neatly shaven lawn were seen groups of blossoming shrubs or flowers of rare excellence, and the camellia and the salvia and the oleander blended with the tulip, the moss-rose, and the carnation, to stud the grass with their gorgeous colors.

Over the front of the cottage, for cottage it really was, a South American creeper, a sort of acanthus, grew, its crimson flowers hanging in rich profusion over cornice and architrave; while a passion-tree of great age covered the entire porch, relieving with its softened tints the almost over-brilliancy of the southern plant.

Seen from the water,—and it came suddenly into view on rounding a little headland,—few could forbear from an exclamation of wonder and admiration at this lovely spot; nor could all the pretentious grandeur of the rich-wooded parks, nor all the more imposing architecture of the great houses, detract from the marvellous charm of this simple home.

A tradition of a swan carried away by some rising of the river from the Castle of Portumna, and swept down the lake till it found refuge in the little bay, had given the name to the place, and for more than a hundred years was it known as the Swan's Nest. The Swan, however, no longer existed, though a little thatched edifice at the water-side marked the spot it had once inhabited, and sustained the truth of the legend.

The owner of the place was a Dr. Lendrick: he had come to it about twenty years before the time at which our story opens,—a widower with two children, a son and a daughter. He was a perfect stranger to all the neighborhood, though by name well known as the son of a distinguished judge, Baron Lendrick of the Court of Exchequer.

It was rumored about, that, having displeased his father, first by adopting medicine instead of law as his profession, and subsequently by marrying a portionless girl of humble family, the Baron had ceased to recognize him in any way. Making a settlement of a few hundreds a year on him, he resolved to leave the bulk of his fortune to a step-son, the child of his second wife, a Colonel Sewell, then in India.

It was with no thought of practising his profession that Dr. Lendrick had settled in the neighborhood; but as he was always ready to assist the poor by his advice and skill, and as the reputation of his great ability gradually got currency, he found himself constrained to yield to the insistence of his neighbors, and consent to practise generally. There were many things which made this course unpalatable to him. He was by nature shy, timid, and retiring; he was fastidiously averse to a new acquaintanceship; he had desired, besides, to live estranged from the world, devoting himself entirely to the education of his children; and he neither liked the forced publicity he became exposed to, nor that life of servitude which leaves the doctor at the hourly mercy of the world around him.

If he yielded, therefore, to the professional calls upon him, he resisted totally all social claims: he went nowhere but as the doctor.

No persuasion, no inducement, could prevail on him to dine out; no exigency of time or season prevent him returning to his home at night. There were in his neighborhood one or two persons whose rank might have, it was supposed, influenced him in some degree to comply with their requests,— and, certainly, whose desire for his society would have left nothing undone to secure it; but he was as obdurate to them as to others, and the Earl of Drum-carran and Sir Reginald Lacy, of Lacy Manor, were not a whit more successful in their blandishments than the Vicar of Killaloe—old Bob Mills, as he was irreverently called—or Lendrick's own colleague, Dr. Tobin, who, while he respected his superior ability and admitted his knowledge, secretly hated him as only a rival doctor knows how to hate a brother practitioner.

For the first time for many years had Dr. Lendrick gone up to Dublin. A few lines from an old family physician, Dr. Beattie, had, however, called him up to town. The Chief Baron had been taken ill in Court, and was conveyed home in a state of insensibility. It was declared that he had rallied and passed a favorable night; but as he was a man of very advanced age, at no time strong, and ever unsparing of himself in the arduous labors of his office, grave doubts were felt that he would ever again resume his seat on the Bench. Dr. Beattie well knew the long estrangement that had separated the father from the son; and although, perhaps, the most intimate friend the Judge had in the world, he never had dared to interpose a word or drop a hint as to the advisability of reconciliation.

Sir William Lendrick was, indeed, a man whom no amount of intimacy could render his friends familiar with. He was positively charming to mere acquaintanceship,—his manner was a happy blending of deference with a most polished wit Full of bygone experiences and reminiscences of interesting people and events, he never overlaid conversation by their mention, but made them merely serve to illustrate the present, either by contrast or resemblance. All this to the world and society was he; to the inmates of his house he was a perfect terror! It was said his first wife had died of a broken heart; his second, with a spirit fierce and combative as his own, had quarrelled with him so often, so seriously, and so hopelessly, that for the last fifteen years of life they had occupied separate houses, and only met as acquaintances, accepting and sending invitations to each other, and outwardly observing all the usages of a refined courtesy.

This was the man of whom Dr. Beattie wrote: "I cannot presume to say that he is *more* favorably disposed towards you than he has shown himself for years, but I would strenuously advise your being here, and sufficiently near, so that if a happier disposition should occur, or an opportunity arise to bring you once more together, the fortunate moment should not be lost. Come up, then, at once, come to my house, where your room is ready for you, and where you will neither be molested by visitors nor interfered with. Manage too, if you can, to remain here for some days."

It is no small tribute to the character of filial affection when one can say, and say truthfully, that scarcely any severity on a parent's part effaces the love that was imbibed in infancy, and that struck root in the heart before it could know what unkindness was! Over and over again in life have I witnessed this deep devotion. Over and over again have I seen a clinging affection to a memory which nothing short of a hallowed tie could have made so dear,—a memory that retained whatever could comfort and sustain, and held nothing that recalled shame or sorrow.

Dr. Lendrick went up to town full of such emotions. All the wrong—it was heavy wrong too—he had suffered was forgotten, all the Injustice wiped out. He only asked to be permitted to see his father,—to nurse and watch by him. There was no thought for himself. By reconciliation he never meant restoration to his place as heir. Forgiveness and love he asked for,—to be taken back to the heart so long closed against him, to hear himself called Tom by that voice he knew so well, and whose accents sounded through his dreams.

That he was not without a hope of such happiness, might be gathered from one circumstance. He had taken up with him two miniatures of his boy and girl to show "Grandfather," if good fortune should ever offer a fitting moment.

The first words which greeted him on reaching his friend's house were: "Better. A tolerably tranquil night. He can move his hand. The attack was paralysis, and his speech is also improved."

"And his mind? how is his mind?"

"Clear as ever it was,—intensely eager to hear what is said about his illness, and insatiable as to the newspaper versions of the attack."

"Does he speak? Has he spoken of—his family at all?" said he, falteringly.

"Only of Lady Lendrick. He desired to see her. He dictated a note to me, in terms of very finished courtesy, asking her if, without incurring inconvenience, she would favor him with an early call. The whole thing was so like himself that I saw at once he was getting better."

"And so you think him better?" asked Lendrick, eagerly.

"Better! Yes—but not out of danger. I fear as much from his irritability as his malady. He will insist on seeing the newspapers, and occasionally his eye falls on some paragraph that wounds him. It was but yesterday that he read a sort of querulous regret from some writer that 'the learned Judge had not retired some years ago, and before failing health, acting on a very irascible temperament, had rendered him a terror alike to the bar and the suitors.' That unfortunate paragraph cost twenty leeches and ice to his temples for eight hours after."

"Cannot these things be kept from him? Surely your authority ought to be equal to this!"

"Were I to attempt it, he would refuse to see me. In fact, any utility I can contribute depends on my apparent submission to him in everything.

Almost his first question to me every morning is, 'Well, sir, who is to be my successor?' Of course I say that we all look with a sanguine hope to see him soon back in his court again. When I said this yesterday, he replied, 'I will sit on Wednesday, sir, to hear appeals; there will be little occasion for me to speak, and I trust another day or two will see the last of this difficulty of utterance. Pemberton, I know, is looking to the Attorney-Generalship, and George Hayes thinks he may order his ermine. Tell them, however, from me, that the Chief Baron intends to preside in his court for many a year to come; that the intellect, such as it is, with which Providence endowed him, is still unchanged and unclouded.' This is his language,—this his tone; and you may know how such a spirit jars with all our endeavors to promote rest and tranquillity."

Lendrick walked moodily up and down the room, his head sunk, and his eyes downcast. "Never to speak of me,—never ask to see me," muttered he, in a voice of intense sadness.

"I half suspected at one time he was about to do so, and indeed he said, 'If this attack should baffle you, Beattie, you must not omit to give timely warning. There are two or three things to be thought of.' When I came away on that morning, I sat down and wrote to you to come up here."

A servant entered at this moment and presented a note to the doctor, who read it hastily and handed it to Lendrick. It ran thus:—

"Dear Dr. Beattie,—The Chief Baron has had an unfavorable turn, partly brought on by excitement. Lose no time in coming here; and believe me, yours sincerely,

"CONSTANTIA LENDRICK."

"They've had a quarrel; I knew they would. I did my best to prevent their meeting; but I saw he would not go out of the world without a scene. As he said last night, 'I mean her to hear my "charge." She must listen to my charge, Beattie;' and I 'd not be astonished if this charge were to prove his own sentence."

"Go to him at once, Beattie; and if it be at all possible, if you can compass it in any way, let me see him once again. Take these with you; who knows but their bright faces may plead better than words for us?" and thus saying, he gave him the miniatuies; and overcome with emotion he could not control, turned away and left the room.

CHAPTER III
A DIFFICULT PATIENT

As Dr. Beattie drove off with all speed to the Chief Baron's house, which lay about three miles from the city, he had time to ponder as he went over his late interview. "Tom Lendrick," as he still called him to himself, he had known as a boy, and ever liked him. He had been a patient, studious, gentle-tempered lad, desirous to acquire knowledge, without any of that ambition that wants to make the knowledge marketable. To have gained a professorship would have appeared to have been the very summit of his ambition, and this rather as a quiet retreat to pursue his studies further than as a sphere wherein to display his own gifts. Anything more unlike that bustling, energetic, daring spirit, his father, would be hard to conceive. Throughout his whole career at the bar, and in Parliament, men were never quite sure what that brilliant speaker and most indiscreet talker would do next. Men secured his advocacy with a half misgiving whether they were doing the very best or the very worst for success. Give him difficulties to deal with, and he was a giant; let all go smoothly and well, and he would hunt up some crotchet,—some obsolete usage,—a doubtful point, that in its discussion very frequently led to the damage of his client's cause, and the defeat of his suit.

Display was ever more to him than victory. Let him have a great arena to exhibit in, and he was proof against all the difficulties and all the casualties of the conflict. Never had such a father a son less the inheritor of his temperament and nature; and this same disappointment rankling on through life—a disappointment that embittered all intercourse, and went so far as to make him disparage the high abilities of his son—created a gulf between them that Beattie knew could never be bridged over. He doubted, too, whether as a doctor he could conscientiously introduce a theme so likely to irritate and excite. As he pondered, he opened the two miniatures, and looked at them. The young man was a fine, manly, daring-looking fellow, with a determined brow and a resolute mouth, that recalled his grandfather's face; he was evidently well grown and strong, and looked one that, thrown where he might be in life, would be likely to assert his own.

The girl, wonderfully like him in feature, had a character of subdued humor in her eye, and a half-hid laughter in the mouth, which the artist had caught up with infinite skill, that took away all the severity of the face, and softened its traits to a most attractive beauty. Through her rich brown hair there was a sort of golden *reflet* that imparted great brilliancy to the expression of the head, and her large eyes of gray-blue were the image of candor and softness, till her laugh gave them a sparkle of drollery whose sympathy there was no resisting. She, too, was tall and beautifully formed, with that slimness of early youth that only escapes being angular, but has in it the charm of suppleness that lends grace to every action and every gesture.

"I wish he could see the originals," muttered Beattie. "If the old man, with his love of beauty, but saw that girl, it would be worth all the arguments in Christendom. Is it too late for this? Have we time for the experiment?"

Thus thinking, he drove along the well-wooded approach, and gained the large ground-space before the door, whence a carriage was about to drive away. "Oh, doctor," cried a voice, "I'm so glad you 're come; they are most impatient for you." It was the Solicitor-General, Mr. Pemberton, who now came up to the window of Beattie's carriage.

"He has become quite unmanageable, will not admit a word of counsel or advice, resists all interference, and insists on going out for a drive."

"I see him at the window," said Beattie; "he is beckoning to me; good-bye," and he passed on and entered the house.

In the chief drawing-room, in a deep recess of a window, sat the Chief Baron, dressed as if to go out, with an overcoat and even his gloves on. "Come and drive with me, Beattie," cried he, in a feeble but harsh voice. "If I take my man Leonard, they 'll say it was a keeper. You know that the 'Post' has it this morning that it is my mind which has given way. They say they 've seen me breaking for years back. Good heavens! can it be possible, think you, that the mites in a cheese speculate over the nature of the man that eats them? You stopped to talk with Pemberton I saw; what did he say to you?"

"Nothing particular,—a mere greeting, I think."

"No, sir, it was not; he was asking you how many hours there lay between him and the Attorney-Generalship. They 've divided the carcase already. The lion has to assist at his autopsy,—rather hard, is n't it? How it embitters death, to think of the fellows who are to replace us!"

"Let me feel your pulse."

"Don't trust it, Beattie; that little dialogue of yours on the grass plot has sent it up thirty beats; how many is it?"

"Rapid,—very rapid; you need rest,—tranquillity."

"And you can't give me either, sir; neither you nor your craft. You are the Augurs of modern civilization, and we cling to your predictions just as our forefathers did, though we never believe you."

"This is not flattery," said Beattie, with a slight smile.

The old man closed his eyes, and passed his hand slowly over his forehead. "I suppose I was dreaming, Beattie, just before you came up; but I thought I saw them all in the Hall, talking and laughing over my death. Burrowes was telling how old I must be, because I moved the amendment to Flood in the Irish Parliament in '97; and Eames mentioned that I was Curran's junior in the great Bagenal record; and old Tysdal set them all in a roar by saying he had a vision of me standing at the gate of heaven, and instead of going in, as St. Peter invited me, stoutly refusing, and declaring I would move for a new trial! How like the rascals!"

"Don't you think you'd be better in your own room? There's too much light and glare here."

"Do you think so?"

"I am sure of it. You need quiet, and the absence of all that stimulates the action of the brain."

"And what do *you*, sir,—what does any one,—know about the brain's operations? You doctors have invented a sort of conventional cerebral organ, which, like lunar caustic, is decomposed by light; and in your vulgar materialism you would make out that what affects *your* brain must act alike upon *mine*. I tell you, sir, it is darkness—obscurity, physical or moral, it matters not which—that irritates *me*, just as I feel provoked this moment by this muddling talk of yours about brain."

"And yet I 'm talking about what my daily life and habits suggest *some* knowledge of," said Beattie, mildly.

"So you are, sir, and the presumption is all on my side. If you'll kindly lend me your arm, I'll go back to my room."

Step by step, slowly and painfully, he returned to his chamber, not uttering a word as he went.

"Yes, this is better, doctor; this half light soothes; it is much pleasanter. One more kindness. I wrote to Lady Lendrick this morning to come up here. I suppose my combative spirit was high in me, and I wanted a round with the gloves,—or, indeed, without them; at all events, I sent the challenge. But *now*, doctor, I have to own myself a craven. I dread the visit Could you manage to interpose? Could you suggest that it is by your order I am not permitted to receive her? Could you hint"—here he smiled half maliciously—"that you do not think the time has come for anodynes,—eh, doctor?"

"Leave it to me. I 'll speak to Lady Lendrick."

"There 's another thing: not that it much matters; but it might perhaps be as well to send a few lines to the morning papers, to say the accounts of the Chief Baron are more favorable to-day; he passed a tranquil night, and so on. Pemberton won't like it, nor Hayes; but it will calm the fears of a very attached friend who calls here twice daily. You'd never guess him. He is the agent of the Globe Office, where I 'm insured. Ah, doctor, it was a bright thought of Philanthropy to establish an industrial enterprise that is bound, under heavy recognizances, to be grieved at our death."

"I must not make you talk, Sir William. I must not encourage you to exert yourself. I 'll say good-bye, and look in upon you this afternoon."

"Am I to have a book? Well; be it so. I I 'll sit and muse over the Attorney-General and his hopes."

"I have got two very interesting miniatures here. I 'll leave them with you; you might like to look at them."

"Miniatures! whose portraits are they?" asked the other, hastily, as he almost snatched them from his hand. "What a miserable juggler! what a stale trick this!" said he, as he opened the case which contained the young man's picture. "So, sir, you lend yourself to such attempts as these."

"I don't understand you," said Beattie, indignantly.

"Yes, sir, you understand me perfectly. You would do, by a piece of legerdemain, what you have not the courage to attempt openly. These are Tom Lendrick's children."

"They are."

"And this simpering young lady is her mother's image; pretty, pretty, no doubt; and a little—a shade, perhaps—of *espièglerie* above what her mother possessed. She was the silliest woman that ever turned a fool's head. She had the ineffable folly, sir, to believe she could persuade me to forgive my son for having married her; and when I handed her to a seat,—for she was at my knees,—she fainted."

"Well. It is time to forgive him now. As for her, she is beyond forgiveness, or favor, either," said Beattie, with more energy than before.

"There is no such trial to a man in a high calling as the temptation it offers him to step beyond it. Take care, sir, that with all your acknowledged ability, this temptation be not too much for you." The tone and manner in which the old judge delivered these words recalled the justice-seat. "It is an honor to me to have you as my doctor, sir. It would be to disparage my own intelligence to accept you as my confessor."

"A doctor but discharges half his trust when he fails to warn his patient against the effects of irritability."

"The man who would presume to minister to my temper or to my nature should be no longer medico of mine. With what intention, sir, did you bring me these miniatures?"

"That you might see two bright and beautiful faces whose owners are bound to you by the strongest ties of blood."

"Do you know, sir,—have you ever heard,—how their father, by his wilfulness, by his folly, by his heartless denial of my right to influence him, ruined the fortune that cost my life of struggle and labor to create?"

The doctor shook his head, and the other continued: "Then I will tell it to you, sir. It is more than seventeen years to-day when the then Viceroy sent for me, and said, 'Baron Lendrick, there is no man, after Plunkett, to whom we owe more than to yourself.' I bowed, and said, 'I do not accept the qualification, my Lord, even in favor of the distinguished Chancellor. I will not believe myself second to any.' I need not relate what ensued; the discussion was a long one,—it was also a warm one; but he came back at last to the object of the interview, which was to say that the Prime Minister was willing to recommend my name to her Majesty for the Peerage,—an honor, he was pleased to say, the public would see conferred upon me with approval; and I refused! Yes, sir, I refused what for thirty-odd years had formed the pride and the prize of my existence! I refused it, because I would not that her Majesty's favor should descend to one so unworthy of it as this fellow, or that his low-born children should inherit a high name of my procuring. I refused, sir, and I told the noble Marquess my reasons. He tried—pretty much as you have tried—to bring me to a more forgiving spirit; but I stopped him by saying, 'When I hear that your Excellency has invited to your table the scurrilous author of the lampoon against you in the "Satirist," I will begin to listen to the claims that may be urged on the score of forgiveness; not till then.'"

"I am wrong—very wrong—to let you talk on themes like this; we must keep them for calmer moments." Beattie laid his finger on the pulse as he spoke, and counted the beats by his watch.

"Well, sir, what says Death? Will he consent to a 'nolle prosequi,' or must the cause go on?"

"You are not worse; and even that, after all this excitement, is something. Good-bye now till evening. No books,—no newspapers, remember. Doze; dream; do anything but excite yourself."

"You are cruel, sir; you cut off all my enjoyments together. You deny me the resources of reading, and you deny me the solace of my wife's society." The cutting sarcasm of the last words was shown in the spiteful sparkle of his eye, and the insolent curl of his mouth; and as the doctor retired, the memory of that wicked look haunted him throughout the day.

CHAPTER IV
HOME DIPLOMACIES

"Well, it's done now, Lucy, and it can't be helped," said young Lendrick to his sister, as, with an unlighted cigar between his lips, and his hands in the pockets of his shooting-jacket, he walked impatiently up and down the drawing-room. "I'm sure if I only suspected you were so strongly against it, I'd not have done it."

"My dear Tom, I'm only against it because I think papa would be so. You know we never see any one here when he is at home, and why should we now, because he is absent?"

"Just for that reason. It's our only chance, girl."

"Oh, Tom!"

"Well, I don't mean that exactly, but I said it to startle you. No, Lucy; but, you see, here's how the matter stands. I have been three whole days in their company. On Tuesday the young fellow gave me that book of flies and the top-joint of my rod. Yesterday I lunched with them. To-day they pressed me so hard to dine with them that I felt almost rude in persisting to refuse; and it was as much to avoid the awkwardness of the situation as anything else that I asked them up to tea this evening."

"I'm sure, Tom, if it would give you any pleasure—"

"Of course it gives me pleasure," broke he in; "I don't suspect that fellows of my age like to live like hermits. And whom do I ever see down here? Old Mills and old Tobin, and Larry Day, the dog-breaker. I ask his pardon for putting him last, for he is the best of the three. Girls can stand this sort of nun's life, but I'll be hanged if it will do for us."

"And then, Tom," resumed she, in the same tone, "remember they are both perfect strangers. I doubt if you even know their names."

"That I do,—the old fellow is Sir Brook something or other. It's not Fogey, but it begins like it; and the other is called Trafford,—Lionel, I think, is his Christian name. A glorious fellow, too; was in the 9th Lancers and in the blues, and is now here with the fifty—th because he went it too hard in the cavalry. He had a horse for the Derby two years ago." The tone of proud triumph in which he made this announcement seemed to say, Now, all discussion about him may cease. "Not but," added he, after a pause, "you might like the old fellow best; he has such a world of stories, and he draws so beautifully. The whole time we were in the boat he was sketching something; and he has a book full of odds and ends; a tea-party in China, quail-shooting in Java, a wedding in Candia,—I can't tell what more; but he 's to bring them up here with him."

"I was thinking, Tom, that it might be as well if you 'd go down and ask Dr. Mills to come to tea. It would take off some of the awkwardness of our receiving two strangers."

"But they 're not strangers, Lucy; not a bit of it. I call him Trafford, and he calls me Lendrick; and the old cove is the most familiar old fellow I ever met."

"Have you said anything to Nicholas yet?" asked she, in some eagerness.

"No; and that's exactly what I want you to do for me. That old bear bullies us all, so that I can't trust myself to speak to him."

"Well, don't go away, and I'll send for him now;" and she rang the bell as she spoke. A smart-looking lad answered the summons, to whom she said, "Tell Nicholas I want him."

"Take my advice, Lucy, and merely say there are two gentlemen coming to tea this evening; don't let the old villain think you are consulting him about it, or asking his advice."

"I must do it my own way," said she; "only don't interrupt. Don't meddle,—mind that, Tom." The door opened, and a very short, thick-set old man, dressed in a black coat and waistcoat, and drab breeches and white stockings, with large shoe-buckles in his shoes, entered. His face was large and red, the mouth immensely wide, and the eyes far set from each other, his low forehead being shadowed by a wig of coarse red hair, which moved when he spoke, and seemed almost to possess a sort of independent vitality.

He had been reading when he was summoned, and his spectacles had been pushed up over his forehead, while he still held the county paper in his hand,—a sort of proud protest against being disturbed.

"You heard that Miss Lucy sent for you?" said Tom Lendrick, haughtily, as his eye fell upon the newspaper.

"I did," was the curt answer, as the old fellow, with a nervous shake of the head, seemed to announce that he was ready for battle.

"What I wanted, Nicholas, was this," interposed the girl, in a voice of very winning sweetness; "Mr. Tom has invited two gentlemen this evening to tea."

"To tay!" cried Nicholas, as if the fact staggered all credulity.

"Yes, to tea; and I was thinking if you would go down to the town and get some biscuits, or a sponge-cake, perhaps—whatever, indeed, you thought best; and also beg Dr. Mills to step in, saying that as papa was away—"

"That you was going to give a ball?"

"No. Not exactly that, Nicholas," said she, smiling; "but that two friends of my brother's—"

"And where did he meet his friends?" cried he, with a marked emphasis on the "friends." "Two strangers. God knows who or what! Poachers as like as anything else. The ould one might be worse."

"Enough of this," said Tom, sternly. "Are you the master here? Go off, sir, and do what Miss Lucy has ordered you."

"I will not,—the devil a step," said the old man, who now thrust the paper into a capacious pocket, and struck each hand on a hip. "Is it when the 'Jidge' is dying, when the newpapers has a column of the names that 's calling to ask after him, you are to be carousing and feastin' here?"

"Dear Nicholas, there's no question of feasting. It is simply a cup of tea we mean to give; sorely there's no carousing in that. And as to grandpapa, papa says that he was certainly better yesterday, and Dr. Beattie has hopes now."

"I have n't, then, and I know him better than Dr. Beattie."

"What a pity they have n't sent for you for the consultation!" said Tom, ironically.

"And look here, Nicholas," said Lucy, drawing the old man towards the door of a small room that led off the drawing-room, "we could have tea here; it will look less formal, and give less trouble; and Mears could wait,— he does it very well; and you need n't be put out at all." These last words fell to a whisper; but he was beyond reserve, beyond flattery. The last speech of her brother still rankled in his memory, and all that fell upon his ear since that fell unheeded.

"I was with your grandfather, Master Tom," said the old man, slowly, "twenty-one years before you were born! I carried his bag down to Court the day he defended Neal O' Gorman for high treason, and I was with him the morning he shot Luke Dillon at Castle Knock; and this I 'll say and stand to, there 's not a man in Ireland, high or low, knows the Chief Baron better than myself."

"It must be a great comfort to you both," said Tom; but his sister had laid her hand on his mouth and made the words unintelligible.

"You'll say to Mr. Mills, Nicholas," said she, in her most coaxing way, "that I did not write, because I preferred sending my message by *you*, who could explain why I particularly wanted him this evening."

"I'll go, Miss Lucy, reserving the point, as they say in the law,—reserving the point! because I don't give in that what you're doin' is right; and when the master comes home, I'm not goin' to defend it."

"We must bear up under that calamity as well as we can," said the young man, insolently; but Nicholas never looked towards or seemed to hear him.

"A barn-a-brack is better than a spongecake, because if there 's some of it left it does n't get stale, and one-and-six-pence will be enough; and I suppose you don't need a lamp?"

"Well, Nicholas, I must say, I think it would be better; and two candles on the small table, and two on the piano."

"Why don't you mentiou a fiddler?" said he, bitterly. "If it's a ball, there ought to be music?"

Unable to control himself longer, young Lendrick wrenched open the sash-door, and walked out into the lawn.

"The devil such a family for temper from this to Bantry!" said Nicholas; "and here's the company comin' already, or I 'm mistaken. There 's a boat makin' for the landing-place with two men in the stern."

Lucy implored him once more to lose no time on his errand, and hastened away to make some change in her dress to receive the strangers. Meanwhile Tom, having seen the boat, walked down to the shore to meet his friends.

Both Sir Brook and Trafford were enthusiastic in their praises of the spot. Its natural beauty was indeed great, but taste and culture had rendered it a marvel of elegance and refinement. Not merely were the trees grouped with reference to foliage and tint, but the flower-beds were so arranged that the laws of color should be respected, and thus these plats of perfume were not less luxuriously rich in odor than they were captivating as pictures.

"It is all the governor's own doing," said Tom, proudly, "and he is continually changing the disposition of the plants. He says variety is a law of the natural world, and it is our duty to imitate it. Here comes my sister, gentlemen."

As though set in a beautiful frame, the lovely girl stood for an instant in the porch, where drooping honeysuckles and the tangled branches of a vine hung around her, and then came courteously to meet and welcome them.

"I am in ecstasy with all I see here, Miss Lendrick," said Sir Brook. "Old traveller that I am, I scarcely know where I have ever seen such a combination of beauty."

"Papa will be delighted to hear this," said she, with a pleasant smile; "it is the flattery he loves best."

"I 'm always saying we could keep up a salmon-weir on the river for a tithe of what these carnations and primroses cost us," said Tom.

"Why, sir, if you had been in Eden you 'd have made it a market garden," said the old man.

"If the governor was a Duke of Devonshire, all these-caprices might be pardonable; but my theory is, roast-beef before roses."

While young Lendrick attached himself to Trafford, and took him here and there to show him the grounds, Sir Brook walked beside Lucy, who did the honors of the place with a most charming courtesy.

"I am almost ashamed, sir," said she, as they turned towards the house, "to have asked you to see such humble objects as these to which we attach value, for my brother tells me you are a great traveller; but it is just possible you have met in your journeys others who, like us, lived so much out of the world that they fancied they had the prettiest spot in it for their own."

"You must not ask me what I think of all I have seen: here, Miss Lendrick, till my enthusiasm calms down;" and his look of admiration, so palpably addressed to herself, sent a flush to her cheek. "A man's belongings are his history," said Sir Brook, quickly turning the conversation into an easier channel: "show me his study, his stable, his garden; let me see his hat, his cane, the volume he thrusts into his pocket, and I 'll make you an indifferent good guess about his daily doings."

"Tell me of papa's. Come here, Tom," cried she, as the two young men came towards her, "and listen to a bit of divination."

"Nay, I never promised a lecture. I offered a confidence," said he, in a half whisper; but she went on: "Sir Brook says that he reads people pretty much as Cuvier pronounced on a mastodon, by some small minute detail that pertained to them. Here's Tom's cigar-case," said she, taking it from his pocket; "what do you infer from that, sir?"

"That he smokes the most execrable tobacco."

"But can you say why?" asked Tom, with a sly twinkle of his eye.

"Probably for the same reason I do myself," said Sir Brook, producing a very cheap cigar.

"Oh, that's a veritable Cuban compared to one of mine," cried Tom; "and by way of making my future life miserable, here has been Mr. Trafford filling my pocket with real havannahs, giving me a taste for luxuries I ought never to have known of."

"Know everything, sir, go everywhere, see all that the world can show you; the wider a man's experiences the larger his nature and the more open his heart," said Foss-brooke, boldly.

"I like the theory," said Trafford to Miss Lendrick; "do you?"

"Sir Brook never meant it for women, I fancy," said she, in a low tone; but the old man overheard her, and said: "You are right. The guide ought to know every part of the mountain; the traveller need only know the path."

"Here comes a guide who is satisfied with very short excursions," cried Tom, laughing; "this is our parson, Dr. Mills."

The little, mellow-looking, well-cared-for person who now joined them was a perfect type of old-bachelorhood, in its aspect of not unpleasant selfishness. Everything about him was neat, orderly, and appropriate; and though you saw at a glance it was all for himself and his own enjoyment it was provided, his good manners and courtesy were ever ready to extend its benefits to others; and a certain genial look he wore, and a manner that nature had gifted him with, did him right good service in life, and made him pass for "an excellent fellow, though not much of a parson."

He was of use now, if only that by his presence Lucy felt more at ease, not to say that his violoncello, which always remained at the Nest, made a pleasant accompaniment when she played, and that he sang with much taste some of those lyrics which arc as much linked to Ireland by poetry as by music.

"I wish he was our chaplain,—by Jove I do!" whispered Trafford to Lendrick; "he's the jolliest fellow of his cloth I have ever met."

"And such a cook," muttered the other.

"A cook!"

"Ay, a cook. I 'll make him ask us to dinner, and you 'll tell me if you ever ate fish as he gives it, or tasted macaroni as dressed by him. I have a salmon for you, doctor, a ten-pound fish. I wish it were bigger! but it is in splendid order."

"Did you set it?" asked the parson, eagerly.

"What does he mean by set it?" whispered Trafford.

"Setting means plunging it in very hot water soon after killing it, to preserve and harden the 'curd.' Yes; and I took your hint about the arbutus leaves, too, doctor. I covered it all up with them."

"You are a teachable youth, and shall be rewarded. Come and eat him to-morrow. Dare I hope that these gentlemen are disengaged, and will honor my poor parsonage? Will you favor me with your company at five o'clock, sir?"

Sir Brook bowed, and accepted the invitation with pleasure.

"And you, sir?"

"Only too happy," said Trafford.

"Lucy, my dear, you must be one of us."

"Oh, I could not; it is impossible, doctor,—you know it is."

"I know nothing of the kind."

"Papa away,—not to speak of his never encouraging us to leave home," muttered she, in a whisper.

"I accept no excuses, Lucy; such a rare opportunity may not occur to me in a hurry. Mrs. Brennan, my housekeeper, will be so proud to see you, that I 'm not sure she 'll not treat these gentlemen to her brandy peaches,—a delicacy, I feel bound to say, she has never conceded to any one less than the bishop of the diocese."

"Don't ask me, doctor. I know that papa—"

But he broke in, saying,—"'You know I 'm your priest, and your conscience is mine;' and besides, I really do want to see how the parsonage will look with a lady at the top of the table: who knows what it may lead to?"

"Come, Lucy, that's the nearest thing to a proposal I 've heard for some time. You really must go now," said Tom.

"Papa will not like it," whispered she in his ear.

"Then he'll have to settle the matter with me, Lucy," said the doctor, "for it was I who overruled you."

"Don't look to me, Miss Lendrick, to sustain you in your refusal," said Sir Brook, as the young girl turned towards him. "I have the strongest interest in seeing the doctor successful."

If Trafford said nothing, the glance he gave her more than backed the old man's speech, and she turned away half vexed, half pleased, puzzled how to act, and flattered at the same time by an amount of attention so new to her and so strange. Still she could not bring herself to promise she would go, and wished them all good-night at last, without a pledge.

"Of course she will," muttered Tom in the doctor's ear. "She's afraid of the governor; but I know he'll not be displeased, — you may reckon on her."

CHAPTER V
THE PICNIC ON HOLY ISLAND

From the day that Sir Brook made the acquaintance of Tom Lendrick and his sister, he determined he would "pitch his tent," as he called it, for some time at Killaloe. They had, so to say, captivated the old man. The young fellow, by his frank, open, manly nature, his ardent love of sport in every shape, his invariable good-humor, and more than all these, by the unaffected simplicity of his character, had strongly interested him; while Lucy had made a far deeper impression by her gentleness, her refinement, an elegance in deportment that no teaching ever gives, and, along with these, a mind stored with thought and reflectiveness. Let us, however, be just to each, and own that her beauty and the marvellous fascination of her smile gave her, even in that old man's eyes, an irresistible charm. It was a very long bygone, but he had once been in love, and the faint flicker of the memory had yet survived in his heart. It was just as likely Lucy bore no resemblance to her he had loved, but he fancied she did, — he imagined that she was her very image. That was the smile, the glance, the tone, the gesture which once had set his heart a-throbbing, and the illusion threw around her an immense fascination.

She liked him too. Through all the strange incongruities of his character, his restless love of adventure and excitement, there ran a gentle liking for quiet pleasures. He loved scenery passionately, and with a painter's taste for color and form; he loved poetry, which he read with a wondrous charm of voice and intonation. Nor was it without its peculiar power, this homage of an old, old man, who rendered her the attentive service of a devoted admirer.

There is very subtle flattery in the obsequious devotion of age to youth. It is, at least, an honest worship, an unselfish offering, and in this way the object of it may well feel proud of its tribute.

From the vicar, Dr. Mills, Fossbrooke had learned the chief events of Dr. Lendrick's history, of his estrangement from his father, his fastidious retirement from the world, and, last of all, his narrow fortune, apparently now growing narrower, since within the last year he had withdrawn his son from the University on the score of its expense.

A gold-medallist and a scholar, Dr. Lendrick would have eagerly coveted such honors for his son. It was, probably, the one triumph in life he would have set most store by, but Tom was one not made for collegiate successes. He had abilities, but they were not teachable qualities; he could pick up a certain amount of almost anything,—he could learn nothing. He could carry away from a chance conversation an amount of knowledge it had cost the talkers years to acquire, and yet set him down regularly to work book-fashion, and either from want of energy, or concentration, or of that strong will which masters difficulties just as a full current carries all before it—whichever of these was his defect,—he arose from his task wearied, worn, but unadvanced.

When, therefore, his father would speak, as he sometimes did, in confidence to the vicar, in a tone of depression about Tom's deficiencies, the honest parson would feel perfectly lost in amazement at what he meant. To his eyes Tom Lendrick was a wonder, a prodigy. There was not a theme he could not talk on, and talk well too. "It was but the other day he told the chief engineer of the Shannon Company more about the geological formation of the river-basin than all his staff knew. Ay, and what's stranger," added the vicar, "he understands the whole Colenso controversy better than I do myself." It is just possible that in the last panegyric there was nothing of exaggeration or excess. "And with all that, sir, his father goes on brooding over his neglected education, and foreshadowing the worst results from his ignorance."

"He is a fine fellow," said Fossbrooke, "but not to be compared with his sister."

"Not for mere looks, perhaps, nor for a graceful manner, and a winning address; but who would think of ranking Lucy's abilities with her brother's?"

"Not I," said Fossbrooke, boldly, "for I place hers far and away above them."

A sly twinkle of the parson's eye showed to what class of advantages he ascribed the other's preference; but he said no more, and the controversy ended.

Every morning found Sir Brook at the "Swan's Nest." He was fond of gardening, and had consummate taste in laying out ground, so that many pleasant surprises had been prepared for Dr. Lendrick's return. He drew, too, with great skill, and Lucy made considerable progress under his teaching; and as they grew more intimate, and she was not ashamed of the confession that she delighted in the Georgics of Virgil, they read whole hours together of those picturesque descriptions of rural life and its occupations, which are as true to nature at this hour as on the day they were written.

Perhaps the old man fancied that it was he who had suggested this intense appreciation of the poet. It is just possible that the young girl believed that she had reclaimed a wild, erratic, eccentric nature, and brought him back ta the love of simple pleasures and a purer source of enjoyment. Whichever way the truth inclined, each was happy, each contented. And how fond are we all, of every age, of playing the missionary, of setting off into the savage districts of our neighbors' natures and combating their false idols, their superstitions and strange rites! The least adventurous and the least imaginative have these little outbursts of conversion, and all are more or less propagandists.

It was one morning, a bright and glorious one too, that, while Tom and Lucy were yet at breakfast, Sir Brook arrived and entered the breakfast-room.

"What a day for a gray hackle, in that dark pool under the larch-trees!" cried Tom, as he saw him.

"What a day for a long walk to Mount Laurel!" said Lucy. "You said, t'other morning, you wanted cloud effects on the upper lake. I 'll show you splendid ones to-day."

"I 'll promise you a full basket before four o'clock," broke in Tom.

"I 'll promise you a full sketch-book," said Lucy, with one of her sweetest smiles.

"And I 'm going to refuse both; for I have a plan of my own, and a plan not to be gainsaid."

"I know it, You want us to go to work on that fish-pond. I'm certain it's that."

"No, Tom; it's the catalogue, — the weary catalogue that he told me, as a punishment for not being able to find Machiavelli's comedies last week, he 'd make me sit down to on the first lovely morning that came."

"Better that than those dreary Georgics which remind one of school, and the third form. But what 's your plan, Sir Brook? We have thought of all the projects that can terrify us, and you look as if it ought to be a terror."

"Mine is a plan for pleasure, and pleasure only; so pack up at once and get ready. Trafford arrived this morning."

"Where is he? I am so glad! Where's Trafford?" cried Tom, delighted.

"I have despatched him with the vicar and two well-filled hampers to Holy Island, where I mean that we shall all picnic. There 's my plan."

"And a jolly plan too! I adhere unconditionally."

"And you, Lucy, what do you say?" asked Sir Brook, as the young girl stood with a look of some indecision and embarrassment.

"I don't say that it's not a very pleasant project, but—"

"But what, Lucy? Where 's the but?"

She whispered a few words in his ear, and he cried out: "Is n't this too bad? She tells me Nicholas does not like all this gayety; that Nicholas disapproves of our mode of life."

"No, Tom; I only said Nicholas thinks that papa would not like it."

"Couldn't we see Nicholas? Couldn't we have a commission to examine Nicholas?" asked Sir Brook, laughingly.

"I 'll not be on it, that 's all I know; for I should finish by chucking the witness into the Shannon. Come along, Lucy; don't let us lose this glorious morning. I 'll get some lines and hooks together. Be sure you 're ready when I come back."

As the door closed after him, Sir Brook drew near to Lucy, where she stood in an attitude of doubt and hesitation. "I mustn't risk your good opinion of me rashly. If you really dislike this excursion, I will give it up," said he, in a low, gentle voice.

"Dislike it? No; far from it. I suspect I would enjoy it more than any of you. My reluctance was simply on the ground that all this is so unlike the life we have been leading hitherto. Papa will surely disapprove of it. Oh, there comes Nicholas with a letter!" cried she, opening the sash-window. "Give it to me; it is from papa."

She broke the seal hurriedly, and ran rapidly over the lines. "Oh, yes! I will go now, and go with delight too. It is full of good news. He is to see grandpapa, if not to-morrow, the day after. He hopes all will be well. Papa knows your name, Sir Brook. He says, 'Ask your friend Sir Brook if he be any relative of a Sir Brook Foss-brooke who rescued Captain Langton some forty years ago from a Neapolitan prison. The print-shops were filled with his likeness when I was a boy.' Was he one of your family?" inquired she, looking at him.

"I am the man," said he, calmly and coldly. "Langton was sentenced to the galleys for life for having struck the Count d'Aconi across the face with his glove; and the Count was nephew to the King. They had him at Capri working in chains, and I landed with my yacht's crew and liberated him."

"What a daring thing to do!"

"Not so daring as you fancy. The guard was surprised, and fled. It was only when reinforced that they showed fight. Our toughest enemies were the galley-slaves, who, when they discovered that we never meant to liberate them, attacked us with stones. This scar on my temple is a memorial of the affair."

"And Langton, what became of him?"

"He is now Lord Burrowfield. He gave me two fingers to shake the last time I met him at the Travellers'."

"Oh, don't say that! Oh, don't tell me of such ingratitude!"

"My dear child, people usually regard gratitude as a debt which, once acknowledged, is acquitted; and perhaps they are right. It makes all intercourse freer and less trammelled."

"Here comes Tom. May I tell him this story, or will you tell him yourself?"

"Not either, my dear Lucy. Your brother's blood is over-hot as it is. Let him not have any promptings to such exploits as these."

"But may I tell papa?"

"Just as well not, Lucy. There were scores of wild things attributed to me in those days. He may possibly remember some of them, and begin to suspect that his daughter might be in better company."

"How was it that you never told me of this exploit?" asked she, looking, not without admiration, at the hard stern features before her.

"My dear child, egotism is the besetting sin of old people, and even the most cautious lapse into it occasionally. Set me once a-talking of myself, all my prudence, all my reserve vanishes; so that, as a measure of safety for my friends and myself too, I avoid the theme when I can. There! Tom is beckoning to us. Let us go to him at once."

Holy Island, or Inishcaltra, to give it its Irish name, is a wild spot, with little remarkable about it, save the ruins of seven churches and a curious well of fabulous depth. It was, however, a favorite spot with the vicar, whose taste in localities was somehow always associated with some feature of festivity, the great merit of the present spot being that you could dine without any molestation from beggars. In such estimation, indeed, did he hold the class, that he seriously believed their craving importunity to be one of the chief reasons of dyspepsia, and was profoundly convinced that the presence of Lazarus at his gate counterbalanced many of the goods which fortune had bestowed upon Dives.

"Here we dine in real comfort," said he, as he seated himself under the shelter of an ivy-covered wall, with a wide reach of the lake at his feet.

"When I come back from California with that million or two," said Tom, "I 'll build a cottage here, where we can all come and dine continually."

"Let us keep the anniversary of the present day as a sort of foundation era," said the vicar.

"I like everything that promises pleasure," said Sir Brook, "but I like to stipulate that we do not draw too long a bill on Fortune. Think how long a year is. This time twelvemonth, for example, you, my dear doctor, may be a bishop, and not over inclined to these harmless levities. Tom there will be, as he hints, gold-crushing, at the end of the earth. Trafford, not improbably, ruling some rajah's kingdom in the far East. Of your destiny, fair Lucy, brightest of all, it is not for me to speak. Of my own it is not worth speaking."

"Nolo episcopari," said the vicar; "pass me the Madeira."

"You forget, perhaps, that is the phrase for accepting the mitre," said Sir Brook, laughing. "Bishops, like belles, say 'No' when they mean 'Yes.'"

"And who told you that belles did?" broke in Lucy. "I am in a sad minority here, but I stand up for my sex."

"I repeat a popular prejudice, fair lady."

"And Lucy will not have it that belles are as illogical as bishops? I see I was right in refusing the bench," said the vicar.

"What bright boon of Fortune is Trafford meditating the rejection of?" said Sir Brook; and the young fellow's cheek grew crimson as he tried to laugh off the reply.

"Who made this salad?" cried Tom.

"It was I; who dares to question it?" said Lucy. "The doctor has helped himself twice to it, and that test I take to be a certificate to character."

"I used to have some skill in dressing a salad, but I have foregone the practice for many a day; my culinary gift got me sent out of Austria in twenty-four hours. Oh, it 's nothing that deserves the name of a story," said Sir Brook, as the others looked at him for an explanation. "It was as long ago as the year 1806. Sir Robert Adair had been our minister at Vienna, when, a rupture taking place between the two Governments, he was recalled. He did not, however, return to England, but continued to live as a private citizen at Vienna. Strangely enough, from the moment that our embassy ceased to be recognized by the Government, our countrymen became objects of especial civility. I myself, amongst the rest, was the *bien-venu* in some of the great houses, and even invited by Count Cobourg Cohari to those *déjeuners* which he gave with such splendor at Maria Hülfe.

"At one of these, as a dish of salad was handed round, instead of eating it, like the others, I proceeded to make a very complicated dressing for it on my plate, calling for various condiments, and seasoning my mess in a most refined and ingenious manner. No sooner had I given the finishing touch to my great achievement than the Grand-Duchess Sophia, who it seems had watched the whole performance, sent a servant round to beg that I would send her my plate. She accompanied the request with a little bow and a smile whose charm I can still recall. Whatever the reason, before I awoke next morning, an agent of the police entered my room and informed me my passports were made out for Dresden, and that his orders were to give me the pleasure of his society till I crossed the frontier. There was no minister, no envoy to appeal to, and nothing left but to comply. They said 'Go,' and I went."

"And all for a dish of salad!" cried the vicar.

"All for the bright eyes of an archduchess, rather," broke in Lucy, laughing.

The old man's grateful smile at the compliment to his gallantry showed how, even in a heart so world-worn, the vanity of youth survived.

"I declare it was very hard," said Tom,—"precious hard."

"If you mean to give up the salad, so think I too," cried the vicar.

"I 'll be shot if I 'd have gone," broke in Trafford.

"You'd probably have been shot if you had stayed," replied Tom.

"There are things we submit to in life, not because the penalty of resistance affrights us, but because we half acquiesce in their justice. You, for instance, Trafford, are well pleased to be here on leave, and enjoy yourself, as I take it, considerably; and yet the call of duty—some very commonplace duty, perhaps—would make you return tomorrow in all haste."

"Of course it would," said Lucy.

"I 'm not so sure of it," murmured Trafford, sullenly; "I 'd rather go into close arrest for a week than I 'd lose this day here."

"Bravo! here's your health, Lionel," cried Tom. "I do like to hear a fellow say he is willing to pay the cost of what pleases him."

"I must preach wholesome doctrine, my young friends," broke in the vicar. "Now that we have dined well, I would like to say aword on abstinence."

"You mean to take no coffee, doctor, then?" asked Lucy, laughing.

"That I do, my sweet child,—coffee and a pipe, too, for I know you are tolerant of tobacco."

"I hope she is," said Tom, "or she 'd have a poor time of it in the house with me."

"I 'll put no coercion upon my tastes on this occasion, for I 'll take a stroll through the ruins, and leave you to your wine," said she, rising.

They protested, in a mass, against her going. "We cannot lock the door, Lucy, *de facto*," said Sir Brook, "but we do it figuratively."

"And in that case I make my escape by the window," said she, springing through an old lancet-shaped orifice in the Abbey wall.

"There goes down the sun and leaves us but a gray twilight," said Sir Brook, mournfully, as he looked after her. "If there were only enough beauty on earth, I verily believe we might dispense with parsons."

"Push me over the bird's-eye, and let me nourish myself till your millennium comes," said the vicar.

"What a charming girl she is! her very beauty fades away before the graceful attraction of her manner!" whispered Sir Brook to the doctor.

"Oh, if you but knew her as I do! If you but knew how, sacrificing all the springtime of her bright youth, she has never had a thought save to make herself the companion of her poor father,—a sad, depressed, sorrow-struck man, only rescued from despair by that companionship! I tell you, sir, there is more courage in submitting one's self to the nature of another than in facing a battery."

Sir Brook grasped the parson's hand and shook it cordially. The action spoke more than any words. "And the brother, doctor,—what say you of the brother?" whispered he.

"One of those that the old adage says 'either makes a spoon or spoils the horn.' That 's Master Tom there."

Low as the words were uttered, they caught the sharp ears of him they spoke of, and with a laughing eye he cried out, "What 's that evil prediction you 're uttering about me, doctor?"

"I am just telling Sir Brook here that it's pure head or tail how you turn out. There's stuff in you to make a hero, but it's just as likely you 'll stop short at a highwayman."

"I think I could guess which of the two would best suit the age we live in," said Tom, gayly. "Are we to have another bottle of that Madeira, for I suspect I see the doctor putting up the corkscrew?"

"You are to have no more wine than what's before you till you land me at the quay of Killaloe. When temperance means safety as well as forbearance, it's one of the first of virtues."

The vicar, indeed, soon grew impatient to depart. Fine as the evening was then, it might change. There was a feeling, too, not of damp, but chilliness; at all events, he was averse to being on the water late; and as he was the great promoter of these little convivial gatherings, his word was law.

It is not easy to explain how it happened that Trafford sat beside Lucy. Perhaps the trim of the boat required it; certainly, however, nothing required that the vicar, who sat next Lucy on the other side, should fall fast asleep almost as soon as he set foot on board. Meanwhile Sir Brook and Tom had engaged in an animated discussion as to the possibility of settling in Ireland as a man settles in some lone island in the Pacific, teaching the natives a few of the needs of civilization and picking up a few convenient ways of theirs in turn, Sir Brook warming with the theme so far as to exclaim at last, "If I only had a few of those thousands left me which I lost, squandered, or gave away, I'd try the scheme, and you should be my lieutenant, Tom."

It was one of those projects, very pleasant in their way, where men can mingle the serious with the ludicrous, where actual wisdom may go hand in hand with downright absurdity; and so did they both understand it, mingling, the very sagest reflections with projects the wildest and most eccentric. Their life, as they sketched it, was to be almost savage in freedom, untrammelled by all the tiresome conventionalities of the outer world, and at the same time offering such an example of contentedness and comfort as to shame the condition of all without the Pale.

They agreed that the vicar must join them; he should be their Bishop. He might grumble a little at first about the want of hot plates or finger-glasses, but he would soon fall into their ways, and some native squaw would console him for the loss of Mrs. Brennan's housekeeping gifts.

And Trafford and Lucy all this time,—what did they talk of? Did they, too, imagine a future and plan out a life-road in company? Far too timid for that,—they lingered over the past, each asking some trait of the other's childhood, eager to hear any little incident which might mark character or indicate temper. And at last they came down to the present,—to the very hour they lived in, and laughingly wondered at the intimacy that had grown up between them. "Only twelve days to-morrow since we first met," said Lucy, and her color rose as she said it, "and here we are talking away as if—as if—"

"As if what?" cried he, only by an effort suppressing her name as it rose to his lips.

"As if we knew each other for years. To me it seems the strangest thing in the world,—I who have never had friendships or companionships. To you, I have no doubt, it is common enough."

"But it is not," cried he, eagerly. "Such fortune never befell me before. I have gone a good deal into life,—seen scores of people in country-houses and the like; but I never met any one before I could speak to of myself,—I mean, that I had courage to tell—not that, exactly—but that I wanted them to know I was n't so bad a fellow—so reckless or so heartless as people thought me."

"And is that the character you bear?" said she, with, though not visible to him, a faint smile on her mouth.

"I think it's what my family would say of me,—I mean now, for once on a time I was a favorite at home."

"And why are you not still?"

"Because I was extravagant; because I went into debt; because I got very easily into scrapes, and very badly out of them,—not dishonorably, mind; the scrapes I speak of were money troubles, and they brought me into collision with my governor. That was how it came about I was sent over here. They meant as a punishment what has turned out the greatest happiness of my life."

"How cold the water is!" said Lucy, as, taking off her glove, she suffered her hand to dip in the water beside the boat.

"Deliciously cold," said he, as, plunging in his hand, he managed, as though by accident, to touch hers. She drew it rapidly away, however, and then, to prevent the conversation returning to its former channel, said aloud: "What *are* you laughing over so heartily, Sir Brook? You and Tom appear to have fallen upon a mine of drollery. Do share it with us."

"You shall hear it all one of these days, Lucy. Jog the doctor's arm now and wake him up, for I see the lights at the boat-house, and we shall soon be on shore."

"And sorry I am for it," muttered Trafford, in a whisper; "I wish this night could be drawn out to years."

CHAPTER VI
WAITING ON

On the sixth day after Dr. Lendrick's arrival in Dublin—a fruitless journey so far as any hope of reconciliation was concerned—he resolved to return home. His friend Beattie, however, induced him to delay his departure to the-next day, clinging to some small hope from a few words-that had dropped from Sir William on that same morning. "Let me see you to-night, doctor; I have a note to show you which I could not to-day with all these people about me." Now, the people in question resolved themselves into one person, Lady Lendrick, who indeed bustled into the room and out of it, slammed doors and upset chairs in a fashion that might well have excused the exaggeration that converted her into a noun of multitude. A very warm altercation had occurred, too, in the doctor's presence with reference to some letter from India, which Lady Lendrick was urging Sir William to reply to, but which he firmly declared he would not answer.

"How I am to treat a man subject to such attacks of temper, so easily provoked, and so incessantly irritated, is not clear to me. At all events I will see him to-night, and hear what he has to say to me. I am sure it has no concern with this letter from India." With these words Beattie induced his friend to defer his journey for another day.

It was a long and anxious day to poor Lendrick. It was not alone that he had to suffer the bitter disappointment of all his hopes of being received by his father and admitted to some gleam of future favor, but he had discovered that certain debts which he had believed long settled by the judge were still outstanding against him, Lady Lendrick having interfered to prevent their payment, while she assured the creditors that if they had patience Dr. Lendrick would one day or other be in a position to acquit them. Between two and three thousand pounds thus hung over him of indebtedness above all his calculations, and equally above all his ability to meet.

"We thought you knew all this, Dr. Lendrick," said Mr. Hack, Sir William's agent; "we imagined you were a party to the arrangement, understanding that you were reluctant to bring these debts under the Chief Baron's eyes, being moneys lent to your wife's relations."

"I believed that they were paid," was all his reply, for the story was a painful one of trust betrayed and confidence abused, and he did not desire to revive it. He had often been told that his stepmother was the real obstacle to all hope of reconciliation with his father, but that she had pushed her enmity to him to the extent of his ruin was more than he was prepared for. They had never met, but at one time letters had frequently passed between them. Hers were marvels of good wishes and kind intentions, dashed with certain melancholy reflections over some shadowy unknown something which had been the cause of his estrangement from his father, but which time and endurance might not impossibly diminish the bitterness of, though with very little hope of leading to a more amicable relation. She would assume, besides, occasionally a kind of companionship in sorrow, and, as though the confession had burst from her unawares, avow that Sir William's temper was more than human nature was called upon to submit to, and that years only added to those violent outbursts of passion which made the existence of all around him a perpetual martyrdom. These always wound up with some sweet congratulations on "Tom's good fortune in his life of peaceful retirement," and the "tranquil pleasures of that charming spot of which every one tells me such wonders, and which the hope of visiting is one of my most entrancing daydreams." We give the passage textually, because it occurred without a change of a word thus in no less than five different letters.

This formal repetition of a phrase, and certain mistakes she made about the names of his children, first opened Lendrick's eyes as to the sincerity and affection of his correspondent, for he was the least suspicious of men, and regarded distrust as a disgrace to him who entertained it.

Over all these things now did he ponder during this long dreary day. He did not like to go out lest he should meet old acquaintances and be interrogated about his father, of whom he knew less than almost every one. He shunned the tone of compassionate interest men met him with, and he dreaded even the old faces that reminded him of the past. He could not read: he tried, but could not. After a few minutes he found that his thoughts wandered off from the book and centred on his own concerns, till his head ached with the weary round of those difficulties which came ever back, and back, and back again undiminished, unrelieved, and unsolved. The embarrassments of life are not, like chess problems, to be resolved by a skilful combination: they are to be encountered by temper, by patience, by daring at one time, by submission at another, by a careful consideration of a man's own powers, and by a clear-sighted estimate of his neighbors; and all these exercised not beforehand, nor in retirement, but on the very field itself where the conflict is raging and the fight at its hottest.

It was late at night when Beattie returned home, and entered the study where Lendrick sat awaiting him. "I am very late, Tom," said he, as he threw himself into an arm-chair, like one fatigued and exhausted; "but it was impossible to get away. Never in all my life have I seen him so full of anecdote, so abounding in pleasant recollections, so ready-witted, and so brilliant. I declare to you that if I could but recite the things he said, or give them even with a faint semblance of the way he told them, it would be the most amusing page of bygone Irish history. It was a grand review of all the celebrated men whom he remembered in his youth, from the eccentric Lord Bristol, the Bishop of Down, to O'Connell and Shiel. Nor did his own self-estimate, high as it was, make the picture in which he figured less striking, nor less memorable his concluding words, as he said, 'These fellows are all in history, Beattie,—every man of them. There are statues to them in our highways, and men visit the spots that gave them birth; and here am I, second to none of them. Trinity College and the Four Courts will tell you if I speak in vanity; and here am I; and the only question about me is, when I intend to vacate the bench, when it will be my good pleasure to resign—they are not particular which—my judgeship or my life. But, sir, I mean not to do either; I mean to live and protest against the inferiority of the men around me, and the ingratitude of the country that does not know how to appreciate the one man of eminence it possesses.' I assure you, Tom, vain and insolent as the speech was, as I listened I thought it was neither. There was a haughty dignity about him, to which his noble bead and his deep sonorous voice and his commanding look lent effect that overcame all thought of attributing to such a man any over-estimate of his powers."

"And this note that he wished to show you,—what was it?"

"Oh, the note was a few lines written in an adjoining room by Balfour, the Viceroy's secretary. It seems that his Excellency, finding all other seductions fail, thought of approaching your father through you."

"Through *me!* It was a bright inspiration."

"Yes; he sent Balfour to ask if the Chief Baron would feel gratified by the post of Hospital Inspector at the Cape being offered to you. It is worth eight hundred a year, and a house."

"Well, what answer did he give?" asked Lendrick, eagerly.

"He directed Balfour, who only saw Lady Lendrick, to reduce the proposal to writing. I don't fancy that the accomplished young gentleman exactly liked the task, but he did not care to refuse, and so he sat down and wrote one of the worst notes I ever read."

"Worst—in what way?"

"In every way. It was scarcely intelligible, without a previous knowledge of its contents, and so worded as to imply that when the Chief Baron had acceded to the proposal, he had so bound himself in gratitude to the Government that all honorable retreat was closed to him. I wish you saw your father's face when he read it. 'Beattie,' said he, 'I have no right to say Tom must refuse this offer; but if he should do so, I will make the document you see there be read in the House, and my name is not William Lendrick if it do not cost them more than they are prepared for. Go now and consult your friend;' it was so he called you. 'If his wants are such that this place is of consequence to him, let him accept it. I shall not ask his reasons for whatever course he may take. *My* reply is already written, and to his Excellency in person.' This he said in a way to imply that its tone was one not remarkable for conciliation or courtesy.

"I thought the opportunity a favorable one to say that you were in town at the moment, that the accounts of his illness had brought you up, and that you were staying at my house.

"'The sooner will you be able to communicate with him, sir,' said he, haughtily."

"No more than that!"

"No more, except that he added, 'Remember, sir, his acceptance or his refusal is to be his own act, not to be intimated in any way to me, nor to come through me.'"

"This is unnecessary harshness," said Lendrick, with a quivering lip; "there was no need to tell me how estranged we are from each other."

"I fancied I could detect a struggle with himself in all his sternness; and his hand trembled when I took it to say 'good-bye.' I was going to ask if you might not be permitted to see him, even for a brief moment; but I was afraid, lest in refusing he might make a reconciliation still more remote, and so I merely said, 'May I leave you those miniatures I showed you a few days ago? 'His answer was, 'You may leave them, sir.'

"As I came down to the hall, I met Lady Lendrick. She was in evening dress, going out, but had evidently waited to Catch me as I passed.

"'You find the Chief much better, don't you?' asked she. I bowed and assented.. 'And he will be better still,' added she, 'when all these anxieties are over.' She saw that I did not or would not apprehend her meaning, and added, 'I mean about this resignation, which, of course, you will advise him to. The Government are really behaving so very well, so liberal, and withal so delicate. If they had been our own people, I doubt if they would have shown anything like the same generosity.'

"'I have heard of nothing but the offer to Dr. Lendrick,' said I.

"She seemed confused, and moved on; and then recovering herself, said, 'And a most handsome offer it is. I hope he thinks so.'

"With this we parted, and I believe now I have told you almost word for word everything that occurred concerning you."

"And what do *you* say to all this, Beattie?" asked Lendrick, in a half-sad tone.

"I say that if in your place, Tom, I would accept. It may be that the Chief Baron will interpose and say, Don't go; or it may be that your readiness to work for your bread should conciliate him; he has long had the impression that you are indisposed to exertion, and too fond of your own ease."

"I know it,—I know it; Lady Lendrick has intimated as much to me."

"At all events, you can make no mistake in entertaining the project; and certainly the offer is not to be despised."

"It is of him, and of him alone, I am thinking, Beattie. If he would let me see him, admit me once more on my old terms of affection, I would go anywhere, do anything that he counselled. Try, my dear friend, to bring this about; do your best for me, and remember I will subscribe to any terms, submit to anything, if he will only be reconciled to me."

"It will be hard if we cannot manage this somehow," said Beattie; "but now let us to bed. It is past two o'clock. Good-night, Tom; sleep well, and don't dream of the Cape or the Caffres."

CHAPTER VII
THE FOUNTAIN OF HONOR

That ancient and incongruous pile which goes by the name of the Castle in Dublin, and to which Irishmen very generally look as the well from which all honors and places flow, is not remarkable for either the splendor or space it affords to the inmates beneath its roof. Upheld by a great prestige perhaps, as in the case of certain distinguished people, who affect a humble exterior and very simple belongings, it may deem that its own transcendent importance has no need of accessories. Certainly the ugliness of its outside is in noway unbalanced by the meanness within; and even the very highest of those who claim its hospitality are lodged in no-princely fashion.

In a corner of the old red brick quadrangle, to the right of the state entrance, in a small room whose two narrow windows looked into a lane, sat a very well-dressed young-gentleman at a writing-table. Short, and disposed to roundness in face as well as figure, Mr. Cholmondely Balfour scarcely responded in appearance to his imposing name. Nature had not been as bountiful, perhaps, as Fortune; for while he was rich, well born, and considerably gifted in abilities, his features were unmistakably common and vulgar, and all the aids of dress could not atone for the meanness in his general look. Had he simply accepted his image as a thing to be quietly borne and submitted to, the case might not have been so very bad; but he took it as something to be corrected, changed, and ameliorated, and the result was a perpetual struggle to make the most ordinary traits and commonplace features appear the impress of one on whom Nature had written gentleman. It would have been no easy task to have imposed on him in a question of his duty. He was the private secretary of the Viceroy, who was his maternal uncle. It would have been a tough task to have misled or deceived him in any matter open to his intelligence to examine; but upon this theme there was not the inventor of a hair-wash, a skin-paste, a whisker-dye, or a pearl-powder that might not have led him captive. A bishop might have found difficulty in getting audience of him,—a barber might have entered unannounced; and while the lieutenant of a county sat waiting in the antechamber, the tailor, with a new waistcoat pattern, walked boldly into the august presence. Entering life by that *petite porte* of politics, an Irish office, he had conceived a very humble estimate of the people amongst whom he was placed. Regarding his extradition from Whitehall and its precincts as a sort of probationary banishment, he felt, however, its necessity; and as naval men are accredited with two years of service for every one year on the coast of Africa, Mr. Balfour was aware that a grateful Government could equally recognize the devotion of him who gave some of the years of his youth to the Fernando Po of statecraft.

This impression, being rarely personal in its consequences, was not of much moment; but it was conjoined with a more serious error, which was to imagine that all rule and governance in Ireland should be carried on with a Machiavellian subtlety. The people, he had heard, were quick-witted; he must therefore out-manoeuvre them. Jobbery had been, he was told, the ruin of Ireland; he would show its inefficiency by the superior skill with which he could wield its weapon. To be sure his office was a very minor one, its influence very restricted, but Mr. Balfour was ambitious; he was a Viceroy's nephew; he had sat for months in the House, from which he had been turned out on a petition. He had therefore social advantages to build on, abilities to display, and wrongs to avenge; and as a man too late for the train speculates during the day how far on his road he might have been by this time or by that, so did Mr. Balfour continually keep reminding himself how, but for that confounded petition, he might now have been a Treasury this or a Board of Trade that,—a corporal, in fact, in that great army whose commissioned officers are amongst the highest in Europe.

Let us now present him to our reader, as he lay back in his chair, and by a hand-bell summoned his messenger.

"I say, Watkins, when Clancey calls about those trousers show him in, and send some one over to the packet-office about the phosphorus blacking; you know we are on the last jar of it. If the Solicitor-General should come—"

"He is here, sir; he has been waiting these twenty minutes. I told him you were with his Excellency."

"So I was,—so I always am," said he, throwing a half-smoked cigar into the fire. "Admit him."

A pale, care-worn, anxious-looking man, whose face was not without traces of annoyance at the length of time he had been kept waiting, now entered and sat down.

"Just where we were yesterday, Pemberton," said Balfour, as he rose and stood with his back to the fire, the tails of his gorgeous dressing-gown hanging over his arms. "Intractable as he ever was; he won't die, and he won't resign."

"His friends say he is perfectly willing to resign if you agree to his terms."

"That may be possible; the question is, What are his terms? Have you a precedent of a Chief Baron being raised to the peerage?"

"It's not, as I understand, the peerage he insists on; he inclines to a moneyed arrangement."

"We are too poor, Pemberton,—we are too poor. There's a deep gap in our customs this quarter. It's reduction we must think of, not outlay."

"If the changes *are* to be made," said the other, with a tone of impatience, "I certainly ought to be told at once, or I shall have no time left for my canvass."

"An Irish borough, Pemberton,—an Irish borough requires so little," said Balfour, with a compassionate smile.

"Such is not the opinion over here, sir," said Pemberton, stiffly; "and I might even suggest some caution in saying it."

"Caution is the badge of all our tribe," said Balfour, with a burlesque gravity. "By the way, Pemberton, his Excellency is greatly disappointed at the issue of these Cork trials; why did n't you hang these fellows?"

"Juries can no more be coerced here than in England; they brought them in not guilty."

"We know all that, and we ask you why? There certainly was little room for doubt in the evidence."

"When you have lived longer in Ireland, Mr. Balfour, you will learn that there are other considerations in a trial than the testimony of the witnesses."

"That's exactly what I said to his Excellency; and I remarked, 'If Pemberton comes into the House, he must prepare for a sharp attack about these trials.'"

"And it is exactly to ascertain if I am to enter Parliament that I have come here to-day," said the other, angrily.

"Bring me the grateful tidings that the Lord Chief Baron has joined his illustrious predecessors in that distinguished court, I 'll answer you in five minutes."

"Beattie declares he is better this morning. He says that he has in all probability years of life before him."

"There 's nothing so hard to kill as a judge, except it be an archbishop. I believe a sedentary life does it; they say if a fellow will sit still and never move he may live to any age."

Pemberton took an impatient turn up and down the room, and then wheeling about directly in front of Balfour, said, "If his Excellency knew, perhaps, that I do not want the House of Commons—"

"Not want the House,—not wish to be in Parliament?"

"Certainly not. If I enter the House, it is as a law-officer of the Crown; personally it is no object to me."

"I'll not tell him that, Pem. I'll keep your secret safe, for I tell you frankly it would ruin you to reveal it."

"It's no secret, sir; you may proclaim it,—you may publish it in the 'Gazette,' But really we are wasting much valuable time here. It is now two o'clock, and I must go down to Court. I have only to say that if no arrangement be come to before this time to-morrow—" He stopped short. Another word might have committed him, but he pulled up in time.

"Well, what then?" asked Balfour, with a half smile.

"I have heard you pride yourself, Mr. Balfour," said the other, recovering, "on your skill in nice negotiation; why not try what you could do with the Chief Baron?"

"Are there women in the family?" said Balfour, caressing his moustache.

"No; only his wife."

"I 've seen her," said he, contemptuously.

"He quarrelled with his only son, and has not spoken to him, I believe, for nigh thirty years, and the poor fellow is struggling on as a country doctor somewhere in the west."

"What if we were to propose to do something for him? Men are often not averse to see those assisted whom their own pride refuses to help."

"I scarcely suspect you 'll acquire his gratitude that way."

"We don't want his gratitude, we want his place. I declare I think the idea a good one. There's a thing now at the Cape, an inspectorship of something,—Hottentots or hospitals, I forget which. His Excellency asked to have the gift of it; what if we were to appoint this man?"

"Make the crier of his Court a Commissioner in Chancery, and Baron Lendrick will be more obliged to you," said Pem-berton, with a sneer. "He is about the least forgiving man I ever knew or heard of."

"Where is this son of his to be found?"

"I saw him yesterday walking with Dr. Beattie. I have no doubt Beattie knows his address. But let me warn you once more against the inutility of the step you would take. I doubt if the old Judge would as much as thank you."

Balfour turned round to the glass and smiled sweetly at himself, as though to say that he had heard of some one who knew how to make these negotiations successful,—a fellow of infinite readiness, a clever fellow, but withal one whose good looks and distinguished air left even his talents in the background.

"I think I 'll call and see the Chief Baron myself," said he. "His Excellency sends twice a day to inquire, and I 'll take the opportunity to make him a visit,—that is, if he will receive me."

"It is doubtful. At all events, let me give you one hint for your guidance. Neither let drop Mr. Attorney's name nor mine in your conversation; avoid the mention of any one whose career might be influenced by the Baron's retirement; and talk of him less as a human being than as an institution that is destined to endure as long as the British constitution."

"I wish it was a woman—if it was only a woman I had to deal with, the whole affair might be deemed settled."

"If you should be able to do anything before the mail goes out to-night, perhaps you will inform me," said Pem-berton, as he bowed and left the room. "And these are the men they send over here to administer the country!" muttered he, as he descended the stairs,—"such are the intelligences that are to rule Ireland! Was it Voltaire who said there was nothing so inscrutable in all the ways of Providence as the miserable smallness of those creatures to whom the destiny of nations was committed?"

Ruminating over this, he hastened on to a *nisi prius* case.

CHAPTER VIII
A PUZZLING COMMISSION

As Colonel Cave re-entered his quarters after morning parade in the Royal Barracks of Dublin, he found the following letter, which the post had just delivered. It was headed "Strictly Private," with three dashes under the words.

"Holt-Trafford.

"My dear Colonel Cave,—Sir Hugh is confined to bed with a severe attack of gout,—the doctors call it flying gout. He suffers greatly, and his nerves are in a state of irritation that makes all attempt at writing impossible. This will be my apology for obtruding upon you, though, perhaps, the cause in which I write might serve for excuse. We are in the deepest anxiety about Lionel. You are already aware how heavily his extravagance has cost us. His play-debts amounted to above ten thousand pounds, and all the cleverness of Mr. Joel has not been able to compromise with the tradespeople for less than as much more; nor are we yet done with demands from various quarters. It is not, however, of these that I desire to speak. Your kind offer to take him into your own regiment, and exercise the watchful supervision of a parent, has relieved us of much anxiety, and his own sincere affection for you is the strongest assurance we can have that the step has been a wise one. Our present uneasiness has however a deeper source than mere pecuniary embarrassment. The boy—he is very little more than a boy in years—has fallen in love, and gravely writes to his father for consent that he may marry. I assure you the shock brought back all Sir Hugh's most severe symptoms; and his left eye was attacked with an inflammation such as Dr. Gole says he never saw equalled. So far as the incoherency of his letter will permit us to guess, the girl is a person in a very humble condition of life, the daughter of a country doctor, of course without family or fortune. That he made her acquaintance by an accident, as he informs us, is also a reason to suppose that they are not people in society. The name, as well as I can decipher it, is Lendrich or Hendrich,—neither very distinguished!

"Now, my dear Colonel, even to a second son, such an alliance would be perfectly intolerable,—totally at variance with all his father's plans for him, and inconsistent with the station he should occupy. But there are other considerations,—too sad ones, too melancholy indeed to be spoken of, except where the best interests of a family are to be regarded, which press upon us here. The last accounts of George from Madeira leave us scarcely a hope. The climate, from which so much was expected, has done nothing. The season has been unhappily most severe, and the doctors agree in declaring that the malady has not yielded in any respect. You will see, therefore, what a change any day may accomplish in Lionel's prospects, and how doubly important it is that he should contract no ties inconsistent with a station of no mean importance. Not that these considerations would weigh with Lionel in the least: he was always headstrong, rash, and self-willed; and if he were, or fancied that he were, bound in honor to do a thing, I know well that all persuasions would be unavailing to prevent him. I cannot believe, however, that matters can have gone so far here. This acquaintanceship must be of the very shortest; and however designing and crafty such people may be, there will surely be some means of showing them that their designs are impracticable, and of a nature only to bring disappointment and disgrace upon themselves. That Sir Hugh would give his consent is totally out of the question,—a thing not to be thought of for a moment; indeed I may tell you in confidence that his first thought on reading L.'s letter was to carry out a project to which George had already consented, and by which the entail should be cut off, and our third son, Harry, in that case would inherit. This will show you to what extent his indignation would carry him.

"Now what is to be done? for, really, it is but time lost in deploring when prompt action alone can save us. Do you know, or do you know any one who does know, these Hendrichs or Lendrichs—who are they, what are they? Are they people to whom I could write myself, or are they in that rank in life which would enable us to make some sort of compromise? Again, could you in anyway obtain L.'s confidence, and make him open his heart to you *first*? This is the more essential, because the moment he hears of anything like coercion or pressure, his whole spirit will rise in resistance, and he will be totally unmanageable. You have perhaps more influence over him than any one else, and even your influence he would resent if he suspected any dominance.

"I am madly impatient to hear what you will suggest. Will it be to see these people, to reason with them, to explain to them the fruitlessness of what they are doing? Will it be to talk to the girl herself?

"My first thought was to send for Lionel, as his father was so ill, but on consideration I felt that a meeting between them might be the thing of all others to be avoided. Indeed, in Sir Hugh's present temper, I dare not think of the consequences.

"Might it be advisable to get Lionel attached to some foreign station? If so, I am sure I could manage it—only, would he go? there 's the question,—would he go? I am writing in such distress of mind, and so hurriedly too, that I really do not know what I have set down and what I have omitted. I trust, however, there is enough of this sad case before you to enable you to counsel me, or, what is much better, act for me. I wish I could send you L.'s letter, but Sir Hugh has put it away, and I cannot lay my hand on it. Its purport, however, was to obtain authority from us to approach this girl's relations as a suitor, and to show that his intentions were known to and concurred in by his family. The only gleam of hope in the epistle was his saying, 'I have not the slightest reason to believe she would accept me, but the approval of my friends will certainly give me the best chance.'

"Now, my dear Colonel, compassionate my anxiety, and write to me at once—something—anything. Write such a letter as Sir Hugh may see; and if you have anything secret or confidential, enclose it as a separate slip. Was it not unfortunate that we refused that Indian appointment for him? All this misery might have been averted. You may imagine how Sir Hugh feels this conduct the more bitterly, coming, as I may say, on the back of all his late indiscretions.

"Remember, finally, happen what may, this project must not go on. It is a question of the boy's whole future and life. To defy his father is to disinherit himself; and it is not impossible that this might be the most effectual argument you could employ with these people who now seek to entangle him.

"I have certainly no reason to love Ireland. It was there that my cousin Cornwallis married that dreadful creature who is now suing him for cruelty, and exposing the family throughout England.

"Sir Hugh gave directions last week about lodging the purchase-money for his company, but he wrote a few lines to Cox's last night—to what purport I cannot say—not impossibly to countermand it. What affliction all this is!"

As Colonel Cave read over this letter for a second time, he was not without misgivings about the even small share to which he had contributed in this difficulty. It was evidently during the short leave he had granted that this acquaintanceship had been formed; and Fossbrooke's companionship was the very last thing in the world to deter a young and ardent fellow from anything high-flown or romantic. "I ought never to have thrown them together," muttered he, as he walked his room in doubt and deliberation.

He rang his bell and sent for the adjutant. "Where 's Trafford?" asked he.

"You gave him three days' leave yesterday, sir. He's gone down to that fishing-village where he went before."

"Confound the place! Send for him at once—telegraph. No—let us see—his leave is up to-morrow?"

"The next day at ten he was to report."

"His father is ill,—an attack of gout," muttered the Colonel, to give some color to his agitated manner. "But it is better, perhaps, not to alarm him. The seizure seems passing off."

"He said something about asking for a longer term; he wants a fortnight, I think. The season is just beginning now."

"He shall not have it, sir. Take good care to warn him not to apply. It will breed discontent in the regiment to see a young fellow who has not been a year with us obtain a leave every ten or fifteen days."

"If it were any other than Trafford, there would be plenty of grumbling. But he is such a favorite!"

"I don't know that a worse accident could befall any man. Many a fine fellow has been taught selfishness by the over-estimate others have formed of him. See that you keep him to his duty, and that he is to look for no favoritism."

The Colonel did not well know why he said this, nor did he stop to think what might come of it. It smacked, to his mind, however, of something prompt, active, and energetic.

His next move was to write a short note to Lady Trafford, acknowledging hers, and saying that, Lionel being absent,—he did not add where,— nothing could be done till he should see him. "To-morrow—next day at farthest—I will report progress. I cannot believe the case to be so serious as you suppose; at all events, count upon me."

"Stay!" cried he to the adjutant, who stood in the window awaiting further instructions; "on second thoughts, do telegraph. Say, 'Return at once.' This will prepare him for something."

CHAPTER IX
A BREAKFAST AT THE VICARAGE

On the day after the picnic Sir Brook went by invitation to breakfast with the vicar.

"When a man asks you to dinner," said Fossbrooke, "he generally wants you to talk; when he asks you to breakfast, he wants to talk to you."

Whatever be the truth of this adage generally, it certainly-had its application in the present case. The vicar wanted very much to talk to Sir Brook.

As they sat, therefore, over their coffee and devilled kidneys, chatting over the late excursion and hinting at another, the vicar suddenly said: "By the way, I want you to tell me something of the young fellow who was one of us yesterday. Tobin, our doctor here, who is a perfect commission-agent for scandal, says he is the greatest scamp going; that about eight or ten months ago the 'Times' was full of his exploits in bankruptcy; that his liabilities were tens of thousands,—assets *nil*. In a word, that, notwithstanding his frank, honest look, and his unaffected manner, he is the most accomplished scapegrace of the age."

"And how much of this do you believe?" asked Sir Brook, as he helped himself to coffee.

"That is not so easy to reply to; but I tell you, if you ask me, that I 'd rather not believe one word of it."

"Nor need you. His Colonel told me something about the young fellow's difficulties; he himself related the rest. He went most recklessly into debt; betted largely on races, and lost; lent freely, and lost; raised at ruinous interest, and renewed at still more ruinous; but his father has paid every shilling of it out of that fortune which one day was to have come to him, so that Lionel's thirty thousand pounds is now about eight thousand. I have put the whole story into the fewest possible words, but that's the substance of it."

"And has it cured him of extravagance?"

"Of course it has not. How should it? *You* have lived some more years in the world than he has, and I a good many more than *you*, and will you tell me that time has cured either of us of any of our old shortcomings? *Non sum quails eram* means, I can't be as wild as I used to be."

"No, no; I won't agree to that. I protest most strongly against the doctrine. Many men are wiser through experience, and, consequently, better."

"I sincerely believe I knew the world better at four-and-twenty than I know it now. The reason why we are less often deceived in after than in early life is not that we are more crafty or more keen-eyed. It is simply because we risk less. Let us hazard as much at sixty as we once did at six-and-twenty, and we 'll lose as heavily."

The vicar paused a few moments over the other's words, and then said, "To come back to this young man, I half suspect he has formed an attachment to Lucy, and that he is doing his utmost to succeed in her favor."

"And is there anything wrong in that, doctor?"

"Not positively wrong; but there is what may lead to a great deal of unhappiness. Who is to say how Trafford's family would like the connection? Who is to answer for Lendrick's approval of Trafford?"

"You induce me to make a confidence I have no right to impart; but I rely so implicitly on your discretion. I will tell you what was intrusted to me as a secret: Trafford has already written to his father to ask his consent."

"Without speaking to Lendrick? without even being sure of Lucy's?"

"Yes, without knowing anything of either; but on my advice he has first asked his father's permission to pay his addresses to the young lady. His position with his family is peculiar; he is a younger son, but not exactly as free as most younger sons feel to act for themselves. I cannot now explain this more fully, but it is enough if you understand that he is entirely dependent on his father. When I came to know this, and when I saw that he was becoming desperately in love, I insisted on this appeal to his friends before he either entangled Lucy in a promise, or even made any declaration himself. He showed me the letter before he posted it. It was all I could wish. It is not a very easy task for a young fellow to tell his father he 's in love; but he, in the very frankness of his nature, acquitted himself well and manfully."

"And what answer has he received?"

"None as yet. Two posts have passed. He might have heard through either of them; but no letter has come, and he is feverishly uneasy and anxious."

The vicar was silent, but a grave motion of his head implied doubt and fear.

"Yes," said Sir Brook, answering the gesture,—"yes, I agree with you. The Traffords are great folk in their own country. Trafford was a strong place in Saxon times. They have pride enough for all this blood, and wealth enough for both pride and blood."

"They 'd find their match in Lendrick, quiet and simple as he seems," said the vicar.

"Which makes the matter worse. Who is to give way? Who is to *céder le pas?*"

"I am not so sure I should have advised that letter. I am inclined to think I would have counselled more time, more consideration. Fathers and mothers are prudently averse to these loves at first sight, and they are merciless in dealing with what they deem a mere passing sentiment."

"Better that than suffer him to engage the girl's affections, and then learn that he must either desert her or marry her against the feeling of his family. Let us have a stroll in the garden. I have made you one confidence; I will now make you another."

They lit their cigars, and strolled out into a long alley fenced on one side by a tall dense hedge of laurels, and flanked on the other by a low wall, over which the view took in the wide reach of the river and the distant mountains of Scariff and Meelick.

"Was not that where we picnicked yesterday?" asked Sir Brook, pointing to an island in the distance.

"No; you cannot see Holy Island from this."

Sir Brook smoked on for some minutes without a word; at last, with a sort of abruptness, he said, "She was so like her, not only in face and figure, but her manner; the very tone of her voice was like; and then that half-caressing, half-timid way she has in conversation, and, more than all, the sly quietness with which she caps you when you fancy that the smart success is all your own."

"Of whom are you speaking?"

"Of another Lucy," said Sir Brook, with a deep melancholy. "Heaven grant that the resemblance follow them not in their lives as in their features! It was that likeness, however, which first attracted me towards Miss Lendrick. The first moment I saw her it overcame me; as I grew to know her better, it almost confused me, and made me jumble in your hearing things of long ago with the present. Time and space were both forgotten, and I found my mind straying away to scenes in the Himalaya with those I shall never see more. It was thus that, one day carried away by this delusion, I chanced to call her Lucy, and she laughingly begged me not to retract it, but so to call her always." For some minutes he was silent, and then resumed: "I don't know if you ever heard of a Colonel Frank Dillon, who served on Napier's staff in Scinde. Fiery Frank was his nickname among his comrades, but it only applied to him on the field of battle, and with an enemy in front. Then he was indeed fiery,—the excitement rose to almost madness, and led him to acts of almost incredible daring. At Meanee he was nearly cut to pieces, and as he lay wounded, and to all appearance dying, he received a lance-wound through the chest that the surgeon declared must prove fatal. He lived, however, for eight months after,—he lived long enough to reach the Himalayas, where his daughter, an only child, joined him from England. On her way out she became acquainted with a young officer, who was coming out as aide-de-camp to the Governor-General. They were constantly thrown together on the journey, and his attentions to her soon showed the sentiments he had conceived for her. In fact, very soon after Lucy had joined her father, Captain Sewell appeared 'in the Hills' to make a formal demand of her in marriage.

"I was there at the time, and I remember well poor Dillon's expression of disappointment after the first meeting with him. His daughter's enthusiastic description of his looks, his manner, his abilities, his qualities generally, had perhaps prepared him for too much. Indeed, Lucy's own intense admiration for the soldierlike character of her father's features assisted the mistake; for, as Dillon said, 'There must be a dash of the *sabreur* in the fellow that will win Lucy.' I came into Dillon's room immediately after the first interview. The instant I caught his eye I read what was going on in his brain. 'Sit down here, Brook,' cried he, 'sit in my chair here;' and he arose painfully as he spoke. 'I'll show you the man.' With this he hobbled over to a table where his cap lay, and, placing it rakishly on one side of his head, he stuck his eyeglass in one eye, and, with a hand in his trousers-pocket, lounged forward towards where I sat, saying, 'How d' ye do, Colonel? Wound doing better, I hope. The breezy climate up here soon set you up.' 'Familiar enough this, sir,' cried Dillon, in his own stern voice; 'but without time to breathe, as it were,—before almost I had exchanged a greeting with him,—he entered upon the object of his journey. I scarcely heard a word he said; I knew its purport,—I could mark the theme,—but no more. It was not the fellow himself that filled my mind; my whole thoughts were upon my daughter, and I went on repeating to myself, "Good heavens! is this Lucy's choice? Am I in a trance? Is it this contemptible cur (for he was a cur, sir) that has won the affections of my darling, high-hearted, generous girl? Is the romantic spirit that I have so loved to see in her to bear no better fruit than this? Does the fellow realize to her mind the hero that fills men's thoughts?" I was so overcome, so excited, so confused, Brook, that I begged him to leave me for a while, that one of my attacks of pain was coming on, and that I should not be able to converse farther He said something about trying one of his cheroots,—some impertinence or other, I forget what; but he left me, and I, who never knew a touch of girlish weakness in my life, who when a child had no mood of softness in my nature,—I felt the tears trickling along my cheeks, and my eyes dimmed with them.' My poor friend," continued Fossbrooke, "could not go on; his emotions mastered him, and he sat with his head buried between his hands and in silence. At last he said, 'She 'll not give him up, Brook; I have spoken to her,—she actually loves him. Good heavens!' he cried, 'how little do we know about our children's hearts! how far astray are we as to the natures that have grown up beside us, imbibing, as we thought, our hopes, our wishes, and our prejudices! We awake some day to discover that some other influence has crept in to undo our teachings, and that the fidelity on which we would have staked our lives has changed allegiance.'

"He talked to me long in this strain, and I saw that the effects of this blow to all his hopes had made themselves deeply felt on his chance of recovery. It only needed a great shock to depress him to make his case hopeless. Within two months after his daughter's arrival he was no more.

"I became Lucy's guardian. Poor Dillon gave me the entire control over her future fortune, and left me to occupy towards her the place he had himself held. I believe that next to her father I held the best place in her affections,—of such affections, I mean, as are accorded to a parent. I was her godfather, and from her earliest infancy she had learned to love me. The reserve—it was positive coldness—with which Dillon had always treated Sewell had caused a certain distance, for the first time in their lives, between the father and daughter. She thought, naturally enough, that her father was unjust; that, unaccustomed to the new tone of manners which had grown up amongst young men,—their greater ease, their less rigid observance of ceremonial, their more liberal self-indulgence,—he was unfairly severe upon her lover. She was annoyed, too, that Sewells attempts to conciliate the old man should have turned out such complete failures. But none of these prejudices extended to me, and she counted much on the good understanding that she expected to find grow up between us.

"If I could have prevented the marriage, I would. I learned many things of the man that I disliked. There is no worse sign of a man than to be at the same time a man of pleasure and friendless. These he was,—he was foremost in every plan of amusement and dissipation, and yet none liked him. Vain fellows get quizzed for their vanity, and selfish men laughed at for their selfishness, and close men for their avarice; but there is a combination of vanity, egotism, small craftiness, and self-preservation in certain fellows that is totally repugnant to all companionship. Their lives are a series of petty successes, not owing to any superior ability or greater boldness of daring, but to a studious outlook for small opportunities. They are ever alive to know the 'right man,' to be invited to the 'right house,' to say the 'right thing.' Never linked with whatever is in disgrace or misfortune, they are always found backing the winning horse, if not riding him.

"Such men as these, so long as the world goes well with them, and events turn out fortunately, are regarded simply as sharp, shrewd fellows, with a keen eye to their own interests. When, however, the weight of any misfortune comes, when the time arrives that they have to bear up against the hard pressure of life, these fellows come forth in their true colors, swindlers and cheats.

"Such was he. Finding that I was determined to settle the small fortune her father had left her inalienably on herself, he defeated me by a private marriage. He then launched out into a life of extravagance to which their means bore no proportion. I was a rich man in those days, and knew nothing better to do with my money than assist the daughter of my oldest friend. The gallant Captain did not balk my good intentions. He first accepted, he then borrowed, and last of all he forged my name. I paid the bills and saved him, not for his sake, I need not tell you, but for hers, who threw herself at my feet, and implored me not to see them ruined. Even this act of hers he turned to profit. He wrote to me to say that he knew his wife had been to my house, that he had long nurtured suspicions against me,—I that was many years older than her own father,—that for the future he desired all acquaintance should cease between us, and that I should not again cross his threshold.

"By what persuasions or by what menaces he led his wife to the step, I do not know; but she passed me when we met without a recognition. This was the hardest blow of all. I tried to write her a letter; but after a score of attempts I gave it up, and left the place.

"I never saw her for eight years. I wish I had not seen her then. I am an old, hardened man of the world, one whom life has taught all its lessons to in the sternest fashion. I have been so baffled and beaten, and thrown back by all my attempts to think well of the world, that nothing short of a dogged resolution not to desert my colors has rescued me from a cold misanthropy; and yet, till I saw, I did not believe there was a new pang of misery my heart had not tasted. What? it is incredible,—surely that is not she who once was Lucy Dillon,—that bold-faced woman with lustrous eyes and rouged cheeks,—brilliant, indeed, and beautiful, but not the beauty that is allied to the thought of virtue,—whose every look is a wile, whose every action is entanglement. She was leaning on a great man's arm, and in the smile she gave him told me how she knew to purchase such distinctions. He noticed me, and shook my hand as I passed. I heard him tell her who I was; and I heard her say that I had been a hanger-on, a sort of dependant of her father's, but she never liked me! I tried to laugh, but the pain was too deep. I came away, and saw her no more."

He ceased speaking, and for some time they walked along side by side without a word. At last he broke out: "Don't believe the people who say that men are taught by anything they experience in life. Outwardly they may affect it. They may assume this or that manner. The heart cannot play the hypocrite, and no frequency of disaster diminishes the smart. The wondrous resemblance Miss Lendrick bears to Lucy Dillon renews to my memory the bright days of her early beauty, when her poor father would call her to sit down at his feet and read to him, that he might gaze at will on her, weaving whole histories of future happiness and joy for her. 'Is it not like sunshine in the room to see her, Brook?' would he whisper to me. 'I only heard her voice as she passed under my window this morning, and I forgot some dark thought that was troubling me.' And there was no exaggeration in this. The sweet music of her tones "vibrated so softly on the ear, they soothed the sense, just as we feel soothed by the gentle ripple of a stream.

"All these times come back to me since I have been here, and I cannot tell you how the very sorrow that is associated with them has its power over me. Every one knows with what attachment the heart will cling to some little spot in a far-away land that reminds one of a loved place at home,— how we delight to bring back old memories, and how we even like to name old names, to cheat ourselves back into the past. So it is that I feel when I see this girl. The other Lucy was once as my daughter; so, too, do I regard her, and with this comes that dreadful sorrow I have told you of, giving my interest in her an intensity unspeakable. When I saw Trafford's attention to her, the only thing I thought of was how unlike he was to him who won the other Lucy. His frank, unaffected bearing, his fine, manly trustfulness, the very opposite to the other's qualities, made me his friend at once. When I say friend, I mean well-wisher, for my friendship now bears no other fruit. Time was when it was otherwise."

"What is it, William?" cried the vicar, as his servant came hurriedly forward.

"There 's a gentleman in the drawing-room, sir, wants to see Sir Brook Fossbrooke."

"Have I your leave?" said the old man, bowing low. "I 'll join you here immediately."

Within a few moments he was back again. "It was Trafford. He has just got a telegram to call him to his regiment. He suspects something has gone wrong; and seeing his agitation, I offered to go back with him. We start within an hour."

CHAPTER X
LENDRICK RECOUNTS HIS VISIT TO TOWN

The vicar having some business to transact in Limerick, agreed to go that far with Sir Brook and Trafford, and accompanied them to the railroad to see them off.

A down train from Dublin arrived as they were waiting, and a passenger, descending, hastily hurried after the vicar, and seized his hand. The vicar, in evident delight, forgot his other friends for a moment, and became deeply interested in the new-comer. "We must say good-bye, doctor," said Fossbrooke; "here comes our train."

"A thousand pardons, my dear Sir Brook. The unlooked-for arrival of my friend here—but I believe you don't know him. Lendrick, come here, I want to present you to Sir Brook Fossbrooke. Captain Trafford, Dr. Lendrick."

"I hope these gentlemen are not departing," said Lendrick, with the constraint of a bashful man.

"It is our misfortune to do so," said Sir Brook; "but I have passed too many happy hours in this neighborhood not to come back to it as soon as I can."

"I hope we shall see you. I hope I may have an opportunity of thanking you, Sir Brook."

"Dublin! Dublin! Dublin! get in, gentlemen: first class, this way, sir," screamed a guard, amidst a thundering rumble, a scream, and a hiss. All other words were drowned, and with a cordial shake-hands the new friends parted.

"Is the younger man his son?" asked Lendrick; "I did not catch the name?"

"No; he's Trafford, a son of Sir Hugh Trafford,—a Lincolnshire man, isn't he?"

"I don't know. It was of the other I was thinking. I felt it so strange to see a man of whom when a boy I used to hear so much. I have an old print somewhere of two over-dressed 'Bloods,' as they were called in those days, with immense whiskers, styled 'Fossy and Fussy,' meaning Sir Brook and the Baron Geramb, a German friend and follower of the Prince."

"I suspect a good deal changed since that day, in person as well as purse," said the vicar, sadly.

"Indeed! I heard of his having inherited some immense fortune."

"So he did, and squandered every shilling of it."

"And the chicks are well, you tell me?" said Lendrick, whose voice softened as he talked of home and his children.

"Could n't be better. We had a little picnic on Holy Island yesterday, and only wanted yourself to have been perfectly happy. Lucy was for refusing at first."

"Why so?"

"Some notion she had that you would n't like it. Some idea about not doing in your absence anything that was not usual when you are here."

"She is such a true girl, so loyal," said Lendrick, proudly.

"Well, I take the treason on my shoulders. I made her come. It was a delightful day, and we drank your health in as good a glass of Madeira as ever ripened in the sun. Now for your own news?"

"First let us get on the road. I am impatient to be back at home again. Have you your car here?"

"All is ready, and waiting for you at the gate."

As they drove briskly along, Lendrick gave the vicar a detailed account of his visit to Dublin. Passing over the first days, of which the reader already has heard something, we take up the story from the day on which Lendrick learned that his father would see him.

"My mind was so full of myself, doctor," said he, "of all the consequences which had followed from my father's anger with me, that I had no thought of anything else till I entered the room where he was. Then, however, as I saw him propped up with pillows in a deep chair, his face pale, his eyes colorless, and his head swathed up in a bandage after leeching, my heart sickened, alike with sorrow and shame at my great selfishness.

"I had been warned by Beattie on no account to let any show of feeling or emotion escape me, to be as cool and collected as possible, and in fact, he said, to behave as though I had seen him the day before.

"'Leave the room, Poynder,' said he to his man, 'and suffer no one to knock at the door—mind, not even to knock—till I ring my bell.' He waited till the man withdrew, and then in a very gentle voice said, 'How are you, Tom? I can't give you my right hand,—the rebellious member has ceased to know me!' I thought I should choke as the words met me; I don't remember what I said, but I took my chair and sat down beside him.

"'I thought you might have been too much agitated, Tom, but otherwise I should have wished to have had your advice along with Beattie. I believe, on the whole, however, he has treated me well.'

"I assured him that none could have done more skilfully.

"The skill of the doctor with an old patient is the skill of an architect with an old wall. He must not breach it, or it will tumble to pieces.

"'Beattie is very able, sir,' said I.

"'No man is able,' replied he, quickly, 'when the question is to repair the wastes of time and years. Draw that curtain, and let me look at you. No; stand yonder, where the light is stronger. What! is it my eyes deceive me,—is your hair white?'

"'It has been so eight years, sir.'

"'And I had not a gray hair till my seventy-second year,—not one. I told Beattie, t' other day, that the race of the strong was dying out. Good heavens, how old you look! Would any one believe in seeing us that you could be my son?'

"'I feel perhaps even more than I look it, sir.'

"'I could swear you did. You are the very stamp of those fellows who plead guilty—"Guilty, my Lord; we throw ourselves on the mercy of the court." I don't know how the great judgment-seat regards these pleas,—with *me* they meet only scorn. Give me the man who says, "Try me, test me." Drop that curtain, and draw the screen across the fire. Speak lower, too, my dear,' said he, in a weak soft voice; 'you suffer yourself to grow excited, and you excite me.'

"'I will be more cautious, sir,' said I.

"'What are these drops he is giving me? They have an acrid sweet taste.'

"'Aconite, sir; a weak solution.'

"'They say that our laws never forgot feudalism, but I declare I believe medicine has never been able to ignore alchemy: drop me out twenty, I see that your hand does not shake. Strange thought, is it not, to feel that a little phial like that could make a new Baron of the Exchequer? You have heard, I suppose, of the attempts—the indecent attempts—to induce me to resign. You have heard what they say of my age. They quote the registry of my baptism, as though it were the date of a conviction. I have yet to learn that the years a man has devoted to his country's service are counts in the indictment against his character. Age has been less merciful to me than to my fellows,—it has neither made me deaf to rancor nor blind to ingratitude. I told the Lord-Lieutenant so yesterday.'

"'You saw him then, sir?' asked I.

"'Yes, he was gracious enough to call here; he sent his secretary to ask if I would receive a visit from him. I thought that a little more tact might have been expected from a man in his station,—it is the common gift of those in high places. I perceive,' added he, after a pause, 'you don't see what I mean. It is this: royalties, or mock royalties, for they are the same in this, condescend to these visits as deathbed attentions. They come to us with their courtesies as the priest comes with his holy cruet, only when they have the assurance that we are beyond recovery. His Excellency ought to have felt that the man to whom he proposed this attention was not one to misunderstand its significance.'

"'Did he remain long, sir?'

"'Two hours and forty minutes. I measured it by my watch.'

"'Was the fatigue not too much for you?'

"'Of course it was; I fainted before he got to his carriage. He twice rose to go away, but on each occasion I had something to say that induced him to sit down again. It was the whole case of Ireland we reviewed,—that is, I did. I deployed the six millions before him, and he took the salute. Yes, sir, education, religious animosities, land-tenure, drainage, emigration, secret societies, the rebel priest and the intolerant parson, even nationality and mendicant insolence, all marched past, and he took the salute! "And now, my Lord," said I, "it is the man who tells you these things, who has the courage to tell and the ability to display them, and it is this man for whose retirement your Ex-lency is so eager, that you have actually deigned to make him a visit, that he may carry away into the next world, perhaps, a pleasing memory of this; it is this man, I say, whom you propose to replace—and by what, my Lord, and by whom? Will a mere lawyer, will any amount of *nisi prius* craft or precedent, give you the qualities you need on that bench, or that you need, sadly need, at this council-board? Go back, my Lord, and tell your colleagues of the Cabinet that Providence is more merciful than a Premier, and that the same overruling hand that has sustained me through this trial will uphold me, I trust, for years to serve my country, and save it for some time longer from your blundering legislation."

"'He stood up, sir, like a prisoner when under sentence; he stood up, sir, and as he bowed, I waved my adieu to him as though saying, You have heard me, and you are not to carry away from this place a hope, the faintest, that any change will come over the determination I have this day declared.

"'He went away, and I fainted. The exertion was too long sustained, too much for me. I believe, after all,' added he, with a smile, 'his Excellency bore it very little better. He told the Archbishop the same evening that he'd not go through another such morning for "the garter." Men in his station hear so little of truth that it revolts them like coarse diet. They 'd rather abstain altogether till forced by actual hunger to touch it. When they come to me, however, it is the only fare they will find before them.'

"There was a long pause after this," continued Lendrick. "I saw that the theme had greatly excited him, and I forbore to say a word, lest he should be led to resume it. 'Too old for the bench!' burst he out suddenly; 'my Lord, there are men who are never too old, as there are those who are never too young. The oak is but a sapling when the pine is in decay. Is there that glut of intellect just now in England, are we so surfeited with ability that, to make room for the coming men, we, who have made our mark on the age, must retire into obscurity?' He tried to rise from his seat; his face was flushed, and his eyes flashing; he evidently forgot where he was, and with whom, for he sank back with a faint sigh, and said, 'Let us talk of it no more. Let us think of something else. Indeed, it was to talk of something else I desired to see you.' He went on, then, to say that he wished something could be done for me. His own means were, he said, sadly crippled; he spoke bitterly, resentfully, I thought. 'It is too long a story to enter on, and were it briefer, too disagreeable a one,' added he. 'I ought to be a rich man, and I am poor; I should be powerful, and I have no influence. All has gone ill with me.' After a silence, he continued, 'They have a place to offer you: the inspectorship, I think they call it, of hospitals at the Cape; it is worth, altogether, nigh a thousand a year, a thing not to be refused.'

"'The offer could only be made in compliment to you, sir; and if my acceptance were to compromise your position—'

"'Compromise *me!*' broke he in. 'I 'll take care it shall not. No man need instruct me in the art of self-defence, sir. Accept at once.'

"'I will do whatever you desire, sir,' was my answer.

"'Go out there yourself, alone,—at first, I mean. Let your boy continue his college career; the girl shall come to me.'

"'I have never been separated from my children, sir,' said I, almost trembling with anxiety.

"'Such separations are bearable,' added he, 'when it is duty dictates them, not disobedience.'

"He fixed his eyes sternly on me, and I trembled as I thought that the long score of years was at last come to the reckoning. He did not dwell on the theme, however, but in a tone of much gentler meaning, went on: 'It will be an act of mercy to let me see a loving face, to hear a tender voice. Your boy would be too rough for me.'

"'You would like him, sir. He is thoroughly truthful and honest.'

"'So he may, and yet be self-willed, be noisy, be over-redolent of that youth which age resents like outrage. Give me the girl, Tom; let her come here, and bestow some of those loving graces on the last hours of my life her looks show she should be rich in. For your sake she will be kind to me. Who knows what charm there may be in gentleness, even to a tiger-nature like mine? Ask her, at least, if she will make the sacrifice.'

"I knew not what to answer. If I could not endure the thought of parting from Lucy, yet it seemed equally impossible to refuse his entreaty,—old, friendless, and deserted as he was. I felt, besides, that my only hope of a real reconciliation with him lay through this road; deny him this, and it was clear he would never see me more. He said, too, it should only be for a season. I was to see how the place, the climate, suited for a residence. In a word, every possible argument to reconcile me to the project rushed to my mind, and I at last said, 'Lucy shall decide, sir. I will set out for home at once, and you shall have her own answer.'

"'Uninfluenced, sir,' cried he,—'mind that. If influence were to be used, I could perhaps tell her what might decide her at once; but I would not that pity should plead for me, till she should have seen if I be worth compassion! There is but one argument I will permit in my favor,—tell her that her picture has been my pleasantest companion these three long days. There it lies, always before me. Go now, and let me hear from you as soon as may be.' I arose, but somehow my agitation, do what I would, mastered me. It was so long since we had met! All the sorrows the long estrangement had cost me came to my mind, together with little touches of his kindness in long-past years, and I could not speak. 'Poor Tom! poor Tom!' said he, drawing me towards him; and he kissed me."

As Lendrick said this, emotion overcame him, and he covered his face with his hands, and sobbed bitterly. More than a mile of road was traversed before a word passed between them. "There they are, doctor! There 's Tom, there's Lucy! They are coming to meet me," cried he. "Good-bye, doctor; you 'll forgive me, I know,—goodbye;" and he sprang off the car as he spoke, while the vicar, respecting the sacredness of the joy, wheeled his horse round, and drove back towards the town.

CHAPTER XI
CAVE CONSULTS SIR BROOK

A few minutes after the Adjutant had informed Colonel Cave that Lieutenant Traflford had reported himself, Sir Brook entered the Colonel's quarters, eager to know what was the reason of the sudden recall of Traflford, and whether the regiment had been unexpectedly ordered for foreign service.

"No, no," said Cave, in some confusion. "We have had our turn of India and the Cape; they can't send us away again for some time. It was purely personal; it was, I may say, a private reason. You know," added he, with a slight smile, "I am acting as a sort of guardian to Trafford just now. His family sent him over to me, as to a reformatory."

"From everything I have seen of him, your office will be an easy one."

"Well, I suspect that, so far as mere wildness goes,—extravagance and that sort of thing,—he has had enough of it; but there are mistakes that a young fellow may make in life—mistakes in judgment—which will damage him more irreparably than all his derelictions against morality."

"That I deny,—totally, entirely deny. I know what you mean,—that is, I think I know what you mean; and if I guess aright, I am distinctly at issue with you on this matter."

"Perhaps I could convince you, notwithstanding. Here's a letter which I have no right to show you; it is marked 'Strictly confidential and private.' You shall read it,—nay, you must read it,—because you are exactly the man to be able to give advice on the matter. You like Traflford, and wish him well. Read that over carefully, and tell me what you would counsel."

Fossbrooke took out his spectacles, and, having seated himself comfortably, with his back to the light, began in leisurely fashion to peruse the letter. "It's his mother who writes," said he, turning to the signature,— "one of the most worldly women I ever met. She was a Lascelles. Don't you know how she married Trafford?"

"I don't remember, if I ever heard."

"It was her sister that Trafford wanted to marry, but she was ambitious to be a peeress; and as Bradbrook was in love with her, she told Sir Hugh, 'I have got a sister so like me nobody can distinguish between us. She 'd make an excellent wife for you. She rides far better than me, and she is n't half so extravagant. I 'll send for her.' She did so, and the whole thing was settled in a week."

"They have lived very happily together."

"Of course they have. They didn't 'go in,' as the speculators say, for enormous profits; they realized very fairly, and were satisfied. I wish her handwriting had been more cared for. What's this she says here about a subscription?"

"That 's supervision,—the supervision of a parent."

"Supervision of a fiddlestick! the fellow is six feet one inch high, and seven-and-twenty years of age; he's quite beyond supervision. Ah! brought back all his father's gout, has he? When will people begin to admit that their own tempers have something to say to their maladies? I curse the cook who made the mulligatawny, but I forget that I ate two platefuls of it. So it's the doctor's daughter she objects to. I wish she saw her. I wish *you* saw her, Cave. You are an old frequenter of courts and drawing-rooms. I tell you you have seen nothing like this doctor's daughter since Laura Bedingfield was presented, and that was before your day."

"Every one has heard of the Beauty Bedingfield; but she was my mother's contemporary."

"Well, sir, her successors have not eclipsed her! This doctor's daughter, as your correspondent calls her, is the only rival of her that I have ever seen. As to wit and accomplishments, Laura could not compete with Lucy Lendrick."

"You know her, then?" asked the Colonel; and then added, "Tell me something about the family."

"With your leave, I will finish this letter first. Ah! here we have the whole secret. Lionel Trafford is likely to be that precious prize, an eldest son. Who could have thought that the law of entail could sway a mother's affections? 'Contract no ties inconsistent with his station.' This begins to be intolerable, Cave. I don't think I can go on."

"Yes, yes; read it through."

"She asks you if you know any one who knows these Hendrichs or Lendrichs; tell her that you do; tell her that your friend is one of those men who have seen a good deal of life, heard more, too, than he has seen. She will understand that, and that his name is Sir Brook Fossbrooke, who, if needed, will think nothing of a journey over to Lincolnshire to afford her all the information she could wish for. Say this, Cave, and take my word for it, she will put very few more questions to you."

"That would be to avow I had already consulted with you. No, no; I must not do that."

"The wind-up of the epistle is charming. 'I have certainly no reason to love Ireland.' Poor Ireland! here is another infliction upon you. Let us hope you may never come to know that Lady Trafford cannot love you."

"Come, come, Fossbrooke, be just, be fair; there is nothing so very unreasonable in the anxiety of a mother that her son, who will have a good name and a large estate, should not share them both with a person beneath him."

"Why must she assume that this is the case,—why take it for granted that this girl must be beneath him? I tell you, sir, if a prince of the blood had fallen in love with her, it would be a reason to repeal the Royal Marriage Act."

"I declare, Fossbrooke, I shall begin to suspect that your own heart has not escaped scathless," said Cave, laughing.

The old man's face became crimson, but not with anger. As suddenly it grew pale; and in a voice of deep agitation he said, "When an old man like myself lays his homage at her feet, it is not hard to believe how a young man might love her."

"How did you come to make this acquaintance?" said Cave, anxious to turn the conversation into a more familiar channel.

"We chanced to fail in with her brother on the river. We found him struggling with a fish far too large for his tackle, and which at last smashed his rod and got away. He showed not alone that he was a perfect angler, but that he was a fine-tempered fellow, who accepted his defeat manfully and well; he had even a good word for his enemy, sir, and it was that which attracted me. Trafford and he, young-men-like, soon understood each other; he came into our boat, lunched with us, and asked us home with him to tea. There 's the whole story. As to the intimacy that followed, it was mostly my own doing. I own to you I never so much as suspected that Trafford was smitten by her; he was always with her brother, scarcely at all in her company; and when he came to tell me he was in love, I asked him how he caught the malady, for I never saw him near the infection. Once that I knew of the matter, however, I made him write home to his family."

"It was by your advice, then, that he wrote that letter?"

"Certainly; I not only advised, I insisted on it,—I read it, too, before it was sent off. It was such a letter as, if I had been the young fellow's father, would have made me prouder than to hear he had got the thanks of Parliament."

"You and I, Fossbrooke, are old bachelors; we are scarcely able to say what we should have done if we had had sons."

"I am inclined to believe it would have made us better, not worse," said Fossbrooke, gravely.

"At all events, as it was at your instigation this letter was written, I can't well suggest your name as an impartial person in the transaction,—I mean, as one who can be referred to for advice or information."

"Don't do so, sir, or I shall be tempted to say more than may be prudent. Have you never noticed, Cave, the effect that a doctor's presence produces in the society of those who usually consult him,—the reserve,—the awkwardness,—the constraint,—the apologetic tone for this or that little indiscretion,—the sitting in the draught or the extra glass of sherry? So is it, but in a far stronger degree, when an old man of the world like myself comes back amongst those he formerly lived with,—one who knew all their past history, how they succeeded here, how they failed there,—what led the great man of fashion to finish his days in a colony, and why the Court beauty married a bishop. Ah, sir, we are the physicians who have all these secrets in our keeping. It is ours to know what sorrow is covered by that smile, how that merry laugh has but smothered the sigh of a heavy heart. It is only when a man has lived to my age, with an unfailing memory too, that he knows the real hollowness of life,—all the combinations falsified, all the hopes blighted,—the clever fellows that have turned out failures, or worse than failures,—the lovely women that have made shipwreck through their beauty. It is not only, however, that he knows this, but he knows how craft and cunning have won where ability and frankness have lost,—how intrigue and trick have done better than genius and integrity. With all this knowledge, sir, in their heads, and stout hearts within them, such men as myself have their utility in life. They are a sort of walking conscience that cannot be ignored. The railroad millionnaire talks less boastfully before him who knew him as an errand-boy; the *grande dame* is less superciliously insolent in the presence of one who remembered her in a very different character. Take my word for it, Cave, Nestor may have been a bit of a bore amongst the young Greeks of fashion, but he had his utility too."

"But how am I to answer this letter? What advice shall I give her?"

"Tell her frankly that you have made the inquiry she wished; that the young lady, who is as well born as her son, is without fortune, and if her personal qualities count for nothing, would be what the world would call a 'bad match.'"

"Yes, that sounds practicable. I think that will do."

"Tell her, also, that if she seriously desires that her son should continue in the way of that reformation he has so ardently followed for some time back, and especially so since he has made the acquaintance of this family, such a marriage as this would give her better reasons for confidence than all her most crafty devices in match-making and settlements."

"I don't think I can exactly tell her that," said Caver smiling.

"Tell her, then, that if this connection be not to her liking, to withdraw her son at once from this neighborhood before this girl should come to care for him; for if she should, by heavens! he shall marry her, if every acre of the estate were to go to a cousin ten times removed!"

"Were not these people all strangers to you t' other day, Fossbrooke?" said Cave, in something like a tone of reprehension.

"So they were. I had never so much as heard of them; but she, this girl, has a claim upon my interest, founded on a resemblance so strong that when I see her, I live back again in the long past, and find myself in converse with the dearest friends I ever had. I vow to Heaven I never knew the bitterness of want of fortune till now! I never felt how powerless and insignificant poverty can make a man till I desired to contribute to this girl's happiness; and if I were not an old worthless wreck,—shattered and unseaworthy,—I 'd set to work to-morrow to refit and try to make a fortune to bestow on her."

If Cave was half disposed to banter the old man on what seemed little short of a devoted attachment, the agitation of Fossbrooke's manner—his trembling lip, his shaking voice, his changing color—all warned him to forbear, and abstain from what might well have proved a perilous freedom.

"You will dine with us at mess, Fossbrooke, won't you?"

"No; I shall return at once to Killaloe. I made Dr. Lendrick's acquaintance just as I started by the train. I want to see more of him. Besides, now that I know what was the emergency that called young Trafford up here, I have nothing to detain me."

"Shall you see him before you go?"

"Of course. I am going over to his quarters now."

"You will not mention our conversation?"

"Certainly not."

"I 'd like to show you my letter before I send it off. I 'd be glad to think it was what you recommended."

"Write what you feel to be a fair statement of the case, and if by any chance an inclination to partiality crosses you, let it be in favor of the young. Take my word for it, Cave, there is a selfishness in age that needs no ally. Stand by the sons; the fathers and mothers will take care of themselves. Good-bye."

CHAPTER XII
A GREAT MAN'S SCHOOLFELLOW

Whether it was that the Chief Baron had thrown off an attack which had long menaced him, and whose slow approaches had gradually impaired his strength and diminished his mental activity, or whether, as some of his "friends" suggested, that the old man's tenure of life had been renewed by the impertinences of the newspapers and the insolent attacks of political foes,—an explanation not by any means far-fetched,—whatever the cause, he came out of his illness with all the signs of renewed vigor, and with a degree of mental acuteness that he had not enjoyed for many years before.

"Beattie tells me that this attack has inserted another life in my lease," said he; "and I am glad of it. It is right that the men who speculated on my death should be reminded of the uncertainty of life by the negative proof. It is well, too, that there should be men long-lived enough to bridge over periods of mediocrity, and connect the triumphs of the past with the coming glories of the future. We are surely not destined to a perpetuity of Pendletons and Fitzgibbons?"

It was thus he discoursed to an old legal comrade,—who, less gifted and less fortunate, still wore his stuff gown, and pleaded for the outer bar,—poor old Billy Haire, the dreariest advocate, and one of the honestest fellows that ever carried his bag into court. While nearly all of his contemporaries had risen to rank and eminence, Billy toiled on through life with small success, liked by his friends, respected by the world, but the terror of attorneys, who only saw in him the type of adverse decisions and unfavorable verdicts.

For forty-odd years had he lived a life that any but himself would have deemed martyrdom,—his law laughed at, his eloquence ridiculed, his manner mimicked, jeered at by the bench, quizzed by the bar, sneered at by the newspapers, every absurd story tagged to his name, every stupid blunder fathered on him, till at last, as it were, by the mere force of years, the world came to recognize the incomparable temper that no provocation had ever been able to irritate, the grand nature that rose above all resentment, and would think better of its fellows than these moods of spiteful wit or impertinent drollery might seem to entitle them to.

The old Judge liked him; he liked his manly simplicity of character, his truthfulness, and his honesty; but perhaps more than all these, did he like his dulness. It was so pleasant to him to pelt this poor heavy man with smart epigrams and pungent sarcasms on all that was doing in the world, and see the hopeless effort he made to follow him.

Billy, too, had another use; he alone, of all the Chief Baron's friends, could tell him what was the current gossip of the hall,—what men thought, or at least what they said of him. The genuine simplicity of Haire's nature gave to his revelations a character so devoid of all spitefulness,—it was so evident that, in repeating, he never identified himself with his story that Lendrick would listen to words from him that, coming from another, his resentment would have repelled with indignation.

"And you tell me that the story now is, my whole attack was nothing but temper?" said the old Judge, as the two men walked slowly up and down on the grass lawn before the door.

"Not that exactly; but they say that constitutional irritability had much to say to it."

"It was, in fact, such a seizure as, with a man like yourself, would have been a mere nothing."

"Perhaps so."

"I am sure of it, sir; and what more do they say?"

"All sorts of things, which, of course, they know nothing about. Some have it that you refused the peerage, others that it was not offered."

"Ha!" said the old man, irritably, while a faint flush tinged his cheek.

"They say, too," continued Haire, "that when the Viceroy informed you that you were not to be made a peer, you said: 'Let the Crown look to it, then. The Revenue cases all come to my court; and so long as I sit there, they shall never have a verdict.'"

"You must have invented that yourself, Billy," said the Judge, with a droll malice in his eye. "Come, confess it is your own. It is *so* like you."

"No, on my honor," said the other, solemnly.

"Not that I would take it ill, Haire, if you had. When a man has a turn for epigram, his friends must extend their indulgence to the humor."

"I assure you, positively, it is not mine."

"That is quite enough; let us talk of something else. By the way, I have a letter to show you. I put it in my pocket this morning, to let you see it; but, first of all, I must show you the writer,—here she is." He drew forth a small miniature case, and, opening it, handed it to the other.

"What a handsome girl! downright beautiful!"

"My granddaughter, sir," said the old man, proudly.

"I declare, I never saw a lovelier face," said Haire. "She must be a rare cheat if she be not as good as she is beautiful. What a sweet mouth!"

"The brow is fine; there is a high intelligence about the eyes and the temples."

"It is the smile, that little lurking smile, that captivates me. What may her age be?"

"Something close on twenty. Now for her letter. Read that."

While Haire perused the letter, the old Judge sauntered away, looking from time to time at the miniature, and muttering some low inaudible words as he went.

"I don't think I understand it. I am at a loss to catch what she is drifting at," said Haire, as he finished the first side of the letter. "What is she so grateful for?"

"You think the case is one which calls for little gratitude, then. What a sarcastic mood you are in this morning, Haire!" said the Judge, with a malicious twinkle of the eye. "Still, there are young ladies in the world who would vouchsafe to bear me company in requital for being placed at the head of such a house as this."

"I can make nothing of it," said the other, hopelessly.

"The case is this," said the Judge, as he drew his arm within the other's. "Tom Lendrick has beeu offered a post of some value—some value to a man poor as he is—at the Cape. I have told him that his acceptance in no way involves me. I have told those who have offered the place that I stand aloof in the whole negotiation,—that in their advancement of my son they establish no claim upon *me*, I have even said I will know nothing whatever of the incident." He paused for some minutes, and then went on: "I have told Tom, however, if his circumstances were such as to dispose him to avail himself of this offer, that—until he assured himself that the place was one to his liking, that it gave a reasonable prospect of permanence, that the climate was salubrious, and the society not distasteful—I would take his daughter to live with me."

"He has a son, too, has n't he?"

"He has, sir, and he fain would have induced me to take *him* instead of the girl; but this I would not listen to. I have not nerves for the loud speech and boisterous vitality of a young fellow of four or five and twenty. His very vigor would be a standing insult to me, and the fellow would know it. When men come to my age, they want a mild atmosphere in morals and manners, as well as in climate. My son's physiology has not taught him this, doctor though he be."

"I see,—I see it all now," said Haire; "and the girl, though sorry to be separated from her father, is gratified by the thought of becoming a tie between him and you."

"That is not in the record, sir," said the Judge, sternly. "Keep to your brief." He took the letter sharply from the other's hand as he spoke. "My granddaughter has not had much experience of life; but her woman's tact has told her that her real difficulty—her only one, perhaps—will be with Lady Lendrick. She cannot know that Lady Lendrick's authority in this house is nothing,—less than nothing. I would never have invited her to come here, had it been otherwise."

"Have you apprised Lady Lendrick of this arrangement?"

"No, sir; nor shall I. it shall be for you to do that 'officiously,' as the French say, to distinguish from what is called 'officially.' I mean you to call upon her and say, in the course of conversation, informally, accidentally, that Miss Lendrick's arrival at the Priory has been deferred, or that it is fixed for such a date,—in fact, sir, whatever your own nice tact may deem the neatest mode of alluding to the topic, leaving to her the reply. You understand me?"

"I 'm not so sure that I do."

"So much the better; your simplicity will be more inscrutable than your subtlety, Haire. I can deal with the one—the other masters me."

"I declare frankly I don't like the mission. I was never, so to say, a favorite with her Ladyship."

"Neither was I, sir," said the other, with a peremptory loudness that was almost startling.

"Hadn't you better intimate it by a few lines in a note? Had n't you better say that, having seen your son during his late visit to town, and learnt his intention to accept a colonial appointment—"

"All this would be apologetic, sir, and must not be thought of. Don't you know, Haire, that every unnecessary affidavit is a flaw in a man's case? Go and see her; your very awkwardness will imply a secret, and she 'll be so well pleased with her acuteness in discovering the mystery, she 'll half forget its offence."

"Let me clearly understand what I' ve got to do. I 'm to tell her or to let her find out that you have been reconciled to your son Tom?"

"There is not a word of reconciliation, sir, in all your instructions. You are to limit yourself to the statement that touches my granddaughter."

"Very well; it will be so much the easier. I'm to say, then, that you have adopted her, and placed her at the head of your house; that she is to live here in all respects as its mistress?"

He paused; and as the Judge bowed a concurrence, he went on: "Of course you will allow me to add that I was never consulted; that you did not ask my opinion, and that I never gave one?"

"You are at liberty to, say all this."

"I would even say that I don't exactly see how the thing will work. A very young girl, with of course a limited experience of life, will have no common difficulties in dealing with a world so new and strange, particularly without the companionship of one of her own sex."

"I cannot promise to supply that want, but she shall see as much of *you* as possible." And the words were uttered with a blended courtesy and malice, of which he was perfect master. Poor Haire, however, only saw the complimentary part, and hurriedly pledged himself to be at Miss Lendrick's orders at all times.

"Come and let me show you how I mean to lodge her. I intend her to feel a perfect independence of me and my humors. We are to see each other from inclination, not constraint: I intend, sir that we should live on good terms; and as the Church will have nothing to say to the compact, it is possible it may succeed.

"These rooms are to be hers," said he, opening a door which offered a *vista* through several handsomely furnished rooms, all looking out upon a neatly kept flower-garden. "Lady Lendrick, I believe, had long since destined them for a son and daughter-in-law of hers, who are on their way home from India. The plan will be now all the more difficult of accomplishment."

"Which will not make my communication to her the pleasanter."

"But redound so much the more to the credit of your adroitness, Haire, if you succeed. Come over here this evening and report progress." And with this he nodded an easy good-bye, and strolled down the garden.

"I don't envy Haire his brief in this case," muttered he. "He'll not have the 'court with him,' that's certain;" and he laughed spitefully to himself as he went.

CHAPTER XIII
LAST DAYS

It may seem a hardship, but not improbably it is in its way an alleviation, that we are never involved in any of the great trials in life without having to deal with certain material embarrassments, questions of vulgar interest which concern our pockets and affect our finances.

Poor Lendrick's was a case in point. He was about to leave his country, — to tear himself from a home he had embellished, — to separate from his children that he loved so dearly, to face a new life in a new land, friendless and alone; and with all these cares on his heart, he had creditors to satisfy, debts to insure payment of by security, and, not least of his troubles, his house to relet. Now, the value the world sets on that which is not for sale is very unlike its estimate for the same commodity when brought to market. The light claret your friend pronounced a very pleasant little wine at your own table, he would discover, when offered for purchase, to be poor, washy, and acrid. The horse you had left him, and whose performance he had encomiumized, if put up to auction, would be found spavined, or windgalled, or broken-down. Such a stern test is money, so fearfully does its coarse jingle jar upon all the music of flattery, and make discord of all compliment. To such a pitch is the process carried, that even pretty women, who as wives were objects of admiration to despairing and disappointed adorers, have become, by widowhood, very ordinary creatures, simply because they are once more "in the market."

It is well for us that heaven itself was not in the "Price Current," or we might have begun to think lightly of it. At all events we 'd have higgled about the cost, and tried to get there as cheaply as might be.

From the day that the Swan's Nest appeared in the Dublin papers "to be let furnished, for the three years of an unexpired term," Lendrick was besieged by letters and applications. All the world apparently wanted the place, but wanted it in some way or other quite out of his power to accord. One insisted on having it unfurnished, and for a much longer period than he could give. Another desired more land, and the right of shooting over several hundred additional acres. A third would like the house and garden, but would not burden himself with the lawn, and could not see why Lendrick might not continue to hold the meadow-land, and come back from the Cape or anywhere else to mow the grass and rick it in due season.

A schoolmistress proposed he should build a dormitory for thirty young ladies, and make the flower-garden into a playground; and a miller from Limerick inquired whether he was willing to join in a suit to establish a right of water-power by diverting a stream from the Shannon through the dining-room to turn an undershot wheel.

It was marvellous with what patience and courtesy Lendrick replied to these and such-like, politely assuring the writers how he regretted his inability to meet their wishes, and modestly confessing that he had neither the money nor the time to make his house other than it was.

All these, however, were as nothing to his trials when the day arrived when the house and grounds, in the language of the advertisement, were "on view," and the world of the curious and idle were free to invade the place, stroll at will through rooms and gardens, comment and criticise not merely the objects before them, but the taste and the fortunes, the habits and the lives of those who had made this their home, and these things part of their own natures.

In a half-jesting humor, but really to save Lendrick from a mortification which, to a nature timid and sensitive as his, would have been torture, Sir Brook and Tom agreed to divide the labors of ciceroneship between them; the former devoting his attentions to the house and furniture, while Tom assumed the charge of grounds and gardens. To complete the arrangement, Lendrick and Lucy were banished to a small summer-house, and strictly enjoined never to venture abroad so long as the stranger horde overran the territory.

"I declare, my dear, I almost think the remedy worse than the disease," said Lendrick to his daughter, as he paced with short feverish steps the narrow limits of his prison-house. "This isolation here has something secret, something that suggests shame about it. I think I could almost rather face all the remarks our visitors might make than sit down here to fancy and brood over them."

"I suspect not, dearest papa; I believe the plan will spare us much that might pain us."

"After all, child, these people have a right to be critical, and they are not bound to know by what associations you and I are tied to that old garden-seat or that bookstand, and we ought to be able to avoid showing them this."

"Perhaps we ought, papa; but could we do so? that's-the question."

"Surely the tradesman affects no such squeamishness about what he offers for sale."

"True, papa; because none of his wares have caught any clew to his identity. They have never been his in the sense which makes possession pleasure."

"I wish they would not laugh without there; their coarse laughter sounds to me so like vulgar ridicule. I hardly thought all this would have made me so irritable; even the children's voices jar on my nerves."

He turned away his head, but her eyes followed him, and two heavy tears stole slowly along her cheek, and her lip quivered as she looked.

"There, they are going away," said he, listening; "I am better now."

"That 's right, dearest papa; I knew it was a mere passing pang," said she, drawing her arm within his, and walking along at his side. "How kind Sir Brook is!"

"How kind every one, we might say. Poor Mills is like a brother, and Tobin too,—I scarcely expected so much heart from him. He gave me his old lancet-case as a keepsake yesterday, and I declare his voice trembled as he said good-bye."

"As for the poor people, I hear, papa, that one would think they had lost their nearest and dearest. Molly Dew says they were crying in her house this morning over their breakfast as if it was a funeral."

"Is it not strange, Lucy, that what touches the heart so painfully should help to heal the pang it gives? There is that in all this affection for us that gladdens while it grieves. All,—all are so kind to us! That young fellow— Trafford I think his name is—he was waiting at the post for his letters this morning when I came up, and it seems that Foss-brooke had told him of my appointment,—indiscreet of him, for I would not wish it talked of; but Trafford turned to him and said, 'Ask Dr. Lendrick, is he decided about going;' and when he heard that I was, he scarcely said goodbye, but jumped into a cab, and drove off full speed.

"'What does that mean?' asked I.

"'He was so fond of Tom,' said Fossbrooke, 'they were never separate this last month or five weeks;' so you see, darling, each of us has his sphere of love and affection."

Lucy was crimson over face and neck, but never spoke a word. Had she spoken it would have been, perhaps, to corroborate Sir Brook, and to say how fond the young men were of each other. I do not affirm this, I only hint that it is likely. Where there are blanks in this narrative, the reader has as much right to fill them as myself.

"Sir Brook," continued Lendrick, "thinks well of the young man; but for my own part I hardly like to see Tom in close companionship with one so much his superior in fortune. He is easily led, and has not yet learned that stern lesson in life, how to confess that there are many things he has no pretension to aspire to."

"Tom loves you too sincerely, papa, ever to do that which would seriously grieve you."

"He would not deliberately,—he would not in cold blood, Lucy; but young men, when together, have not many moods of deliberation or cold blood. But let us not speculate on trouble that may never come. It is enough for the present that he and Trafford are separated, if Trafford was even likely to lead him into ways of extravagance."

"What 's that! Is n't it, Tom? He's laughing heartily at something. Yes; here he comes."

"You may come out; the last of them has just driven off," cried Tom, knocking at the door, while he continued to laugh on immoderately.

"What is it, Tom? What are you laughing at?"

"You should have seen it; it's nothing to tell, but it was wonderful to witness. I'll never forget it as long as I live."

"But what was it?" asked she, impatiently.

"I thought we had fully done with all our visitors,—and a rum set they were, most of them, not thinking of taking the place, but come out of mere curiosity,—when who should drive up with two postilions and four spicy grays but Lady Drumcarran and a large party, three horsemen following? I just caught the word 'Excellency,' and found out from one of the servants that a tall old man with white hair and very heavy eyebrows was the Lord-Lieutenant. He stooped a good deal, and walked tenderly; and as the Countess was most eager about the grounds and the gardens, they parted company very soon, he going into the house to sit down, while she prosecuted her inquiries without doors.

"I took him into the library; we had a long chat about fishing, and fish-curing, and the London markets, and flax, and national education, and land-tenure, and such-like. Of course I affected not to know who he was, and I took the opportunity to say scores of impertinences about the stupidity of the Castle, and the sort of men they send over here to govern us; and he asked me if I was destined for any career or profession, and I told him frankly that whenever I took up anything I always was sure to discover it was the one very thing that didn't suit me; and as I made this unlucky discovery in law, medicine, and the Church, I had given up my college career, and was now in a sort of interregnal period, wondering what it was to be next. I did n't like to own that the *res angusto* had anything to say to it. It was no business of his to know about that.

"'You surely have friends able and willing to suggest something that would fit you,' said he. 'Is not the Chief Baron your grandfather?'

"'Yes, and he might make me crier of his court; but I think he has promised the reversion to his butler. The fact is, I 'd not do over well with any fixed responsibilities attached to me. I 'd rather be a guerilla than serve in the regulars, and so I 'll just wait and see if something won't turn up in that undisciplined force I 'd like to serve with.'

"'I 'll give you my name,' said he, 'before we part, and possibly I may know some one who might be of use to you.'

"I thanked him coolly, and we talked of something else, when there came a short plump little fellow, all beard and gold chains, to say that Lady Drumcarran was waiting for him. 'Tell her I'm coming,' said he; 'and, Balfour,' he cried out, 'before you go away, give this gentleman my address, and if he should call, take care that I see him.'

"Balfour eyed me, and I eyed him, with, I take it, pretty much the same result, which said plainly enough, 'You 're not the man for me.'

"'What in heaven's name is this?' cried the Viceroy, as he got outside and saw Lady Drumcarran at the head of a procession carrying plants, slips, and flower-pots down to the carriage.

"'Her Ladyship has made a raid amongst the greeneries,' said Balfour, 'and tipped the head-gardener, that tall fellow there with the yellow rose-tree; as the place is going to be sold, she thought she might well do a little genteel pillage.' Curious to see who our gardener could be, all the more that he was said to be 'tall,' I went forward, and what do you think I saw? Sir Brook, with a flower-pot under one arm, and a quantity of cuttings under the other, walking a little after the Countess, who was evidently giving him ample directions as to her intentions. I could scarcely refrain from an outburst of laughing, but I got away into the shrubbery and watched the whole proceedings. I was too far off to hear, but this much I saw. Sir Brook had deposited his rose-tree and his slips on the rumble, and stood beside the carriage with his hat off. When his Excellency came up, a sudden movement took place in the group, and the Viceroy, seeming to push his way through the others, cried out something I could not catch, and then grasped Sir Brook's hand with both his own. All was tumult in a moment. My Lady, in evident confusion and shame,—that much I could see,—was courtesying deeply to Sir Brook, who seemed not to understand her apologies—, at least, he appeared stately and courteous, as usual, and not in the slightest degree put out or chagrined by the incident. Though Lady Drumcarran was profuse of her excuses, and most eager to make amends for her mistake, the Viceroy took Sir Brook's arm and led him off to a little distance, where they talked together for a few moments.

"'It's a promise, then, Fossbrooke,—you promise me!' cried he aloud, as he approached the carriage.

"'Rely upon me,—and within a week, or ten days at farthest,' said Sir Brook, as they drove away.

"I have not seen him since, and I scarcely know if I shall be able to meet him without laughing."

"Here he comes," cried Lucy; "and take care, Tom, that you do nothing that might offend him."

The caution was so far unnecessary that Sir Brook's manner, as he drew near, had a certain stately dignity that invited no raillery.

"You have been detained a long time a prisoner, Dr. Len-drick," said Fossbrooke, calmly; "but your visitors were so charmed with all they saw that they lingered on, unwilling to take their leave."

"Tom tells me we had some of our county notabilities,—Lord and Lady Drumcarran, the Lacys, and others," said Lendrick.

"Yes; and the Lord-Lieutenant, too, whom I used to know at Christ Church. He would have been well pleased to have met you. He told me your father was the ablest and most brilliant talker he ever knew."

"Ah! we are very unlike," said Lendrick, blushing modestly. "Did he give any hint as to whether his party are pleased or the reverse with my father's late conduct?"

"He only said, 'I wish you knew him, Fossbrooke; I sincerely wish you knew him, if only to assure him that he will meet far more generous treatment from us than from the Opposition.' He added that we were men to suit each other; and this, of course, was a flattery for which I am very grateful."

"And the tall man with the stoop was the Lord-Lieutenant?" asked Tom. "I passed half an hour or more with him in the library, and he invited me to call upon him, and told a young fellow, named Balfour, to give me his address, which he forgot to do."

"We can go together, if you have no objection; for I, too, have promised to pay my respects," said Sir Brook.

Tom was delighted at the suggestion, but whispered in his sister's ear, as they passed out into the garden, "I thought I 'd have burst my sides laughing when I met him; but it's the very last thing in my thoughts now. I declare I 'd as soon pull a tiger's whiskers as venture on the smallest liberty with him."

"I think you are right, Tom," said she, squeezing his arm affectionately, to show that she not alone agreed with him, but was pleased that he had given her the opportunity of doing so.

"I wonder is he telling the governor what happened this morning? It can scarcely be that, though, they look so grave."

"Papa seems agitated too," said Lucy.

"I just caught Trafford's name as they passed. I hope he 's not saying anything against him. It is not only that Lionel Trafford is as good a fellow as ever lived, but that he fully believes Fossbrooke likes him. I don't think he could be so false; do you, Lucy?"

"I 'm certain he is not. There, papa is beckoning to you; he wants you;" and Lucy turned hurriedly away, anxious to conceal her emotion, for her cheeks were burning, and her lips trembled with agitation.

CHAPTER XIV
TOM CROSS-EXAMINES HIS SISTER

It was decided on that evening that Sir Brook and Tom should set out for Dublin the next morning. Lucy knew not why this sudden determination had been come to, and Tom, who never yet had kept a secret from her, was now reserved and uncommunicative. Nor was it merely that he held aloof his confidence, but he was short and snappish in his manner, as though she had someway vexed him, and vexed him in some shape that he could not openly speak of or resent.

This was very new to her from him, and yet how was it? She had not courage to ask for an explanation. Tom was not exactly one of those people of whom it was pleasant to ask explanations., Where the matter to be explained might be one of delicacy, he had a way of abruptly blurting out the very thing one would have desired might be kept back. Just as an awkward surgeon will tear off the dressing, and set a wound a-bleeding, would he rudely destroy the work of time in healing by a moment of rash impatience. It was knowing this—knowing it well—that deterred Lucy from asking what might lead to something not over-agreeable to hear.

"Shall I pack your portmanteau, Tom?" asked she. It was a task that always fell to her lot.

"No; Nicholas can do it,—any one can do it," said he, as he mumbled with an unlit cigar between his teeth.

"You used to say I always did it best, Tom,—that I never forgot anything," said she, caressingly.

"Perhaps I did,—perhaps I thought so. Look here, Lucy," said he, as though by an immense effort he had got strength to say what he wanted, "I am half vexed with you, if not more than half."

"Vexed with me, Tom,—vexed with *me!* and for what?"

"I don't think that you need ask. I am inclined to believe that you know perfectly well what I mean, and what I would much rather not say, if you will only let me."

"I do not," said she, slowly and deliberately.

"Do you mean to say, Lucy," said he, and his manner was almost stern as he spoke, "that you have no secrets from me, that you are as frank and outspoken with me today as you were three months ago?"

"I do say so."

"Then what's the meaning of this letter?" cried he, as, carried away by a burst of passion, he overstepped all the prudential reserve he had sworn to himself to regard. "What does this mean?"

"I know nothing of that letter, nor what it contains," said she, blushing till her very brow became crimson.

"I don't suppose you do, for though it is addressed to you, the seal is unbroken; but you know whose handwriting it's in, and you know that you have had others from the same quarter."

"I believe the writing is Mr. Trafford's," said she, as a deathlike paleness spread over her face, "because he himself once asked me to read a letter from him in the same handwriting."

"Which you did?"

"No; I refused. I handed the letter back to him unopened, and said that, as I certainly should not write to him without my father's knowledge and permission, I would not read a letter from him without the same."

"And what was the epistle, then, that the vicar's housekeeper handed him from you?"

"That same letter I have spoken of. He left it on my table, insisting and believing that on second thoughts I would read it. He thought so because it was not to me, though addressed to me, but the copy of a letter he had written to his mother, about me certainly." Here she blushed deeply again. "As I continued, however, of the same mind, determined not to see what the letter contained, I re-enclosed it and gave it to Mrs. Brennan to hand to him."

"And all this you kept a secret from me?"

"It was not my secret. It was his. It was his till such time as he could speak of it to my father, and this he told me had not yet come."

"Why not?"

"I never asked him that. I do not think, Tom," said she, with much emotion, "it was such a question as you would have had me ask."

"Do you love—Come, darling Lucy, don't be angry with me. I never meant to wound your feelings. Don't sob that way, my dear, dear Lucy. You know what a rough coarse fellow I am; but I'd rather die than offend you.

Why did you not tell me of all this? I never liked any one so well as Trafford, and why leave me to the chance of misconstruing him? Would n't it have been the best way to have trusted me as you always have?"

"I don't see what there was to have confided to you. Mr. Trafford might, if he wished. I mean, that if there was a secret at all. I don't know what I mean," cried she, covering her face with her handkerchief, while a convulsive motion of her shoulders showed how she was moved.

"I am as glad as if I had got a thousand pounds, to know you have been so right, so thoroughly right, in all this, Lucy; and I am glad, too, that Trafford has done nothing to make me think less well of him. Let's be friends; give me your hand, like a dear, good girl, and forgive me if I have said what pained you."

"I am not angry, Tom," said she, giving her hand, but with her head still averted.

"God knows it's not the time for us to fall out," said he, with a shaking voice. "Going to separate as we are, and when to be together again not so easy to imagine."

"You are surely going out with papa?" asked she, eagerly.

"No; they say not."

"Who says not?"

"The governor himself—Sir Brook—old Mills—everybody, in fact. They have held a committee of the whole house on it. I think Nicholas was present too; and it has been decided that as I am very much given to idleness, bitter beer, and cigars, I ought not to be anywhere where these ingredients compose the chief part of existence. Now the Cape is precisely one of these places; and if you abstract the idleness, the bitter beer, and the tobacco, there is nothing left but a little Hottentotism, which is neither pleasant nor profitable. Voted, therefore, I am not to go to the Cape. It is much easier, however, to open the geography books, and show all the places I am unfit for, than to hit upon the one that will suit me. And so I am going up to Dublin to-morrow with Sir Brook to consult—I don't well know whom, perhaps a fortune-teller—what 's to be done with me. All I do know is, I am to see my grandfather, and to wait on the Viceroy, and I don't anticipate that any of us will derive much pleasure from either event."

"Oh, Tom! what happiness it would be to me if grandpapa—" She stopped, blushed, and tried in vain to go on.

"Which is about the least likely thing in the world, Lucy," said he, answering her unspoken sentence. "I am just the sort of creature he could n't abide,—not to add that, from all I have heard of him, I 'd rather take three years with hard labor at the hulks than live with him. It will do very well with you. You have patience, and a soft forgiving disposition. You 'll fancy yourself, besides, Heaven knows what of a heroine, for submitting to his atrocious temper, and imagine slavery to be martyrdom. Now, I could n't. I 'd let him understand that I was one of the family, and had a born right to be as ill-tempered, as selfish, and as unmannerly as any other Lendrick."

"But if he should like you, Tom? If you made a favorable impression upon him when you met?"

"If I should, I think I 'd go over to South Carolina, and ask some one to buy me as a negro, for I 'd know in my heart it was all I could be fit for."

"Oh, my dear, dear Tom, I wish you would meet him in a different spirit, if only for poor papa's sake. You know what store he lays by grandpapa's affection."

"I see it, and it puzzles me. If any one should continue to ill-treat me for five-and-twenty years, I 'd not think of beginning to forgive him till after fifty more, and I 'm not quite sure I 'd succeed then."

"But you are to meet him, Tom," said she, hopefully. "I trust much to your meeting."

"That 's more than I do, Lucy. Indeed, I 'd not go at all, except on the condition which I have made with myself, to accept nothing from him. I had not meant to tell you this; but it has escaped me, and can't be helped. Don't hang your head and pout your lip over that bad boy, brother Tom. I intend to be as submissive and as humble in our interview as if I was going to owe my life to him, just because I want him to be very kind and gracious to you; and I 'd not wish to give him any reason for saying harsh things of me, which would hurt you to listen to. If I only knew how—and I protest I do not—I'd even try and make a favorable impression upon him, for I 'd like to be able to come and see you, Lucy, now and then, and it would be a sore blow to me if he forbade me."

"You don't think I'd remain under his roof if he should do so?" asked she, indignantly.

"Not if you saw him turn me away,—shutting the door in my face; but what scores of civil ways there are of intimating that one is not welcome! But why imagine all these?—none of them may happen; and, as Sir Brook says, the worst misfortunes of life are those that never come to us; and I, for one, am determined to deal only with real, actual, present enemies. Is n't he a rare old fellow?—don't you like him, Lucy?"

"I like him greatly."

"He loves you, Lucy,—he told me so; he said you were so like a girl whose godfather he was, and that he had loved her as if she were his own. Whether she had died, or whether something had happened that estranged them, I could n't make out; but he said you had raised up some old half-dead embers in his heart, and kindled a flame where he had thought all was to be cold forever; and the tears came into his eyes, and that great deep voice of his grew fainter and fainter, and something that sounded like a sob stopped him. I always knew he was a brave, stout-hearted, gallant fellow; but that he could feel like this I never imagined. I almost think it was some girl he was going to be married to once that you must be so like. Don't you think so?" "I don't know; I cannot even guess," said she, slowly. "It's not exactly the sort of nature where one would expect to find much sentiment; but, as he said one day, some old hearts are like old chateaux, with strange old chambers in them that none have traversed for years and years, and with all the old furniture moth-eaten and crumbling, but standing just where it used to be. I 'd not wonder if it was of himself he was speaking."

She remained silent and thoughtful, and he went on,—"There's a deal of romance under that quaint stern exterior. What do you think he said this morning?—'Your father's heart is wrapped up in this place, Tom; let us set to work to make money and buy it for him. 'I did not believe he was serious, and I said some stupid nonsense about a diamond necklace and ear-rings for you on the day of presentation; and he turned upon me with a fierce look, and in a voice trembling with anger, said, 'Well, sir, and whom would they become better? Is it her birth or her beauty would disparage them, if they were the jewels of a crown?' I know I 'll not cross another whim of his in the same fashion again; though he came to my room afterwards to make an apology for the tone in which he had spoken, and assured me it should never be repeated." "I hope you told him you had not felt offended." "I did more,—I did, at least, what pleased him more,—I said I was delighted with that plan of his about buying up the Nest, and that the very thought gave a zest to any pursuit I might engage in; and so, Lucy, it is settled between us that if his Excellency won't make me something with a fine salary and large perquisites, Sir Brook and I are to set out I'm not very sure where, and we are to do I'm not quite certain what; but two such clever fellows, uniting experience with energy, can't fail, and the double event—I mean the estate and the diamonds—are just as good as won already. Well, what do you want, Nicholas?" cried Tom, as the grim old man put his head inside the door and retired again, mumbling something as he went. "Oh, I remember it now; he has been tormenting the governor all day about getting him some place,—some situation or other; and the old rascal thinks we are the most ungrateful wretches under the sun, to be so full of our own affairs and so forgetful of his: we are certainly not likely to leave him unprovided for; he can't imagine that. Here he comes again. My father is gone into Killaloe, Nicholas; but don't be uneasy, he 'll not forget you."

"Forgettin's one thing, Master Tom, and rememberin's the right way is another," said Nicholas, sternly. "I told him yesterday, and I repeated it to-day, I won't go among them Hottentots."

"Has he asked you?"

"Did he ask me?" repeated the old man, leaning forward and eying him fiercely,—"did he ask me?"

"My brother means, Nicholas, that papa could n't expect you to go so far away from your home and your friends."

"And where's my home and my friends?" cried the irascible old fellow; "and I forty-eight years in the family? Is that the way to have a home or friends either?"

"No, Tom, no,—I entreat—I beg of you," said Lucy, standing between her brother and the old man, and placing her hand on Tom's lips; "you know well that he can't help it."

"That's just it," cried Nicholas, catching the words; "I can't help it. I 'm too old to help it. It is n't after eight-and-forty years one ought to be looking out for new sarvice."

"Papa hopes that grandpapa will have no objection to taking you, Nicholas; he means to write about it to-day; but if there should be a difficulty, he has another place."

"Maybe I'm to 'list and be a sodger; faix, it wouldn't be much worse than going back to your grandfather."

"Why, you discontented old fool," burst in Tom, "have n't you been teasing our souls out these ten years back by your stories of the fine life you led in the Chief Baron's house?"

"The eatin' was better, and the drinkin' was better," said Nicholas, resolutely. "Wherever the devil it comes from, the small beer here bangs

Banagher; but for the matter of temper he was one of yourselves! and by my sowl, it's a family not easily matched!"

"I agree with you; any other man than my father would have pitched you neck and crop into the Shannon years ago,—I 'll be shot if I would n't."

"Mind them words. What you said there is a threat; it's what the law makes a constructive threat, and we 'll see what the Coorts say to it."

"I declare, Nicholas, you would provoke any one; you will let no one be your friend," said Lucy; and taking her brother's arm she led him away, while the old man, watching them till they entered the shrubbery, seated himself leisurely in a deep arm-chair, and wiped the perspiration from his forehead. "By my conscience," muttered he, "it takes two years off my life every day I have to keep yez in order."

CHAPTER XV
MR. HAIRE'S MISSION

Although the Chief Baron had assured Haire that his mission had no difficulty about it, that he 'd find her Ladyship would receive him in a very courteous spirit, and, finally, that "he'd do the thing" admirably, the unhappy little lawyer approached his task with considerable misgivings, which culminated in actual terror as he knocked at the door of the house where Lady Lendrick resided in Merrion Square, and sent up his name.

"The ladies are still in committee, sir," said a bland-looking, usher-like personage, who, taking up Haire's card from the salver, scanned the name with a half-supercilious look.

"In committee! ah, indeed, I was not aware," stammered out Haire. "I suspect—that is—I have reason to believe her Ladyship is aware—I mean my name is not unknown to Lady Lendrick—would you kindly present my card?"

"Take it up, Bates," said the man in black, and then turned away to address another person, for the hall was crowded with people of various conditions and ranks, and who showed in their air and manner a something of anxiety, if not of impatience.

"Mr. MacClean,—where's Mr. MacClean?" cried a man in livery, as he held forth a square-shaped letter. "Is Mr. MacClean there?"

"Yes, I'm Mr. MacClean," said a red-faced, fussy-looking man. "I'm Mr. George Henry MacClean, of 41 Mount Street."

"Two tickets for Mr. MacClean," said the usher, handing him the letter with a polite bow.

"Mr. Nolan, Balls Bridge,—does any one represent Mr. Nolan of Balls Bridge?" said the usher, haughtily.

"That 's me," said a short man, who wiped the perspiration from his face with a red-spotted handkerchief, as large as a small bed-quilt,—"that's me."

"The references not satisfactory, Mr. Nolan," said the usher, reading from a paper in his hand.

"Not satisfactory?—what do you mean? Is Peter Arkins, Esquire, of Clontarf, unsatisfactory? Is Mr. Ryland, of Abbey Street, unsatisfactory?"

"I am really, sir, unable to afford you the explanation you desire. I am simply deputed by her Ladyship to return the reply that I find written here. The noise is really so great here I can hear nothing. Who are you asking for, Bates?"

"Mr. Mortimer O'Hagan."

"He's gone away," cried a voice; "he was here since eleven o'clock."

"Application refused. Will some one tell Mr. O'Hagan his application is refused?" said the usher, austerely.

"Might I be bold enough to ask what is going forward?" whispered Haire.

"Mr. W. Haire, Ely Place," shouted out the man in livery. "Card refused for want of a reference."

"You ought to have sent up two names,—well-known names, Mr. Haire," said the usher, with a politeness that seemed marked. "It's not too late yet; let me see," and he looked at his watch, "we want a quarter to one; be back here in half an hour. Take a car,—you 'll find one at the door. Get your names, and I 'll see if I can't do it for you."

"I am afraid I don't understand you, and I am sure you don't understand me. I came here by appointment—" The rest of the sentence was lost by a considerable bustle and movement that now ensued, for a number of ladies descended the stairs, chatting and laughing freely; while servants rushed hither and thither, calling up carriages, or inquiring for others not yet come. The usher, frantically pushing the crowd aside to clear a path for the ladies, was profuse of apologies for the confusion; adding at the same time that "it was twice as bad an hour ago. There were n't less than two hundred here this morning."

A number of little pleasantries passed as the bland usher handed the ladies to their carriages; and it was evident by their laughter that his remarks were deemed pungent and witty. Meanwhile the hall was becoming deserted. The persons who had crowded there, descending singly or in groups, went their several ways, leaving Haire the only one behind. "And now, sir," said the usher, "you see it's all over. You would n't take my advice. They are all gone, and it's the last meeting."

"Will you favor me so far as to say for what did they meet? What was the object of the gathering?"

"I suppose, sir, you are not a reader of the morning papers?"

"Occasionally. Indeed, I always glance at them."

"Well, sir, and has not your glance fallen upon the announcement of the ball,—the grand ball to be given at the-Rotundo for the orphan asylum called the 'Rogues Redemptory,' at Rathmines, at the head of whose patronesses stands my Lady's name?"

Haire shook his head in negative.

"And have you not come like the rest with an application for permission to attend the ball?"

"No; I have come to speak to Lady Lendrick—and by appointment too."

A faint but prolonged "Indeed!" expressed the usher's-astonishment, and he turned and whispered a few words to-a footman at his side. He disappeared, and returned in & moment to say that her Ladyship would see Mr. Haire.

"I trust you will forgive me, sir," said Lady Lendrick,—a very large, very showy, and still handsome woman,—as she motioned him to be seated. "I got your card when my head was so full of this tiresome ball, and I made the absurd mistake of supposing you came for tickets. You are, I think your note says, an old friend of Mr. Thomas-Lendrick?"

"I am an old friend of his father's. Madam! The Chief Baron and myself were schoolfellows."

"Yes, yes: I have no doubt," said she, hurriedly; "but from your note—I have it here somewhere," and she rummaged amongst a lot of papers that littered the table,—"your note gave me to understand that your visit to me regarded Mr. Thomas Lendrick, and not the Chief Baron. It is possible, however, I may have mistaken your meaning. I wish I could find it. I laid it out of my hand a moment ago. Oh, here it is! now we shall see which of us is right," and with a sort of triumph she opened the letter and read aloud, slurring over the few commencing lines till she came to "that I may explain to your Ladyship the circumstances by which Mr. Thomas Lendrick's home will for the present be broken up, and entreat of you to extend to his daughter the same kind interest and favor you have so constantly extended to her father." "Now, sir, I hope I may say that it is not *I* have been mistaken. If I read this passage aright, it bespeaks my consideration for a young lady who will shortly need a home and a protectress."

"I suppose I expressed myself very ill. I mean, Madam, I take it, that in my endeavor not to employ any abruptness, I may have fallen into some obscurity. Shall I own, besides," added he, with a tone of half-desperation in his voice, "that I had no fancy for this mission of mine at all,—that I undertook it wholly against my will? Baron Len-drick's broken health, my old friendship for him, his insistence,—and you can understand what *that* is, eh?"—he thought she was about to speak; but she only gave a faint equivocal sort of smile, and he went on: "All these together overcame my scruples, and I agreed to come." He paused here as though he had made the fullest and most ample explanation, and that it was now her turn to speak.

"Well, sir," said she, "go on; I am all ears for your communication."

"There it is: that 's the whole of it, Madam. You are to understand distinctly that with the arrangement itself I had no concern whatever. Baron Lendrick never asked my advice; I never tendered it. I 'm not sure that I should have concurred with his notions,—but that 's nothing to the purpose; all that I consented to was to come here, to tell you the thing is so, and why it is so—there!" and with this he wiped his forehead, for the exertion had heated and fatigued him.

"I know I 'm very dull, very slow of comprehension; and in compassion for this defect, will you kindly make your explanation a little, a very little, fuller? What is it that is *so?*" and she emphasized the last word with a marked sarcasm in her tone.

"Oh, I can see that your Ladyship may not quite like it. There is no reason why you should like it,—all things considered; but, after all, it may turn out very well. If she suit him, if she can hit it off with his temper,—and she may,—young folks have often more forbearance than older ones,—there 's no saying what it may lead to."

"Once for all, sir," said she, haughtily, for her temper was sorely tried, "what is this thing which I am not to like, and yet bound to bear?"

"I don't think I said that; I trust I never said your Ladyship was bound to bear anything. So well as I can recall the Chief Baron's words,—and, God forgive me, but I wish I was—no matter what or where—when I heard them,—this is the substance of what he said: 'Tell her,' meaning your Ladyship,—'tell her that, rightly understood, the presence of my granddaughter as mistress of my house—'"

"What do you say, sir?—is Miss Lendrick coming to reside at the Priory?"

"Of course—what else have I been saying this half-hour?"

"To take the position of lady of the house?" said she, not deigning to notice his question.

"Just so, Madam."

"I declare, sir, bold as the step is," —she arose as she spoke, and drew herself haughtily up,—"bold as the step is, it is not half so bold as your own courage in coming to tell of it. What the Chief Baron had not the hardihood to communicate in writing, you dare to deliver to me by word of mouth,— you dare to announce to me that my place, the station I ought to fill, is to be occupied by another, and that whenever I pass the threshold of the Priory, I come as the guest of Lucy Lendrick! I do hope, sir, I may attribute to the confusion of your faculties—a confusion of which this short interview has given me proof—that you really never rightly apprehended the ignominy of the mission your friend intrusted to you."

"You 're right there," said he, placing both his hands on the side of his head; "confusion is just the name for it."

"Yes, sir; but I apprehend you must have undertaken this office in a calm moment, and let me ask you how you could have lent yourself to such a task? You are aware, for the whole world is aware, that in living apart from the Chief Baron I am yielding to a necessity imposed by his horrible, his insufferable temper; now, how long will this explanation be valid, if my place in any respect should be occupied by another? The isolation in which he now lives, his estrangement from the world, serve to show that he has withdrawn from society, and accepted the position of a recluse. Will this continue now? Will these be the habits of the house with a young lady at its bead, free to indulge all the caprices of ignorant girlhood? I declare, sir, I wonder how a little consideration for your friend might not have led you to warn him against the indiscretion he was about to commit. The slight to me," said she, sarcastically, and flushing deeply, "it was possible you might overlook; but I scarcely see how you could have forgotten the stain that must attach to that 'large intellect,—that wise and truly great man.' I am quoting a paragraph I read in the 'Post' this morning, with which, perhaps, you are familiar."

"I did not see it," said Haire, helplessly.

"I declare, sir, I was unjust enough to think you wrote it. I thought no one short of him who had come on your errand to-day could have been the author."

"Well, I wish with all my heart I 'd never come," said he, with a melancholy gesture of his hands.

"I declare, sir, I am not surprised at your confession. I suppose you are not aware that in the very moment adopted for this—this—this new establishment, there is something like studied insult to me. It is only ten days ago I mentioned to the Chief Baron that my son, Colonel Sewell, was coming back from India on a sick-leave. He has a wife and three little children, and, like most soldiers, is not over-well off. I suggested that as the Priory was a large roomy house, with abundant space for many people without in the slightest degree interfering with each other, he should offer the Sewells to take them in. I said nothing more,—nothing about *ménage*,—no details of any kind. I simply said: "Could n't you give the Sewells the rooms that look out on the back lawn? Nobody ever enters them; even when you receive in the summer evenings, they are not opened. It would be a great boon to an invalid to be housed so quietly, so removed from all noise and bustle.' And to mark how I intended no more, I added, 'They would n't bore you, nor need you ever see them unless you wished for it.' And what was his reply? 'Madam, I never liked soldiers. I 'm not sure that his young wife would n't be displeasing to me, and I know that his children would be insufferable.'

"I said, 'Let me take the dear children, then.' 'Do, by all means, and their dear parents also,' he broke in. 'I should be in despair if I thought I had separated you.' Yes, sir, I give you his very words. This wise and truly great man, or truly wise and great—which is it?—had nothing more generous nor more courteous to say to me than a sarcasm and an impertinence. Are you not proud of your friend?"

Never was there a more unlucky peroration, from the day when Lord Denman concluded an eloquent defence of a queen's innocence by appealing to the unhappy illustration which called forth the touching words, "Let him that is without sin cast the first stone at her." Never was there a more signal blunder than to ask this man to repudiate the friendship which had formed the whole pride and glory of his life.

"I should think I *am* proud of him, Madam," said he, rising, and speaking with a boldness that amazed even himself. "I was proud to be his class-fellow at school; I was proud to sit in the same division with him in college,—proud when he won his gold medal and carried off his fellowship. It was a proud day to me when I saw him take his seat on the bench; and my heart nearly burst with pride when he placed me on his right hand at dinner, and told the Benchers and the Bar that we had walked the road of life together, and that the grasp of my hand—he called it my honest hand— had been the ever-present earnest of each success he had achieved in his career. Yes, Madam, I am very proud of him; and my heart must be cold indeed before I cease to be proud of him."

"I declare, sir, you astonish, you amaze me. I was well aware how that truly great and wise man had often inspired the eloquence of attack. Many have assailed—many have vituperated him; but that any one should have delivered a panegyric on the inestimable value of his friendship!—his friendship, of all things!—is what I was not prepared for."

Haire heard the ringing raillery of her laugh; he was stung by he knew not what tortures of her scornful impertinence; bitter, biting words, very cruel words, too, fell over and around him like a sort of hail; they beat on his face and rattled over his head and shoulders. He was conscious of a storm, and conscious too that he sought neither shelter nor defence, but only tried to fly before the hurricane, whither he knew not.

How he quitted that room, descended the stairs, and escaped from the house, he never was able to recall. He was far away outside the city wandering along through an unfrequented suburb ere he came to his full consciousness, murmuring to himself ever as he went, "What a woman, what a woman! what a temper,—ay, and what a tongue!" Without any guidance of his own—without any consciousness of it—he walked on and on, till he found himself at the gate-lodge of the Priory; a carriage was just passing in, and he stopped to ask whose it was. It was the Chief Baron's granddaughter who had arrived that morning by train. He turned back when he heard this, and returned to town. "Whether you like it or not, Lady Lendrick, it is done now, and there 's no good in carrying on the issue after the verdict." And with this reflection, embodying possibly as much wisdom as his whole career had taught him, he hastened homeward, secretly determining, if he possibly could, never to reveal anything to the Chief Baron of his late interview with Lady Lendrick.

CHAPTER XVI
SORROWS AND PROJECTS

Dr. Lendrick and his son still lingered at the Swan's Nest after Lucy's departure for the Priory. Lendrick, with many things to arrange and prepare for his coming voyage, was still so overcome by the thought of breaking up his home and parting from his children, that he could not address his mind to anything like business. He would wander about for hours through the garden and the shrubberies, taking leave, as he called it, of his dear plants and flowers, and come back to the house distressed and miserable. Often and often would he declare to Sir Brook, who was his guest, that the struggle was too much for him. "I never was a man of ardor or energy, and it is not now, when I have passed the middle term of life, that I am to hope for that spring and elasticity which were denied to my youth. Better for me send for Lucy, and stay where I am; nowhere shall I be so happy again." Then would come the sudden thought that all this was mere selfishness, that in this life of inaction and indolence he was making no provision for that dear girl be loved so well. Whatever hopes the reconciliation with his father might lead to, would of course be utterly scattered to the winds by an act so full of disobedience as this. "It is true," thought he, "I may fail abroad as I have failed at home. Success and I are scarcely on speaking terms,—but the grandfather cannot leave the granddaughter whom he has taken from her home, totally uncared and unprovided for."

As for young Tom, Sir Brook had pledged himself to take care of him. It was a vague expression enough; it might mean anything, everything, or nothing. Sir Brook Fossbrooke had certainly, in worldly parlance, not taken very good care of himself,—far from it; he had squandered and made away with two large estates and an immense sum in ready money. It was true he had friends everywhere,—some of them very great people with abundant influence, and well able to help those they cared for; but Fossbrooke was not one of those who ask; and the world has not yet come to the millennial beatitude in which one's friends importune them with inquiries how they are to be helped, what and where they wish for.

Many a time in the course of country-house life—at breakfast, as the post came in, and during the day, as a messenger would deliver a telegram—

some great man would say, "There is a vacancy there—such a one has died—so-and-so has retired. There's a thing to suit you, Fossbrooke,"—and Sir Brook would smile, say a word or two that implied nothing, and so would end the matter. If "my Lord" ever retained any memory of the circumstance some time after, it would be that he had offered something to Fossbrooke, who would n't take it, did n't care for it. For so is it throughout life; the event which to one is the veriest trifle of the hour, is to another a fate and a fortune; and then, great folk who lead lives of ease and security are very prone to forget that humble men have often a pride very disproportioned to their condition, and are timidly averse to stretch out the hand for what it is just possible it may not be intended they should touch.

At all events, Fossbrooke went his way through the world a mystery to many and a puzzle,—some averring that it was a shame to his friends in power that he had "got nothing," others as stoutly declaring that he was one whom no office would tempt, nor would any place requite him for the loss of liberty and independence.

He himself was well aware of each of these theories, but too proud to say a word to those who professed either of them. If, however, he was too haughty to ask for himself, he was by no means above being a suitor for his friends; and many a one owed to his active solicitude the advancement which none stood more in need of than himself.

"We shall make the Viceroy do something for us, Tom," he would say. "Think over what it shall be,—for that's the invariable question, What is it you want? And it's better far to say, Make me an archbishop, than have to own that you want anything, and are, maybe, fit for nothing."

Though Lendrick was well disposed towards Fossbrooke, and fully sensible of his manly honesty and frankness, he could not help seeing that he was one of those impulsive sanguine natures that gain nothing from experience beyond the gift of companionship. They acquire all that can make them delightful in society,—boons they are,—and especially to those whose more prudent temperament inclines them to employ their gifts more profitably. Scores of these self-made men, rich to overflowing with all that wealth could buy around them, would say, What a happy fellow was Fossbrooke! what a blessing it was to have his nature, his spirits, buoyancy, and such-like,—to be able to enjoy life as he did! Perhaps they believed all that they said too,—who knows? When they made such speeches to himself, as they would at times, he heard them with the haughty humility of one who hears himself praised for that which the flatterer deems a thing too low for envy. He well understood how cheaply others estimated his wares, for they were a scrip that figured in no share-list, and never were quoted at a premium.

Lendrick read him very correctly, and naturally thought that a more practical and a more worldly guide would have been better for Tom,—some one to hold him back, not to urge him forward; some one to whisper prudence, restraint, denial,—not daring, and dash, and indulgence. But somehow these flighty, imaginative, speculative men have very often a wonderful persuasiveness about them, and can give to the wildest dreams a marvellous air of substance and reality. A life so full of strange vicissitudes as Fossbrooke's seemed a guarantee for any—no matter what—turn of fortune. Hear him tell of where he had been, what he had done, and with whom, and you at once felt you were in presence of one to whom no ordinary laws of worldly caution or prudence applied.

That his life had compassed many failures and few successes was plain enough. He never sought to hide the fact.

Indeed, he was candor itself in his confessions, only that he accompanied them by little explanations, showing the exact spot and moment in which he had lost the game. It was wonderful what credit he seemed to derive from these disclosures. It was like an honest trader showing his balance-sheet to prove that, but for the occurrence of such ills as no prudence could ward off, his condition must have been one of prosperity.

Never did he say anything more truthful than that "he had never cared for money." So long as he had it he used it lavishly, thoughtlessly, very often generously. When he ceased to have it, the want scarcely appeared to touch him personally. Indeed, it was only when some necessity presented itself to aid this one or extricate that, he would suddenly remember his impotence to be of use, and then the sting of his poverty would sorely pain him.

Like all men who have suffered reverses, he had to experience the different acceptance he met with in his days of humble fortune from what greeted him in his era of prosperity. If he felt this, none could detect it. His bearing and manner betrayed nothing of such consciousness. A very slight increase of stateliness might possibly have marked him in his poverty, and an air of more reserved dignity, which showed itself in his manner to strangers. In all other respects he was the same.

That such a character should have exercised a great influence over a young man like Tom Lendrick—ardent, impetuous, and desirous of adventure—was not strange.

"We must make a fortune for Lucy, Tom," said Sir Brook. "Your father's nature is too fine strung to be a money-maker, and she must be cared for." This was a desire which he continued to utter day after day; and though Fossbrooke usually smoked on after he had said it without any intimation as to where and when and how this same fortune was to be amassed, Tom Lendrick placed the most implicit faith in the assurance that it would be done "somehow."

One morning as Lendrick was walking with his son in the garden, making, as he called it, his farewell visit to his tulips and moss-roses, he asked Tom if any fixed plan had been decided on as to his future.

"We have got several, sir. The difficulty is the choice. Sir Brook was at one time very full of buying a great tract in Donegal, and stocking it with all sorts of wild animals. We began with deer, antelopes, and chamois; and last night we got to wolves, bears, and a tiger. We were to have a most commodious shooting-box, and invite parties to come and sport, who, instead of going to Bohemia, the Rocky Mountains, and to Africa, would find all their savagery near home, and pay us splendidly for the privilege.

"There are some difficulties in the plan, it is true; our beasts might not be easy to keep within bounds. The jaguar might make an excursion into the market-town; the bear might eat a butcher. Sir Brook, besides, doubts if *fero* could be preserved under the game laws. He has sent a case to Brewster for his opinion."

"Don't tell me of such absurdities," said Lendrick, trying to repress his quiet laugh. "I want you to speak seriously and reasonably."

"I assure you, sir, we have the whole details of this on paper, even to the cost of the beasts, and the pensions to the widows of the keepers that may be devoured. Another plan that we had, and it looked plausible enough too, was to take out a patent for a wonderful medical antidote. As Sir Brook says, there is nothing like a patent medicine to make a man rich; and by good luck he is possessed of the materials for one. He has the secret for curing the bite of the rattlesnake. He got it from a Tuscarora Indian, who, I believe, was a sort of father-in-law to him. Three applications of this to the wound have never been known to fail."

"But we are not infested with rattlesnakes, Tom."

"That's true, sir. We thought of that, and decided that we should alter the prospectus of our company, and we have called it 'The antidote to an evil of stupendous magnitude and daily recurrence.

"A new method of flotation in water, by inflating the cellular membrane to produce buoyancy; a translation of the historical plays of Shakspeare into Tonga, for the interesting inhabitants of those islands; artificial rainfall by means of the voltaic battery: these are a few of his jottings down in a little book in manuscript he has entitled 'Things to be Done.'

"His favorite project, however, is one he has revolved for years in his mind, and he is fully satisfied that it contains the germ of boundless wealth. It has been shown, he says, that in the smoke issuing from the chimneys of great smelt-ing-furnaces, particles of subtilized metal are carried away to the amount of thousands of pounds sterling: not merely is the quantity great, but the quality, as might be inferred, is of the most valuable and precious kind. To arrest and precipitate this waste is his project, and he has been for years making experiments to this end. He has at length, he believes, arrived at the long-sought-for problem; and as he possesses a lead-mine in the island of Sardinia, he means that we should set out there, and at once begin operations."

Dr. Lendrick shook his head gravely as he listeued; indeed, Tom's manner in detailing Sir Brook's projects was little calculated to inspire serious confidence.

"I know, father," cried he, "what you mean. I know well how wild and flighty these things appear; but if you had only heard them from him,—had you but listened to his voice, and heard him speak of his own doubts and fears,—how he canvasses, not merely the value of his project, but what the world will say of it and of him,—how modestly he rates himself,—how free of all the cant of the discoverer he is,—how simply he enters into explanations,—how free to own the difficulties that bar success,—I say, if you had experienced these, I feel sure you would not escape from him without catching some of that malady of speculation which has so long beset him. Nor is one less disposed to trust him that he makes no parade of these things. Indeed, they are his deepest, most inviolable secrets. In his intercourse with the world no one has ever heard him allude to one of these projects, and I have given him my solemn pledge not to speak of them, save to you."

"It is a reason to think better of the man, Tom, but not to put more faith in the discoveries."

"I believe I take the man and his work together; at all events, when I am along with him, and listening to him, he carries me away captive, and I am ready to embark in any enterprise he suggests. Here he comes, with two letters, I see, in his hand. Did you ever see a man less like a visionary, father? Is not every trait of his marked with thought and struggle?" This was not the way Tom's father read Fossbrooke, but there was no time to discuss the point further.

"A letter for each of you," said Sir Brook, handing them; and then taking out a cigar, he strolled down an alley, while they were engaged in reading.

"We have got a tenant at last," said Lendrick. "The Dublin house-agent has found some one who will take the place as it stands; and now, to think of my voyage."

CHAPTER XVII
A LUNCHEON AT THE PRIORY

It was well for poor Lendrick that he was not to witness the great change which, in a few short weeks, had been effected in his once home. So complete, indeed, was the transformation, there was but very little left beyond the natural outline of the scenery to remind one of that lovely nook in which the tasteful cottage nestled. The conservatory had been converted into a dining-room; the former dinner-room being fitted up for a billiard-room. The Swiss cowhouse, a pretty little conceit, on which Lendrick had lavished some money and more time, was turned into a stable, with three loose boxes; and the neat lawn, whose velvet sward was scarce less beautiful than the glittering flower-beds that studded it, was ruthlessly cut up into a racecourse, with hurdles and fences and double ditches, to represent a stiff country, and offer all the features of a steeple-chase.

It needed not the assurance of Mr. Kimball, the house-agent, to proclaim that his client was very unlike the last occupant of the place. "*He* was no recluse, no wretched misanthropist, hiding his discontent amongst shrubs and forcing-beds; he was a man of taste and refinement, with knowledge of life and its requirements. He would be an acquisition to any neighborhood."

Now, the last phrase—and he invariably made it his peroration—has a very wide and sweeping acceptation. It appeals to the neighborhood with all the charms that pertain to social intercourse; a guest the more and a host the more are no small claims in small places. It appeals to the parson, as another fountain from which to draw draughts of benevolence. To the doctor it whispers fees and familiar dinners. Galen knows that the luckiest of men are not exempt from human ills, and that gout comes as a frequent guest where the cook is good and the wine tempting; and the butcher himself revels in the thought of a "good family" that consumes sirloins and forestalls sweetbreads.

It was somewhat trying to young Tom Lendrick, who had gone down to the Nest to fetch away some remnants of fishing-tackle he had left there, to hear these glowing anticipations of the new-comer, so evidently placed in contrast with the quiet and inexpensive life his father had led. How unlike were his father and this "acquisition to any neighborhood," was impressed upon him at any moment! How could a life of unobtrusive kindness, of those daily ministerings to poor men's wants, compete with the glitter and display which were to adorn a neighborhood?

Already were people beginning to talk of Lendrick as odd, eccentric, peculiar; to set down his finest qualities as strange traits of a strange temperament, and rather, on the whole, to give themselves credit for the patience and forbearance which they had shown to one who, after all, was "simply an egotist."

Yes, such are not unfrequent judgments in this same world of ours; and if you would have men's suffrages for the good you do, take care that you do it conventionally. Be in all things like those around you; and if there be a great man in your vicinity, whenever a doubt arises in your mind as to any course of action, do as you may imagine he might do.

Young Lendrick came away not a little disgusted with this taste of human fickleness. The sight of their old home changed even to desecration was bad enough, but this cold ingratitude was worse.

Had he gone into the cabins of the poor, had he visited the humble dwellings where his father's generous devotion had brought him face to face with famine and fever, he would have heard much to redress the balance of these opinions. He would have heard those warm praises that come from sorrow-stricken hearts, the wail of the friendless and forlorn. Tom heard not these, and he returned to town with a feeling of anger and resentment against the world he had never known before.

"How absurd it is in old Fossbrooke," thought he, "to go on saying money cannot do this, that, and t'other! Why, it can do everything. It does not alone make a man great, powerful, and influential, but it gains him the praise of being good and kind and generous. Look at my poor father, who never had a thought but for others, who postponed himself to all around him; and yet here is some one, whose very name is unknown, more eagerly looked for, more ardently desired, than would he be were it to be announced to-morrow he was coming back to live amongst them. What nonsense it is to say that the world cares for any qualities save those it can utilize; and I am only amazed how a man could have seen so much of life as Sir Brook and gained so little by his experience."

It was in this mood he got back to the little lodging in a humble suburb called Cullen's Wood, where Sir Brook awaited him. It is not impossible that the disparities of temperament in this world are just as beneficial, just as grateful, as are the boundless variety and change we find in nature. To Tom Lendrick's depression, almost disgust with life, Sir Brook brought that bright, hopeful, happy spirit which knew how to throw sunlight on every path to be travelled.

He had received good news, or what he thought was good news, from Sardinia. A new vein of ore had been struck,—very "fat" ore they called it,—some eighty-odd per cent, and a fair promise of silver in it. "They ask me for thirty thousand francs, though, Tom," said he, with a smile; "they might as well have written 'pounds' when they were about it. They want to repair the engine and erect a new crane. They say, too, the chains are worn and unsafe,—a thing to be looked to, or we shall have some accidents. In fact, they need fully double what they ask for; and seeing how impossible was the performance, I am astonished at their modesty."

"And what do you mean to do, sir?" asked Tom, bluntly.

"I have been thinking of two courses: my first thought was to make a formal conveyance of the mine to you and your sister, for your joint use and benefit. This done, and I standing aloof from all possible interest in it, I bethought me of a loan to be raised on the security of the property,—not publicly, not generally, but amongst your father's friends and well-wishers,—beginning with the neighborhood where he has lived so long, and around which he has sowed the seeds of such benefits as needs must ripen in gratitude."

"Indulge no delusions on that score, sir. There is not a man in the county, except old Mills the vicar, perhaps, has a good word for us; and as to going to one of them for assistance, I 'd rather sweep a crossing. You shake your head, Sir Brook, and you smile at my passionate denunciation; but it is true, every word of it. I heard, in the few hours I spent there, scores of stories of my poor father's eccentricity,—his forgetfulness, his absence, and what not,—but never a syllable of his noble liberality, his self-sacrifice, or his gentleness."

"My dear Tom," said the old man, solemnly, "when you have lived to one-half my age, you will discover that the world is not so much cursed with ill-nature as with levity, and that when men talk disparagingly of their fellows, they do so rather to seem witty than to be just. There was not, perhaps, one of those who tried to raise a laugh at your father's oddities, or who assumed to be droll at his expense, who would not in a serious mood have conceded to him every good and great trait of his nature. The first step in worldly knowledge is to rise above all consideration of light gossip. Take my word for it, we often confirm men in wrong thinking by opposition, who, if left to themselves and their own hearts, would review their judgments, and even retract them."

Tom took a hasty turn up and down the room; a ready reply was on his lip; indeed, it was with difficulty he repressed it, but he did so, and stood in seeming acquiescence to what he had heard. At last he said, "And the other plan, Sir Brook, — what was that?"

"Perhaps a more likely one, Tom," said the old man, cheerfully. "It was to apply directly to your grandfather, a man whose great intelligence would enable him to examine a project with whose details he had not ever before versed himself, and ask whether he would not make the advance we require on mortgage or otherwise."

"I don't think I 'd like to ask him," said Tom, with a grim smile.

"The proposal could come from me," said Sir Brook, proudly, "if he would graciously accord me an interview."

Tom turned away to hide a smile, for he thought, if such a meeting were to take place, what he would give to be an unseen witness of it, — to watch the duel between antagonists so different, and whose weapons were so unlike.

"My sister knows him better than any of us," said Tom, at last; "might I consult her as to the likelihood of any success with him?"

"By all means; it is what I would have myself advised."

"I will do so, then, to-day. I ought to have gone to see her yesterday; but I will go to-day, and report progress when I come back. I have a long budget for her," added he, with a sigh, — "a catalogue of all the things I am not going to do. I am not going to be a medallist, nor win a fellowship, nor even be a doctor; it will, however, give me great courage if I can say, I 'll be a miner."

Tom Lendrick was right when he said he should have gone to see his sister on the day before, though he was not fully aware how right. The Chief Baron, in laying down a few rules for Lucy's guidance, made a point of insisting that she should only receive visitors on one day of the week; and in this regulation he included even her brother. So averse was the old man to be exposed to even a passing meeting with strangers, that on these Tuesdays he either kept his room or retired to a little garden of which he kept the key, and from whose precincts all were rigorously excluded.

Well knowing her brother's impatience of anything like restricted liberty, and how rapidly he would connect such an injunction as this with a life of servitude and endurance, Lucy took care to make the time of receiving him appear a matter of her own choice and convenience, and at the time of parting would say, "Good-bye till Tuesday, Tom; don't forget Tuesday, for we shall be sure to be alone and to ourselves." He the more easily believed this, that on these same Tuesdays the whole place seemed deserted and desolate. The grave-looking man in black, who preceded him up the stairs, ushered him along the corridor, and finally announced him, awaited him like a piece of machinery, repeating every movement and gesture with an unbroken uniformity, and giving him to understand that not only his coming was expected, but all the details of his reception had been carefully prescribed and determined on.

"As I follow that fellow along the passage, Lucy," said Tom, one day, "I can't help thinking that I experience every sensation of a man going to be hanged,—his solemn face, his measured tread, the silence, and the gloom,—only needing pinioned arms to make the illusion perfect."

"Tie them around me, dearest Tom," said she, laughing, and drawing him to a seat beside her on the sofa; "and remember," added she, "you have a long day. Your sentence will not come off for another week;" and thus jestingly did she contrive to time his coming without ever letting him know the restrictions that defined his visits.

Now, the day before this conversation between Sir Brook and Tom took place being a Tuesday, Lucy had watched long and anxiously for his coming. She knew he had gone down to Killaloe on the preceding Saturday, but he had assured her he would be back and be with her by Tuesday. Lucy's life was far from unhappy, but it was one of unbroken uniformity, and the one sole glimpse of society was that meeting with her brother, whose wayward thoughts and capricious notions imparted to all he said a something striking and amusing. He usually told her how his week had been passed,—where he had been and with whom,—and she had learned to know his companions, and ask after them by name. Her chief interest was, however, about Sir Brook, from whom Tom usually brought a few lines, but always in an unsealed envelope, inscribed, "By the favor of Mr. Lendrick, jun."

How often would Tom quiz her about the respectful devotion of her old admirer, and jestingly ask her if she could consent to marry him. "I know he'll ask you the question one of these days, Lucy, and it's your own fault if you give him such encouragement as may mislead him." And then they would talk over the romance of the old man's nature, wondering whether the real world would be rendered more tolerable or the reverse by that ideal tone which so imaginative a temperament could give it "Is it not strange," said Tom, one day, "that I can see all the weakness of his character wherever my own interests do not come, but the moment he presents before me some bright picture of a splendid future, a great name to achieve, a great fortune to make, that moment he takes me captive, and I regard him not as a visionary or a dreamer, but as a man of consummate shrewdness and great knowledge of life?"

"In this you resemble Sancho Panza, Tom," said she, laughing. "He had little faith in his master's chivalry, but he implicitly believed in the island he was to rule over;" and from that day forward she called her brother Sancho and Sir Brook the Don.

On the day after that on which Tom's visit should have been but was not paid, Lucy sat at luncheon with her grandfather in a small breakfast-room which opened on the lawn. The old Judge was in unusual spirits; he had just received an address from the Bar, congratulating him on his recovery, and expressing hope that he might be soon again seen on that Bench he had so much ornamented by his eloquence and his wisdom. The newspapers, too, with a fickleness that seems their most invariable feature, spoke most flatteringly of his services, and placed his name beside those who had conferred highest honor on the judgeship.

"It is neatly worded, Lucy," said the old man, taking up the paper on which the address was written; "and the passage that compares me with Mansfield is able as well as true. Both Mansfield and myself understood how there stands above all written law that higher, greater, grander law, that is based in the heart of all humanity, in the hope of an eternal justice, and soars above every technicality, by the intense desire of truth. It would have been, however, no more than fair to have added that, to an intellect the equal of Mansfield, I brought a temper which Mansfield had not, and a manner which if found in the courts of royalty, is seldom met with on the Bench. I do not quite like that phrase, 'the rapid and unerring glance of Erskine.' Erskine was brilliant for a Scotchman, but a brilliant Scotchman is but a third-rate Irishman. They who penned this might have known as much. I am better pleased with the words, 'the noble dignity of Lord Eldon.' There, my child, there, they indeed have hit upon a characteristic. In Eldon nature seemed to have created the judicial element in a high degree. It would be the vulgarity of modesty to pretend not to recognize in my own temperament a like organization.

"May I read you, Lucy, the few words in which I mean to reply to this courteous address? Will it bore you, my dear?"

"On the contrary, sir, I shall feel myself honored as well as interested."

"Sit where you are, then, and I will retire to the far corner of the room. You shall judge if my voice and delivery be equal to the effort; for I mean to return my thanks in person, Lucy. I mean to add the force of my presence to the vigor of my sentiments. I have bethought me of inviting those who have signed this document to luncheon here; and it may probably be in the large drawing-room that I shall deliver this reply. If not, it may possibly be in my court before rising,—I have not fully determined." So saying, he arose, and with feeble steps—assisting himself, as he went, by the table, and then grasping a chair—he moved slowly across the room. She knew him too well to dare to offer her arm, or appear in any way to perceive his debility. That he felt, and felt bitterly, "the curse of old age," as he once profanely called it, might be marked in the firm compression of his lips and the stern frown that settled on him, while, as he sank into a seat, a sad weary sigh declared the utter exhaustion that overcame him.

It was not till after some minutes that he rallied sufficiently to unroll his manuscript and adjust his spectacles. The stillness in the room was now perfect; not a sound was heard save the faint hum of a bee which had strayed into the room, and was vaguely floating about to find an exit. Lucy sat in an attitude of patient attention,—her hands crossed before her, and her eyes slightly downcast.

A faint low cough, and he began, but in a voice tremulous and faint, "'Mr. Chief Sergeant, and Gentlemen of the Bar'—do you hear me, Lucy?"

"Yes, sir, I hear you."

"I will try to be more audible; I will rest for a moment." He laid his paper on his knees, closed his eyes, and sat immovable for some seconds.

It was at this moment, when to the intense stillness was added a sense of expectancy, the honeysuckle that grew across the window moved, the frail branches gave way, and a merry voice called out, "Scene the first: a young lady discovered at luncheon!" and with a spring Tom Lendrick bounced into the room, and, ere her cry of alarm had ended, was clasping his sister in his arms.

"Oh, Tom, dearest Tom, why to-day? Grandpapa—grandpapa is here," sighed she, rather than whispered, in his ear.

The young man started back, more struck by the emotion he had shown than by her words, and the Chief Baron advanced towards him with a manner of blended courtesy and dignity, saying, "I am glad to know you. Your sister's brother must be very welcome to me."

"I wish I could make a proper excuse for this mode of entry, sir. First of all, I thought Lucy was alone; and, secondly—"

"Never mind the second plea; I submit to a verdict on the first," said the Judge, smiling.

"Tom forgot; it was Tuesday was his day," began Lucy.

"I have no day; days are all alike to me, Lucy. My occupations of Monday could be transferred to a Saturday, or, if need be, postponed indefinitely beyond it."

"The glorious leisure of the fortunate," said the Judge, with a peculiar smile.

"Or the vacuity of the unlucky, possibly," said Tom, with an easy laugh.

"At all events, young gentleman, you carry your load jauntily."

"One reason is, perhaps, that I never knew it was a load. I have always paraded in heavy marching order, so that I don't mind the weight of my pack."

For the first time did the old man's features relax into a look of kindly meaning. To find the youth not merely-equal to appreciate a figure of speech, but able to carry on the illustration, seemed so to identify him with his own blood and kindred that the old Judge felt himself instinctively drawn towards him.

"Lucy, help your brother to something; there was an excellent curry there awhile ago, — if it be not cold."

"I have set my affections on that cold beef. It seems tome an age since I have seen a real sirloin."

A slight twitch crossed the Judge's face, — a pang he felt at what might be an insinuated reproach at his in hospitality; and he said, in a tone of almost apology, "We see no one—-absolutely no one—here. Lucy resigns herself to the companionship of a very dreary old man whom all else have forgotten."

"Don't say so, grandpapa, on the day when such a testimony of esteem and affection reaches you."

Young Lendrick looked up from his plate, turning his eyes first towards his sister, then towards his grandfather; his glance was so palpably an interrogatory, there was no-mistaking it. Perhaps the old man's first impulse was not to reply; but his courtesy or his vanity, or a blending of both, carried the day, and he said, in a voice of much feeling: "Your sister refers to an address I have just received,—an address which the Irish Bar have deemed proper to transmit to me with their congratulations on my recovery. It is as gratifying, it is as flattering, as she says. My brethren have shown that they can rise above all consideration of sect or party in tendering their esteem to a man whom no administration has ever been able to convert into a partisan."

"But you have always been a Whig, sir, haven't you?" said Tom, bluntly.

"I have been a Whig, sir, in the sense that a King is a Royalist," said the old man, haughtily; and though Tom felt sorely provoked to reply to this pretentious declaration, he only gave a wicked glance at his sister, and drank off his wine.

"It was at the moment of your unexpected appearance," continued the Judge, "that I was discussing with your sister whether my reply to this compliment would come better if delivered here, or from my place on the Bench."

"I 'd say from the Bench," said Tom, as he helped himself to another slice of beef.

The old man gave a short cough, with a start. The audacity of tendering advice so freely and positively overcame him; and his color, faint indeed, rose to his withered cheek, and his eye glittered as he said, "Might I have the benefit of hearing the reasons which have led you to this opinion?"

"First of all," said Tom, in a careless off-hand way, "I take it the thing would have more—what shall I say?—dignity; secondly, the men who have signed the address might feel they were treated with more consideration; and lastly,—it 's not a very good reason, but I 'm bound to own it,—I 'd like to hear it myself, which I could if it were delivered in public, but which I am not so likely to do if spoken here."

"Oh, Tom, dear Tom!" whispered his sister, in dismay at a speech so certain to be accepted in its least pleasing signification.

"You have already to-day reminded me of my deficiencies in hospitality, sir. This second admonition was uncalled for. It is happy for *me* that my defence is unassailable. It is happy for *you* that your impeachment is unwitnessed."

"You have mistaken me, sir," said Tom, eagerly. "I never thought of reflecting on your hospitality. I simply meant to say that as I find myself here to-day by a lucky accident, I scarcely look to Fortune to do me such another good turn in a hurry."

"Your father's fault—a fault that would have shipwrecked fourfold more ability than ever he possessed—was a timidity that went to very cowardice. He had no faith in himself, and he inspired no confidence in others. Yours is, if possible, a worse failing. You have boldness without knowledge. You have the rashness that provokes a peril, and no part of the skill that teaches how to meet it. It was with a wise prescience that I saw we should not be safe company for each other."

He arose as he spoke, and, motioning back Lucy as she approached to offer her arm, he tottered from the room, to all seeming more overcome by passion than even by years and infirmity.

"Well!" said Tom, as he threw his napkin on the table, and pushed his chair back, "I 'll be shot if I know how I provoked that burst of anger, or to what I owe that very neat and candid appreciation of my character."

Lucy threw her arm around his neck, and, bending over his shoulder till her face touched his own, said, "Oh, my dearest Tom, if you only knew how nervous and susceptible he is, in part from his nature, but more, far more, from suffering and sorrow! Left to the solitude of his own bitter thoughts for years, without one creature to whisper a kind word or a hopeful thought, is it any wonder if his heart has begun to consume itself?"

"Devilish bitter diet it must find it! Pass me over the Madeira, Lucy. I mean to have my last glass to the old gentleman's health and better temper."

"He has moments of noble generosity that would win all your love," said she, enthusiastically.

"You have a harder lot than ever I thought it, my poor Lucy," said he, looking into her eyes with an affectionate solicitude. "This is so unlike our old home."

"Oh, so unlike!" said she; and her lip quivered and her eyes grew glazy.

"And can you bear it, girl? Does it not seem to you like a servitude to put up with such causeless passion, such capricious anger as this?"

She shook her head mournfully, but made no answer.

"If it be your woman's nature enables you to do it, all I can say is, I don't envy you your sex."

"But, Tom, remember his years,—remember his age."

"By Jove, he took good care to remind me of my own!—not that he was so far wrong in what he said of me, Lucy. I felt all the while he had 'hit the blot,' and I would have owned it too, if he had n't taken himself off so quickly."

"If you had, Tom,—if you had said but one word to this purport,—you would have seen how nobly forgiving he could be in an instant."

"Forgiving,—humph! I don't think the forgiveness was to have come from *him*."

"Sir William wishes to speak with you, Miss Lucy," said the butler, entering hastily.

"I must go, Tom,—good-bye. I will write to you tomorrow,—to-night, if I can,—good-bye, my dearest brother; be sure to come on Tuesday,—mind, Tuesday. You will be certain to find me alone."

CHAPTER XVIII
THE FIRST LETTER HOME

The post of the morning after the events of our last chapter brought Lucy a letter from her father. It was the first since his departure. What chapters in life are these first letters after absence! How do they open to us glimpses of not only new scenes and incidents, but of emotions and sentiments which, while we had relied upon them, we had never so palpably realized before! There is such ecstasy in thinking that time and space are no barriers against love, and that, even as we read, the heart that sent the message is beating with affection for us.

Lendrick's letter to his daughter was full of fondness; her image had evidently gone with him through all the changes of the voyage, and their old home mingled in every thought of the new life before him. It was plain enough how unwillingly he turned from the past to the present, and how far rather he would revel in the scenes around the Shannon than turn to the solitary existence that awaited him beyond the seas.

"I console myself, dear Lucy," wrote he, "as well as I may, by thinking that in my great sacrifice I have earned the love of my father,—that love from which I have lived so long estranged, and for which my heart had never ceased to yearn; and I delight to think how by this time you must have grown into his heart, soothed many a care for him, and imparted to his solitary life the blessing of that bright hopefulness which gave even to my own dull existence a glow of glad sunshine. Out of my selfishness I cannot help asking you to remind him of all I have given him. And now that my egotism is so fully aroused, let me tell of myself. The voyage was less dreary than my fears had made it. I suffered at first, it is true; and when at last use had inured me to the sea, I fell into a sort of low feverish state, more the result of homesickness, perhaps, than real malady. It was a condition of rather depression than disease. Nothing could engage, nothing interest me. I could not read, neither could I partake in any of the various pastimes by which my fellow-voyagers beguiled the hours; and I found myself in that pitiable state of sinking daily lower and lower, without what I could call a cause for the depression.

"I have more than once in my experience as a doctor had to deal with such cases, and I own now that I have neither valued their intensity nor understood their importance. I did not, it is true, go to the vulgar extent of calling them hippishness; but I did the next worse thing,—I treated them as the offspring of an over-easy existence, of a placid frictionless life.

"With much shame do I recall how often I have rallied these poor sufferers on the vast space that separated them from real sorrow. There is no unreality, dearest Lucy, in whatever so overcomes the brain that thought is all but madness, and so pains the heart that the whole wish is for death. There are subtler influences in our nature than those that work by the brain or the blood, and the maladies of these have but one physician.

"It was my great good-fortune to have a fellow-traveller who took the kindest interest in me. If he could not cure, he certainly did much to console me. He was a young man, lately gazetted on the commander-in-chief's staff, and who came on board of us in the Downs from a frigate bound for England. It was the merest accident that he did not miss us and lose his passage.

"I am not a very attractive person, and it was with some astonishment that I heard he desired to make my acquaintance; and on meeting he said, 'Though you have forgotten me, Dr. Lendrick, I had the honor of being presented to you at Killaloe by my friend Sir Brook Fossbrooke;' and I then remembered all about it, and how it was his features were so familiar to me,—very good features, too, they were, with much candor and manliness in the expression,—altogether a handsome young fellow, and with an air of good birth about him just as distinctive as his good looks.

"I am so unused to being singled out by a stranger as the object of attentions, that I never fully got over the surprise which this young man's attachment to me inspired; and I am not using too strong a word, Lucy, when I call it attachment. There might have been, at least to his eyes, something in our respective fortunes that suggested this drawing towards me. Who knows whether he too might not have parted from a loved home and friends!

"When he first came on board, his manner was wild,—almost incoherent; he ran here and there, like one in search of something or of somebody, but whose name he had forgotten. Indeed he actually startled me by the eagerness with which he addressed me; and when I informed him that I was alone, quite alone, and as friendles as himself on board, I thought he would have fainted. In all this suffering and emotion I suspected that I found what led him to a companionship with one as sorrow-stricken as himself.

"As it was, there was no care he did not bestow on me. My own dear boy himself could not have nursed me more tenderly, nor tried to rally my spirits with more affectionate solicitude. He read for me, played chess with me, he even lent himself to the sort of reading I liked best, to become more companionable to me, withdrawing all this while from the gay and pleasant society of young fellows like himself. In a word, Lucy, by his devotion to me, he sent through my heart a lurking thought, almost like a hope, that I must somehow have certain qualities for which the world at large had not yet credited me, which could make me of interest to a young, bright-natured creature, fresh to life and all its enjoyments; and from the self-esteem of this notion I really believe I drew more encouragement than from any amount of more avowed approbation.

"I feel I am not wearying you, my darling Lucy, by dwelling even with prolixity on what beguiled the long hours of absence, the weary, weary days at sea.

"When we landed, for a time at least, I only met him now and then; he had his duties, and I had mine. I had to look out for a house. My predecessor's family are still occupying the official residence, and have begged of me leave to remain there a little longer. I had my visits of duty or compliment to make, and a whole round of little courtesies to perform, for which I well know I have all your sympathy. Every one was, however, kind and polite; some were even friendly. Indeed, my very want of manner, my awkward bashfulness and deficient tact, have, I can see, not injured me in the esteem of those whose worldly breeding and knowledge have taught them to be compassionate as well as courteous.

"Amongst the many persons to whom I was presented I made two acquaintances of more than common interest to me,—I will not go farther, and say of any great degree of gratification. In dining with the Governor, yesterday week, he said, 'You will meet a relation to-day, Dr. Lendrick. His ship has just put in to coal, and he and his wife dine with us.' Though quite persuaded the Governor was laboring under some mistake, I waited with anxiety as the different arrivals were announced, and at last came Colonel and Mrs. Sewell,—the Colonel being Lady Lendrick's son by her first marriage,—what relation to myself all my skill in genealogy is unable to pronounce.

"We met, however, shook hands very cordially, and I had the honor to conduct Mrs. Sewell to table. I am unfortunately terribly prone to first impressions, and all those that I entertain regarding the Colonel are adverse. He is a tall, handsome man, easy in manner, and with the readiness in speech and address that shows familiarity with life. He however will never suffer your eyes to meet his, never exchange a frank look with you, and seems, from some cause or other, to be always laboring under an impatient anxiety to be somewhere else than where he stands at the moment.

"He asked about my father, and never waited for my reply; and he laughingly said, with a bad taste that shocked me, 'My mother and he never could hit it off together.'

"Mrs. Sewell interested me more than her husband. She is still very handsome; she must at one time have been perfectly beautiful. She is very gentle, low-voiced, and quiet, talking with a simplicity that even I can detect only covers a deep knowledge of life and the world. The dread of her husband seems, however, to pervade all she says or does. She changes color when he looks at her, and if he addresses her, she sometimes seems about to faint. His slightest word is accepted as a command; and yet with all this terror—terror it was—I caught a look that once passed between them that actually overwhelmed me with amazement. It was the very look that two accomplices might have interchanged in a moment when they could not communicate more freely. Don't think that there is any exaggeration in this, Lucy, or that I am assuming to possess a finer insight into human motives than my neighbors; but my old craft as a doctor supplies me with a technical skill that no acquaintance with the mere surface-life of the world could have given; for the *Medico* reads mankind by a stronger and steadier light than ever shone out of conventionalities or social usages.

"'We are on our way to England, to Ireland, perhaps,' he said to me, in a careless way; but she, not aware of his speech, told me they had been invited to the Priory,—a piece of information which I own startled me. First of all, they are not by any means like people who would be agreeable to my father, nor, so far as I can guess, are they persons who would easily sacrifice their own modes of life and habits to the wishes of a recluse. Least of all, dearest Lucy, do I desire this lady to be your companion. She has, I see, many attractive qualities; she may have others as good and excellent; but if I do not greatly err, her whole nature and being are in subjection to a very stern, cold, and unscrupulous man, and she is far from being all that she should be with such gifts as she possesses, and farther again from what she might have been with a happier destiny in marriage.

"If it were not that you are so certain to meet, and not improbably see much of these people, I should not have filled so much of my letter with them; but I confess to you, since I saw them they have never been out of my thoughts. Our relationship—if that be the name for it—led us rapidly into considerable intimacy; he brought his children—two lovely girls, and a little cherub of a boy of three years old—to see me yesterday, and Mrs. Sewell comes to take me to drive every day after luncheon. She expresses the most ardent desire to meet you, and says she knows you will love each other. She carried off your picture t' other day, and I was in real terror till I got it back again. She seemed in ecstasy on being told you were living with your grandfather; but I saw a look she shot across to her husband as I told it, and I saw his reply by another glance that revealed to me how my tidings had caused surprise, and something more than surprise.

"You must not set me down as fanciful or captious, dear Lucy; but the simple truth is, I have never had a quiet moment since I knew these people. They inspire me with the same sort of anxiety I have often felt when, in the course of my profession, some symptom has supervened in a case not very grave or startling in itself, but still such as I have always found heralding in very serious combinations. It is therefore the doctor as much as the father that takes alarm here.

"It is just possible—mind, I say possible—that I am a little jealous of these Sewells, for they have already seduced from me my young friend Lionel, who was so kind to me on the voyage. I scarcely see him now, he is always with them; and yesterday I heard—it may not be true—that he is already weary of Cape Town, and means to return home by the next ship,—that is, along with the Sewells, who are to sail on Friday.

"I am certain that Sewell is neither a good nor a safe companion for a young fellow so bashful and unsuspecting as Lionel Trafford.

"There are men who read the world the way certain dishonest critics quote a book or an article, by extracting all that is objectionable, and, omitting context and connection, place passage after passage in quick sequence. By such a process as this, human life is a pandemonium. I half suspect Sewell to be one of this scornful school; and if so, a most dangerous intimate. The heartfelt racy enjoyment of his manner, as he records some trait of rascality or fraud, is not more marked than the contemptuous sneer with which he receives a story that bears testimony to generosity or trustfulness, throwing over his air in each that tone of knowledge of life and the world that seems to say, 'These are the things we all of us know well, though only a few have either the manliness or the honesty to declare them openly.'

"I may have tired you with this long tirade, my dear Lucy, but I am pouring out to you my thoughts as they come,—come, too, out of the fulness of much reflection. Remember, too, my sweet child, that I have often told you, 'It is just some half-dozen people with whom we are intimate who make or mar our fate in life.' Big as the world is, we play a very small game in one corner of the board, and it behoves us to look well to those with whom we are to play it.

"If I am jealous of the Sewells for having robbed me of my young friend, I am envious of himself also, for he is going back to England,—going back to the loved faces and scenes he has left,—going back to Home. There 's the word, Lucy, that gathers all that we come to live for, when life really is a blessing.

"It would seem too early to pronounce, but I think I can already see this is not a place to which I would like to bring you; but I will not prejudge it. It may be that time will reconcile me to some things I now dislike; it may be, too, that the presence of my own around me will dispose me to take a cheerier view of much that now depresses me. I have a great deal to do; I am employed during the whole day, and never really free till evening, when society claims me. This latter is my only severe burden. You can imagine me daily dining out, and fancy the martyrdom it costs me.

"I am most anxious to hear of you, and how you like your new life,—I mean how you bear it. Liking is not the word for that which entails separation. I feel assured that you will love my father. You will be generous towards those traits which the host of mere acquaintanceship took pleasure in exaggerating, and you will be fair enough not to misjudge his great qualities because of certain faults of temper. He has great gifts, Lucy; and as you will see, the two pendulums of his nature, heart and head, swing together, and he is as noble in sentiment as he is grand in action.

"It almost consoles me for separation when I think that I have transferred to him the blessings of that presence that made my own sunshine. Mind that you send me a diary of your life. I want your whole day; I want to see how existence is filled, so that whenever my mind flies back to you I may say, 'She is in her garden,—she is working,—she is at her music,—she is reading to him.'

"It was a mistake to send me here, Lucy. There are men in scores who would rejoice in the opportunities of such a place, and see in it the road to rapid fortune. I only look at one feature of it,—the banishment. Not that by nature I am discontented,—I hope and believe this is not so,—but I feel that there are many things in life far worse than poverty. I have not the same dread of narrow means most men have. I do not feel depressed in spirit when I lie beneath a very humble roof, and sit down to a coarse meal; nor has splendor the power to exhilarate or elevate me. I am essentially humble, and I need nothing that is not generally within the reach of the humble; and I vow to you in all truth, I 'd rather be your grandfather's gardener than be the governor of this great colony. There 's an ignoble confession, but keep it for yourself.

"I have written a long letter to Tom by this post, and addressed it to Mr. Dempster, who will forward it if he should have left before this. It distresses me greatly when I think that I have not been able to give him any definite career in life before we parted. Mere aptitude has no value with the world. You may be willing and ready to do fifty things, but some fourth-rate fellow who *knows* how to do one will beat you. The marketable quality in life is skill; the thing least in request is genius. Tom has this harsh lesson yet to learn, but learn it he must, for the world is a schoolmaster that will stand no skulking, and however little to our taste be its tasks, we must come up when called on, and go on with our lesson as well as we may.

"In many respects Sir Brook Fossbrooke was an unfortunate companion for him to have chanced upon. A man of considerable resources, who has employed them all unprofitably, is a bad pilot. The very waywardness of such a nature was exactly the quality to be avoided in Tom's case; but what was to be done? Poverty can no more select its company than its climate; and it would have been worse than ungracious to have rejected a friendship so generously and freely offered.

"I am curious—I am more than curious, I am anxious—to know if Tom should ever have met my father. They are so intensely alike in many things that I fear me their meeting could not lead to-good. I know well that Tom resents, and would like to show that he resents, what he deems the harsh treatment evinced towards me, and I dread anything like interchange of words between them. My whole hope is that you would prevent such a mischance, or, if it did occur, would take measures to obviate its dangers.

"Tell me particularly about this when you write. Tell me also, have you met Lady Lendrick, and if so, on what terms? I have ever found her obliging and good-natured, and with many qualities which the world has not given her credit for. Give her my most respectful regards when you see her.

"It is daybreak; the hot sun of Africa is already glancing into the room, and I must conclude. I cannot bear to think of the miles these lines must travel ere they meet you, but they will be with you at last, and they are in this more fortunate than your loving father,

"T. Lendrick."

Lucy sat long pondering over this letter. She read it too, again and again, and by a light which was certainly not vouchsafed to him who wrote it. To *her* there was no mystery in Trafford's conduct. It was plain enough he had gone out, expecting to find her as his fellow-passenger. His despair—his wretchedness—his devotion to her father, the last resource of that disappointment he could not subdue—were all intelligible enough. Less easy, however, to read the sudden attachment he had formed for the Sewells. What did this mean? Had it any meaning; and if so, was it one that concerned her to know?

CHAPTER XIX
OFFICIAL MYSTERIES

"I think I had better see him myself," said Fossbrooke, after patiently listening to Tom Lendrick's account of his meeting with his grandfather. "It is possible I may be able to smooth down matters a little, and dispose the old gentleman, besides, to accord us some aid in our Sardinian project, for I have resolved upon that, Tom."

"Indeed, sir; the gold-mine?"

"No, the lead,—the lead and silver. In the rough calculation I made last night on this slip of paper, I see my way to something like seven thousand a year to begin with; untold wealth will follow. There are no less than eleven products available,—the black lead of pencils and the white used by painters being the chief; while in my new salt, which I am disposed to call the 'pyrochloride of plumbium,' we have a sedative that will allay the pangs of hydrophobia."

"I wish it would quiet the Chief Baron," muttered Tom; and Sir Brook, not hearing him correctly, continued,—"I think so,—I think the Chief Baron eminently calculated to take a proper estimate of my discovery. A man of fine intellect is ever ready to accept truth, albeit it come in a shape and through a channel in which he has himself not pursued it. Will you write a line to your sister and ask if it would be his Lordship's convenience to receive me, and at what time?"

"Of course, sir, whatever you wish," said Tom, in some confusion; "but might I ask if it be your intention to ask my grandfather to aid me with his purse?"

"Naturally. I mean that he should, by advancing, let us say, eight hundred pounds, put you in a position to achieve a speedy fortune. He shall see, too, that our first care has been your sister's interests. Six-sixteenths of the profits for fifty years are to be hers; three each we reserve for ourselves; the remaining four will form a reserve fund for casualties, a capital for future development, and a sum at interest to pay superannuations, with some other objects that you will find roughly jotted down here, for which, however, they will amply suffice. I take it his Lordship knows something of metallurgy, Tom?" "I believe he knows a little of everything." "Chemistry I feel sure he must have studied." "I won't answer for the study; but you 'll find that when you come to talk with him, you 'll scarcely wander very far out of his geography. But I was going to say, sir, that I 'm not quite easy at the thought of asking him for money."

"It's not money—at least, it's no gift—we require of him. We are in possession of a scheme certain to secure a fortune. We know where a treasure lies hid, and we want no more than the cost of the journey to go and fetch it. He shall be more than repaid. The very dispositions we make in your sister's favor will show him in what spirit we mean to deal. It is possible—I am willing to own it—it is possible I might approach a man of inferior intelligence with distrust and fear, but in coming before Baron Lendrick I have no misgivings. All my experience of life has shown me that the able men are the generous men. In the ample stretch of their minds they estimate mankind by larger averages, and thus they come to see that there is plenty of good in human nature."

"I believe the old Judge is clever enough, and some speak very well of his character; but his temper—his temper is something that would swallow up all the fine qualities that ever were accorded to one man; and even if you were about to go on a mission I liked better, I 'd say, Don't ask to see him, don't expose yourself to the risk of some outrageous affront,—something you could n't bear and would n't resent."

"I have never yet found myself in the predicament you speak of," said Sir Brook, drawing himself up haughtily, "nor do I know of any contingency in life from which I could retreat on account of its perils. It may be, indeed it is, more than likely, from what you tell me, that I shall make no appeal to your grandfather's generosity; but I shall see him to tender your regrets for any pain you may have caused him, and to tell also so much of our future intentions as it is becoming the head of your house should hear. I also desire to see your sister, and say good-bye."

"Ask her to let me do so too. I can't go away without seeing her again." Tom took a turn or two up and down the room as though he had not made up his mind whether to say something or not. He looked out of the window, possibly in search of something to distract his thoughts, and then turning suddenly about, he said: "I was thinking, sir, that if it was your opinion—mind, I don't want to insinuate that it ought to be, or even that it is my own—but that if you came to the conclusion that my sister was not happy with my grandfather—that her life was one of depression and suffering—what would you say to her coming along with us?"

"To Sardinia! Coming to Sardinia, do you mean, Tom?" said the old man, in astonishment.

"Yes, sir, that is what I meant."

"Have I not told you the sort of life that lies before us in the island,—the hardships, the dangers, the bitter privations we shall have to endure? Is it to these we can invite a young girl, trained and accustomed to every elegance and every comfort?"

"She 'd not shrink from her share,—that much I 'll warrant you; and the worst roughing of that rugged life would be easier to bear than this old man's humor."

"No, no; it must not be thought of," said Fossbrooke, sternly. "What meaning has our enterprise if it be not to secure her future fortune? She cannot—she shall not—pay any part of the price. Let me think over this, Tom. It may be that we ought not to leave her; it may be that we should hit upon something nearer home. I will go up to the Castle and see the Viceroy."

He made a light grimace as he said this. Such a visit was by no means to his taste. If there was anything totally repugnant to his nature, it was to approach men whom he had known as friends or intimates with anything like the request for a favor. It seemed to him to invert all the relations which ought to subsist between men in society. The moment you had stooped to such a step, in his estimation you had forfeited all right to that condition of equality which renders intercourse agreeable.

"I must have something for this young fellow,—something that may enable him to offer his sister a home if she should need it. I will accept nothing for myself,—on that I am determined. It is a sorry part, that of suppliant, but so long as it is for another it is endurable. Not that I like it, though,—not that it sits easy on me,—and I am too old to acquire a new manner." Thus muttering to himself, he went along till he found himself at the chief entrance of the Castle.

"You will have to wait on Mr. Balfour, sir, his Excellency's private secretary, the second door from the corner," said the porter, scarcely deigning a glance at one so evidently unversed in viceregal observances. Sir Brook nodded and withdrew. From a groom who was holding a neat-looking cob pony Fossbrooke learned that Mr. Balfour was about to take his morning's ride. "He'll not see you now," said the man. "You 'll have to come back about four or half-past."

"I have only a question to ask," said Sir Brook, half to himself as he ascended the stairs. As he gained the landing and rang, the door opened and Mr. Balfour appeared. "I regret to detain you, sir," began Sir Brook, as he courteously raised his hat. "Mr. Balfour, I believe."

"You are right as to my name, but quite as wrong if you fancy that you will detain me," said that plump and very self-satisfied gentleman, as he moved forward.

"And yet, sir, such is my intention," said Sir Brook, placing himself directly in front of him.

"That is a matter very soon settled," said Balfour, returning to the door and calling out, "Pollard, step down to the lower yard, and send a policeman here."

Sir Brook heard the order unmoved in manner, and even made way for the servant to pass down the stairs. No sooner, however, was the man out of hearing than he said, "It would be much better, sir, not to render either of us ridiculous. I am Sir Brook Fossbrooke, and I come here to learn at what time it would be his Excellency's pleasure to receive me."

The calm quiet dignity in which he spoke, even more than the words, had its effect on Balfour, who, with more awkwardness than he would like to have owned, asked Sir Brook to walk in and be seated. "I have had a message for you from his Excellency these three or four days back, and knew not where to find you."

"Did it never occur to you to try what assistance the police might afford, sir?" said he, with deep gravity.

"One thinks of these generally as a last resource," said Balfour, coolly, and possibly not sorry to show how imperturbable he could be under a sarcasm.

"And now for the message, sir," said Fossbrooke.

"I'll be shot if I remember it. Wasn't it something about an election riot? You thrashed a priest, named Malcahy, eh?"

"I opine not, sir," said Sir Brook, with a faint smile.

"No, no; you are the great man for acclimatization; you want to make the ornithorhynchus as common as the turkey. Am I right?"

Sir Brook shook his head.

"I never have my head clear out of office hours, that 's the fact," said Balfour, impatiently. "If you had called on me between twelve and three, you 'd have found me like a directory."

"Put no strain upon your recollection, sir. When I see the Viceroy, it is probable he will repeat the message."

"You know him, then?"

"I have known him eight-and-forty years."

"Oh, I have it,—I remember it all now. You used to be with Colonel Hanger and Hugh Seymour and O'Kelly and all the Carlton House lot."

Fossbrooke bowed a cold assent.

"His Excellency told us the other evening that there was not a man in England who had so many stories of the Prince. Didn't Moore go to you about his Life of Sheridan?—yes, of course,—and you promised him some very valuable documents; and sent him five-and-twenty protested bills of poor Brinsley's, labelled 'Indubitable Records.'"

"This does not lead us to the message, sir," said Foss-brooke, stiffly.

"Yes, but it does though,—I'm coming to it. I have a system of artificial memory, and I have just arrived at you now through Carlton House, milk-punch, and that story about Lord Grey and yourself riding postilions to Ascot, and you on the wheelers tipping up Grey with your whip till he grew frantic. Was n't that a fact?"

"I wait for the message, sir; or rather I grow impatient at not hearing it."

"I remember it perfectly. It's a place he wants to offer you; it's a something under the Courts of Law. You are to do next to nothing,—nothing at all, I believe, if you prefer it, as the last fellow did. He lived in Dresden for the education of his children, and he died there, and we did n't know when he died,—at least they suspect he signed some dozen life certificates that his doctor used to forward at quarter-day. Mind, I don't give you the story as mine; but the impression is that he held the office for eight years after his death."

"Perhaps, sir, you would now favor me with the name and nature of the appointment."

"He was called the Deputy-Assistant Sub-something of somewhere in the Exchequer; and he had to fill, or to register, or to put a seal, or, if not a seal, a stamp on some papers; but the marrow of the matter is, he had eight hundred a year for it; and when the Act passed requiring two seals, he asked for an increase of salary and an assistant clerk, and they gave him two hundred more, but they refused the clerk. They do such shabby things in those short sittings over the Estimates!"

"And am I to understand that his Excellency makes me an offer of this appointment?"

"Well, not exactly; there's a hitch in it,—I may say there are two hitches: first of all, we 're not sure it's in our gift; and, secondly—"

"Perhaps I may spare you the secondly,—the firstly is more than enough for me."

"Yes, but I'd like to explain. Here's how it is: the Chief Baron claimed the patronage about twenty years ago, and we made, or the people who were in power made, some sort of a compromise about an ultimate nomination, and he was to have the first. Now this man only died t' other day, having held the office, as I said, upwards of twenty years,—a most unconscionable thing,—just one of those selfish acts small official fellows are always doing; and so I thought, as I saw your name down for something on his Excellency's list, that I 'd mention *you* for the post as a sort of sop to Baron Lendrick, saying, 'Look at our man; we are not going to saddle the country with one of your long-annuity fellows,—*he* 's eighty if he's a day.' I say, I 'd press this point, because the old Judge says he is no longer bound by the terms of the compromise, for that the office was abolished and reconstructed by the 58th of Victoria, and that he now insists on the undivided patronage."

"I presume that the astute reasons which induced you to think of *me* have not been communicated to the Viceroy."

"I should think not. I mention them to you frankly, because his Excellency said you were one of those men who must be dealt with openly. 'Play on the square with Foss-brooke,' said he; 'and whether he win or lose, you 'll see no change in him. Try to overreach him, and you 'll catch a tiger.'"

"I am very grateful for his kind estimate of me. It is, however, no more than I looked for at his hands." This he said with a marked feeling, and then added, in a lighter tone, "I have also a debt of gratitude to yourself, of which I know not how to acquit myself better than by accepting this appointment, and taking the earliest opportunity to die afterwards."

"No, don't do that; I don't mean that. You can do like that fellow they made Pope because he looked on the verge of the grave, and who pitched his crutch into the air when he had put on the tiara."

"I understand; so that it is only in Baron Lendrick's eyes I am to look short-lived."

"Just so; call on him,—have a meeting with him; say that his Excellency desires to act with every delicacy towards him,—that should it be discovered hereafter the right of nomination lies with the Court and not with us, we 'll give him an equivalent somewhere else, till—till—"

"Till I shall have vacated the post," chimed in Sir Brook, blandly; "a matter, of course, of very brief space."

"You see the whole thing,—you see it in all its bearings; and now if you only could know something about the man you have to deal with, there would be nothing more to tell you."

"I have heard about him passingly."

"Oh, yes, his eccentricities are well known. The world is full of stories of him, but he is one of those men who play wolf on the species,—he must be worrying somebody to keep him from worrying himself; he smashed the last two Governments here, and he 'd have upset *us* too if *I* had n't been here. He hates *me* cordially; and if you don't want to rouse his anger, don't let your lips murmur the name, Cholmondely Balfour."

"You may rely upon me, sir," said Sir Brook, bowing. "I have scarcely ever met a gentleman whose name I am not more likely to recall than your own."

"Sharp, that; did you mean it?" said Balfour, with his glass to his eye.

"I am never ambiguous, sir, though it occasionally happens to me to say somewhat less than I feel. I wish you a good day."

CHAPTER XX
IN COURT

When the day arrived that the Chief Baron was to resume his place on the Bench, no small share of excitement was seen to prevail within the precincts of the Four Courts. Many opined that his recovery was far from perfect, and that it was not his intention ever to return to the justice-seat. Some maintained that the illness had been far less severe than was pretended, and that he had employed the attack as a means of pressure on the Government, to accord to his age and long services the coveted reward. Less argumentative partisans there were who were satisfied to wager that he would or would not reappear on the Bench, and bets were even laid that he would come for one last time, as though to show the world in what full vigor of mind and intellect was the man the Government desired to consign to inactivity and neglect.

It is needless to say that he was no favorite with the Bar. There was scarcely a man, from the highest to the lowest, whom he had not on some occasion or another snubbed, ridiculed, or reprimanded. Whose law had he not controverted? Whose acuteness had he not exposed, whose rhetoric not made jest of? The mere presence of ability before him seemed to stimulate his combative spirit, and incite him to a passage at arms with one able to defend himself. No first-rate man could escape the shafts of his barbed and pointed wit; it was only dulness, hopeless dulness, that left his court with praise of his urbanity and an eulogy over his courteous demeanor.

Now, hopeless dulness is not the characteristic of the Irish Bar, and with the majority the Chief Baron was the reverse of popular.

No small tribute was it therefore to his intellectual superiority, to that mental power that all acknowledged while they dreaded, that his appearance was greeted with a murmur of approbation, which swelled louder and louder as he moved across the hall, till it burst out at last into a hoarse, full cheer of welcome. Mounting the steps with difficulty, the pale old man, seared with age and wrinkled with care, turned round towards the vast crowd, and with an eye of flashing brightness, and a heightened color, pressed his hand upon his heart, and bowed. A very slight motion it was,—less, far less, perhaps, than a sovereign might have accorded; but in its dignity and grace it was a perfect recognition of all the honor he felt had been done him.

How broken! how aged! how fearfully changed! were the whispered remarks that were uttered around as he took his seat on the Bench, and more significant even than words were the looks interchanged when he attempted to speak, and instead of that clear metallic ring which once had been audible even outside the court, a faint murmuring sound was only heard.

A few commonplace motions were made and discharged. A somewhat wearisome argument followed on a motion for a new trial, and the benches of the Bar gradually grew thinner and thinner, as the interest of the scene wore off, and as each in turn had scanned, and, after his own fashion, interpreted, the old Judge's powers of mind and body; when suddenly, and as it were without ostensible cause, the court began to fill,—bench after bench was occupied, till at last even all the standing-space was crowded; and when the massive curtain moved aside, vast numbers were seen without, eagerly trying to enter. At first the Chief Baron appeared not to notice the change, but his sharp eye no sooner detected it than he followed with his glance the directed gaze of the crowd, and saw it fixed on the gallery, opposite the jury-box, now occupied by a well-dressed company, in the midst of whom, conspicuous above all, sat Lady Lendrick. So well known were the relations that subsisted between himself and his wife, such publicity had been given to their hates and quarrels, that her presence here was regarded as a measure of shameless indelicacy. In the very defiant look, too, that she bestowed on the body of the court she seemed to accept the imputation, and to dare it.

Leisurely and calmly did she scan the old man's features through her double eyeglass, while from time to time, with a simpering smile, she would whisper some words to the lady at her side,—words it was not needful to overhear, they were so palpably words of critical comment upon him she gazed at.

So engrossed was attention by the indecency of this intrusion, which had not even the shallow pretext of an interesting cause to qualify it, that it was only after a considerable time it was perceived that the lady who sat next Lady Lendrick was exceedingly beautiful. If no longer in her first youth, there were traits of loveliness in her perfectly formed features which even years respect; and in the depth of her orbits and the sculptural elegance of her nostrils and her mouth, there was all that beauty we love to call Greek, but in which no classic model ever could compete with the daughters of England.

Her complexion was of exceeding delicacy, as was the half-warm tint of her light-brown hair. But it was when she smiled that the captivation of her beauty became perfect; and it seemed as though each and all there appropriated that radiant favor to himself, and felt his heart bound with a sort of ecstasy. It had been rumored in the morning through the hall that the Chief Baron, at the rising of the Court, would deliver a short reply to the address of the Bar; and now, as the last motion was being disposed of, the appearance of eager expectation and curiosity became conspicuous on every side.

That the unlooked-for presence of his wife had irritated and embarrassed the old man, was plain to the least observant. The stern expression of his features; the steadfast way in which he gazed into the body of the court, to avoid even a chance glance at the gallery; the fretful impatience with which he moved his hands restlessly amongst his papers,—all showed discomposure and uneasiness. Still, it was well known that the moment he was called on for a mental effort intellect ever assumed the mastery over temper, and all felt that when he should arise not a trace of embarrassment would remain to mar the calm dignity of his manner.

It was amidst a hushed silence that he stood up, and said: "Mr. Chief Sergeant, and Gentlemen of the Bar: I had intended to-day,—I had even brought down with me some notes of a reply which I purposed to make to the more than flattering address which you so graciously offered to me. I find, however, that I have overrated the strength that remains to me. I find I have measured my power to thank you by the depth of my gratitude, and not by the vigor of my frame. I am too weak to say all that I feel, and too deeply your debtor to ask you to accept less than I owe you. Had the testimony of esteem you presented to me only alluded to those gifts of mind and intellect with which a gracious Providence was pleased to endow me,— had you limited yourself to the recognition of the lawyer and the judge,—I might possibly have found strength to assure you that I accepted your praise with the consciousness that it was not all unmerited. The language of your address, however, went beyond this; your words were those of regard, even of affection. I am unused to such as these, gentlemen,—they unsettle—they unman me. Physicians tell us that the nerves of the student acquire a morbid and diseased acuteness for want of those habits of action and physical exertion which more vulgar organizations practise. So do I feel that the mental faculties gain an abnormal intensity in proportion as the affections are neglected, and the soil of the heart left untilled.

"Mine have been worse than ignored," said he, with an elevated tone, and in a voice that rang through the court,—"they have been outraged; and when the time comes that biography will have to deal with my character and my fortunes, if there be but justice in the award, the summing-up will speak of me as one ever linked with a destiny that was beneath him. He was a lawyer,—he ought to have been a legislator. He sat on the Bench, while his place was the Cabinet; and when at the end of a laborious life his brethren rallied round him with homage and with tender regard, they found him like a long beleaguered city starved into submission, carrying a bold port towards the enemy, but torn by dissension within, and betrayed by the very garrison that should have died in its defence."

The savage fierceness of these words turned every eye in the court to the gallery, where Lady Lendrick sat, and where, with a pleasant smile on her face, she not only listened with seeming pleasure, but beat time with her fan to the rhythm of the well-rounded periods.

A quivering of the lip, and a strange flattening of the cheek of one side, succeeded to the effort with which he delivered these words, and when he attempted to speak again his voice failed him; and after a few attempts he placed his hand on his brow, and with a look of intense and most painful significancy, bowed around him to both sides of the court and retired.

"That woman, that atrocious woman, has killed him," muttered poor Haire, as he hastened to the Judge's robing-room.

"I am sorry, my dear, you should not have heard him in a better vein, for he is really eloquent at times," said Lady Lendrick to her beautiful companion, as they moved through the crowd to their carriage.

"I trust his present excitement will not have bad consequences," said the other, softly. "Don't you think we ought to wait and ask how he is?"

"If you like. I have only one objection, and that is, that we may be misconstrued. There are people here malicious enough to impute the worst of motives to our anxiety. Oh, here is Mr. Pemberton! Mr. Pemberton, will you do me the great favor to inquire how the Chief Baron is? Would you do more, and say that I am most eager to know if I could be of any use to him?"

If Mr. Pemberton had no fancy for his mission, he could not very well decline it. While he was absent, the ladies took a turn through the hall, inspecting the two or three statues of distinguished lawyers, and scanning the living faces, whose bewigged expression seemed to blend the over-wise and the ridiculous in the strangest imaginable manner.

A sudden movement in the crowd betokened some event; and now, through a lane formed in the dense mass, the Chief Baron was seen approaching. He had divested himself of his robes, and looked the younger for the change. Indeed, there was an almost lightness in his step, as he came forward, and with a bland smile said: "I am most sensible of the courtesy that led you here. I only wish my strength had been more equal to the occasion." And he took Lady Lendrick's hand with a mingled deference and regard.

"Sir William, this is my daughter-in-law. She only arrived yesterday, but was determined not to lose the opportunity of hearing you."

He raised the young lady's hand to his lips.

"To have *heard* me to-day was disappointment," said the old man, as he raised the young lady's hand to his lips; "to see her is none. I am charmed to meet one so closely tied to me,—of such exquisite beauty. Ah, Madam! it's a dear-bought privilege, this candid appreciation of loveliness we old men indulge in. May I offer you my arm?"

And now through the dense crowd they passed along,—all surprised and amazed at the courteous attentions of the old Judge, whom but a few moments before they had seen almost convulsed with passion.

"She almost had won the game, Haire," said the Chief Baron, as, having handed the ladies to their carriage, he went in search of his own. "But I have mated her. My sarcasm has never given me one victory with that woman," said he, sternly. "I have never conquered her except by courtesy."

"Why did she come down to court at all?" blurted out Haire; "it was positively indecent."

"The Spanish women go to bull-fights, but I never heard that they stepped down into, the arena. She has great courage,—very great courage."

"Who was the handsome woman with her?"

"Her daughter-in-law, Mrs. Sewell. Now, that is what I call beauty, Haire. There is the element which is denied to us men,—to subdue without effort, to conquer without conflict."

"Your granddaughter is handsomer, to my thinking."

"They are like each other,—strangely like. They have the same dimpling of the cheek before they smile, and her laugh has the same ring as Lucy's."

Haire muttered something, not very intelligibly, indeed, but certainly not sounding like assent.

"Lady Lendrick had asked me to take these Sewells in at the Priory, and I refused her. Perhaps I 'd have been less peremptory had I seen this beauty. Yes, sir! There is a form of loveliness—this woman has it—as distinctly an influence as intellectual superiority, or great rank, or great riches. To deny its power you must live out of the world, and reject all the ordinances of society."

"Coquettes, I suppose, have their followers; but I don't think you or I need be of the number."

"You speak with your accustomed acuteness, Haire; but coquetry is the exercise of many gifts, beauty is the display of one. I can parry off the one; I cannot help feeling the burning rays of the other. Come, come, don't sulk; I am not going to undervalue your favorite Lucy. They have promised to dine with me on Sunday; you must meet them."

"Dine with you!—dine with you, after what you said today in open court!"

"That I could invite them, and they accept my invitation, is the best reply to those who would, in their malevolence, misinterpret whatever may have fallen from me. The wound of a sharp arrow is never very painful till some inexpert bungler endeavors to withdraw the weapon. It is then that agony becomes excruciating, and peril imminent."

"I suppose I am the bungler, then?"

"Heaven forbid I should say so! but as I have often warned you, Haire, your turn for sarcasm is too strong for even your good sense. When you have shotted your gun with a good joke, you will make a bull's eye of your best friend."

"By George, then, I don't know myself, that's all; and I could as easily imagine myself a rich man as a witty one."

"You are rich in gifts more precious than money; and you have the quintessence of all wit in that property that renders you suggestive; it is like what chemists call latent heat. But to return to Mrs. Sewell: she met my son at the Cape, and reports favorably of his health and prospects."

"Poor fellow! what a banishment he must feel it!"

"I wonder, sir, how many of us go through life without sacrifices! She says that he goes much into the world, and is already very popular in the society of the place,—a great and happy change to a man who had suffered his indolence and self-indulgence to master him. Had he remained at home, I might have been able to provide for him. George Ogle's place is vacant, and I am determined to exercise my right of appointment."

"First Registrar, was he not?"

"Yes; a snug berth for incapacity,—one thousand a year. Ogle made more of it by means we shall not inquire into, but which shall not be repeated."

"You ought to give it to your grandson," said Haire, bluntly.

"You ought to know better than to say so, sir," said the Judge, with a stern severity. "It is to men like myself the public look for example and direction, and it would be to falsify all the teaching of my life if I were to misuse my patronage. Come up early on Saturday morning, and go over the lists with me. There are one hundred and twenty-three applicants, backed by peers, bishops, members of Parliament, and men in power."

"I don't envy you your patronage."

"Of course not, sir. The one hundred and twenty-two disappointed candidates would present more terror to a mind like yours than any consciousness of a duty fulfilled would compensate for; but I am fashioned of other stuff."

"Well, I only hope it may be a worthy fellow gets it."

"If you mean worthy in what regards a devotion to the public service, I may possibly be able to assure you on that head."

"No, no; I mean a good fellow,—a true-hearted, honest fellow, to whom the salary will be a means of comfort and happiness."

"Sir, you ask far too much. Men in my station investigate fitness and capacity; they cannot descend to inquire how far the domestic virtues influence those whom they advance to office."

"You may drop me here: I am near home," said Haire, who began to feel a little weary of being lectured.

"You will not dine with me?"

"Not to-day. I have some business this evening. I have a case to look over."

"Come up on Saturday, then,—come to breakfast; bring me any newspapers that treat of the appointment, and let us see if we cannot oppose this spirit of dictation they are so prone to assume; for I am resolved I will never name a man to office who has the Press for his patron."

"It may not be his fault."

"It shall be his misfortune, then. Stop, Drab; Mr. Haire wishes to get down. To the Priory," said he, as his friend went his way; and now, leaning back in his carriage, the old man continued to talk aloud, and, addressing an imaginary audience, declaim against the encroaching spirit of the newspapers, and inveigh against the perils to which their irresponsible counsels exposed the whole framework of society; and thus speaking, and passionately gesticulating, he reached his home.

CHAPTER XXI
A MORNING CALL

As Sir William waited breakfast for Haire on Saturday morning, a car drove up to the door, and the butler soon afterwards entered with a card and a letter. The card bore the name "Sir Brook Fossbrooke," and the letter was sealed with the viceregal arms, and had the name "Wilmington" on the corner. Sir William broke it open, and read,—

"My dear Chief Baron,—This will come to your hand through Sir Brook Fossbrooke, one of my oldest and choicest friends. He tells me he desires to know you, and I am not aware of any more natural or legitimate ambition. It would be presumption in me to direct your attention to qualities you will be more quick to discover and more able to appreciate than myself. I would only add that your estimate will, I feel assured, be not less favorable that it will be formed of one of whose friendship I am proud. It may be that his visit to you will include a matter of business; if so, give it your courteous attention: and believe me ever, my dear Chief Baron, your faithful friend,

"Wilmington."

"Show the gentleman in," said the Judge; and he advanced towards the door as Sir Brook entered. "I am proud to make your acquaintance, Sir Brook," said he, presenting his hand.

"I would not have presumed to call on you at such an hour, my Lord Chief Baron, save that my minutes are numbered. I must leave for England this evening; and I wished, if possible, to meet you before I started."

"You will, I hope, join me at breakfast?"

"I breakfasted two hours ago,—if I dare to dignify by the name my meal of bread and milk. But, pray, let me not keep you from yours,—that is, if you will permit me to speak to you while so occupied."

"I am at your orders, sir," said the old Judge, as he seated himself and requested his visitor to sit beside him.

"His Excellency tells me, my Lord, that there is just now vacant a situation of which some doubt exists as to the patron,—a Registrarship, I think he called it, in your Court?"

"There is no doubt whatever, sir. The patronage is mine."

"I merely quote the Viceroy, my Lord,—I assert nothing of myself."

"It may not impossibly save time, sir, when I repeat that his Excellency has misinformed you. The office is in my gift."

"May I finish the communication with which he charged me?"

"Sir, there is no case before the court," said the Judge. "I can hear you, as a matter of courtesy; but it cannot be your object to be listened to on such terms?"

"I will accept even so little. If it should prove that the view taken by his Excellency is the correct one—pray, sir, let me proceed—"

"I cannot; I have no temper for a baseless hypothesis. I will not, besides, abuse your time any more than my own forbearance; and I therefore say that if any portion of your interest in making my acquaintance concerns that question you have so promptly broached, the minutes employed in the discussion would be thrown away by us both."

"Mr. Haire," said the servant, at this moment; and the Chief Baron's old friend entered, rather heated by his walk.

"You are late by half an hour, Haire; let me present you to Sir Brook Fossbrooke, whose acquaintance I am now honored in making. Sir Brook is under a delusive impression, Haire, which I told you a few days ago would demand some decisive step on my part; he thinks that the vacant registrarship is at the disposal of the Crown."

"I ask pardon," said Fossbrooke. "As I understood his Excellency, they only claim the alternate appointment."

"And they shall not assert even that, sir."

"Sir William's case is strong,—it is irrefutable. I have gone over it myself," broke in Haire.

"There, sir! listen to that. You have now wherewithal to go back and tell the Viceroy that the opinion of the leading man of the Irish Bar has decided against his claim. Tell him, sir, that accident timed your visit here at the same moment with my distinguished friend's, and that you in this way obtained a spontaneous decision on the matter at issue. When you couple with that judgment the name of William Haire, you will have said enough."

"I bow to this great authority," said Sir Brook, with deep courtesy, "and accepting your Lordship's statement to the fullest, I would only add, that as it was his Excellency's desire to have named me to this office, might I so far presume, on the loss of the good fortune that I had looked for, to approach you with a request, only premising that it is not on my own behalf?"

"I own, sir, that I do not clearly appreciate the title to your claim. You are familiar with the turf, Sir Brook, and you know that it is only the second horse has a right to demand his entry."

"I have not been beaten, my Lord. You have scratched my name and prevented my running."

"Let us come back to fact, sir," said the Chief Baron, not pleased with the retort. "How can you base any right to approach me with a request on the circumstance that his Excellency desired to give you what belonged to another?"

"Yes, that puts it forcibly—unanswerably—to my thinking," said Haire.

"I may condole with disappointment, sir, but I am not bound to compensate defeat," said the old Judge; and he arose and walked the room with that irritable look and manner which even the faintest opposition to him often evoked, and for which even the utterance of a flippant rebuke but partly compensated him.

"I take it, my Lord Chief Baron," said Fossbrooke, calmly, "that I have neither asked for condolence nor compensation. I told you, I hoped distinctly that what I was about to urge was not on my own behalf."

"Well, sir, and I think the plea is only the less sustainable. The Viceroy's letter might give a pretext for the one; there is nothing in our acquaintance would warrant the other."

"If you knew, sir, how determined I am not to take offence at words which certainly imperil patience, you would possibly spare me some of these asperities. I am in close relations of friendship with your grandson; he is at present living with me; I have pledged myself to his father to do my utmost in securing him some honorable livelihood, and it is in his behalf that I have presented myself before you to-day. Will you graciously accord me a hearing on this ground?"

There was a quiet dignity of manner in which he said this, a total forgetfulness of self, and a manly simplicity of purpose so palpable, that the old Judge felt he was in presence of one whose character called for all his respect; at the same time he was not one to be suddenly carried away by a sentiment, and in a very measured voice he replied, "If I 'm flattered, sir, by the interest you take in a member of my family, I am still susceptible of a certain displeasure that it should be a stranger should stand before me to ask me for any favor to my own."

"I am aware, my Lord Chief Baron, that my position is a false one, but so is your own."

"Mine, sir! mine? What do you mean? Explain yourself."

"If your Lordship's interest had been exerted as it might have been, Dr. Lendrick's son would never have needed so humble a friend as he has found in me."

"And have you come here, sir, to lecture me on my duty to my family? Have you presented yourself under the formality of a viceregal letter of introduction to tell a perfect stranger to you how he should have demeaned himself to his own?"

"Probably I might retort, and ask by what right you lecture me on my manners and behavior? But I am willing to be taught by so consummate a master of everything; and though I was once a courtier, I believe that I have much to learn on the score of breeding. And now, my Lord, let us leave this unpromising theme, and come to one which has more interest for each of us. If this registrarship, this place, whatever it be, would be one to suit your grandson, will the withdrawal of *my* claim serve to induce your Lordship to support *his*? In one word, my Lord, will you let him have the appointment?"

"I distinctly refuse, sir," said the Judge, waving his hand with an air of dignity. "Of the young gentleman for whom you intercede I know but little; but there are two disqualifications against him, more than enough, either of them, to outweigh your advocacy."

"May I learn them?" asked Sir Brook, meekly.

"You shall, sir. He carries my name without its prestige; he inherits *my* temper, but not my intellect." The blood rushed to his face as he spoke, and his chest swelled, and his whole bearing bespoke the fierce pride that animated him; when suddenly, as it were, recollecting himself, he added: "I am not wont to give way thus, sir. It is only in a moment of forgetfulness that I could have obtruded a personal consideration into a question of another kind. My friend here will tell you if it has been the habit of my life to pension my family on the public."

"Having failed in one object of my coming, let me hope for better success in another. May I convey to your Lordship your grandson's regret for having offended you? It has caused him sincere sorrow and much self-reproach. May I return with the good tidings of your forgiveness?"

"The habits of my order are opposed to rash judgments, and consequently to hasty reversions. I will consider the case, and let you hear my opinion upon it."

"I think that is about as much as you will do with him," muttered Haire in Sir Brook's ear, and with a significant gesture towards the door.

"Before taking my leave, my Lord, would it be too great a liberty if I beg to present my personal respects to Miss Lendrick?"

"I will inform her of your wish, sir," said the Judge, rising, and ringing the bell. After a pause of some minutes, in which a perfect silence was maintained by all, the servant returned to say, "Miss Lendrick would be happy to see Sir Brook."

"I hope, sir," said the Chief Baron, as he accompanied him to the door, "I have no need to request that no portion of what has passed here to-day be repeated to my granddaughter."

A haughty bow of assent was all the reply.

"I make my advances to her heart," said the Judge, with a tone of more feeling in his voice, "through many difficulties. Let these not be increased to me,—let her not think me unmindful of my own."

"Give her no reason to think so, my Lord, and you may feel very indifferent to the chance words of a passing acquaintance."

"For the third time to-day, sir, have you dared to sit in judgment over my behavior to my family. You cannot plead want of experience of life, or want of converse with men, to excuse this audacity. I must regard your intrusion, therefore, as a settled project to insult me. I accept no apologies, sir," said the old man, with a haughty wave of his hand, while his eyes glittered with passion. "I only ask, and I hope I ask as a right, that I may not be outraged under my own roof. Take your next opportunity to offend me when I may not be hampered by the character of your host. Come down into the open arena, and see how proud you will feel at the issue of the encounter." He rang the bell violently as he spoke, and continued to ring it till the servant came.

"Accompany this gentleman to the gate," said he to the man.

Not a change came over Sir Brook's face during the delivery of this speech; and as he bowed reverentially and withdrew, his manner was all that courtesy could desire.

"I see he's not going to visit Lucy," muttered Haire, as Sir Brook passed the window.

"I should think not, sir. There are few men would like to linger where they have been so ingloriously defeated." He walked the room with a proud defiant look for some minutes, and then, sinking faintly into a chair, said, in a weak, tremulous tone, "Haire, these trials are too much for me. It is a cruel aggravation of the ills of old age to have a heart and a brain alive to the finest sense of injury."

Haire muttered something like concurrence.

"What is it you say, sir? Speak out," cried the Judge.

"I was saying," muttered the other, "I wish they would not provoke—would not irritate you; that people ought to see the state your nerves are in, and should use a little discretion how they contradict and oppose you." The bland smile of the Chief-Justice, and an assenting gesture of his hand, emboldened Haire to continue, and he went on: "I have always said, Keep away such as excite him; his condition is not one to be bettered by passionate outbreaks. Calm him, humor him."

"What a pearl above price is a friend endowed with discretion! Leave me, Haire, to think over your nice words. I would like to ponder them alone and to myself. I 'll send for you by and by."

CHAPTER XXII
COMING-HOME THOUGHTS

Had a mere stranger been a guest on that Sunday when the Chief Baron entertained at dinner Lady Lendrick, the Sewells, and his old schoolfellow Haire, he might have gone away under the impression that he had passed an evening in the midst of a happy and united family.

Nothing could be more perfect than the blending of courtesy and familiarity. The old Chief himself was in his best of humors, which means that, with the high polish of a past age, its deference, and its homage, he combined all the readiness and epigrammatic smartness of a later period. Lady Lendrick was bland, courteous, and attentive. Colonel Sewell took the part assigned him by his host, alternate talker and listener; and Mrs. Sewell herself displayed, with true woman's wit, that she knew how to fall in with the Judge's humor, as though she had known him for years, and that, in each sally of his wit and each flash of his repartee he was but reviving memories of such displays in long-past years. As for Haire, no enchantment could be more complete; he found himself not only listened to but appealed to. The Chief asked him to correct him about some fact or other of recent history; he applied to him to relate some incident in a trial he had taken part in; and, greatest triumph of all, he was called on to decide some question about the dressing of Mrs. Sewell's hair, his award being accepted as the last judgment of connoisseurship.

Lucy talked little, but seemed interested by all around her. It was a bit of high-life comedy, really amusing, and she had that mere suspicion—it was no more—of the honesty and loyalty of the talkers to give an added significance to all she saw and heard. This slight distrust, however, gave way, when Mrs. Sewell sat down beside her in the drawing-room, and talked to her of her father. Oh, how well she appeared to know him; how truly she read the guileless simplicity of his noble nature; how she distinguished— it was not all who did so—between his timid reserve and pride; how she saw that what savored of haughtiness was in reality an excess of humility shrouding itself from notice; how she dwelt on his love for children, and the instantaneous affection he inspired in them towards himself. Last of all, how she won the poor girl's heart as she said, "It will never do to leave him there, Lucy; we must have him here, at home with us. I think you may intrust it to me; I generally find my way in these sort of things."

Lucy could have fallen at her feet with gratitude as she heard these words, and she pressed her hand to her lips and kissed it fervently. "Why isn't your brother here? Is he not in Dublin?" asked Mrs. Sewell, suddenly.

"Yes, he is in town," stammered out Lucy, "but grandpapa scarcely knows him, and when they did meet, it was most unfortunate. I 'll tell you all about it another time."

"We have many confidences to make each other," said Mrs. Sewell, with a sigh so full of sorrow that Lucy instinctively pressed her hand with warmth, as though to imply her trustfulness would, not be ill deposited.

At last came the hour of leave-taking, and the Judge accompanied his guests to the door, and even bareheaded handed Lady Lendrick to her carriage. To each, as they said "Good-night," he had some little appropriate speech,—a word or two of gracious compliment, uttered with all his courtesy.

"I call this little dinner a success, Lucy," said he, as he stood to say "Good-night" on the stairs. "Lady Lendrick was unusually amiable, and her daughter-in-law is beyond praise."

"She is indeed charming," said Lucy, fervently.

"I found the Colonel also agreeable,—less dictatorial than men of his class generally are. I suspect we shall get on well together with further acquaintance; but, as Haire said, I was myself to-night, and would have struck sparks out of the dullest rock, so that I must not impute to him what may only have been the reflex of myself. Ah, dear! there was a time when these exertions were the healthful stimulants of my life; now they only weary and excite,—good-night, dear child, good-night."

As Lady Lendrick and her party drove homeward, not a word was uttered for some minutes after they had taken their seats. It was not till after they had passed out of the grounds, and gained the high-road, that she herself broke silence. "Well, Dudley," said she at last, "is he like my description? Was my portrait too highly colored?"

"Quite the reverse. It was a faint weak sketch of the great original. In all my life I never met such inordinate vanity and such overweening pretension. I give him the palm as the most conceited man and the greatest bore in Christendom."

"Do you wonder now if I could n't live with him?" asked she, half triumphantly.

"I 'll not go that far. I think I could live with him if I saw my way to any advantage by it."

"I'm certain you could not! The very things you now reprobate are the few endurable traits about him. It is in the resources of his intense conceit he finds whatever renders him pleasant and agreeable. I wish you saw his other humor."

"I can imagine it may not be all that one would desire; but still—"

"It comes well from you to talk of submitting and yielding," burst out Lady Lendrick. "I certainly have not yet detected these traits in your character; and I tell you frankly, you and Sir William could not live a week under the same roof together. Don't you agree with me, Lucy?"

"What should she know about it?" said he, fiercely; and before she could reply, "I don't suspect she knows a great deal about me,—she knows nothing at all about *him*."

"Well, would you like to live with him yourself, Lucy?" asked Lady Lendrick.

"I don't say I 'd *like* it, but I think it might be done," said she, faintly, and scarcely raising her eyes as she spoke.

"Of course, then, my intractable temper is the cause of all our incompatibility; my only consolation is that I have a son and a daughter-in-law so charmingly endowed that their virtues are more than enough to outweigh my faults."

"What I say is this," said the Colonel, sternly,—"I think the man is a bore or a bully, but that he need n't be both if one does n't like it. Now I 'd consent to be bored, to escape being bullied, which is precisely the reverse of what you appear to have done."

"I am charmed with the perspicuity you display. I hope, Lucy, that it tends to the happiness of your married life to have a husband so well able to read character."

Apparently this was a double-headed shot, for neither spoke for several minutes.

"I declare I almost wish he would put you to the test," said Lady Lendrick. "I mean, I wish he'd ask you to the Priory."

"I fancy it is what he means to do," said Mrs. Sewell, in the same low tone,—"at least he came to me when I was standing in the small drawing-room, and said, 'How would you endure the quiet stillness and uniformity of such a life as I lead here? Would its dulness overpower you?'"

"Of course, you said it would be paradise," broke in her Ladyship; "you hinted all about your own resources, and such-like."

"She did no such thing; she took the pathetic line, put her handkerchief to her eyes, and implied how she would love it, as a refuge from the cruel treatment of a bad husband,—eh, am I right?" Harsh and insolent as the words were, the accents in which they were uttered were far more so. "Out with it, Madam! was it not something like that you said?"

"No," said she, gently. "I told Sir William I was supremely happy, blessed in every accident and every relation of my life, and that hitherto I had never seen the spot which could not suit the glad temper of my heart."

"You keep the glad temper confoundedly to yourself then," burst he out. "I wish you were not such a niggard of it."

"Dudley, Dudley, I say," cried Lady Lendrick, in a tone of reproof.

"I have learned not to mind these amenities," said Mrs. Sewell, in a quiet voice, "and I am only surprised that Colonel Sewell thinks it worth while to continue them."

"If it be your intention to become Sir William's guest, I must say such habits will require to be amended," said her Ladyship, gravely.

"So they shall, mother. Your accomplished and amiable husband, as you once called him in a letter to me, shall only see us in our turtle moods, and never be suffered to approach our cage save when we are billing and cooing."

The look of aversion he threw at his wife as he spoke was something that words cannot convey; and though she never raised eyes to meet it, a sickly pallor crept over her cheek as the blight fell on her.

"I am to call on him to-morrow, by appointment. I wish he had not said twelve. One has not had his coffee by twelve; but as he said, 'I hope that will not be too early for you,' I felt it better policy to reply, 'By no means;' and so I must start as if for a journey."

"What does he mean by asking you to come at that hour? Have you any notion what his business is?"

"Not the least. We were in the hall. I was putting on my coat, when he suddenly turned round and asked me if I could without inconvenience drop in about twelve."

"I wonder what it can be for."

"I'll tell you what I hope it may not be for! I hope it may not be to show me his conservatory, or his Horatian garden, as he pedantically called it, or his fish-ponds. If so, I think I 'll invite him some fine morning to turn over all my protested bills, and the various writs issued against me. Bore for Bore, I suspect we shall come out of the encounter pretty equal."

"He has some rare gems. I'd not wonder if it was to get you to select a present for Lucy."

"If I thought so, I'd take a jeweller with me, as though my friend, to give me a hint as to the value."

"He admires you greatly, Lucy; he told me so as he took me downstairs."

"She has immense success with men of that age: nothing over eighty seems able to resist her."

This time she raised her eyes, and they met his, not with their former expression, but full of defiance, and of an insolent meaning, so that after a moment he turned away his gaze, and with a seeming struggle looked abashed and ashamed. "The first change I will ask you to make in that house," said Lady Lendrick, who had noticed this by-play, "if ever you become its inmates, will be to dismiss that tiresome old hanger-on, Mr. Haire. I abhor him."

"My first reform will be in the sherry,—to get rid of that vile sugary compound of horrid nastiness he gives you After soup. The next will be the long-tailed black coach-horses. I don't think a man need celebrate his own funeral every time he goes out for a drive."

"Haire," resumed Lady Lendrick, in a tone of severity, meant, perhaps, to repress all banter on a serious subject, — "Haire not only supplies food to his vanity, but stimulates his conceit by little daily stories of what the world says of him. I wish he would listen to *me* on that subject,—I wish he would take *my* version of his place in popular estimation."

"I opine that the granddaughter should be got rid of," said the Colonel.

"She is a fool,—only a fool," said Lady Lendrick.

"I don't think her a fool," said Mrs. Sewell, slowly.

"I don't exactly mean so much; but that she has no knowledge of life, and knows nothing whatever of the position she is placed in, nor how to profit by it."

"I'd not even go that far," said Mrs. Sewell, in the same quiet tone.

"Don't pay too much attention to *that*," said the Colonel to his mother. "It's one of her ways always to see something in every one that nobody else has discovered."

"I made that mistake once too often for my own welfare," said she, in a voice only audible to his ear.

"She tells me, mother, that she made that same mistake once too often for her own welfare; which being interpreted, means in taking me for her husband,—a civil speech to make a man in presence of his mother."

"I begin to think that politeness is not the quality any of us are eager about," said Lady Lendrick; "and I must say I am not at all sorry that the drive is over."

"If I had been permitted to smoke, you'd not have been distressed by any conversational excesses on my part," said the Colonel.

"I shall know better another time, Dudley; and possibly-it would be as well to be suffocated with tobacco as half-choked with anger. Thank heaven we are at the door!"

"May I take your horses as far as the Club?" asked Sewell, as he handed her out.

"Yes, but not to wait. You kept them on Tuesday night till past four o'clock."

"On second thought, I'll walk," said he, turning away. "Good-night;" and leaving his wife to be assisted down the steps by the footman, he lighted his cigar, and walked away.

CHAPTER XXIII
A VERY HUMBLE DWELLING

The little lodging occupied by Sir Brook and young Lendrick was in a not very distinguished suburb near Cullen's Wood. It was in a small one-storied cottage, whose rickety gate bore the inscription "Avoca Villa" on a black board, under which, in the form of permanence that indicated frequent changes of domicile, were the words, "Furnished Apartments, and Board if required." A small enclosure, with three hollyhocks in a raised mound in the centre, and a luxurious crop of nettles around, served as garden: a narrow path of very rough shingle conducted to the door.

The rooms within were very small, low, and meanly furnished; they bespoke both poverty and neglect; and while the broken windows, the cobwebbed ceiling, and the unwashed floor all indicated that no attention was bestowed on comfort or even decency, over the fireplace, in a large black frame, was a painting representing the genealogical tree of the house of the proprietor, Daniel O'Reardon, Esquire, the lineal descendant of Frenok-Dhubh-na-Bochlish O'Reardon, who was King of West Carbarry, a.d. 703, and who, though at present only a doorkeeper in H. M. Court of Exchequer, had royal blood in his veins, and very kingly thoughts in his head.

If a cruel destiny compelled Mr. O'Reardon to serve the Saxon, he "took it out" in a most hearty hatred of his patron. He denounced him when he talked, and he reviled him when he sang. He treasured up paragraphs of all the atrocities of the English press, and he revelled in the severe strictures which the Irish papers bestowed on them. So far as hating went, he was a true patriot.

If some people opined that Mr. O'Reardon's political opinions rather partook of what was in vogue some sixty-odd years ago than what characterized a time nearer our own day, there were others, less generous critics, who scrupled not to say that he was a paid spy of the Government, and that all the secret organization of treason—all the mysterious plotting of rebellion that seems never to die completely out in Ireland—were known to and reported by this man to the Castle. Certain it was that he lived in a way his humble salary at the Four Courts could not have met, and indulged in convivial excesses far beyond the reach of his small income.

When Sir Brook and Tom Lendrick became his lodgers, he speedily saw that they belonged to a class far above what usually resorted to his humble house. However studiously simple they might be in all their demands, they were unmistakably gentlemen; and this fact, coupled with their evident want of all employment or occupation, considerably puzzled Mr. O'Reardon, and set him a-thinking what they could be, who they were, and, as he phrased it, "what they were at." No letters came for them, nor, as they themselves gave no names, was there any means of tracing their address; and to his oft-insinuated request, "If any one asks for you, sir, by what name will I be able to answer?" came the same invariable "No one will call;" and thus was Mr. O'Reardon reduced to designate them to his wife as the "old chap" and the "young one,"—titles which Sir Brook and Tom more than once overheard through the frail partitions of the ill-built house.

It is not impossible that O'Reardon's peculiar habits and line of life disposed him to attach a greater significance to the seeming mystery that surrounded his lodgers than others might have ascribed; it is probable that custom had led him to suspect everything that was in any way suspicious. These men draw many a cover where there is no fox, but they rarely pass a gorse thicket and leave one undetected. His lodgers thus became to him a study. Had he been a man of leisure, he would have devoted the whole of it to their service; he would have dogged their steps, learned their haunts, and watched their acquaintances,—if they had any. Sunday was, however, his one free day, and by some inconceivable perversity they usually spent the entire of it at home.

The few books they possessed bore no names, some of them were in foreign languages, and increased thereby Mr. O'Reardon's suspicious distrust; but none gave any clew to their owners. There was another reason for his eagerness and anxiety; for a long time back Ireland had been generally in a condition of comparative quiet and prosperity; there was less of distress, and, consequently, less of outrage. The people seemed at length to rely more upon themselves and their own industry than on the specious promises of trading politicians, and Mr. O'Reardon, whose functions, I fear, were not above reproach in the matter of secret information, began to fear lest some fine morning he might be told his occupation was gone, and that his employers no longer needed the fine intelligence that could smell treason, even by a sniff; he must, he said, do something to revive the memory of his order, or the chance was it would be extinguished forever.

He had to choose between denouncing them as French emissaries or American sympathizers. A novel of Balzac's that lay on the table decided for the former, for he knew enough to be aware it was in French; and fortified with this fact, he proceeded to draw up his indictment for the Castle.

It was, it must be confessed, a very meagre document; it contained little beyond the writer's own suspicions. Two men who were poor enough to live in Avoca Villa, and yet rich enough to do nothing for their livelihood, who gave no names, went out at unseasonable hours, and understood French, ought to be dangerous, and required to be watched, and therefore he gave an accurate description of their general appearance, age, and dress, at the office of the Private Secretary, and asked for his "instructions" in consequence.

Mr. O'Reardon was not a bad portrait-painter with his pen, and in the case of Sir Brook there were peculiarities enough to make even a caricature a resemblance; his tall narrow head, his long drooping moustache, his massive gray eyebrows, his look of stern dignity, would have marked him, even without the singularities of dress which recalled the fashions of fifty years before.

Little, indeed, did the old man suspect that his high-collared coat and bell-shaped hat were subjecting him to grave doubts upon his loyalty. Little did he think, as he sauntered at evening along the green lanes in this retired neighborhood, that his thoughts ought to have been on treason and bloodshed.

He had come to the little lodging, it is true, for privacy. After his failure in that memorable interview with Sir William Lendrick, he had determined that he would not either importune the Viceroy for place, or would he be in any way the means of complicating the question between the Government and the Chief Baron by exciting the Lord-Lieutenant's interest in his behalf.

"We must change our lodging, Tom," said he, when he came home on that night. "I am desirous that, for the few days we remain here, none should trace nor discover us. I will not accept what are called compensations, nor will I live on here to be either a burden or a reproach to men who were once only my equals."

"You found my worthy grandfather somewhat less tractable than you thought for, sir?" asked Tom.

"He was very fiery and very haughty; but on the whole, there was much that I liked in him. Such vitality in a man of his years is in itself a grand quality, and even in its aggressiveness suggests much to regard. He refused to hear of me for the vacant office, and he would not accept *you*."

"How did he take your proposal to aid us by a loan?"

"I never made it. The terms we found ourselves on after half an hour's discussion of other matters rendered such a project impossible."

"And Lucy, how did she behave through it all?"

"She was not there; I did not see her."

"So that it turned out as I predicted,—a mere meeting to exchange amenities."

"The amenities were not many, Tom; and I doubt much if your grandfather will treasure up any very delightful recollections of my acquaintance."

"I'd like to see the man, woman, or child," burst out Tom, "who ever got out of his cage without a scratch. I don't believe that Europe contains his equal for irascibility."

"Don't dwell on these views of life," said Sir Brook, almost sternly. "You, nor I, know very little what are the sources of those intemperate outbreaks we so often complain of,—what sore trials are ulcerating the nature, what agonizing maladies, what secret terrors, what visions of impending misery; least of all do we know or take count of the fact that it is out of these high-strung temperaments we obtain those thrilling notes of human passion and tenderness coarser natures never attain to. Let us bear with a passing discord in the instrument whose cadences can move us to very ecstasy."

Tom hung his head in silence, but he certainly did not seem convinced. Sir Brook quietly resumed: "How often have I told you that the world has more good than bad in it,—yes, and what's more, that as we go on in life this conviction strengthens in us, and that our best experiences are based on getting rid of our disbeliefs. Hear what happened me this morning. You know that for some days back I have been negotiating to raise a small loan of four hundred pounds to take us to Sardinia and start our mine. Mr. Waring, who was to have lent me this sum on the security of the mine itself, took it into his head to hesitate at the last hour, and inserted an additional clause that I should insure my life in his behalf.

"I was disconcerted, of course, by this,—so much so, that had I not bought a variety of tools and implements on trust, I believe I would have relinquished the bargain and tried elsewhere. It was, however, too late for this; I was driven to accept his terms, and, accredited with a printed formula from an insurance office, I waited on the doctor who was to examine me.

"A very brief investigation satisfied him that I was not seaworthy; he discovered I know not what about the valves of my heart, that implied mischief, and after 'percussing' me, as he called it, and placing his ear to my chest, he said, 'I regret to say, sir, that I cannot pronounce you insurable.'

"I could have told him that I came of a long-lived race on either side; that during my life I had scarcely known an illness, that I had borne the worst climates without injury, and such-like,—but I forbore; I had too much deference for his station and his acquirements to set my judgment against them, and I arose to take my leave. It is just possible, though I cannot say I felt it, that his announcement might have affected me; at all events, the disappointment did so, and I was terrified about the difficulties in which I saw myself involved. I became suddenly sick, and I asked for a glass of water; before it came I had fainted, a thing that never in my whole life had befallen me. When, I rallied, he led me to talk of my usual habits and pursuits, and gradually brought me to the subject which had led me-to his house. 'What!' said he, 'ask for any security beyond the property itself! It is absurd; Waring is always-doing these things. Let me advance this money. I know a great deal more about you, Sir Brook, than you think; my friend Dr. Lendrick has spoken much of you, and of all your kindness to his son; and though you may not have heard of my name,—Beattie,—I am very familiar with yours.'

"In a word, Tom, he advanced the money. It is now in that writing-desk; and I have—I feel it—a friend the-more in the world. As I left his door, I could not help saying to myself, What signify a few days more or less of life, so long as such generous traits as this follow one to the last? He made me a happier man by his noble trust in me than if he had declared me a miracle of strength and vigor. Who is that looking in at the window, Tom? It's the second time I have seen a face there."

Tom started to his feet and hurried to the door. There was, however, no one there; and the little lane was silent and deserted. He stopped a few minutes to listen, but not a footfall could be heard, and he returned to the room believing it must have been a mere illusion.

"Let us light candles, Tom, and have out our maps. I want to see whether Marseilles will not be our best and cheapest route to the island."

They were soon poring eagerly over the opened map, Sir Brook carefully studying all the available modes of travel; while Tom, be it owned, let his eyes wander from land to land, till following out the Danube to the Black Sea, he crossed over and stretched away into the mountain gorges of Circassia, where Schamyl and his brave followers were then fighting for liberty. For maps, like the lands they picture, never offer to two minds kindred thoughts; each follows out in space the hopes and ambitions that his heart is charged with; and where one reads wars and battle-fields, another but sees pastoral pleasures and a tranquil existence,—home and home-happiness.

"Yes, Tom; here I have it. These coasting-craft, whose sailing-lines are marked here, will take us and our traps to Cagliari for a mere trifle,—here is the route."

As the young man bent over the map, the door behind opened, and a stranger entered. "So I have found you, Fossbrooke!" cried he, "though they insisted you had left Ireland ten days ago."

"Mercy on me! Lord Wilmington!" said Sir Brook, as he shaded his eyes to stare at him. "What could have brought you here?"

"I 'll tell you," said he, dropping his voice. "I read a description so very like you in the secret report this morning, that I sent my servant Curtis, who knows you well, to see if it was not yourself; when he came back to me—for I waited for him at the end of the lane—with the assurance that I was right, I came on here. I must tell you that I took the precaution to have your landlord detained, as if for examination, at the Under-Secretary's office; and he is the only one here who knows me. Mr. Lendrick, I hope you have not forgotten me? We met some months ago on the Shannon."

"What can I offer you?" said Sir Brook. "Shall it be tea? We were just going to have it."

"I 'll take whatever you like to give me; but let us profit by the few moments I can stay. Tell me how was it you failed with the Chief Baron?"

"He wouldn't have me; that's all. He maintains his right to an undivided patronage, and will accept of no dictation."

"Will he accept of your friend here? He has strong claims on him."

"As little as myself, my Lord; he grew eloquent on his public virtue, and of course became hopeless."

"Will he retire and let us compensate him?"

"I believe not. He thinks the country has a vested interest in his capacity, and as he cannot be replaced, he has no right to retire."

"He may make almost his own terms with us, Fossbrooke," said the Viceroy. "We want to get rid of himself and an intractable Solicitor-General together. Will you try what can be done?"

"Not I, my Lord. I have made my first and last advances in that quarter."

"And yet I believe you are our last chance. He told Pemberton yesterday you were the one man of ability that ever called on him with a message from a Viceroy."

"Let us leave him undisturbed in his illusion, my Lord."

"I 'd say, let us profit by it, Fossbrooke. I have been in search of you these eight days, to beg you would take the negotiation in hand. Come, Mr. Lendrick, you are interested in this; assist me in persuading Sir Brook to accept this charge. If he will undertake the mission, I am ready to give him ample powers to treat."

"I suspect, my Lord," said Tom, "you do not know my grandfather. He is not a very manageable person to deal with."

"It is for that reason I want to place him in the hands of my old friend here."

"No, no, my Lord; it is quite hopeless. Had we never met, I might have come before him with some chance of success; but I have already prejudiced myself in his eyes, and our one interview was not very gratifying to either of us."

"I'll not give in, Fossbrooke, even though I am well aware I can do nothing to requite the service I ask of you."

"We leave Ireland to-morrow evening. We have a project which requires our presence in the island of Sardinia. We are about to make our fortunes, my Lord, and I 'm sure you 're not the man to throw any obstacle in the way."

"Give me half an hour of your morning, Fossbrooke; half an hour will suffice. Drive out to the Priory; see the Chief Baron; tell him I intrusted the negotiation to you, as at once more delicate to each of us. You are disconnected with all party ties here. Say it is not a question of advancing this man or that, — that we well know how inferior must any successor be to himself, but that certain changes are all-essential to us. We have not — I may tell you in confidence — the right man as our law adviser in the House; and add, 'It is a moment to make your own terms; write them down and you shall have your reply within an hour, — a favorable one I may almost pledge myself it will be. At all events, every detail of the meeting is strictly between us, and on honor.' Come, now, Fossbrooke; do this for me as the greatest service I could entreat of you."

"I cannot refuse you any longer. I will go. I only premise that I am to limit myself strictly to the statement you shall desire me to repeat. I know nothing of the case; and I cannot be its advocate."

"Just so. Give me your card. I will merely write these words, — 'See Sir Brook for me. — Wilmington.' Our object is his resignation, and we are prepared to pay handsomely for it. Now, a word with you, Mr. Lendrick. I heard most honorable mention of you yesterday from the vice-provost; he tells me that your college career was a triumph so long as you liked it, and that you have abilities for any walk in life. Why not continue, then, on so successful a path? Why not remain, take out your degree, and emulate that distinguished relative who has thrown such lustre on your family?"

"First of all, my Lord, you have heard me much overrated. I am not at all the man these gentlemen deem me; secondly, if I were, I 'd rather bring my abilities to any pursuit my friend here could suggest. I 'd rather be *his* companion than be my grandfather's rival. You have heard what he said awhile ago,—we are going to seek our fortune."

"He said to make it," said Lord Wilmington, with a smile.

"Be it so, my Lord. I *'ll* seek, and *he 'll* find; at all events, I shall be his companion; and I'm a duller dog than I think myself if I do not manage to be the better of it."

"You are not the only one he has fascinated," said the Viceroy, in a whisper. "I 'm not sure I 'd disenchant you if I had the power."

"Must I positively undertake this negotiation?" asked Fossbrooke, with a look of entreaty.

"You must"

"I know I shall fail."

"I don't believe it."

"Well, as Lady Macbeth says, if we fail *we fail*; and though murdering a king be an easier thing than muzzling a Chief Baron,—here goes."

As he said this, the door was gently moved, and a head protruded into the room.

"Who is that?" cried Tom, springing rapidly towards the door; but all was noiseless and quiet, and no one to be seen. "I believe we are watched here," said he, coming back into the room.

"Good-night, then. Let me have your report as early as may be, Fossbrooke. Good-night."

CHAPTER XXIV
A MORNING AT THE PRIORY

The morning after this interview was that on which the Chief Baron had invited Colonel Sewell to inspect his gardens and hothouses,—a promise of pleasure which, it is but fair to own, the Colonel regarded with no extravagant delight. To his thinking, the old Judge was an insupportable bore. His courtesy, his smartness, his anecdotes, his reminiscences were all Boredom. He was only endurable when by the excess of his conceit he made himself ridiculous. Then alone did Sewell relish his company; for he belonged to that class of men, and it is a class, who feel their highest enjoyment whenever they witness any trait in human nature that serves to disparage its dignity or tarnish its lustre.

That a man of unquestionable ability and power like the Chief Baron should render himself absurd through his vanity, was a great compensation to such a person as Sewell. To watch the weaknesses and note the flaws in a great nature, to treasure up the consolation that, after all, these "high intelligences" occasionally make precious fools of themselves, are very congenial pastimes to small folk. Perhaps, indeed, they are the sole features of such men they are able to appreciate, and, like certain reptiles, they never venture to bite save where corruption has preceded them.

Nothing in his manner betrayed this tendency; he was polished and courteous to a degree. A very critical eye might have detected in his bearing that he had been long a subordinate. His deference was a little—a very little—overstrained; he listened with a slight tinge of over-attention; and in his humility as he heard an order, and his activity as he obeyed it, you could read at once the aide-decamp in waiting.

It is not necessary to remind the reader that all this lacquer of good breeding covered a very coarse and vulgar nature. In manner he was charming,—his approach, his address, his conversation were all perfect; he knew well when to be silent,—when to concur by a smile with what he was not expected to confirm by a word,—when to seem suddenly confronted with a new conviction, and how to yield assent as though coerced to what he would rather have resisted. In a word, he was perfect in all the training of those superb poodles who fetch and carry for their masters, that they may have the recompense of snarling at all the rest of mankind.

As there are heaven-born doctors, lawyers, divines, and engineers, so are there men specially created for the antechamber, and Sewell was one of them.

The old Judge had given orders for a liberal breakfast. He deemed a soldier's appetite would be a hearty one, and he meant to treat him hospitably. The table was therefore very generously spread, and Sewell looked approvingly at the fare, and ventured on a few words of compliment on the ample preparations before him.

"It is the only real breakfast-table I have seen since I left Calcutta," said he, smiling graciously.

"You do me honor, sir," replied the old man, who was not quite sure whether or not he felt pleased to be complimented on a mere domestic incident.

Sewell saw the hitch at once, and resumed: "I remember an observation Lord Commorton made me when I joined his staff in India. I happened to make some remark on a breakfast set out pretty much like this, and he said, 'Bear in mind, Captain Sewell, that when a man who holds a high function sits down to a well-served breakfast, it means that he has already completed the really important work of the day. The full head means the empty stomach.'"

"His Excellency was right, sir; had he always been inspired with sentiments of equal wisdom, we should never have been involved in that unhappy Cantankankarabad war."

"It was a very disastrous affair, indeed," sighed Sewell; "I was through the whole of it."

"When I first heard of the project," continued the Judge, "I remarked to a friend who was with me,—one of the leading men at the Bar,—'This campaign will tarnish our arms, and imperil our hold on India. The hill-tribes are eminently warlike, and however specious in their promises to us, their fidelity to their chiefs has never been shaken.'"

"If your judgment had been listened to, it would have saved us a heavy reverse, and saved me a very painful wound; both bones were fractured here," said Sewell, showing his wrist.

The Chief Baron scarcely deigned a glance at the cicatrix; he was high above such puny considerations. He was at that moment Governor-General of India and Prime Minister of England together. He was legislating for hundreds of millions of dark-skins, and preparing his explanations of his policy for the pale faces at home.

"'Mark my words, Haire,' said I," continued the Judge, with increased pomposity of manner, "'this is the beginning of insurrection in India.' We have a maxim in law, Colonel Sewell, Like case, like rule. So was it there. May I help you to this curry?"

"I declare, my Lord, I was beginning to forget how hungry I was. Shall I be deemed impertinent if I ask how you obtained your marvellous—for it is marvellous—knowledge of India?"

"Just as I know the Japanese constitution; just as I know Central Africa; just as I know, and was able to quote some time back, that curious chapter of the Brehon laws on substitutes in penal cases. My rule of life has been, never to pass a day without increasing the store of my acquirements."

"And all this with the weighty charge and labor of your high office."

"Yes, sir; I have been eighteen years on the Bench. I have delivered in that time some judgments which have come to be deemed amongst the highest principles of British law. I have contributed largely to the periodical literature of the time. In a series of papers—you may not have heard of them—signed 'Icon,' in the 'Lawyer's Treasury of Useful Facts,' I have defended the Bar against the aggressive violence of the Legislature, I hope it is not too much to say, triumphantly."

"I remember Judge Beale, our Indian Chief-Justice, referring to those papers as the most splendid statement of the position and claims of the barrister in Great Britain."

"Beale was an ass, sir; his law was a shade below his logic,—both were pitiable."

"Indeed?—yes, a little more gravy. Is your cook a Provençal? that omelette would seem to say so."

"My cook is a woman, and an Irishwoman, sir. She came to me from Lord Manners, and, I need not say, with the worst traditions of her art, which, under Lady Lendrick's training, attained almost to the dignity of poisoning."

Sewell could not restrain himself any longer, but laughed out at this sudden outburst. The old Judge was, however, pleased to accept the emotion as complimentary; he smiled and went on: "I recognized her aptitude, and resolved to train her, and to this end I made it a practice to detain her every morning after prayers, and read to her certain passages from approved authors on cookery, making her experiment on the receipts for the servants' hall. We had at first some slight cases of illness, but not more serious than colic and violent cramps. In the end she was successful, sir, and has become what you see her."

"She would be a *cordon bleu* in Paris."

"I will take care, sir, that she hears of your approval. Would you not like a glass of Maraschino to finish with?"

"I have just tasted your brandy, and it is exquisite."

"I cannot offer you a cigar, Colonel; but you are at liberty to smoke if you have one."

"If I might have a stroll in that delicious garden that I see there, I could ask nothing better. Ah, my Lord," said he, as they sauntered down a richly scented alley, "India has nothing like this,—I doubt if Paradise has any better."

"You mean to return to the East?"

"Not if I can help it,—not if an exchange is possible. The fact is, my Lord, my dear wife's health makes India impossible so far as she is concerned; the children, too, are of the age that requires removal to Europe; so that, if I go back, I go back alone." He said this with a voice of deep depression, and intending to inspire the sorrow that overwhelmed him. The old Judge, however, fancied he had heard of heavier calamities in life than living separated from the wife of his bosom; he imagined, at least, that with courage and fortitude the deprivation might be endured; so he merely twitched the corners of his mouth in silence.

The Colonel misread his meaning, and went on: "Aspiring to nothing in life beyond a home and home-happiness, it is, of course, a heavy blow to me to sacrifice either my career or my comfort. I cannot possibly anticipate a return earlier than eight or ten years; and who is to count upon eight or ten years in that pestilent climate? Assuredly not a man already broken down by wounds and jungle fever!"

The justice of the remark was, perhaps, sufficient for the Chief Baron. He paid no attention to its pathetic side, and *so* did not reply.

Sewell began to lose patience, but he controlled himself, and, after a few puffs of his cigar, went on: "If it were not for the children, I 'd take the thing easy enough. Half-pay is a beggarly thing, but I 'd put up with it. I 'm not a man of expensive tastes. If I can relish thoroughly such sumptuous fare as you gave me this morning, I can put up with very humble diet. I 'm a regular soldier in that."

"An excellent quality, sir," said the old man, dryly.

"Lucy, of course, would suffer. There are privations which fall very heavily on a woman, and a woman, too, who has always been accustomed to a good deal of luxury."

The Chief bowed an assent.

"I suppose I might get a depot appointment for a year or two. I might also—if I sold out—manage a barrack-mastership, or become an inspector of yeomanry, or some such vulgar makeshift; but I own, my Lord, when a man has filled the places I have,—held staff appointments,—been a private secretary,—discharged high trusts, too, for in Mooraghabad I acted as Deputy-Resident for eight months,—it does seem a precious come-down to ask to be made a paymaster in a militia regiment, or a subaltern in the mounted police."

"Civil life is always open to a man of activity and energy," said the Judge, calmly.

"If civil life means a profession, it means the sort of labor a man is very unfit for after five-and-thirty. The Church, of course, is open on easier terms; but I have scruples about the Church. I really could not take orders without I could conscientiously say, This is a walk I feel called to."

"An honorable sentiment, sir," was the dry rejoinder.

"So that the end will be, I suppose, one of these days I shall just repack my bullock-trunk, and go back to the place from whence I came, with the fate that attends such backward journeys!"

The Chief Baron made no remark. He stooped to fasten, a fallen carnation to the stick it had been attached to, and then resumed his walk. Sewell was so provoked by the sense of failure—for it had been a direct assault—that he walked along silent and morose. His patience could endure no longer, and he was ready now to resent whatever should annoy him.

"Have you any of the requirements, sir, that civil services demand?" asked the Judge, after a long pause.

"I take it I have such as every educated gentleman possesses," replied Sewell, tartly.

"And what may these be, in your estimation?"

"I can read and write, I know the first three rules of arithmetic, and I believe these are about the qualifications that fit a man for a place in the Cabinet."

"You are right, sir. With these, and the facility to talk platitudes in Parliament, a man may go very far and very high in life. I see that you know the world."

Sewell, for a moment, scarcely knew whether to accept the speech as irony or approval; but a sidelong glance showed him that the old man's face had resumed its expression of mingled insolence and vanity, and convinced him that he was now sincere. "The men," said the Judge, pompously, "who win their way to high station in these days are either the crafty tricksters of party or the gross flatterers of the people; and whenever a man of superior mould is discovered, able to leave his mark on the age, and capable of making his name a memory, they have nothing better to offer him, as their homage, than an entreaty that he would resign his office and retire."

"I go with every word you say, my Lord," cried Sewell, with a well-acted enthusiasm.

"I want no approval, sir; I can sustain my opinions without a following!" A long silence ensued; neither was disposed to speak: at last the Judge said,—and he now spoke in a more kindly tone, divested alike of passion and of vanity,—"Your friends must see if something cannot be done for you, Colonel Sewell. I have little doubt but that you have many and warm friends. I speak not of myself; I am but a broken reed to depend on. Never was there one with less credit with his party. I might go farther, and say, never was there one whose advocacy would be more sure to damage a good cause; therefore exclude *me* in all questions of your advancement. If you could obliterate our relationship, it might possibly serve you."

"I am too proud of it, my Lord, to think so."

"Well, sir," said he, with a sigh, "it is possibly a thing a man need not feel ashamed of; at least I hope as much. But we must take the world as it is, and when we want the verdict of public opinion, we must not presume to ask for a special jury. What does that servant want? Will you have the kindness to ask him whom he is looking for?"

"It is a visitor's card, my Lord," said Sewell, handing it to the old man as he spoke.

"There is some writing on it. Do me the favor to read it."

Sewell took the card and read, "See Sir B. for me.—Wilmington. Sir Brook Fossbrooke." The last words Sewell spoke in a voice barely above a whisper, for a deadly sickness came over him, and he swayed to and fro like one about to faint.

"What! does he return to the charge?" cried the old man, fiercely. "The Viceroy was a diplomatist once. Might it not have taught him that, after a failure, it would be as well to employ another envoy?"

"You have seen this gentleman already, then?" asked Sewell, in a low faint tone.

"Yes, sir. We passed an hour and half together,—an hour and half that neither of us will easily forget."

"I conjecture, then, that he made no very favorable impression upon you, my Lord?"

"Sir, you go too fast. I have said nothing to warrant your surmise; nor am I one to be catechised as to the opinions I form of other men. It is enough on the present occasion if I say I do not desire to receive Sir Brook Fossbrooke, accredited though he be from so high a quarter. Will you do me the very great favor"—and now his voice became almost insinuating in its tone—"will you so deeply oblige me ate to see him for me? Say that I am prevented by the state of my health; that the rigorous injunctions of my doctor to avoid all causes of excitement—lay stress on excitement— deprive me of the honor of receiving him in person; but that *you*—mention our relationship—have been deputed by me to hear, and if necessary to convey to me, any communication he may have to make. You will take care to impress upon him that if the subject-matter of his visit be the same as that so lately discussed between ourselves, you will avail yourself of the discretion confided to you not to report it to me. That my nerves have not sufficiently recovered from the strain of that excitement to return to a topic no less full of irritating features than utterly hopeless of all accommodation. Mind, sir, that you employ the word as I give it,—'accommodation.' It is a Gallicism, but all the better, where one desires to be imperative, and yet vague. You have your instructions, sir."

"Yes, I think I understand what you desire me to do. My only difficulty is to know whether the matters Sir Brook Fossbrooke may bring forward be the same as those you discussed together. If I had any clew to these topics, I should at once be in a position to say, These are themes I must decline to present to the Chief Baron."

"You have no need to know them, sir," said the old man, haughtily. "You are in the position of an attesting witness; you have no dealing with the body of the document. Ask Sir Brook the question as I have put it, and reply as I have dictated."

Sewell stood for a moment in deep thought. Had the old man but known over what realms of space his mind was wandering,—what troubles and perplexities that brain was encountering,—he might have been more patient and more merciful as he gazed on him.

"I don't think, sir, I have confided to you any very difficult or very painful task," said the Judge at last.

"Nothing of the kind, my Lord," replied he, quickly; "my anxiety is only that I may acquit myself to your perfect satisfaction. I 'll go at once."

"You will find me here whenever you want me."

Sewell bowed, and went his way; not straight towards the house, however, but into a little copse at the end of the garden, to recover his equanimity and collect himself. Of all the disasters that could befall him, he knew of none he was less ready to confront than the presence of Sir Brook Fossbrooke in the same town with himself. No suspicion ever crossed his mind that he would come to Ireland. The very last he had heard of him was in New Zealand, where it was said he was about to settle. What, too, could be his business with the Chief Baron? Had he discovered their relationship, and was he come to denounce and expose him? No,—evidently not. The Viceroy's introduction of him could not point in this direction, and then the old Judge's own manner negatived this conjecture. Had he heard but one of the fifty stories Sir Brook could have told of him, there would be no question of suffering him to cross his threshold.

"How shall I meet him? how shall I address him?" muttered he again and again to himself, as he walked to and fro in a perfect agony of trouble and perplexity. With almost any other man in the world, Sewell would have relied on his personal qualities to carry him through a passage of difficulty. He could assume a temper of complete imperturbability; he could put on calm, coldness, deference, if needed, to any extent; he could have acted his part—it would have been mere acting—as man of honor and man of courage to the life, with any other to confront him but Sir Brook.

This, however, was the one man on earth who knew him,—the one man by whose mercy he was able to hold up his head and maintain his station; and that this one man should now be here! here, within a few yards of where he stood!

"I could murder him as easily as I go to meet him," muttered Sewell, as he turned towards the house.

CHAPTER XXV
AN UNEXPECTED MEETING

As Sir Brook sat in the library waiting for the arrival of the Chief Baron, Lucy Lendrick came in to look for a book she had been reading. "Only think, sir," said she, flushing deeply with joy and astonishment together,—"to find you here! What a delightful surprise!"

"I have come, my dear child," said he, gravely, "to speak with Sir William on a matter of some importance; and evidently he is not aware that my moments are precious, for I have been here above half an hour alone."

"But now that I am with you," said she, coquettishly, "you 'll surely not be so churlish of your time, will you?"

"There is no churlishness, my darling Lucy, in honest thrift. I have nothing to give away." The deep sadness of his voice showed how intensely his words were charged with a stronger significance. "We are off to-night."

"To-night!" cried she, eagerly.

"Yes, Lucy. It's no great banishment,—only to an island in the Mediterranean, and Tom came up here with me in the vague, very vague hope he might see you. I left him in the shrubbery near the gate, for he would not consent to come farther."

"I 'll go to him at once. We shall meet again," said she, as she opened the sash-door and hastened down the lawn at speed.

After another wait of full a quarter of an hour, Foss-brooke's patience became exhausted, and he drew nigh the bell to summon a servant; his hand was on the rope, when the door opened, and Sewell entered. Whatever astonishment Fossbrooke might have felt at this unexpected appearance, nothing in his manner or look betrayed it. As for Sewell, all his accustomed ease had deserted him, and he came forward with an air of assumed swagger, but his color came and went, and his hands twitched almost convulsively.

He bowed, and, smiling courteously, invited Fossbrooke to be seated. Haughtily drawing himself up to his full height, Sir Brook said, in his own deep sonorous voice, "There can be nothing between us, sir, that cannot be dismissed in a moment—and as we stand."

"As you please, sir," rejoined Sewell, with an attempt at the same haughty tone. "I have been deputed by my stepfather, the Chief Baron, to make his excuses for not receiving you,—his health forbids the excitement. It is his-wish that you may make to *me* whatever communication you had destined for *him*."

"Which I refuse, sir, at once," interrupted Sir Brook. "I opine, then, there is no more to be said," said Sewell, with a faint smile.

"Nothing more, sir,—not a word; unless perhaps you will be gracious enough to explain to the Chief Baron the reasons—they cannot be unknown to you—why I refuse all and any communication with Colonel Sewell."

"I have no presumption to read your mind and know your thoughts," said Sewell, with quiet politeness.

"You would discover nothing in either to your advantage, sir," said Fossbrooke, defiantly.

"Might I add, sir," said Sewell, with an easy smile, "that all your malevolence cannot exceed my indifference to it?"

Fossbrooke waived his hand haughtily, as though to dismiss the subject and all discussion of it, and after a few seconds' pause said: "We have a score that must be settled one day. I have deferred the reckoning out of reverence to the memory of one whose name must not be uttered between us, but the day for it shall come. Meanwhile, sir, you shall pay me interest on your debt."

"What do you assume me to owe you?" asked Sewell, whose agitation could no longer be masked.

"You would laugh if I said, your character before the world and the repute through which men keep your company; but you will not laugh—no, sir, not even smile—when I say that you owe me the liberty by which you are at large, instead of being, as I could prove you, a forger and a felon."

Sewell threw a hurried and terrified look around the room, as though there might possibly be some to overhear the words; he grasped the back of a chair to steady himself, and in the convulsive effort seemed as if he was about to commit some act of violence.

"None of that, sir," said Fossbrooke, folding his arms.

"I meant nothing; I intended nothing; I was faint, and wanted support," stammered out Sewell, in a broken voice. "What do you mean by interest? How am I to pay interest on an indefinite sum?"

"It may relieve you of some anxiety to learn that I am not speaking of money in the interest I require of you. What I want—what I shall exact—is this: that you and yours—" He stopped and grew scarlet; the fear lest something coarse or offensive might fall from him in a moment of heat and anger arrested his words, and he was silent.

Sewell saw all the difficulty. A less adroit man would have deemed the moment favorable to assert a triumph; Sewell was too acute for this, and waited without speaking a word.

"My meaning is this," said Fossbrooke, in a voice of emotion. "There is a young lady here for whom I have the deepest interest. I desire that, so long as she lives estranged from her father's roof, she should not be exposed to other influences than such as she has met there. She is new to life and the world, and I would not that she should make acquaintance with them through any guidance save of her own nearest and dearest friends."

"I hear, sir; but, I am free to own, I greatly mistrust myself to appreciate your meaning."

"I am sorry for it," said Fossbrooke, sighing. "I wanted to convey my hope that in your intercourse here Miss Lendrick might be spared the perils of—of—"

"My wife's friendship, you would say, sir," said Sewell, with a perfect composure of voice and look.

Fossbrooke hung his head. Shame and sorrow alike crushed him down. Oh that the day should come when he could speak thus of Frank Dillon's daughter!

"I will not say with what pain I hear you, Sir Brook," said Sewell, in a low gentle voice. "I am certain that you never uttered such a speech without much suffering. It will alleviate your fears when I tell you that we only remain a few days in town. I have taken a country house, some sixty or seventy miles from the capital, and we mean to live there entirely."

"I am satisfied," said Sir Brook, whose eagerness to make reparation was now extreme.

"Of course I shall mention nothing of this to my wife," said Sewell.

"Of course not, sir; save with such an explanation as I could give of my meaning, it would be an outrage."

"I was not aware that there was—that there could be—an explanation," said Sewell, quietly; and then seeing the sudden flash that shot from the old man's eyes, he added hastily, "This is far too painful to dwell on; let it suffice, sir, that I fully understand you, and that you shall be obeyed."

"I ask no more," said Fossbrooke, bowing slightly.

"You will comprehend, Sir Brook," resumed Sewell, "that as I am precluded from making this conversation known to my wife, I shall not be able to limit any intimacy between her and Miss Lendrick farther than by such intimations and hints as I may offer without exciting suspicion. It might happen, for instance, that in coming up to town we should be Sir William's guests. Am I to suppose that you interdict this?"

"I hope I am not capable of such a condition," said Sir Brook, flushing, for at every step and stage of the negotiation he felt that his zeal had outrun his judgment, and that he was attempting not only more than he could, but more than he ought to do.

"In fairness, Sir Brook," said Sewell, with an assumed candor that sat very well on him, "I ought to tell you that your conditions are very easy ones My wife has come to this country to recruit her health and look after her children. I myself shall probably be on my way back to India soon after Christmas. Our small means totally preclude living in the gay world; and," added he, with a laugh, "if we really had any blandishments or captivations at our disposal, they would be best bestowed on the Horse Guards, to extend my leave, or assist me to an exchange."

There was high art in the way in which Sewell had so contrived to get the old man involved in the conflict of his own feelings that he was actually grateful for the easy and even familiar tone employed towards him.

"I have wounded this man deeply," said Fossbrooke to himself. "I have said to him things alike unfeeling and ungenerous, and yet he has temper enough to treat me amicably, even courteously."

It was almost on his lips to say that he had still some influence with the Horse Guards, that a great man there had been one of his most intimate friends in life, and that he was ready to do anything in his power with him, when a sudden glance at Sewell's face recalled him at once to himself, and he stammered out, "I will detain you no longer, sir. Be kind enough to explain to the Lord Chief Baron that my communication was of a character that could not be made indirectly. His Excellency's name on my card probably suggested as much. It might be proper to add that the subject was one solely attaching to his Lordship and to his Lordship's interest. He will himself understand what I mean."

Sewell bowed acquiescence. As he stood at the half-open door, he was disposed to offer his hand. It was a bold step, but he knew if it should succeed it would be a great victory. The opportunity was too good to be lost, and just as Sir Brook turned to say good-morning, Sewell, like one carried away by a sudden impulse, held out his hand, and said, "You may trust me, Sir Brook."

"If you wish me to do so, sir, let me not touch your hand," said the old man, with a look of stern and haughty defiance, and he strode out without a farewell.

Sewell staggered back into the room and sat down. A clammy cold perspiration covered his face and forehead, for the rancor that filled his heart sickened him like a malady. "You shall pay for this, by heaven! you shall," muttered he, as he wiped the great drops from his brow. "The old fool himself has taught me where he was vulnerable, and as I live he shall feel it."

"His Lordship wants to see you, sir; he is in the garden," said a servant; and Sewell rose and followed him. He stopped twice as he went to compose his features and regain his calm. On the last time he even rehearsed the few words and the smile by which he meant to accost the Judge. The little artifice was, however, forestalled, as Sir William met him abruptly with the words, "What a time you have been, sir,—forty-eight minutes by my watch!"

"I assure you, my Lord, I'd have made it shorter if I could," said Sewell, with a smile of some significance.

"I am unable to see why you could not have done so. The charge I gave you was to report to me, not to negotiate on your own part."

"Nor did I, my Lord. Sir Brook Fossbrooke distinctly declared that he would only communicate with yourself personally,—that what he desired to say referred to yourself, and should be answered by yourself."

"On hearing which, sir, you withdrew?"

"So far as your Lordship was concerned, no more was said between us. What passed after this I may be permitted to call private."

"What, sir! You see a person in *my* house, at *my* instance, and with *my* instructions,—who comes to see and confer with *me*; and you have the hardihood to tell me that you took that opportunity to discuss questions which you call private!"

"I trust, my Lord, you will not press me in this matter; my position is a most painful one."

"It is worse than painful, sir; it is humiliating. But," added he, after a short pause, "I have reason to be grateful to you. You have rescued me from, perhaps, a very grave indiscretion. Your position—your wife's health—your children's welfare had all interested me. I might have—No matter what, sir. I have recovered the balance of my mind. I am myself again."

"My Lord, I will be open with you."

"I will accept of no forced confidences, sir," said the Judge, waving his hand haughtily.

"They are not forced, my Lord, farther than my dislike to give you pain renders them so. The man to whom you sent me this morning is no stranger to me—would that he had been!—would that I had never known nor heard of him! Very few words will explain why, my Lord. I only entreat that, before I say them, they may be in strictest confidence between us."

"If they require secrecy, sir, they shall have it."

"Quite enough, my Lord,—amply sufficient for me is this assurance. This person, then, my Lord, was the old friend and brother officer of Sir Frank Dillon, my father-in-law. They lived as young men in closest friendship together; shared perils, amusements, and purse together. For many years nothing occurred to interrupt the relations between them, though frequent remonstrances from Dillon's family against the intimacy might possibly have caused a coolness; for the world had begun to talk of Fossbrooke with a certain distrust, comparing his mode of living with the amount of his fortune, and half hinting that his successes at play were more than accidental.

"Still Dillon held to him; and to break the tie at last, his family procured an Indian appointment for him, and sent him to Calcutta. Fossbrooke no sooner heard of it than he sold off his town house and horses, and actually sailed in the same packet with him."

"Let us sit down, Colonel Sewell; I am wearied with walking, and I should like to hear the remainder of this story."

"I will make it very brief, my Lord. Here is a nice bench to rest on. Arrived in India, they commenced a style of living the most costly and extravagant imaginable. Their receptions, their dinners, their equipages, their retinues, completely eclipsed the splendors of the native princes. For a while these were met promptly by ready money; later on came bills, at first duly met, and at last dishonored. On investigation, however, it was found that the greater number—far the greater number—of the acceptances were issued by Dillon alone,—a circumstance which puzzled none so much as Dillon himself, who never remembered the emergencies that had called for them."

"They were forgeries by Fossbrooke," said the Judge.

"You are right, my Lord, they were, but so adroitly done that Dillon was the first to declare the signatures his own; nor was the fraud ever discovered. To rescue his friend, as it were, Dillon sold off everything, and paid, I know not what amount, and they both left for Ceylon, where Dillon was named Commander of the Forces.

"Here Dillon married, and, on the birth of his first child, Fossbrooke was the godfather, their affection being stronger than ever. Once more the life of extravagance burst forth, and now, besides the costly household and reckless expenditure, the stories of play became rife and frequent, several young fellows being obliged to leave the service and sell their commissions to meet their debts. The scandal reached England, and Dillon was given his choice to resign or resume active service at his old rank. He accepted the last, and went back to India. For a while they were separated. My father-in-law made a brilliant campaign, concluding with the victory of Atteyghur. He was named Political Resident at the seat of government, and found himself in the receipt of a large revenue, and might in a few years have become wealthy and honored. His evil genius, however, was soon at his side. Fossbrooke arrived, as he said, to see him before leaving for Europe; he never left him till his death. From that day dated my father-in-law's inevitable ruin. Maladministration, corruption, forced loans on every side. Black-mail was imposed on all the chiefs, and a system of iniquity instituted that rendered the laws a farce, and the office of judge a degradation.

"Driven almost to desperation by his approaching ruin, and yet blind to the cause of it, Sir Frank took service against the Affghans, and fell, severely wounded, at Walhalla. Fossbrooke followed him to the Hills, where he went to die. The infatuation of that fatal man was unbroken, and on his deathbed he not only confided to him all the deeds and documents that concerned his fortune, but gave him the guardianship and control of his daughter. In the very last letter he ever penned are these words: 'Scandal may some day or other dare to asperse him (Sir Brook),—the best have no immunity on that score,—but I charge you, however fortune may deal with you, share it with him if he need it; your father never had so true, so noble, so generous a friend. Have full courage in any course he approves of, and never distrust yourself so completely as when he differs from you; above all, believe no ill of him.'

"I have seen this letter,—I have read it more than once; and with my full knowledge of the man, with my memory stored with stories about him, it was very hard to see him exercise an influence in my house, and a power over my wife. For a while I tried to respect what had been the faith of her childhood; I could not bear to destroy what formed one of the links that bound her to her father's memory; but the man's conduct obliged me to abandon this clemency. He insisted on living upon us, and living in a style not merely costly, but openly, flagrantly disreputable. Of his manner to myself I will not speak; he treated me not alone as a dependant, but as one whose character and fortune were in his hands. To what comments this exposed me in my own house I leave you to imagine: I remonstrated at first, but my endurance became exhausted, and I turned him from my house.

"Then began his persecution of me,—not alone of myself, but my wife, and all belonging to me. I must not dwell on this, or I should forget myself.

"We left India, hoping never to hear more of him. There was a story that he had gone on a visit to a Rajah in Oude, and would in all likelihood live there till he died. Imagine what I felt, my Lord, when I read his name on that visiting-card. I knew, of course, what his presence meant, a pretended matter of business with you,—the real object being to traduce and vilify me. He had ascertained the connection between us, and determined to turn it to profit. So long as I followed my career in India,—a poor soldier of fortune,—I was not worth persecution; but here at home, with friends, possibly with friends able and willing to aid me, I at once assumed importance in his eyes. He well knows how dear to us is the memory of my wife's father, what sacrifices we have made, what sacrifices we would make again, that his name should not be harshly dealt with by the world. He feels, too, all the power and weight he can yield by that letter of poor Dillon's, given so frankly, so trustfully, and so unfortunately on his deathbed. In one word, my Lord, this man has come back to Europe to exert over me the pressure which he once on a time used over my father-in-law. For reasons I cannot fathom, the great people who knew him once, and who ought to know whom and what he has become, are still willing to acknowledge him. It is true he no longer frequents their houses and mixes in their society,—but they recognize him. The very card he sent in this morning bore the Viceroy's name,—and from this cause alone, even if there were not others, he would be dangerous. I weary you, my Lord, and I will conclude. By an accidental admission he let drop that he would soon leave Ireland for a while; let it seem, my Lord, so long as he remains here, that I am less intimate here, less frequent as a visitor, than he has imagined. Let him have grounds to imagine that my presence here was a mere accident, and that I am not at all likely to enjoy any share of your Lordship's favor,—in fact, let him believe me as friendless here as he saw me in India, and he will cease to speculate on persecuting me."

"There would be indignity in such a course, sir," cried the Judge, fiercely; "the man has no terrors for *me*."

"Certainly not, my Lord, nor for me personally. I speak on my wife's behalf; it is for her sake and for her peace of mind I am alone thinking here."

"I will speak to her myself on this head."

"I entreat you not, my Lord. I implore you never to approach the subject. She has for years been torn between the terrible alternative of obeying the last injunctions of her father or yielding to the wishes of her husband. Her life has been a continual struggle, and her shattered health has been the consequence. No, my Lord; let us go down for a few weeks or months—as it may be—to this country place they have taken for us; a little quietness will do us both good. My leave will not expire till March; there is still time to look about me."

"Something shall be done for you, sir," said the Judge, pompously. Sewell bowed low: he knew how to make his bow a very deep acknowledgment of gratitude; he knew the exact measure of deference and trustfulness and thankfulness to throw into his expression as he bent his head, while he seemed too much overpowered to speak.

"Yes, sir, you shall be cared for," said the old man. "And if this person, this Sir Brook Fossbrooke, return here, it is with *me* he will have to deal,— not *you*."

"My Lord, I entreat you never to admit him; neither see nor correspond with him. The man is a desperado, and holds his own life too cheap to care for another's."

"Sir, you only pique my curiosity to meet with him. I have heard of such fellows, but never saw one."

"From all I have heard, my Lord, *your* courage requires no proofs."

"You have heard the truth, sir. It has been tested in every way, and found without alloy. This man came here a few days ago to ask me to nominate my grandson to an office in my gift; but, save a lesson for his temerity, he 'took nothing by his motion.'" The old Judge walked up and down with short impatient steps, his eyebrows moving fiercely, And his mouth twitching angrily. "The Viceroy must be taught that it is not through such negotiators he can treat with men like myself. We hear much about the dignity of the Bench. I would that his Excellency should know that the respect for it is a homage to be rendered by the highest as well as the lowest, and that I for one will accept of nothing less than all the honors that befit my station."

Relieved, as it were, by this outburst of vanity, his heart unburdened of a load of self-conceit, the old man felt freer And better; and in the sigh he heaved there seemed a something that indicated a sense of alleviation. Then, turning to Sewell, with a softened voice, he said, "How grieved I am that you should have passed such a morning! It was certainly not what I had intended for you."

"You are too good to me, my Lord,—far too good, and too thoughtful of me," said Sewell, with emotion.

"I am one of those men who must go to the grave misconstrued and misrepresented. He who would be firm in an age of cowardice, he who would be just in an age of jobbery, cannot fail to be calumniated. But, sir, there is a moral stature, as there is a material stature, that requires distance for its proportions; and it is possible posterity will be more just to me than my contemporaries."

"I would only hope, my Lord, that the time for such a judgment may be long deferred."

"You are a courtier, sir," said the Judge, smiling. "It was amongst courtiers I passed my early youth, and I like them. When I was a young man, Colonel Sewell, it was the fashion to make the tour of Europe as a matter of education and good breeding. The French Court was deemed, and justly deemed, the first school of manners, and I firmly believe France herself has suffered in her forms of politeness from having ceased to be the centre of supply to the world. She adulterated the liquor as the consumers decreased in taste and increased in number."

"How neatly, how admirably expressed!" said Sewell, bowing.

"I had some of that gift once," said the old man, with a sigh; "but it is a weapon out of use nowadays. Epigram has its place in a museum now as rightfully as an Andrea Ferrara."

"I declare, my Lord, it is two o'clock. Here is your servant coming to announce luncheon. I am ashamed to think what a share of your day I have monopolized."

"You will stay and take some mutton broth, I hope?"

"No, my Lord. I never eat luncheon, and I am, besides, horrified at inflicting you so long already."

"Sir, if I suffer many of the miseries of old age, I avail myself of some of its few privileges. One of the best of these is, never to be bored. I am old and feeble enough to be able to say to him who wearies me, Leave me—

leave-me to myself and my own dreariness. Had you 'inflicted' me, as you call it, I 'd have said as much two hours ago. Your company was, however, most agreeable. You know how to talk, and, what is rarer, you know how to listen."

Sewell bowed respectfully and in silence.

"I wish the school that trains aides-de-camp could be open to junior barristers and curates," muttered he, half to himself; then added aloud, "Come and see me soon again. Come to breakfast, or, if you prefer it, to dinner. We dine at seven;" and without further adieu than a slight wave of his hand, he turned away and entered the house.

CHAPTER XXVI
SIR BROOK IN CONFUSION

Tom Lendrick had just parted with his sister as Fossbrooke came up, and, taking his arm in silence, moved slowly down the road.

Seeing his deep preoccupation, Tom did not speak for some time, but walked along without a word. "I hope you found my grandfather in better temper, sir?" asked Tom, at last.

"He refused to receive me; he pleaded illness, or rather he called it by its true name, indisposition. He deputed another gentleman to meet me,—a Colonel Sewell, his stepson."

"That 's the man my father saw at the Cape; a clever sort of person he called him, but, I suspect, not one to his liking; too much man of the world,—too much man of fashion for poor Dad."

"I hope so," muttered Fossbrooke, unconsciously.

"Indeed, sir; and why?" asked Tom, eagerly.

"What of Lucy?" said Sir Brook, abruptly; "how did you think she was looking?"

"Well, sir, on the whole, well. I've seen her jollier; but, to be sure, it was a leave-taking to-day, and that's not the occasion to put one in high spirits. Poor girl, she said, 'Is it not hard, Tom? There are only three of us, and we must all live apart.'"

"So it is,—hard, very hard. I 'd have tried once more to influence the old Judge if he 'd have given me a meeting. He may do worse with that office than bestow it on you, Tom. I believe I'd have told him as much."

"It's perhaps as well, sir, that you did not see him," said Tom, with a faint smile.

"Yes," said Fossbrooke, following along the train of his own thoughts, and not noticing the other's remark. "He may do worse; he may give it to *him*, and thus draw closer the ties between them; and if *that* man once gets admission there, he'll get influence."

"Of whom are you talking, sir?"

"I was not speaking, Tom. I was turning over some things in my mind. By the way, we have much to do before evening. Go over to Hodgen's about those tools; he has not sent them yet: and the blasting-powder, too, has not come down. I ought, if I could manage the time, to test it; but it 's too late. I must go to the Castle for five minutes,—five minutes will do it; and I 'll pass by Grainger's on my way back, and buy the flannel—miners' flannel they call it in the advertisement. We must look our *métier*, Tom, eh? You told Lucy where to write, and how to address us, I hope?"

"Yes, sir, she wrote it down. By the way, that reminds me of a letter she gave me for you. It was addressed to her care, and came yesterday."

The old man thrust it in his pocket without so much as a look at it.

"I think the post-mark was Madeira," said Tom, to try and excite some curiosity.

"Possibly. I have correspondents everywhere."

"It looked like Trafford's writing, I thought."

"Indeed! let us see;" and he drew forth the letter, and broke the envelope. "Right enough, Tom,—it is Trafford."

He ran his eyes rapidly over the first lines, turned to the next side, and then to the end of the letter, and then once more began at the beginning.

"This is his third attempt, he says, to reach me, having written twice without any acknowledgment; hence he has taken the liberty—and a very great liberty too—to address the present to the care of your sister. His brother died in March last, and the younger brother has now shown symptoms of the same malady, and has been sent out to Madeira. 'I could not,' he writes,—'I could not refuse to come out here with him, however eager I was to go to Ireland. You can well believe,'"—here the old man slurred over the words, and murmured inaudibly for some seconds. "I see," added he at last, "he has gone back to his old regiment, with good hopes of the majority. 'Hinks is sick of the service, and quite willing to leave. Harvey, however, stands above me, and deems it a cruel thing to be passed over. I must have your advice about this, as well as about—'" Here again he dropped his voice and mumbled unintelligibly. At length he read on: "'What is Tom doing? What a shame it would be if a fellow with such abilities should not make his way!'"

"A crying shame," burst in Tom, "but I neither see the abilities nor the way; would he kindly indicate how to find either or both?"

"'My mother suggested,'" read on Sir Brook, "'two or three things which my father could readily obtain, but you know the price of the promotion;

you know what I would have to—'" Here, once more, the old man stopped abruptly.

"Pray go on, sir," cried Tom, eagerly; "this interests me much, and as it touches myself I have half a claim to hear it."

Sir Brook gave no heed to the request, but read on in silence and to himself. Turning to the last page, he said: "'I may then hope to be in England by the end of the month. I shall not go down to Holt, but straight to Dublin. My leave will expire on the 28th, and this will give me a good excuse for not going home. I am sure you will agree with me that I am doing the right thing.

"'If I am fortunate enough to meet you in Dublin, I can ask your advice on many things which press for solution; but if you should have left Ireland and gone heaven knows where, what is to become of me?'"

"Got into debt again, evidently," said Tom, as he puffed his cigar.

"Nothing of the kind. I know thoroughly what he alludes to, though I am not at liberty to speak of it. He wishes me to leave our address with Colonel Cave at the barracks, and that if we should have left Ireland already, he'll try and manage a month's leave, and pay us a visit."

"I declare I guessed that!" burst out Tom. "I had a dread of it, from the very day we first planned our project. I said to myself, So sure as we settle down to work,—to work like men who have no thought but how to earn their bread,—some lavender-gloved fellow, with a dressing-case and three hat-boxes, will drop down to disgust us alike with our own hardships and *his* foppery."

"He'll not come," said Sir Brook, calmly; "and if he should, he will be welcome."

"Oh! as to that," stammered out Tom, somewhat ashamed of his late warmth, "Trafford is perhaps the one exception to the sort of thing I am afraid of. He is a fine, manly, candid fellow, with no affectations nor any pretensions."

"A gentleman, sir,—just a gentleman, and of a very good type."

The last few lines of the letter were small and finely written, and cost the old man some time to decipher. At last he read them aloud. "'Am I asking what you would see any objection to accord me, if I entreat you to give me some letter of introduction or presentation to the Chief t Baron? I presume that you know him; and I presume that he might not refuse to know *me*. It is possible I may be wrong in either or both of these assumptions. I am sure you will be frank in your reply to this request of mine, and say No, if you dislike to say Yes. I made the acquaintance of Colonel Sewell, the Judge's step-son, at the Cape; but I suspect—I may be wrong—but I suspect that to be presented by the Colonel might not be the smoothest road to his Lordship's acquaintance,—I was going to write "favor," but I have no pretension, as yet at least, to aspire that far.'

"'The Colonel himself told me that his mother and Sir William never met without a quarrel. His affectionate remark was that the Chief Baron was the only creature in Europe whose temper was worse than Lady Lendrick's, and it would be a blessing to humanity if they could be induced to live together.

"'I saw a good deal of the Se wells at the Cape. She is charming! She was a Dillon, and her mother a Lascelles, some forty-fifth cousin of my mother's,—quite enough of relationship, however, to excuse a very rapid intimacy, so that I dined there when I liked, and uninvited. I did not like *him* so well; but then he beat me at billiards, and always won my money at *écarté*, and of course these are detracting ingredients which ought not to be thrown into the scale.

"'How she sings! I don't know how you, with your rapturous love of music, would escape falling in love with her: all the more that she seems to me one who expects that sort of homage, and thinks herself defrauded if denied it. If the Lord Chief Baron is fond of ballads, he has been her captive this many a day.

"'My love to Tom, if with you or within reach of you; and believe me, ever yours affectionately,—Lionel Trafford.'"

"It was the eldest son who died," said Tom, carelessly.

"Yes, the heir. Lionel now succeeds to a splendid fortune and the baronetcy."

"He told me once that his father had made some sort of compact with his eldest son about cutting off the entail, in case he should desire to do it. In fact, he gave me to understand that he was n't a favorite with his father, and that, if by any course of events he were likely to succeed to the estate, it was more than probable his father would use this power, and merely leave him what he could not alienate,—a very small property that pertained to the baronetage."

"With reference to what did he make this revelation to you? What had you been talking of?"

"I scarcely remember. I think it was about younger sons,—how hardly they were treated, and how unfairly."

"Great hardship truly that a man must labor! not to say that there is not a single career in life he can approach without bringing to it greater advantages than befall humbler men,—a better and more liberal education, superior habits as regards society, powerful friends, and what in a country like ours is inconceivably effective,—the prestige of family. I cannot endure this compassionate tone about younger sons. To my thinking they have the very best opening that life can offer, if they be men to profit by it; and if they are not, I care very little what becomes of them."

"I do think it hard that my elder brother should have fortune and wealth to over-abundance, while my pittance will scarcely keep me in cigars."

"You have no right, sir, to think of his affluence. It is not in the record; the necessities of your position have no-relation to his superfluities. Bethink you of yourself, and if cigars are too expensive for you, smoke cavendish. Trafford was full of this cant about the cruelty of primogeniture, but I would have none of it. Whenever a man tells me that he deems it a hardship that he should do anything for his livelihood, I leave him, and hope never to see more of him."

"Trafford surely did not say so."

"No,—certainly not; there would have been no correspondence between us if he had. But I want to see these young fellows showing the world that they shrink from no competitorship with any. They have long proved that to confront danger and meet death they are second to none. Let me show that in other qualities they admit of no inferiority,—that they are as ready for enterprise, as well able to stand cold and hunger and thirst, to battle with climate and disease. I know well they can do it, but I want the world to know it."

"As to intellectual distinctions," said Tom, "I think they are the equals of any. The best man in Trinity in my day was a fellow-commoner."

This speech seemed to restore the old man to his best humor. He slapped young Lendrick familiarly on the shoulder and said: "It would be a grand thing, Tom, if we could extend the application of that old French adage, 'noblesse oblige,' and make it apply to every career in life and every success. Come along down this street; I want to buy some nails,—we can take them home with us."

They soon made their purchases; and each, armed with a considerably sized brown-paper parcel, issued from the shop,—the old man eagerly following up the late theme, and insisting on all the advantages good birth and blood conferred, and what a grand resource was the gentleman element in moments of pressure and temptation.

"His Excellency wishes to speak to you, sir," said a footman, respectfully standing hat in hand before him "The carriage is over the way."

Sir Brook nodded an assent, and then, turning to Torn, said, "Have the kindness to hold this for me for a moment; I will not detain you longer;" and placing in young Lendrick's hands a good-sized parcel, he stepped across the street, totally forgetting that over his left arm, the hand of which was in his pocket, a considerable coil of strong rope depended, being one of his late purchases. As he drew nigh the carriage, he made a sign that implied defeat; and mortified as the Viceroy was at the announcement, he could not help smiling at the strange guise in which the old man presented himself.

"And how so, Fossbrooke?" asked he, in answer to the other's signal.

"Simply, he would not see me, my Lord. Our first meeting had apparently left no very agreeable memories of me, and he scarcely cared to cultivate an acquaintance that opened so inauspiciously."

"But you sent him your card with my name?"

"Yes; and his reply was to depute another gentleman to receive me and take my communication."

"Which you refused, of course, to make?"

"Which I refused."

"Do you incline to suppose that the Chief Baron guessed the object of your visit?"

"I have no means of arriving at that surmise, my Lord. His refusal of me was so peremptory that it left me no clew to any guess."

"Was the person deputed to receive you one with whom it was at all possible to indicate such an intimation of your business as might convey to the Chief Baron the necessity of seeing you?"

"Quite the reverse, my Lord; he was one with whom, from previous knowledge, I could hold little converse."

"Then there is, I fear, nothing to be done."

"Nothing."

"Except to thank you heartily, my dear Fossbrooke, and ask you once more, why are you going away?"

"I told you last night I was going to make a fortune. I have—to my own astonishment I own it—begun to feel that narrow means are occasionally most inconvenient; that they limit a man's action in so many ways that he comes at last to experience a sort of slavery; and instead of chafing against this, I am resolved to overcome it, and become rich."

"I hope, with all my heart, you may. There is no man whom wealth will more become, or who will know how to dispense it more reputably."

"Why, we have gathered a crowd around us, my Lord," said Fossbrooke, looking to right and left, where now a number of people had gathered, attracted by the Viceroy's presence, but still more amused by the strange-looking figure with the hank of rope over his arm, who discoursed so freely with his Excellency. "This is one of the penalties of greatness, I take it," continued he. "It's your Excellency's Collar of St. Patrick costs you these attentions—"

"I rather suspect it's *your* 'grand cordon,' Fossbrooke," said the Viceroy, laughing, while he pointed to the rope.

"Bless my stars!" exclaimed Sir Brook, blushing deeply, "how forgetful I am growing! I hope you forgive me. I am sure you could not suppose—"

"I could never think anything but good of you, Fossbrooke. Get in, and come out to 'the Lodge' to dinner."

"No, no; impossible. I am heartily ashamed of myself. I grow worse and worse every day; people will lose patience at last, and cut me; good-bye."

"Wait one moment. I want to ask you something about young Lendrick. Would he take an appointment in a colonial regiment? Would he—" But Fossbrooke had elbowed his way through the dense crowd by this time, and was far out of hearing,—shocked with himself, and overwhelmed with the thought that in his absurd forgetfulness he might have involved another in ridicule.

"Think of me standing talking to his Excellency with this on my arm, Tom!" said he, flushing with shame and annoyance: "how these absent fits keep advancing on me! When a man begins to forget himself in this fashion, the time is not very distant when his friends will be glad to forget him. I said so this moment to Lord Wilmington, and I am afraid that he agreed with me. Where are the screws, Tom,—have I been forgetting them also?"

"No, sir, I have them here; the holdfasts were not finished, but they will be sent over to us this evening, along with the cramps you ordered."

"So, then, my head was clear so far," cried he, with a smile. "In my prosperous days, Tom, these freaks of mine were taken as good jokes, and my friends laughed at them over my Burgundy; but when a man has no longer Burgundy to wash down his blunders with, it is strange how different becomes the criticism, and how much more candid the critic."

"So that, in point of enlightenment, sir, it is better to be poor."

"It is what I was just going to observe to you," said he, calmly. "Can you give me a cigar?"

CHAPTER XXVII
THE TWO LUCYS

Within a week after this incident, while Fossbrooke and young Lendrick were ploughing the salt sea towards their destination, Lucy sat in her room one morning engaged in drawing. She was making a chalk copy from a small photograph her brother had sent her, a likeness of Sir Brook, taken surreptitiously as he sat smoking at a window, little heeding or knowing of the advantage thus taken of him.

The head was considerably advanced, the brow and the eyes were nearly finished, and she was trying for the third time to get an expression into the mouth which the photograph had failed to convey, but which she so often observed in the original. Eagerly intent on her work, she never heard the door open behind her, and was slightly startled as a very gentle hand was laid on her shoulder.

"Is this a very presumptuous step of mine, dear Lucy?" said Mrs. Sewell, with one of her most bewitching smiles: "have I your leave for coming in upon you in this fashion?"

"Of course you have, my dear Mrs. Sewell; it is a great pleasure to me to see you here."

"And I may take off my bonnet and my shawl and my gloves and my company manner, as my husband calls it?"

"Oh! *you* have no company manner," broke in Lucy.

"I used to think not; but men are stern critics, darling, and especially when they are husbands. You will find out, one of these days, how neatly your liege lord will detect every little objectionable trait in your nature, and with what admirable frankness he will caution you against—yourself."

"I almost think I 'd rather he would not."

"I 'm very certain of it, Lucy," said the other, with greater firmness than before. "The thing we call love in married life has an existence only a little beyond that of the bouquet you carried to the wedding-breakfast; and it would be unreasonable in a woman to expect it, but she might fairly ask for courtesy and respect, and you would be amazed how churlish even gentlemen can become about expending these graces in their own families."

Lucy was both shocked and astonished at what she heard, and the grave tone in which the words were uttered surprised her most of all.

Mrs. Sewell had by this time taken off her bonnet and shawl, and, pushing back her luxuriant hair from her forehead, looked as though suffering from headache, for her brows were contracted, and the orbits around her eyes dark and purple-looking.

"You are not quite well to-day," said Lucy, as she sat down on the sofa beside her, and took her hand.

"About as well as I ever am," said she, sighing; and then, as if suddenly recollecting herself, added, "India makes such an inroad on health and strength! No buoyancy of temperament ever resisted that fatal climate. You would n't believe it, Lucy, but I was once famed for high spirits."

"I can well believe it."

"It was, however, very long ago. I was little more than a child at the time—that is, I was about fourteen or fifteen—when I left England, to which I returned in my twentieth year. I went back very soon afterwards to nurse my poor father, and be married."

The depth of sadness in which she spoke the last words made the silence that followed intensely sad and gloomy.

"Yes," said she, with a deep melancholy smile, "papa called me madcap. Oh dear, if our fathers and mothers could look back from that eternity they have gone to, and see how the traits they traced in our childhood have saddened and sobered down into sternest features, would they recognize us as their own? I don't look like a madcap now, Lucy, do I?" As she said this, her eyes swam in tears, and her lip trembled convulsively. Then standing hastily up, she drew nigh the table, and leaned over to look at the drawing at which Lucy had been engaged.

"What!" cried she, with almost a shriek,—"what is this? Whose portrait is this? Tell me at once; who is it?"

"A very dear friend of mine and of Tom's. One you could not have ever met, I'm sure."

"And how do you know whom I have met?" cried she, fiercely. "What can you know of my life and my associates?"

"I said so, because he is one who has lived long estranged from the world," said Lucy, gently; for in the sudden burst of the other's passion she only saw matter for deep compassion. It was but another part of a nature torn and distracted by unceasing anxieties.

"But his name,—his name?" said Mrs. Sewell, wildly.

"His name is Sir Brook Fossbrooke."

"I knew it, I knew it!" cried she, wildly,—"I knew it!" and said it over and over again. "Go where we will we shall find him. He haunts; us like a curse,—like a curse!" And it was in almost a shriek the last word came forth.

"You cannot know the man if you say this of him," said Lucy, firmly.

"Not know him!—not know him! You will tell me next that I do not know myself,—not know my own name,—not know the life of bitterness I have lived,—the shame of it,—the ineffable shame of it!" and she threw herself on her face on the sofa, and sobbed convulsively. Long and anxiously did Lucy try all in her power to comfort and console her. She poured out her whole heart in pledges of sisterly love and affection. She assured her of a sympathy that would never desert her; and, last of all, she told her that her judgment of Sir Brook was a mistaken one,—that in the world there lived not one more true-hearted, more generous, or more noble.

"And where did you learn all this, young woman?" said the other, passionately. "In what temptations and trials of your life have these experiences been gained? Oh, don't be angry with me, dearest Lucy; forgive this rude speech of mine; my head is turning, and I know not what I say. Tell me, child, did this man speak to you of my husband?"

"No."

"Nor of myself?"

"Not a word. I don't believe he was aware that we were related to each other."

"He not aware? Why, it's his boast that he knows every one and every one's connections. You never heard him speak without this parade of universal acquaintanceship. But why did he come here? How did you happen to meet him?"

"By the merest accident. Tom found him one day fishing the river close to our house, and they got to talk together; and it ended by his coming to us to tea. Intimacy followed very quickly, and then a close friendship."

"And do you mean to tell me that all this while he never alluded to us?"

"Never."

"This is so unlike him,—so unlike him," muttered she, half to herself. "And the last place you saw him,—where was it?"

"Here in this house."

"Here! Do you mean that he came here to see you?"

"No; he had some business with grandpapa, and called one morning, but he was not received. Grandpapa was not well, and sent Colonel Sewell to meet him."

"He sent my husband! And did he go?"

"Yes."

"Are you sure of that?"

"I know it."

"I never heard of this," said she, holding her hands to her temples. "About what time was it?"

"It was on Friday last. I remember the day, because it was the last time I saw poor Tom."

"On Friday last," said she, pondering. "Yes, you are right. I do remember that Friday;" and she drew up the sleeve of her dress, and looked at a dark-blue mark upon the fair white skin of her arm; but so hastily was the action done that Lucy did not remark it.

"It was on Friday morning. It was on the forenoon of Friday, was it not?"

"Yes. The clock struck one, I remember, as I got back to the house."

"Tell me, Lucy," said she in a caressing tone, as she drew her arm round the girl's waist,—"tell me, darling, how did Colonel Sewell look after that interview? Did he seem angry or irritated? I'll tell you why I ask this some other time,—but I want to know if he seemed vexed or chagrined by meeting this man."

"I did not see him after; he went away almost immediately after Sir Brook. I heard his voice talking with grandpapa in the garden, but I went to my room, and we did not meet."

"As they spoke in the garden, were their voices raised? Did they talk like men excited or in warmth?"

"Yes. Their tone and manner were what you say,—so much so that I went away, not to overhear them. Grandpapa, I know, was angry at something; and when we met at luncheon, he barely spoke to me."

"And what conclusion did you draw from all this?"

"None! There was nothing to induce me to dwell on the circumstance; besides," added she, with some irritation, "I am not given to reason upon the traits of people's manner, or their tone in speaking."

"Nor perhaps accustomed to inquire, when your grandfather is vexed, what it is that has irritated him."

"Certainly not. It is a liberty I should not dare to take."

"Well, darling," said she, with a saucy laugh, "he is more fortunate in having *you* for a granddaughter than me. I 'm afraid I should have less discretion,—at all events, less dread."

"Don't be so sure of that," said Lucy, quietly. "Grandpapa is no common person. It is not his temper but his talent that one is loath to encounter."

"I do not suspect that either would terrify me greatly. As the soldiers say, Lucy, I have been under fire pretty often, and I don't mind it now. Do you know, child, that we have got into a most irritable tone with each other? Each of us is saying something that provokes a sharp reply, and we are actually sparring without knowing it."

"I certainly did not know it," said Lucy, taking her hand within both her own, "and I ask pardon if I have said anything to hurt you."

Leaving her hand to Lucy unconsciously, and not heeding one word of what she had said, Mrs. Sewell sat with her eyes fixed on the floor deep in thought. "I 'm sure, Lucy," said she at last, "I don't know why I asked you all those questions awhile ago. That man—Sir Brook, I mean—is nothing to me; he ought to be, but he is not. My father and he were friends; that is, my father thought he was his friend, and left him the guardianship of me on his deathbed."

"Your guardian,—Sir Brook your guardian?" cried Lucy, with intense eagerness.

"Yes; with more power than the law, I believe, would accord to any guardian." She paused and seemed lost in thought for some seconds, and then went on: "Colonel Sewell and he never liked each other. Sir Brook took little trouble to be liked by him; perhaps Dudley was as careless on his side. What a tiresome vein I have got in! How should *you* care for all this?"

"But I do care—I care for all that concerns you."

"I take it, if you were to hear Sir Brook's account, we should not make a more brilliant figure than himself. He 'd tell you about our mode of life, and high play, and the rest of it; but, child, every one plays high in India, every one does scores of things there they would n't do at home, partly because the *ennui* of life tempts to anything,—anything that would relieve it; and then all are tolerant because all are equally—I was going to say wicked; but I don't mean wickedness,—I mean bored to that degree that there is no stimulant left without a breach of the decalogue."

"I think that might be called wickedness," said Lucy, dryly.

"Call it what you like, only take my word for it you 'd do the selfsame things if you lived there. I was pretty much what you are now when I left England; and if any naughty creature like myself were to talk, as I am doing to you now, and make confession of all her misdeeds and misfortunes, I'm certain I'd have known how to bridle up and draw away my hand, and retire to a far end of the sofa, and look unutterable pruderies, just as you do this moment."

"Without ever suspecting it, certainly," said Lucy laughing.

"Tear up that odious drawing, dear Lucy," said she, rising and walking the room with impatience. "Tear it up; or, if you won't do that, let me write a line under it—one line, I ask for no more—so that people may know at whom they are looking."

"I will do neither; nor will I sit here to listen to one word against him."

"Which means, child, that your knowledge of life is so-much greater than mine, you can trust implicitly to your own judgment. I can admire your courage, certainly, though I am not captivated by your prudence."

"It is because I have so little faith in my own judgment that I am unwilling to lose the friend who can guide me."

"Perhaps it would be unsafe if I were to ask you to choose between *him* and me," said Mrs. Sewell, very slowly, and with her eyes fully bent on Lucy.

"I hope you will not."

"With such a warning I certainly shall not do so. Who-could have believed it was so late?" said she, hastily looking at her watch; "What a seductive creature you must be, child, to slip over one's whole morning without knowing it,—two o'clock already. You lunch about this time?"

"Yes, punctually at two."

"Are you sufficiently lady of the house to invite me, Lucy?"

"I am sure *you* need no invitation here; you are one of us."

"What a little Jesuit it is!" said Mrs. Sewell, patting her cheek. "Come, child, I 'll be equal with you. I 'll enter the room on your arm, and say, 'Sir William, your granddaughter insisted on my remaining; I thought it an awkwardness, but she tells me she is the mistress here, and I obey.'"

"And you will find he will be too well-bred to contradict you," said Lucy, while a deep blush covered her face and throat.

"Oh, I think him positively charming!" said Mrs. Sewell, as she arranged her hair before the glass; "I think him charming. My mother-in-law and I have a dozen pitched battles every day on the score of his temper and his character. *My* theory is, the only intolerable thing on earth is a fool; and whether it be that Lady Lendrick suspects me of any secret intention to designate one still nearer to her by this reservation, I do not know, but the declaration drives her half crazy. Come, Lucy, we shall be keeping grandpapa waiting for us."

They moved down the stairs arm-in-arm, without a word; but as they gained the door of the dining-room, Mrs. Sewell turned fully round and said, in a low deep voice, "Marry anything,—rake, gambler, villain,—anything, the basest and the blackest; but never take a fool, for a fool means them all combined."

CHAPTER XXVIII
THE NEST WITH STRANGE "BIRDS" IN IT

To the Swan's Nest, very differently tenanted from what we saw it at the opening of our story, we have now to conduct our reader. Its present occupant—"the acquisition to any neighborhood," as the house-agent styled him—was Colonel Sewell.

Lady Lendrick had taken the place for her son on finding that Sir William would not extend his hospitality to him. She had taken the precaution not merely to pay a year's rent in advance, but to make a number of changes in the house and its dependencies, which she hoped might render the residence more palatable to him, and reconcile him in some degree to its isolation and retirement.

The Colonel was, however, one of those men—they are numerous enough in this world—who canvass the mouth of the gift-horse, and have few scruples in detecting the signs of his age. He criticised the whole place with a most commendable frankness. It was a "pokey little hole." It was dark; it was low-ceilinged. It was full of inconveniences. The furniture was old-fashioned. You had to mount two steps into the drawing-room and go down three into the dining-room. He had to cross a corridor to his bath-room, and there was a great Tudor window in the small breakfast-parlor, that made one feel as if sitting in a lantern.

As for the stables, "he would n't put a donkey into them." No light, no ventilation,—no anything, in short. To live surrounded with so many inconveniences was the most complete assertion of his fallen condition, and, as he said, "he had never realized his fall in the world till he settled down in that miserable Nest."

There are men whose especial delight it is to call your attention to their impaired condition, their threadbare coat, their patched shoes, their shabby equipage, or their sorry dwelling, as though they were framing a sort of indictment against Fate, and setting forth the hardships of persons of merit like them being subjected to this unjustifiable treatment by Fortune.

"I suppose you never thought to see me reduced to this," is the burden of their song; and it is very strange how, by mere repetition and insistence, these people establish for themselves a sort of position, and oblige the world to yield them a black-mail of respect and condolence.

"This was not the sort of tipple I used to set before you once on a time, old fellow," will be uttered by one of whose hospitalities you have never partaken. "It was another guess sort of beast I gave you for a mount when we met last," will be said by a man who never rose above a cob pony; and one is obliged to yield a kind of polite assent to such balderdash, or stand forward as a public prosecutor and arraign the rascal for a humbug.

In this self-commiseration Sewell was a master, and there was not a corner of the house he did not make the butt of his ridicule,—to contrast its littleness and vulgarity with the former ways and belongings of his own once splendor.

"You're capital fellows," said he to a party of officers from the neighboring garrison, "to come and see me in this dog-hole. Try and find a chair you can sit on, and I 'll ask my wife if we can give you some dinner. You remember me up at Rangoon, Hobbes? Another guess sort of place, wasn't it? I had the Rajah's palace and four elephants at my orders. At Guzerat, too, I was the Resident, and, by Jove, I never dreamed of coming down to this!"

Too indolent or too indifferent to care where or how she was lodged, his wife gave no heed to his complaints, beyond a little half-supercilious smile as he uttered them. "If a fellow will marry, however, he deserves it all," was his usual wind-up to all his lamentations; and in this he seemed to console himself by the double opportunity of pitying himself and insulting his wife.

All that Colonel Cave and his officers could say in praise of the spot, its beauty, its neatness, and its comfort, were only fresh aliment to his depreciation, and he more than half implied that possibly the place was quite good enough for *them*, but that was not exactly the question at issue.

Some men go through life permitted to say scores of things for which their neighbor would be irrevocably cut and excluded from society. Either that the world is amused at their bitterness, or that it is regarded as a malady, far worse to him who bears than to him who witnesses it,—whatever the reason,—people endure these men, and make even a sort of vicious pets of them. Sewell was of this order, and a fine specimen too.

All the men around him were his equals in every respect, and yet there was not one of them who did not accept a position of quiet, unresisting inferiority to him for the sake of his bad temper and his bad tongue. It was "his way," they said, and they bore it.

He was a consummate adept in all the details of a household; and his dinners were perfection, his wine good, and his servants drilled to the very acme of discipline. These were not mean accessories to any pretension; and as they sat over their claret, a pleasanter and more social tone succeeded than the complaining spirit of their host had at first promised.

The talk was chiefly professional. Pipeclay will ever assert its pre-eminence, and with reason, for it is a grand leveller; and Digges, who joined three months ago, may have the Army List as well by heart as the oldest major in the service: and so they discussed, Where was Hobson? what made Jobson sell out? how did Bobson get out of that scrape with the paymaster? and how long will Dobson be able to live at his present rate in that light-cavalry corps? Everything that fell from them showed the most thorough intimacy with the condition, the fortune, and the prospects of the men they discussed,—familiarity there was enough of, but no friendship. No one seemed to trouble himself whether the sick-leave or the sell-out meant hopeless calamity,—all were dashed with a species of well-bred fatalism that was astonished with nothing, rejoiced at nothing, repined at nothing.

"I wish Trafford would make up his mind!" cried one. "Three weeks ago he told me positively he would leave, and now I hear he offered Craycroft three thousand pounds to retire from the majority."

"That 's true; Craycroft told me so himself; but old Joe is a wily bird, and he 'll not be taken so easily."

"He's an eldest son now!" broke in another. "What does he care whether he be called major or captain?"

"An eldest son!" cried Sewell, suddenly; "how is that? When I met him at the Cape, he spoke of an elder brother."

"So he had, then, but he's 'off the hooks.'"

"I don't think it matters much," said the Colonel. "The bulk of the property is disentailed, and Sir Hugh can leave it how he likes."

"That's what I call downright shameful," said one; but he was the minority, for a number of voices exclaimed,—"And perfectly right; that law of primogeniture is a positive barbarism."

While the dispute waxed warm and noisy, Sewell questioned the Colonel closely about Trafford,—how it happened that the entail was removed, and why there was reason to suppose that Sir Hugh and his son were not on terms of friendship.

Cave was frank enough when he spoke of the amount of the fortune and the extent of the estate, but used a careful caution in speaking of family matters, merely hinting that Trafford had gone very fast, spent a deal of money, had his debts twice paid by his father, and was now rather in the position of a reformed spendthrift, making a good character for prudence and economy.

"And where is he?—not in Ireland?" asked Se well, eagerly.

"No; he is to join on Monday. I got a hurried note from him this morning, dated Holyhead. You said you had met him?"

"Yes, at the Cape; he used to come and dine with us there occasionally."

"Did you like him?"

"In a way. Yes, I think he was a nice fellow,—that is, he might be made a nice fellow, but it was always a question into what hands he fell; he was at the same time pliant and obstinate. He would always imitate,—he would never lead. So he seemed to me; but, to tell you the truth, I left him a good deal to the women; he was too young and too fresh for a man like myself."

"You are rather hard on him," said Cave, laughing; "but you are partly right. He has, however, fine qualities,—he is generous and trustful to any extent."

"Indeed!" said Sewell, carelessly, as he bit off the end of a cigar.

"Nothing would make him swerve from his word; and if placed in a difficulty where a friend was involved, his own interests would be the last he 'd think of."

"Very fine, all that. Are you drinking claret?—if so, finish that decanter, and let's have a fresh bottle."

Cave declined to take more wine, and he arose, with the rest, to repair to the drawing-room for coffee.

It was not very usual for Sewell to approach his wife or notice her in society; now, however, he drew a chair near her as she sat at the fire, and in a low whisper said, "I have some pleasant news for you."

"Indeed!" she said coldly,—"what a strange incident!"

"You mean it is a strange channel for pleasant news to come through, perhaps," said he, with a curl of his lip.

"Possibly that is what I meant," said she, as quietly as before.

"None of these fine-lady airs with me, Madam," said he, reddening with anger; "there are no two people in Europe ought to understand each other better than we do."

"In that I quite agree with you."

"And as such is the case, affectations are clean thrown away, Madam; we *can* have no disguises for each other."

A very slight inclination of her head seemed to assent to this remark, but she did not speak.

"We came to plain speaking many a day ago," said he, with increased bitterness in his tone. "I don't see why we are to forego the advantage of it now,—do you?"

"By no means. Speak as plainly as you wish; I am quite ready to hear you."

"You have managed, however, to make people observe us," muttered he, between his teeth,—"it's an old trick of yours, Madam. You can play martyr at the shortest notice." He rose hastily and moved to another part of the room, where a very noisy group were arranging a party for pool at billiards.

"Won't you have me?" cried Sewell, in his ordinary tone. "I'm a perfect boon at pool; for I am the most unlucky dog in everything."

"I scarcely think you'll expect us to believe *that*," said Cave, with a glance of unmistakable admiration towards Mrs. Sewell.

"Ay," cried Sewell, fiercely, and answering the unspoken sentiment,— "ay, sir, and *that*,"—he laid a stern emphasis on the word,—"and *that* the worst luck of all."

"I 've been asking Mrs. Sewell to play a game with us, and she says she has no objections," said a young subaltern, "if Colonel Sewell does not dislike it."

"I'll play whist, then," said Sewell. "Who 'll make a rubber?—Cave, will you? Here's Houghton and Mowbray,—eh?"

"No, no," said Mowbray,—"you are all too good for me."

"How I hate that,—too good for me," said Sewell. "Why, man, what better investment could you ask for your money than the benefit of good teaching? Always ride with the best hounds, play with the best players, talk with the best talkers."

"And make love to the prettiest women," added Cave, in a whisper, as Mowbray followed Mrs. Sewell into the billiard-room.

"I heard you, Cave," whispered Sewell, in a still lower whisper; "there's devilish little escapes my ears, I promise you." The bustle and preparation of the card-table served in part to cover Cave's confusion, but his cheek tingled and his hand shook with mingled shame and annoyance.

Sewell saw it all, and knew how to profit by it. He liked high play, to which Cave generally objected; but he well knew that on the present occasion Cave would concur in anything to cover his momentary sense of shame.

"Pounds and fives, I suppose," said Sewell; and the others bowed, and the game began.

As little did Cave like three-handed whist, but he was in no mood to oppose anything; for, like many men who have made an awkward speech, he exaggerated the meaning through his fears, and made it appear absolutely monstrous to himself.

"Whatever you like," was therefore his remark; and he sat down to the game.

Sewell was a skilled player; but the race is no more to the swift in cards than in anything else,—he lost, and lost heavily. He undervalued his adversaries too, and, in consequence, he followed up his bad luck by increased wagers. Cave tried to moderate the ardor he displayed, and even remonstrated with him on the sums they were staking, which, he good-humoredly remarked, were far above his own pretensions; but Sewell resented the advice, and replied with a coarse insinuation about winners' counsels. The ill-luck continued, and Sewell's peevishness and ill-temper increased with every game. "What have I lost to you?" cried he, abruptly, to Cave; "it jars on my nerves every time you take out that cursed memorandum, so that all I can do is not to fling it into the fire."

"I'm sure I wish you would, or that you would let me do it," said Cave, quietly.

"How much is it?—not short of three hundred, I'll be bound."

"It is upwards of five hundred," said Cave, handing the book across the table.

"You'll have to wait for it, I promise you. You must give me time, for I am in all sorts of messes just now." While Cave assured him that there was no question of pressing for payment,—to take his own perfect convenience,—Sewell, not heeding him, went on: "This confounded place has cost me a pot of money. My wife, too, knows how to scatter her five-pound notes; in short, we are a wasteful lot. Shall we have one rubber more, eh?"

"As you like. I am at your orders."

"Let us say double or quits, then, for the whole sum."

Cave made no reply, and seemed not to know how to answer.

"Of course, if you object," said Sewell, pushing back his chair from the table, as though about to rise, "there's no more to be said."

"What do *you* say, Houghton?" asked Cave.

"Houghton has nothing to say to it; *he* hasn't won twenty pounds from me," said Sewell, fiercely.

"Whatever you like, then," said Cave, in a tone in which it was easy to see irritation was with difficulty kept under, and the game began.

The game began in deep silence. The restrained temper of the players and the heavy sum together impressed them, and not a word was dropped. The cards fell upon the table with a clear, sharp sound, and the clink of the counters resounded through the room, the only noises there.

As they played, the company from the billiard-room poured in and drew around the whist-table, at first noisily enough; but seeing the deep preoccupation of the players, their steadfast looks, their intense eagerness, made more striking by their silence, they gradually lowered their voices, and at last only spoke in whispers and rarely.

The first game of the rubber had been contested trick by trick, but ended by Cave winning it. The second game was won by Sewell, and the third opened with his deal.

As he dealt the cards, a murmur ran through the bystanders that the stake was something considerable, and the interest increased in consequence. A few trifling bets were laid on the issue, and one of the group, in a voice slightly raised above the rest, said, "I'll back Sewell for a pony."

"I beg you will not, sir," said Sewell, turning fiercely round. "I'm in bad luck already, and I don't want to be swamped altogether. There, sir, your interference has made me misdeal," cried he, passionately, as he flung the cards on the table.

Not a word was said as Cave began his deal. It was too plain to every one that Sewell's temper was becoming beyond control, and that a word or a look might bring the gravest consequences.

"What cards!" said Cave, as he spread his hand on the table: "four honors and nine trumps." Sewell stared at them, moved his fingers through them to separate and examine them, and then, turning his head round, he looked behind. It was his wife was standing at the back of his chair, calm, pale, and collected. "By Heaven!" cried he, savagely, "I knew who was there as well as if I saw her. The moment Cave spread out his cards, I 'd have taken my oath that *she* was standing over me."

She moved hastily away at the ruffianly speech, and a low murmur of indignant anger filled the room. Cave and Houghton quitted the table, and mingled with the others; but Sewell sat still, tearing up the cards one by one, with a quiet, methodical persistence that betrayed no passion. "There!" said he, as he threw the last fragment from him, "you shall never bring good or bad luck to any one more." With the ease of one to whom such paroxysms were not un-frequent, he joined in the conversation of a group of young men, and with a familiar jocularity soon set them at their ease towards him; and then, drawing his arm within Cave's, he led him apart, and said: "I 'll go over to the Barrack to-morrow and breakfast with you. I have just thought of how I can settle this little debt."

"Oh, don't distress yourself about that," said Cave. "I beg you will not let it give you a moment's uneasiness."

"Good fellow!" said Sewell, clapping him on the shoulder; "but I have the means of doing it without inconvenience, as I 'll show you to-morrow. Don't go yet; don't let your fellows go. We are going to have a broil, or a devilled biscuit, or something." He walked over and rang the bell, and then hastily passed on into a smaller room, where his wife was sitting on a sofa, an old doctor of the regiment seated at her side.

"I won't interrupt the consultation," said Sewell, "but I have just one word to say." He leaned over the back of the sofa, and whispered in her ear, "Your friend Trafford is become an eldest son. He is at the Bilton Hotel, Dublin; write and ask him here. Say I have some cock-shooting,—there are harriers in the neighborhood. Are you listening to me, Madam?" said he, in a harsh hissing voice, for she had half turned away her head, and her face had assumed an expression of sickened disgust. She nodded, but did not speak. "Tell him that I've spoken to Cave—he'll make his leave all right—that I 'll do my best to make the place pleasant to him, and that—in fact, I needn't toy to teach you to write a sweet note. You understand me, eh?"

"Oh, perfectly," said she, rising; and a livid paleness now spread over her face, and even her lips were bloodless.

"I was too abrupt with my news. I ought to have been more considerate; I ought to have known it might overcome you," said he, with a sneering bitterness. "Doctor, you 'll have to give Mrs. Se well some cordial, some restorative,—that's the name for it. She was overcome by some tidings I brought her. Even pleasant news will startle us occasionally. As the French comedy has it, *La joie fait peur;*" and with a listless, easy air, he sauntered away into another room.

CHAPTER XXIX
SEWELL VISITS CAVE

Punctual to his appointment, Sewell appeared at breakfast the next morning with Colonel Cave. Of all the ill-humor and bad conduct of the night before, not a trace now was to be seen. He was easy, courteous, and affable. He even made a half-jesting apology for his late display of bad temper; attributing it to an attack of coming gout. "So long as the malady," said he, "is in a state of menace, one's nerves become so fine-strung that there is no name for the irritability; but when once a good honest seizure has taken place, a man recovers himself, and stands up to his suffering manfully and well.

"To-day, for instance," said he, pointing to a shoe divided by long incisions, "I have got my enemy fixed, and I let him do his worst."

The breakfast proceeded pleasantly; Cave was in admiration of his guest's agreeability; for he talked away, not so much of things as of people. He had in a high degree that-man-of-the-world gift of knowing something about every one. No name could turn up of which he could not tell you something the owner of it had said or done, and these "scratch" biographies are often very amusing, particularly when struck off with the readiness of a practised talker.

It was not, then, merely that Sewell obliterated every memory of the evening before, but he made Cave forget the actual object for which he had come that morning. Projects, besides, for future pleasure did Sewell throw out, like a man who had both the leisure, the means, and the taste for enjoyment. There was some capital shooting he had just taken; his neighbor, an old squire, had never cared for it, and let him have it "for a song." They were going to get up hack races, too, in the Park,—"half-a-dozen hurdles and a double ditch to tumble over," as he said, "will amuse our garrison fellows,—and my wife has some theatrical intentions—if you will condescend to help her."

Sewell talked with that blended munificence and shiftiness, which seems a specialty with a certain order of men. Nothing was too costly to be done, and yet everything must be accomplished with a dexterity that was almost a dodge. The men of this gift are great scene-painters. They dash you off a view—be it a wood or a rich interior, a terraced garden or an Alpine hut—in a few loose touches. Ay! and they "smudge" them out again before criticism has had time to deal with them. "By the way," cried he, suddenly, stopping in the full swing of some description of a possible regatta, "I was half forgetting what brought me here this morning. I am in your debt, Cave."

He stopped as though his speech needed some rejoinder, and Cave grew very red and very uneasy—tried to say something—anything—but could not. The fact was, that, like a man who had never in all his life adventured on high play or risked a stake that could possibly be of importance to him, he felt pretty much the same amount of distress at having won as he would have felt at having lost. He well knew that if by any mischance he had incurred such a loss as a thousand pounds, it would have been a most serious embarrassment—by what right, then, had he won it? Now, although feelings of this sort were about the very last to find entrance into Sewell's heart, he well knew that there were men who were liable to them, just as there were people who were exposed to plague or yellow fever, and other maladies from which he lived remote. It was, then, with a sort of selfish delight that he saw Cave's awkward hesitating manner, and read the marks of the shame that was overwhelming him.

"A heavy sum too," said Sewell, jauntily; "we went the whole 'pot' on that last rubber."

"I wish I could forget it—I mean," muttered Cave, "I wish we could both forget it."

"I have not the least objection to that," said Sewell gayly; "only let it first be paid."

"Well, but—what I meant was—what I wanted to say, or rather, what I hoped—was—in plain words, Sewell," burst he out, like a man to whom desperation gave courage,—"in plain words, I never intended to play such stakes as we played last night,—I never have—I never will again."

"Not to give me my revenge?" said Sewell, laughing.

"No, not for anything. I don't know what I'd have done—I don't know what would have become of me—if I had lost; and I pledge you my honor, I think the next worst thing is to have won."

"Do you, by George!"

"I do, upon my sacred word of honor. My first thoughts on waking this morning were more wretched than they have been for any day in the last twenty years of life, for I was thoroughly ashamed of myself."

"You 'll not find many men afflicted with your malady, Cave; and, at all events, it's not contagious."

"I know nothing about that," said Cave, half irritably; "I never was a play man, and have little pretension to understand their feelings."

"They have n't got any," said Sewell, as he lit his cigar.

"Perhaps not; so much the worse for them. I can only say, if the misery of losing be only proportionate to the shame of winning, I don't envy a gambler. Such an example, too, to exhibit to my young officers! It was too bad—too bad."

"I declare I don't understand this," said Sewell, carelessly; "when I commanded a battalion, I never imagined I was obliged to be a model to the subs or the junior captains." The tone of banter went, this time, to the quick; and Cave flushed a deep crimson, and said,—"I'm not sorry that my ideas of my duty are different; though, in the present case, I have failed to fulfil it."

"Well, well, there's nothing to grow angry about," said Sewell, laughing, "even though you won't give me my revenge. My present business is to book up;" and, as he spoke, he sat down at the table, and drew a roll of papers from his pocket and laid it before him.

"You distress me greatly by all this, Sewell," said Cave, whose agitation now almost overcame him. "Cannot we hit upon some way? can't we let it lie over? I mean,—is there no arrangement by which this cursed affair can be deferred? You understand me?"

"Not in the least. Such things are never deferred without loss of honor to the man in default. The stake that a man risks is supposed to be in his pocket, otherwise play becomes trade, and accepts all the vicissitudes of trade."

"It's the first time I ever heard them contrasted to the disparagement of honest industry."

"And I call billiards, tennis, whist, and écarté honest industries, too, though I won't call them trades. There, there," said he, laughing at the other's look of displeasure, "don't be afraid; I am not going to preach these doctrines to your young officers, for whose morals you are so much concerned. Sit down here, and just listen to me for one moment."

Cave obeyed, but his face showed in every feature how reluctantly.

"I see, Cave," said Sewell, with a quiet smile,—"I see you want to do me a favor,—so you shall. I am obliged to own that I am an exception to the theory I have just now enunciated. I staked a thousand pounds, and I had *not* the money in my pocket. Wait a moment,—don't interrupt me. I had not the money in gold or bank-notes, but I had it here"—and he touched the papers before him—"in a form equally solvent, only that it required that he who won the money should be not a mere acquaintance, but a friend,—a friend to whom I could speak with freedom and in confidence. This," said he, "is a bond for twelve hundred pounds, given by my wife's guardian in satisfaction of a loan once made to him; he was a man of large fortune, which he squandered away recklessly, leaving but a small estate, which he could neither sell nor alienate. Upon this property this is a mortgage. As an old friend of my father-in-law,—a very unworthy one, by the way,—I could of course not press him for the interest, and, as you will see, it has never been paid; and there is now a balance of some hundred pounds additional against him. Of this I could not speak, for another reason,—we are not without the hope of inheriting something by him, and to allude to this matter would be ruinous. Keep this, then. I insist upon it. I declare to you, if you refuse, I will sell it to-morrow to the first moneylender I can find, and send you my debt in hard cash. I 've been a play-man all my life, but never a defaulter."

There was a tone of proud indignation in the way he spoke that awed Cave to silence; for in good truth he was treating of themes of which he knew nothing whatever: and of the sort of influences which swayed gamblers, of the rules that guided and the conventionalities that bound them, he was profoundly ignorant.

"You 'll not get your money, Cave," resumed Sewell, "till this old fellow dies; but you will be paid at last,—of that I can assure you. Indeed, if by any turn of luck I was in funds myself, I 'd like to redeem it. All I ask is, therefore, that you 'll not dispose of it, but hold it over in your own possession till the day—and I hope it may be an early one—it will be payable."

Cave was in no humor to dispute anything. There was no condition to which he would not have acceded, so heartily ashamed and abashed was he by the position in which he found himself. What he really would have liked best, would have been to refuse the bond altogether, and say, Pay when you like, how you like, or, better still, not at all. This of course was not possible, and he accepted the terms proposed to him at once.

"It shall be all as you wish," said he, hurriedly. "I will do everything you desire; only let me assure you that I would infinitely rather this paper remained in *your* keeping than in *mine*. I'm a careless fellow about documents," added he, trying to put the matter on the lesser ground of a safe custody. "Well, well, say no more; you don't wish it, and that's enough."

"I must be able to say," said Sewell, gravely, "that I never lost over night what I had not paid the next morning; and I will even ask of you to corroborate me so far as this transaction goes. There were several of your fellows at my house last night; they saw what we played for, and that I was the loser. There will be—there always is—plenty of gossip about these things, and the first question is, 'Has he-booked up?' I'm sure it's not asking more than you are ready to do, to say that I paid my debt within twenty-four hours."

"Certainly; most willingly. I don't know that any one has a right to question me on the matter."

"I never said he had. I only warned you how people will talk, and how necessary it is to be prepared to stifle a scandal even before it has flared out."

"It shall be cared for. I'll do exactly as you wish," said Cave, who was too much flurried to know what was asked of him, and to what he was pledged.

"I'm glad this is off my mind," said Sewell, with a long sigh of relief. "I lay awake half the night thinking of it; for there are scores of fellows who are not of your stamp, and who would be for submitting these documents to their lawyer, and asking, Heaven knows, what this affair related to. Now I tell you frankly, I 'd have given no explanations. He who gave that bond is, as I know, a consummate rascal, and has robbed me—that is, my wife—out of two-thirds of her fortune; but *my* hands are tied regarding him. I could n't touch him, except he should try to take my life,—a thing, by the way, he is quite capable of. Old Dillon, my wife's father, believed him to be the best and truest of men, and my wife inherited this belief, even in the face of all the injuries he had worked us. She went on saying, 'My father always said, "Trust Fossy: there's at least one man in the world that will never deceive you."'"

"What was the name you said?" asked Cave, quickly.

"Oh, only a nickname. I don't want to mention his name. I have sealed up the bond, with this superscription,—'Colonel Sewell's bond.' I did this believing you would not question me farther; but if you desire to read it over, I 'll break the envelope at once."

"No, no; nothing of the kind. Leave it just as it is."

"So that," said Sewell, pursuing his former line of thought, "this man not alone defrauded me, but he sowed dissension between me and my wife. Her faith is shaken in him, I have no doubt, but she 'll not confess it. Like a genuine woman, she will persist in asserting the convictions she has long ceased to be held by, and quote this stupid letter of her father in the face of every fact.

"I ought not to have got into these things," said Sewell, as he walked impatiently down the room. "These family bedevilments should be kept from one's friends; but the murder is out now, and you can see how I stand—and see besides, that if I am not always able to control my temper, a friend might find an excuse for me."

Cave gave a kindly nod of assent to this, not wishing, even by a word, to increase the painful embarrassment of the scene.

"Heigh ho!" cried Sewell, throwing himself down in a chair, "there's one care off my heart, at least! I can remember a time when a night's bad luck would n't have cost me five minutes of annoyance; but nowadays I have got it so hot and so heavy from fortune, I begin not to know myself." Then, with a sudden change of tone, he added: "When are you coming out to us again? Shall we say Tuesday?"

"We are to be inspected on Tuesday. Trafford writes me that he is coming over with General Halkett,—whom, by the way, he calls a Tartar,—and says, 'If the Sewells are within hail, say a kind word to them on my part.'"

"A good sort of fellow, Trafford," said Sewell, carelessly.

"An excellent fellow,—no better living!"

"A very wide-awake one too," said Sewell, with one eye closed, and a look of intense cunning.

"I never thought so. It is, to my notion, to the want of that faculty he owes every embarrassment he has ever suffered. He is unsuspecting to a fault."

"It's not the way I read him; though, perhaps, I think as well of him as you do. I 'd say that for his years he is one of the very shrewdest young fellows I ever met."

"You astonish me! May I ask if you know him well?"

"Our acquaintance is not of very old date, but we saw a good deal of each other at the Cape. We rode out frequently, dined, played, and conversed freely together; and the impression he made upon me was that every sharp lesson the world had given him he 'd pay back one day or other with a compound interest."

"I hope not,—I fervently hope not!" cried Cave. "I had rather hear to-morrow that he had been duped and cheated out of half his fortune than learn he had done one act that savored of the—the—" He stopped, unable to finish, for he could not hit upon the word that might be strong enough for his meaning, and yet not imply an offence.

"Say blackleg. Is n't that what you want? There's my wife's pony chaise. I 'll get a seat back to the Nest. Goodbye, Cave. If Wednesday is open, give it to us, and tell Trafford I'd be glad to see him."

Cave sat down as the door closed after the other, and tried to recall his thoughts to something like order. What manner of man was that who had just left him? It was evidently a very mixed nature. Was it the good or the evil that predominated? Was the unscrupulous tone he displayed the result of a spirit of tolerance, or was it the easy indifference of one who trusted nothing,—believed nothing?

Was it possible his estimate of Trafford could be correct? and could this seemingly generous and open manner cover a nature cold, calculating, and treacherous? No, no. *That* he felt to be totally out of the question.

He thought long and intently over the matter, but to no end; and as he arose to deposit the papers left by Sewell in his writing-desk, he felt as unsettled and undecided as when he started on the inquiry.

CHAPTER XXX
THE RACES ON THE LAWN

A bright October morning, with a blue sky and a slight, very slight feeling of frost in the air, and a gay meeting on foot and horseback on the lawn before the Swan's Nest, made as pretty a picture as a painter of such scenes could desire. I say of such scenes, because in the *tableau de genre* it is the realistic element that must predominate, and the artist's skill is employed in imparting to very commonplace people and costumes whatever poetry can be lent them by light and shade, by happy groupings, and, more than all these, by the insinuation of some incident in which they are the actors,—a sort of storied interest pervading the whole canvas, which gives immense pleasure to those who have little taste for the fine arts.

There was plenty of color even in the landscape. The mountains had put on their autumn suit, and displayed every tint from a pale opal to a deep and gorgeous purple, while the river ran on in those circling eddies which come to the surface of water under sunshine as naturally as smiles to the face of flattered beauty.

Colonel Sewell had invited the country-side to witness hack-races in his grounds, and the country-side had heartily responded to the invitation. There were the county magnates in grand equipages,—an earl with two postilions and outriders, a high sheriff with all his official splendors, squires of lower degree in more composite vehicles, and a large array of jaunting-cars, through all of which figured the red coats of the neighboring garrison, adding to the scene that tint of warmth in color so dear to the painter's heart.

The wonderful beauty of the spot, combining, as it did, heath-clad mountain, and wood, and winding river, with a spreading lake in the distance, dotted with picturesque islands, was well seconded by a glorious autumnal day,—one of those days when the very air has something of champagne in its exhilarating quality, and gives to every breath of it a sense of stimulation.

The first three races—they were on the flat—had gone off admirably. They were well contested, well ridden, and the "right horse" the winner. All was contentment, therefore, on every side, to which the interval of a pleasant moment of conviviality gave hearty assistance, for now came the hour of luncheon; and from the "swells" in the great marquée, and the favored intimates in the dining-room, to the assembled unknown in the jaunting-cars, merry laughter issued, with clattering of plates and popping of corks, and those commingled sounds of banter and jollity which mark such gatherings.

The great event of the day was, however, yet to come off. It was a hurdle race, to which two stiff fences were to be added, in the shape of double ditches, to test the hunting powers of the horses. The hurdles were to be four feet eight in height, so that the course was by no means a despicable one, even to good cross-country riders. To give increased interest to the race, Sewell himself was to ride, and no small share of eagerness existed amongst the neighboring gentry to see how the new-comer would distinguish himself in the saddle,—some opining he was too long of leg; some, that he was too heavy; some, that men of his age—he was over five-and-thirty—begin to lose nerve; and many going so far as to imply "that he did not look like riding,"—a judgment whose vagueness detracts nothing from its force.

"There he goes now, and he sits well down too!" cried one, as a group of horsemen swept past, one of whom, mounted on a "sharp" pony, led the way, a white macintosh and loose overalls covering him from head to foot. They were off to see that the fences were all being properly put up, and in an instant were out of sight.

"I'll back Tom Westenra against Sewell for a twenty-pound note," cried one, standing up on the seat of his car to proclaim the challenge.

"I'll go further," shouted another,—"I'll do it for fifty."

"I'll beat you both," cried out a third,—"I'll take Tom even against the field."

The object of all this enthusiasm was a smart, cleanshaven little fellow, with a good blue eye, and a pleasant countenance, who smoked his cigar on the seat of a drag near, and nodded a friendly recognition to their confidence.

"If Joe Slater was well of his fall, I'd rather have him than any one in the county," said an old farmer, true to a man of his own class and standing.

"Here's one can beat them both!" shouted another; "here's Mr. Creagh of Liskmakerry!" and a thin, ruddy-faced, keen-eyed man of about fifty rode by on a low-sized horse, with that especial look of decision in his mouth, and a peculiar puckering about the corners that seem to belong to those who traffic in horse-flesh, and who, it would appear, however much they may know about horses, understand humanity more thoroughly still.

"Are you going to ride, Creagh?" cried a friend from a high tax-cart.

"Maybe so, if the fences are not too big for me;" and a very malicious drollery twinkled in his gray eye.

"Faix, and if they are," said a farmer, "the rest may stay at home."

"I hope you 'll ride, Creagh," said the first speaker, "and not let these English fellows take the shine out of us. Yourself and Tom are the only county names on the card."

"Show it to me," said Creagh, listlessly; and he took the printed list in his hand and conned it over, as though it had all been new to him. "They 're all soldiers, I see," said he. "It's Major This, and Captain That—Who is the lady?" This question was rapidly called forth by a horsewoman who rode past at an easy canter in the midst of a group of men. She was dressed in a light-gray habit and hat of the same color, from which a long white feather encircling the hat hung on one side.

"That's Mrs. Sewell,—what do you think of her riding?"

"If her husband has as neat a hand, I 'd rather he was out of the course. She knows well what she 's about."

"They say there's not her equal in the park in London."

"That's not park riding; that's something very different, take my word for it. She could lead half the men here across the country."

Nor was she unworthy of the praise, as, with her hand low, her head a little forward, but her back well curved in, she sat firmly down in her saddle; giving to the action of the horse that amount of movement that assisted the animal, but never more. The horse was mettlesome enough to require all her attention. It was his first day under a sidesaddle, and he chafed at it, and when the heavy skirt smote his flank, bounded with a lunge and a stroke of his head that showed anger.

"That's a four-hundred guinea beast she 's on. He belongs to the tall young fellow that's riding on her left."

"I like his own horse better,—the liver-chestnut with the short legs. I wish I had a loan of him for the hurdle-race."

"Ask him, Phil; or get the mistress there to ask him," said another, laughing. "I 'm mighty mistaken or he wouldn't refuse her."

"Oh, is that it?" said Creagh, with a knowing look.

"So they tell me here, for I don't know one of them myself; but the story goes that she was to have married that young fellow when Sewell earned her off."

"I must go and get a better look at her," said Creagh, as he spurred his horse and cantered away.

"Is any one betting?" said little Westenra, as he descended from his seat on the drag. "I have not seen a man to-day with five pounds on the race."

"Here's Sewell," muttered another; "he's coming up now, and will give or take as much as you like."

"Did you see Mrs. Sewell, any of you?" asked Sewell, cavalierly, as he rode up with an open telegram in his hand; and as the persons addressed were for the most part his equals, none responded to the insolent demand.

"Could you tell me, sir," said Sewell, quickly altering his tone, while he touched his hat to Westenra, "if Mrs. Sewell passed this way?"

"I haven't the honor to know Mrs. Sewell, but I saw a lady ride past, about ten minutes ago, on a black thoroughbred."

"Faix, and well she rode him too," broke in an old farmer.

"She took the posy out of that young gentleman's button-hole, while her beast was jumping, and stuck it in her breast, as easy as I 'm sitting here."

Sewel's face grew purple as he darted a look of savage anger at the speaker, and, turning his horse's head, he dashed out at speed and disappeared.

"Peter Delaney," said Westenra, "I thought you had more discretion than to tell such a story as that."

"Begorra, Mister Tom! I didn't know the mischief I was making till I saw the look he gave me!"

It was not till after a considerable search that Sewell came up with his wife's party, who were sauntering leisurely along the river-side, through a gorse-covered slope.

"I 've had a devil of a hunt after you!" he cried, as he rode up, and the ringing tone of his voice was enough to intimate to her in what temper he spoke. "I 've something to say to you," said he, as though meant for her private ear; and the others drew back, and suffered them to ride on together. "There 's a telegram just come from that old beast the Chief Baron; he desires to see me to-night. The last train leaves at five, and I shall only hit it by going at once. Can't you keep your horse quiet, Madam, or must you show off while I 'm speaking to you?"

"It was the furze that stung him," said she, coldly, and not showing the slightest resentment at his tone.

"If the old bear means anything short of dying, and leaving me his heir, this message is a shameful swindle."

"Do you mean to go?" asked she, coldly.

"I suppose so; that is," added he, with a bitter grin, "if I can tear myself away from *you*;" but she only smiled.

"I 'll have to pay a forfeit in this match," continued he, "and my book will be all smashed, besides. I say," cried he, "would Trafford ride for me?"

"Perhaps he would."

"None of your mock indifference, Madam. I can't afford to lose a thousand pounds every time you have a whim. Ay, look astonished if you like! but if you had n't gone into the billiard-room on Saturday evening and spoiled my match, I 'd have escaped that infernal whist-table. Listen to me now! Tell him that I have been sent for suddenly,—it might be too great a risk for me to refuse to go,—and ask him to ride Cressy; if he says Yes,—and he will say yes if you ask him as you *ought*,"—her cheek grew crimson as he uttered the last word with a strong emphasis,—"tell him to take up my book. Mind you use the words 'take up;' *he'll* understand you."

"But why not say all this yourself?—he 's riding close behind at this minute."

"Because I have a wife, Madam, who can do it so much better; because I have a wife who plucks a carnation out of a man's coat, and wears it in her bosom, and this on an open race-course, where people can talk of it! and a woman with such rare tact ought to be of service to her husband, eh?" She swayed to and fro in her saddle for an instant as though about to fall, but she grasped the horn with both hands and saved herself.

"Is that all," muttered she faintly.

"Is that all?" muttered she, faintly.

"Not quite. Tell Trafford to come round to my dressing-room, and I 'll give him a hint or two about the horse. He must come at once, for I have only time to change my clothes and start. You can make some excuse to the people for my absence; say that the old Judge has had another attack, and I only wish it may be true. Tell them I got a telegram, and *that* may mean anything. Trafford will help you to do the honors, and I 'll swear him in as viceroy before I go. Is n't that all that could be asked of me?" The insolence of his look as he said this made her turn away her head as though sickened and disgusted.

"They want you at the weighing-stand, Colonel Sewell," said a gentleman, riding up.

"Oh, they do! Well, say, please, that I 'm coming. Has he given you that black horse?" asked he, in a hurried whisper.

"No; he offered him, but I refused."

"You had no right to refuse; he's strong enough to carry *me*; and the ponies that I saw led round to the stable-yard, whose are they?"

"They are Captain Trafford's."

"You told him you thought them handsome, I suppose, didn't you?"

"Yes, I think them very beautiful."

"Well, don't take them as a present. Win them if you like at piquet or écarté,—any way you please, but don't take them as a gift, for I heard Westenra say they were meant for you."

She nodded; and as she bent her head, a smile, the very strangest, crossed her features. If it were not that the pervading expression of her face was at the instant melancholy, the look she gave him would have been almost devilish.

"I have something else to say, but I can't remember it."

"You don't know when you'll be back?" asked she, carelessly.

"Of course not,—how can I? I can only promise that I'll not arrive unexpectedly, Madam; and I take it that's as much as any gentleman can be called on to say. Bye-bye."

"Good-bye," said she, in the same tone.

"I see that Mr. Balfour is here. I can't tell who asked him; but mind you don't invite him to luncheon; take no notice of him whatever; he'll not bet a guinea; never plays; never risks anything,—even his *affections!*"

"What a creature!"

"Isn't he! There! I'll not detain you from pleasanter company; good-bye; see you here when I come back, I suppose?"

"Most probably," said she, with a smile; and away he rode, at a tearing gallop, for his watch warned him that he was driven to the last minute.

"My husband has been sent for to town, Captain Traf-ford," said she, turning her head towards him as he resumed his place at her side; "the Chief Baron desires to see him immediately, and he sets off at once."

"And his race? What 's to become of his match?"

"He said I was to ask you to ride for him."

"Me—I ride! Why, I am two stone heavier than he is."

"I suppose he knew that," said she, coldly, and as if the matter was one of complete indifference to her. "I am only delivering a message," continued she, in the same careless tone; "he said, 'Ask Captain Trafford to ride for me and take up my book;' I was to be particular about the phrase 'take up;' I conclude you will know what meaning to attach to it."

"I suspect I do," said he, with a low soft laugh.

"And I was to add something about hints he was to give you, if you 'd go round to his dressing-room at once; indeed, I believe you have little time to spare."

"Yes, I'll go,—I 'll go now; only there 's one thing I 'd like to ask—that is—I'd be very glad to know—"

"What is it?" said she, after a pause, in which his confusion seemed to increase with every minute.

"I mean, I should like to know whether you wished me to ride this race or not?"

"Whether *I* wished it?" said she, in a tone of astonishment.

"Well, whether you cared about the matter one way or other?" replied he, in still deeper embarrassment.

"How could it concern me, my dear Captain Trafford?" said she, with an easy smile; "a race never interests me much, and I 'd just as soon see Blue and Orange come in as Yellow and Black; but you 'll be late if you intend to see my husband; I think you 'd better make haste."

"So I will, and I 'll be back immediately," said he, not sorry to escape a scene where his confusion was now making him miserable.

"You *are* a very nice horse!" said she, patting the animal's neck, as he chafed to dash off after the other. "I 'd like very much to own you; that is, if I ever was to call anything my own."

"They 're clearing the course, Mrs. Sewell," said one of her companions, riding up; "we had better turn off this way, and ride down to the stand."

"Here's a go!" cried another, coming up at speed. "Big Trafford is going to ride Cressy; he 's well-nigh fourteen stone."

"Not thirteen: I 'll lay a tenner on it."

"He can ride a bit," said a third.

"I 'd rather he 'd ride his own horse than mine."

"Sewell knows what he 's about, depend on 't."

"That's his wife," whispered another; "I'm certain she heard you."

Mrs. Sewell turned her head as she cantered along, and, in the strange smile her features wore, seemed to confirm the speaker's words; but the hurry and bustle of the moment drowned all sense of embarrassment, and the group dashed onward to the stand.

Leaving that heaving, panting, surging tide of humanity for an instant, let us turn to the house, where Sewell was already engaged in preparing for the road.

"You are going to ride for me, Trafford?" said Sewell, as the other entered his dressing-room, where, with the aid of his servant, he was busily packing up for the road.

"I 'm not sure; that is, I don't like to refuse, and I don't see how to accept."

"My wife has told you; I 'm sent for hurriedly."

"Yes."

"Well?" said he, looking round at him from his task.

"Just as I have told you already; I 'd ride for you as well as a heavy fellow could take a light-weight's place, but I don't understand about your book—am I to stand your engagements?"

"You mean, are you to win all the money I'm sure to pocket on the match?"

"No, I don't mean that," said he, laughing; "I never thought of trading on another man's brains; I simply meant, am I to be responsible for the losses?"

"If you ride Crescy as you ought to ride him, you needn't fret about the losses?"

"But suppose that I do not—and the case is a very possible one—that, not knowing your horse—"

"Take this portmanteau down, Bob, and the carpet-bag; I shall only lose my train," said Sewell, with a gesture of hot impatience; and as the servant left the room, he added: "Pray don't think any more about this stupid race; scratch Crescy, and tell my wife that it was a change of mind on "my" part,—that I did not wish you to ride; good-bye;" and he waved a hasty adieu with his hand, as though to dismiss him at once.

"If you 'll let me ride for you, I 'll do my best," blundered out Trafford; "when I spoke of your engagements, it was only to prepare you for what perhaps you were not aware of, that I 'm not very well off just now, and that if anything like a heavy sum—"

"You are a most cautious fellow; I only wonder how you ever did get into a difficulty; but I 'm not the man to lead you astray, and wreck such splendid principles; adieu!"

"I 'll ride, let it end how it may!" said Trafiford, angrily, and left the room at once, and hurried downstairs.

Sewell gave a parting look at himself in the glass; and as he set his hat jauntily on one side, said, "There 's nothing like a little mock indignation to bully fellows of *his* stamp; the keynote of their natures is the dread of being thought mean, and particularly of being thought mean by a woman." He laughed pleasantly at this conceit, and went on his way.

CHAPTER XXXI
SEWELL ARRIVES IN DUBLIN

It was late at night when Sewell reached town. An accidental delay to the train deferred the arrival for upwards of an hour after the usual time; and when he reached the Priory, the house was all closed for the night, and not a light to be seen.

He knocked, however, and rang boldly; and after a brief delay, and considerable noise of unbolting and unbarring, was admitted. "We gave you up, sir, after twelve o'clock," said the butler, half reproachfully, "and his Lordship ordered the servants to bed. Miss Lendrick, however, is in her drawing-room still."

"Is there anything to eat, my good friend? That is what I stand most in need of just now."

"There's a cold rib of beef, sir, and a grouse pie; but if you 'd like something hot, I 'll call the cook."

"No, no, never mind the cook; you can give me some sherry, I 'm sure?"

"Any wine you please, sir. We have excellent Madeira, which ain't to be had everywhere nowadays."

"Madeira be it, then; and order a fire in my room. I take it you have a room for me?"

"Yes, sir, all is ready; the bath was hot about an hour ago, and I 'll have it refreshed in a minute."

"Now for the grouse pie. By the way, Fenton, what is the matter with his Lordship? He was n't ill, was he, when he sent off that despatch to me?"

"No, sir; he was in court to-day, and he dined at the Castle, and was in excellent spirits before he went out."

"Has anything gone wrong, then, that he wanted me up so hurriedly?"

"Well, sir, it ain't so easy to say, his Lordship excites himself so readily; and mayhap he had words with some of the judges,—mayhap with his Excellency, for they 're always at him about resigning, little knowing that if they 'd only let him alone he 'd go of himself, but if they press him he 'll stay on these twenty years."

"I don't suspect he has got so many as twenty years before him."

"If he wants to live, sir, he 'll do it. Ah, you may laugh, sir, but I have known him all my life, and I never saw the man like him to do the thing he wishes to do."

"Cut me some of that beef, Fenton, and fetch me some draught beer. How these old tyrants make slaves of their servants," said he, aloud, as the man left the room,—"a slavery that enthralls mind as well as body." A gentle tap came to the door, and before Sewell could question the summons, Miss Lendrick entered. She greeted him cordially, and said how anxiously her grandfather had waited for him till midnight. "I don't know when I saw him so eager or so impatient," she said.

"Have you any clew to his reason for sending for me?" said he, as he continued to eat, and assumed an air of perfect unconcern.

"None whatever. He came into my room about two o'clock, and told me to write his message in a good bold hand; he seemed in his usual health, and his manner displayed nothing extraordinary. He questioned me about the time it would take to transmit the message from the town to your house, and seemed satisfied when I said about half an hour."

"It's just as likely, perhaps, to be some caprice,—some passing fancy."

She shook her head dissentingly, but made no reply.

"I believe the theory of this house is, 'he can do no wrong,'" said Sewell, with a laugh.

"He is so much more able in mind than all around him, such a theory might prevail; but I 'll not go so far as to say that it does."

"It's not his mind gives him his pre-eminence, Miss Lucy,—it's his temper; it's that same strong will that overcomes weaker natures by dint of sheer force. The people who assert their own way in life are not the most intellectual, they are only the best bullies."

"You know very little of grandpapa, Colonel Sewell, that's clear."

"Are you so sure of that?" asked he, with a dubious-smile.

"I *am* sure of it, or in speaking of him you would never have used such a word as bully."

"You mistake me,—mistake me altogether, young lady. I spoke of a class of people who employ certain defects of temper to supply the place of certain gifts of intellect; and if your grandfather, who has no occasion for it, chooses to take a weapon out of their armory, the worse taste his."

Lucy turned fiercely round, her face flushed, and her lip trembling. An angry reply darted through her mind, but she repressed it by a great effort, and in a faint voice she said, "I hope you left Mrs. Sewell well?"

"Yes, perfectly well, amusing herself vastly. When I saw her last, she had about half a dozen young fellows cantering on either side of her, saying, doubtless, all those pleasant things that you ladies like to hear."

Lucy shrugged her shoulders, without answering.

"Telling you," continued he, in the same strain, "that if you are unmarried you are angels, and that if married you are angels and martyrs too; and it is really a subject that requires investigation, how the best of wives is not averse to hearing her husband does not half estimate her. Don't toss your head so impatiently, my dear Miss Lucy; I am giving you the wise precepts of a very thoughtful life."

"I had hoped, Colonel Sewell, that a very thoughtful life might have brought forth pleasanter reflections." "No, that is precisely what it does not do. To live as long as I have, is to arrive at a point when all the shams have been seen through, and the world exhibits itself pretty much as a stage during a day rehearsal."

"Well, sir, I am too young to profit by such experiences, and I will wish you a very good-night,—that is, if I can give no orders for anything you wish."

"I have had everything. I will finish this Madeira—to your health—and hope to meet you in the morning, as beautiful and as trustful as I see you now,—*felice notte*." He bowed as he opened the door for her to pass out, and she went, with a slight bend of the head and a faint smile, and left him.

"How I could make you beat your wings against your cage, for all your bravery, if I had only three days here, and cared to do it," said he, as he poured the rest of the wine into his glass. "How weary I could make you of this old house and its old owner. Within one month—one short month—I 'd have you repeating as wise saws every sneer and every sarcasm that you just now took fire at. And if I am to pass three days in this dreary old dungeon, I don't see how I could do better. What can he possibly want with me?" All the imaginable contingencies he could conjure up now passed before his mind. That the old man was sick of solitude, and wanted him to come and live with them; that he was desirous of adopting one of the children, and which of them? then, that he had held some correspondence with Fossbrooke, and wanted some explanations,—a bitter pang, that racked and tortured him while he revolved it; and, last of all, he came back to his first guess,—it was about his will he had sent for him. He had been struck by the beauty of the children, and asked their names and ages twice or thrice over; doubtless he was bent on making some provision for them. "I wish I could tell him that I'd rather have ten thousand down, than thrice the sum settled on Reginald and the girls. I wish I could explain to him that mine is a ready-money business, and that cash is the secret of success; and I wish I could show him that no profits will stand the reverses of loans raised at two hundred per cent! I wonder how the match went off to-day; I'd like to have the odds that there were three men down at the double rail and bank." Who got first over the brook, was his next speculation, and where was Trafford? "If he punished Crescy, I think I could tell *that*," muttered he, with a grin of malice. "I only wish I was there to see it;" and in the delight this thought afforded he tossed off his last glass of wine, and rang for his bedroom candle.

"At what time shall I call you, sir?" asked the butler.

"When are you stirring here,—I mean, at what hour does Sir William breakfast?"

"He breakfasts at eight, sir, during term; but he does not expect to see any one but Miss Lucy so early."

"I should think not. Call me at eleven, then, and bring me some coffee and a glass of rum when you come. Do you mean to tell me," said he, in a somewhat stern tone, "that the Chief Baron gets up at seven o'clock?"

"In term-time, sir, he does every day."

"Egad! I'm well pleased that I have not a seat on the Bench. I'd not be Lord Chancellor at that price."

"It's very hard on the servants, sir,—very hard indeed."

"I suppose it is," said Sewell, with a treacherous twinkle of the eye.

"If it wasn't that I'm expecting the usher's place in the Court, I'd have resigned long ago."

"His Lordship's pleasant temper, however, makes up for everything, Fenton, eh?"

"Yes, sir, that's true;" and they both laughed heartily at the pleasant conceit; and in this merry humor they went their several ways to bed.

CHAPTER XXXII
MORNING AT THE PRIORY

Sewell was awoke from a sound and heavy sleep by the Chief Baron's valet asking if it was his pleasure to see his Lordship before he went down to Court, in which case there was not much time to be lost.

"How soon does he go?" asked Sewell, curtly.

"He likes to be on the Bench by eleven exactly, sir, and he has always some business in Chamber first."

"All that tells me nothing, my good friend. How much time have I now to catch him in before he starts?"

"Half an hour, sir. Forty minutes, at most."

"Well, I 'll try and do it. Say I 'm in my bath, and that I 'll be with him immediately."

The man was not well out of the room when Sewell burst out into a torrent of abuse of the old Judge and his ways: "His inordinate vanity, his consummate conceit, to imagine that any activity of an old worn-out intellect like his could be of service to the public! If he knew but all, he is just as useful in his nightcap as in his wig, and it would be fully as dignified to sleep in his bed as in the Court of Exchequer." While he poured forth this invective, he dressed himself with all possible haste; indeed his ill-temper stimulated his alacrity, and he very soon issued from his room, trying to compose his features into a semblance of pleasure on meeting with his host.

"I hope and trust I have not disturbed you unreasonably," said the Judge, rising from the breakfast-table, as Sewell entered. "I know you arrived very late, and I 'd have given you a longer sleep if it were in my power."

"An old soldier, my Lord, knows how to manage with very little. I am only sorry if I have kept you waiting."

"No man ever presumed to keep me waiting, sir. It is a slight I have yet to experience."

"I mean, my Lord, it would have grieved me much had I occasioned you an inconvenience."

"If you had, sir, it might have reacted injuriously upon yourself."

Sewell bowed submissively, for what he knew not; but he surmised that as there was an opening for regret, there might also be a reason for gratitude; he waited to see if he were right.

"My telegram only told you that I wanted you; it could not say for what," continued the Judge; and his voice still retained the metallic ring the late irritation had lent it.

"There has been a contested question between the Crown and myself as to the patronage to an office in my Court. I have carried my point. They have yielded. They would have me believe that they have submitted out of deference to myself personally, my age, and long services. I know better, sir. They have taken the opinion of the Solicitor-General in England, who, with no flattering opinion of what is called 'Irish law,' has pronounced against them. The gift of the office rests with me, and it is my intention to confer it upon *you*."

"Oh, my Lord, I have no words to express my gratitude!"

"Very well, sir, it shall be assumed to have been expressed. The salary is one thousand a year. The duties are almost nominal."

"I was going to ask, my Lord, whether my education and habits are such as would enable me to discharge these duties?"

"I respect your conscientious scruple, sir. It is creditable and commendable. Your mind may, however, be at ease. Your immediate predecessor passed the last thirteen years at Tours, in France, and there was never a complaint of official irregularity till, three years ago, when he came over to afford his substitute a brief leave of absence, he forgot to sign his name to certain documents,—a mistake the less pardonable that his signature formed his whole and sole official drudgery."

It was on Sewell's lips to say, "that if *he* had not signed his name a little too frequently in life, his difficulties would not have been such as they now were."

"I am afraid I did not catch what you said, sir," said the Judge.

"I did not speak, my Lord," replied he, bowing.

"You will see, therefore, sir, that the details of your official life need not deter you, although I have little doubt the Ministerial press will comment sharply upon your absence, if you give them the opportunity, and will reflect severely upon your unfitness, if they can detect a flaw in you. Is there anything, therefore, in your former life to which these writers can refer—I will not say disparagingly—but unpleasantly?"

"I am not aware, my Lord, of anything."

"Of course, sir, I could not mean what might impugn your honor or affect your fame. I spoke simply of what soldiers are, perhaps, more exposed to than civilians,—the lighter scandals of society. You apprehend me?"

"I do, my Lord; and, I repeat that I have a very easy conscience on this score: for though I have filled some rather responsible stations at times, and been intrusted with high functions, all my tastes and habits have been so domestic and quiet—I have been so much more a man of home than a man of pleasure—that I have escaped even the common passing criticisms bestowed on people who are before the world."

"Is this man—this Sir Brook Fossbrooke—one likely to occasion you any trouble?"

"In the first place, my Lord, he is out of the country, not very likely to return to it; and secondly, it is not in his power—not in any man 's power—to make me a subject for attack."

"You are fortunate, sir; more fortunate than men who have served their country longer. It will scarcely be denied that I have contributed to the public service, and yet, sir, *I* have been arraigned before the bar of that insensate jury they call Public Opinion, and it is only in denying the jurisdiction I have deferred the award."

Sewell responded to the vainglorious outburst by a look of admiring wonder, and the Judge smiled a gracious acceptance of the tribute. "I gather, therefore, sir, that you can accept this place without fear of what scandal or malignity may assail you by—"

"Yes, my Lord, I can say as much with confidence."

"It is necessary, sir, that I should be satisfied on this-head. The very essence of the struggle between the Crown and myself is in the fact that *my* responsibility is pledged, *my* reputation is in bond for the integrity and the efficiency of this officer, and I will not leave to some future biographer of the Irish Chief Barons of the Exchequer the task of apology for one who was certainly not the least eminent of the line."

"Your Lordship's high character shall not suffer through me," said Sewell, bowing respectfully.

"The matter, then, is so far settled; perhaps, however, you would like to consult your wife? She might be averse to your leaving the army."

"No, my Lord. She wishes—she has long wished it. We are both domestic in our tastes, and we have always-been looking to the time when we could live more for each other, and devote ourselves to the education of our children."'

"Commendable and praiseworthy," said the Judge, with a half grunt, as though he had heard something of this-same domesticity and home-happiness, but that his own experiences scarcely corroborated the report. "There are-certain steps you will have to take before leaving the service; it may, then, be better to defer your public nomination to this post till they be taken?"

This, which was said in question, Sewell answered at once, saying, "There need be no delay on this score, my Lord; by this day week I shall be free."

"On this day week, then, you shall be duly sworn in. Now, there is another point—I throw it out simply as a suggestion—you will not receive it as more if you are indisposed to it. It may be some time before you can find a suitable house or be fully satisfied where to settle down. There is ample room here; one entire wing is unoccupied. May I beg to place it at your disposal?"

"Oh, my Lord, this is really too much kindness. You overwhelm me with obligations. I have never heard of such generosity."

"Sir, it is not all generosity,—I reckon much on the value of your society. Your companionable qualities are gifts I would secure by a 'retainer.'"

"In your society, my Lord, the benefits would be all on my side."

"There was a time, sir,—I may say it without boastful-ness,—men thought me an agreeable companion. The three Chiefs, as we were called from our separate Courts, were reputed to be able talkers. I am the sole survivor; and it would be a gain to those who care to look back on the really great days of Ireland, if some record should remain of a time when there were giants in the land. I have myself some very curious materials—masses of letters and such-like—which we may turn over some winter's evening together."

Sewell professed his delight at such a prospect; and the Judge then, suddenly bethinking himself of the hour,—it was already nigh eleven,— arose. "Can I set you down anywhere? Are you for town?" asked he.

"Yes, my Lord; I was about to pay my mother a visit."

"I'll drop you there; perhaps you would convey a message from me, and say how grateful I should feel if she would give us her company at dinner,—

say seven o'clock. I will just step up to say good-bye to my granddaughter, and be with you immediately."

Sewell had not time to bethink him of all the strange events which a few minutes had grouped around him, when the Chief Baron appeared, and they set out.

As they drove along, their converse was most agreeable. Sewell's attentive manner was an admirable stimulant, and the old Judge was actually sorry to lose his companion, as the carriage stopped at Lady Lendrick's door.

"What on earth brought you up, Dudley?" said she, as he entered the room where she sat at breakfast.

"Let me have something to eat, and I'll tell you," said he, seating himself at table, and drawing towards him a dish of cutlets. "You may imagine what an appetite I have when I tell you whose guest I am."

"Whose?"

"Your husband's."

"You! at the Priory! and how came that to pass?"

"I told you already I must eat before I talk. When I got downstairs this morning, I found the old man just finishing his breakfast, and instead of asking me to join him, he entertained me with the siege of Derry, and some choice anecdotes of Lord Bristol and 'the Volunteers.' This coffee is cold."

"Ring, and they'll bring you some."

"If I am to take him as a type of Irish hospitality as well as Irish agreeability, I must say I get rid of two delusions together."

"There's the coffee. Will you have eggs?"

"Yes, and a rasher along with them. You can afford to be liberal with the larder, mother, for I bring you an invitation to dine."

"At the Priory?"

"Yes; he said seven o'clock."

"Who dines there?"

"Himself and his granddaughter and I make the company, I believe."

"Then I shall not go. I never do go when there's not a party."

"He's safer, I suppose, before people?"

"Just so. I could not trust to his temper under the temptation of a family circle. But what Drought you to town?"

"He sent for me by telegraph; just, too, when I had the whole county with me, and was booked to ride a match I had made with immense trouble. I got his message,—'Come up immediately.' There was not the slightest reason for haste, nor for the telegraph at all. The whole could have been done by letter, and replied to at leisure, besides—"

"What was it, then?"

"It is a place he has given me,—a Registrarship of something in his Court, that he has been fighting the Castle people about for eighteen years, and to which Heaven knows if he has the right of appointment this minute."

"What's it worth?"

"A thousand a year net. There were pickings,—at least, the last man made a good thing of them,—but there are to be no more. We are to inaugurate, as the newspapers say, a reign of integrity and incorruptibility."

"So much the better."

"So much the worse," say I. "My motto is, Full batta and plenty of loot; and it's every man's motto, only that every man is not honest enough to own it."

"And when are you to enter upon the duties of your office?"

"Immediately. I 'm to be sworn in—there's an oath, it seems—this day week, and we 're to take up our abode at the Priory till we find a house to suit us."

"At the Priory?"

"Yes. May I light a cigarette, mother: only one? He gave the invitation most royally. A whole wing is to be at our disposal. He said nothing about the cook or the wine-cellar, and these are the very ingredients I want to secure."

She shook her head dubiously, but made no answer.

"You don't think, then, that he meant to have us as his guests?"

"I think it unlikely."

"How shall I find out? It's quite certain I 'll not go live under his roof—which means his surveillance—without an adequate compensation. I 'll only consent to being bored by being fed."

"House-rent is something, however."

"Yes, mother, but not everything. That old man would be inquiring who dined with me, how late he stayed, who came to supper, and what they did afterwards. Now, if he take the whole charge of us, I 'll put up with a great deal, because I could manage a little *'pied à terre'* somewhere about Kingstown or Dalkey, and 'carry on' pleasantly enough. You must find out his intentions, mother, before I commit myself to an acceptance. You must, indeed."

"Take my advice, Dudley, and look out for a house at once. You 'll not be in *his* three weeks."

"I can submit to a great deal when it suits me, mother," said he, with a derisive smile, and a look of intense treachery at the same time.

"I suppose you can," said she, nodding in assent. "How is she?"

"As usual," said he, with a shrug of the shoulders.

"And the children?"

"They are quite well. By the way, before I forget it, don't let the Judge know that I have already sent in my papers to sell out. I want him to believe that I do so now in consequence of his offer."

"It is not likely we shall soon meet, and I may not have an opportunity of mentioning the matter."

"You 'll come to dinner to-day, won't you?"

"No."

"You ought, even out of gratitude on *my* account. It would be only commonly decent to thank him."

"I could n't."

"Couldn't what? Couldn't come, or couldn't thank him?".

"Could n't do either. You don't know, Dudley, that whenever our intercourse rises above the common passing courtesies of mere acquaintanceship, it is certain to end in a quarrel. We must never condemn or approve. We must never venture upon an opinion, lest it lead to a discussion, for discussion means a fight."

"Pleasant, certainly,—pleasant and amiable too!"

"It would be better, perhaps, that I had some of that happy disposition of my son," said she, with a cutting tone, "and could submit to whatever suited me."

He started as if he had seen something, and turning on her a look of passionate anger, began: "Is it from *you* that this should come?" Then suddenly recollecting himself, he subdued his tone, and said: "We 'll not do better by losing our tempers. Can you put me in the way to raise a little money? I shall have the payment for my commission in about a fortnight; but I want a couple of hundred pounds at once."

"It's not two months since you raised five hundred."

"I know it, and there's the last of it. I left Lucy ten sovereigns when I came away, and this twenty pounds is all that I now have in the world."

"And all these fine dinners and grand entertainments that I have been told of,—what was the meaning of them?"

"They were what the railway people call 'preliminary expenses,' mother. Before one can get fellows to come to a house where there is play, there must be a sort of easy style of good living established that all men like: excellent dinners and good wine are the tame elephants, and without them you'll not get the wild ones into your 'compounds.'"

"And to tell me that this could pay!"

"Ay, and pay splendidly. If I had three thousand pounds in the world to carry on with, I'd see the old Judge and his rotten place at Jericho before I'd accept it. One needs a little capital, that's all. It's just like blockade-running,—you must be able to lose three for one you succeed with."

"I see nothing but ruin—disreputable ruin—in such a course."

"Come down and look at it, mother, and you'll change your mind. You 'll own you never saw a better ordered society in your life,—the *beau idéal* of a nice country-house on a small scale. I admit our *chef* is not a Frenchman, and I have only one fellow out of livery; but the thing is well done, I promise you. As for any serious play, you'll never hear of it—never suspect it—no more than a man turning over Leech's sketches in a dentist's drawing-room suspects there's a fellow getting his eye-tooth extracted in the next room."

"I disapprove of it all, Dudley. It is sure to end ill."

"For that matter, mother, so shall I! All I have asked from Fate this many a year is a deferred sentence; a long day, my Lord,—a long day!"

"Tell Sir William I am sorry I can't dine at the Priory to-day. It is one of my cruel headache-days. Say you found me looking very poorly. It puts him in good-humor to hear it; and if you can get away in the evening, come in to tea."

"You will think of this loan I want,—won't you?"

"I'll think of it, but I don't know what good thinking will do." She paused, and after a few minutes' silence, said, "If you really are serious about taking up your abode at the Priory, you'll have to get rid of the granddaughter."

"We could marry her off easily enough."

"You might, and you mightn't. If she marry to Sir William's satisfaction, he'll leave her all he has in the world."

"Egad, he must have a rare taste in a son-in-law if he likes the fellow I 'll promote to the place."

"You seem to forget, Dudley, that the young lady has a will of her own. She's a Lendrick too."

"With all my heart, mother. She 'll not be a match for Lucy."

"And would *she*—"

"Ay, would she," interrupted he, "if her pride as a woman—if her jealousy was touched. I have made her do more than that when I wounded her self-love!"

"You are a very amiable husband, I must say."

"We might be better, perhaps, mother; but I suspect we are pretty much like our neighbors. And it's positive you won't come to dinner?"

"No! certainly not."

"Well, I 'll try and look in at tea-time. You 'll not forget what I spoke of. I shall be in funds in less than three weeks."

She gave a little incredulous laugh as she said "Goodbye!" She had heard of such pledges before, and knew well what faith to attach to them.

CHAPTER XXXIII
EVENING AT THE PRIORY

The Chief Baron brought his friend Haire back from Court to dine with him. The table had been laid for five, and it was only when Sewell entered the drawing-room that it was known Lady Lendrick had declined the invitation. Sir William heard the apology to the end; he even waited when Sewell concluded, to see if he desired to add anything more, but nothing came.

"In that case," said he, at length, "we 'll order dinner." That his irritation was extreme needed no close observation to detect, and the bell-rope came down with the pull by which he summoned the servant.

The dinner proceeded drearily enough. None liked to adventure on a remark which might lead to something unpleasant in discussion, and little was spoken on any side. Sewell praised the mutton, and the Chief Baron bowed stiffly. When Haire remarked that the pale sherry was excellent, he dryly told the butler to "fill Mr. Haire's glass;" and though Lucy, with more caution, was silent, she did not escape, for he turned towards her and said, "We have not been favored with a word from your lips, Miss Lendrick; I hope these neuralgic headaches are not becoming a family affection."

"I am perfectly well, sir," said she, with a smile.

"It is Haire's fault, then," said the Judge, with one of his malicious twinkles of the eye, — "all Haire's fault if we are dull. It is ever so with wits, Colonel Sewell; they will not perform to empty benches."

"I don't know whom you call a wit," began Haire.

"My dear friend, the men of pleasantry and happy conceits must no more deny the reputation that attaches to them than must a rich merchant dishonor his bill; nor need a man resent more being called a Wit, than being styled a Poet, a Painter, a Chief Baron, or" —here he waved his hand towards Sewell, and bowing slightly, added—"a Chief Registrar to the Court of Exchequer."

"Oh, have you got the appointment?" said Haire to the Colonel. "I am heartily glad of it. I 'm delighted to know it has been given to one of the family."

"As I said awhile ago," said the Judge, with a smile of deeper malice, "these witty fellows spare nobody! At the very moment he praises the sherry he disparages the host. Why should not this place be filled by one of my family, Haire? I call upon you to show cause."

"There's no reason against it. I never said there was. Nay, I was far from satisfied with you on the day you refused my prayer on behalf of one belonging to you."

"Sir, you are travelling out of the record," said the Judge, angrily.

"I can only say," added Haire, "that I wish Colonel Sewell joy with all my heart; and if he 'll allow me, I 'll do it in a bumper."

"'A reason fair to drink his health again!' That 's not the line. How does it go, Lucy? Don't you remember the verse?"

"No, sir; I never heard it."

"'A reason fair,—a reason fair.' I declare I believe the newspapers are right. I am losing my memory. One of the scurrilous rascals t'other day said they saw no reason Justice should be deaf as well as blind. Haire, was that yours?"

"A thousand a year," muttered Haire to Sewell.

"What is that, Haire?" cried the old Judge. "Do I hear you aright? You utter one thousand things just as good every year?"

"I was speaking of the Registrar's salary," said Haire, half testily.

"A thousand a year is a pittance,—a mere pittance, sir, in a country like England. It is like the place at a window to see a procession. You may gaze on the passing tide of humanity, but must not dare to mix in it."

"And yet papa went half across the globe for it," said Lucy, with a flushed and burning cheek.

"In your father's profession the rewards are less money, Lucy, than the esteem and regard of society. I have ever thought it wise of our rulers not to bestow titles on physicians, but to leave them the unobtrusive and undistinguished comforters of every class and condition. The equal of any,—the companion of all."

It was evident that the old Judge was eager for discussion on anything. He had tried in vain to provoke each of his guests, and he was almost irritable at the deference accorded him.

"Do I see you pass the decanter, Colonel Sewell? Are you not drinking any wine?"

"No, my Lord."

"Perhaps you like coffee? Don't you think, Lucy, you could give him some?"

"Yes, sir. I shall be delighted."

"Very well. Haire and I will finish this magnum, and then join you in the drawing-room."

Lucy took Sewells arm and retired. They were scarcely well out of the room when Sewell halted suddenly, and in a voice so artificial that, if Lucy had been given to suspectfulness, she would have detected at once, said, "Is the Judge always as pleasant and as witty as we saw him today?"

"To-day he was very far from himself; something, I 'm sure, must have irritated him, for he was not in his usual mood."

"I confess I thought him charming; so full of neat reply, pleasant apropos, and happy quotation."

"He very often has days of all that you have just said, and I am delighted with them."

"What an immense gain to a young girl—of course, I mean one whose education and tastes have fitted her for it—to be the companion of such a mind as his! Who is this Mr. Haire?"

"A very old friend. I believe he was a schoolfellow of grandpapa's."

"Not his equal, I suspect, in ability or knowledge."

"Oh, nothing like it; a most worthy man, respected by every one, and devotedly attached to grandpapa, but not clever."

"The Chief, I remarked, called him witty," said Sewell with a faint twinkle in his eye.

"It was done in jest. He is fond of fathering on him the smart sayings of the day, and watching his attempts to disown them."

"And Haire likes that?"

"I believe he likes grandpapa in every mood he has."

"What an invaluable friend! I wish to Heaven he could find such another for me. I want—there 's nothing I want more than some one who would always approve of me."

"Perhaps you might push this fidelity further than grandpapa does," said she, with a smile.

"You mean that it might not always be so easy to applaud *me*."

She only laughed, and made no effort to disclaim the assertion.

"Well," said he, with a sigh, "who knows but if I live to be old and rich I may be fortunate enough to have such an accommodating friend? Who are the other 'intimates' here? I ask because we are going to be domesticated also."

"I heard so this morning."

"I hope with pleasure, though you have n't said as much."

"With pleasure, certainly; but with more misgiving than pleasure."

"Pray explain this."

"Simply that the very quiet life we lead here would not be endurable by people who like the world, and whom the world likes. We never see any one, we never go out, we-have not even those second-hand glances at society that people have who admit gossiping acquaintances; in fact, regard what you have witnessed to-day as a dinner-party, and then fashion for yourself our ordinary life."

"And do *you* like it?"

"I know nothing else, and I am tolerably happy. If papa and Tom were here, I should be perfectly happy."

"By Jove! you startle me," said he, throwing away the unlighted cigar he had held for some minutes in his fingers; "I did n't know it was so bad."

"It is possible he may relax for you and Mrs. Sewell; indeed, I think it more than likely that he will."

"Ay, but the relaxation might only be in favor of a few more like that old gent we had to-day. No, no; the thing will never work. I see it at once. My mother said we could not possibly stand it three weeks, and I perceive it is your opinion too."

"I did not say so much," said she, smiling.

"Joking apart," said he, in a tone that assuredly bespoke sincerity, "I could n't stand such a dinner as we had to-day very often. I can bear being bullied, for I was brought up to it. I served on Rolffe's staff in Bombay for four years, and when a man has been an aide-de-camp he knows what being bullied means; but what I could not endure is that outpouring of conceit mingled with rotten recollections. Another evening of it would kill me."

"I certainly would not advise your coming here at that price," said she, with a gravity almost comical.

"The difficulty is how to get off. He appears to me to resent as an affront everything that differs from his own views."

"He is not accustomed to much contradiction."

"Not to any at all!"

The energy with which he said this made her laugh heartily, and he half smiled at the situation himself.

"They are coming upstairs," said she; "will you ring for tea?—the bell is beside you."

"Oh, if they 're coming I 'm off. I promised my mother a short visit this evening. Make my excuses if I am asked for;" and with this he slipped from the room and went his way.

"Where's the Colonel, Lucy? Has he gone to bed?"

"No, sir, he has gone to see his mother; he had made some engagement to visit her this evening."

"This new school of politeness is too liberal for my taste. When we were young men, Haire, we would not have ventured to leave the house where we had dined without saluting the host."

"I take it we must keep up with the spirit of our time." "You mistake, Haire,—it is the spirit of our time is in arrear. It is that same spirit lagging behind, and deserting the post it once occupied, makes us seem in default. Let us have the cribbage-board, Lucy. Haire has said all the smart things he means to give us this evening, and I will take my revenge at the only game at which I am his master. Haire, who reads men like a book, Lucy," continued the Chief, as he dealt the cards, "says that our gallant friend will rebel against our humdrum life here. I demur to the opinion,—what say you?" But he was now deep in his game, and never heeded the answer.

CHAPTER XXXIV
SEWELL'S TROUBLES

"A letter for you by the post, sir, and his Lordship's compliments to say he is waiting breakfast," were the first words which Sewell heard the next morning.

"Waiting breakfast! Tell him not to wait,—I mean, make my respects to his Lordship, and say I feel very poorly to-day,—that I think I 'll not get up just yet."

"Would you like to see Dr. Beattie, sir? He's in the drawing-room."

"Nothing of the kind. It's a complaint I caught in India; I manage it myself. Bring me up some coffee and rum in about an hour, and mind, don't disturb me on any account till then. What an infernal house!" muttered he, as the man withdrew. "A subaltern called up for morning parade has a better life than this. Nine o'clock only! What can this old ass mean by this pretended activity? Upon whom can it impose? Who will believe that it signifies a rush whether he lay abed till noon or rose by daybreak?" A gentle tap came to the door, but as he made no reply there came after a pause another, a little louder. Sewell still preserved silence, and at last the sound of retiring footsteps along the corridor. "Not if I know it," muttered he to himself, as he turned round and fell off asleep again.

"The coffee, sir, and a despatch; shall I sign the receipt for you?" said the servant, as he reappeared about noon.

"Yes; open the window a little, and leave me."

Leaning on his arm, he tore open the envelope and glanced at the signature,—"Lucy." He then read, "Send down Eccles or Beattie by next train; he is worse." He read and re-read this at least half-a-dozen times over before he bethought him of the letter that lay still unopened on the bed.

He now broke the seal; it was also from his wife, dated the preceding evening, and very brief:—

"Dear Dudley,—Captain Trafford has had a severe fall. Cressy balked at the brook and fell afterwards. Trafford was struck on the head as he rose by Mr. Creagh's horse. It is feared the skull is fractured. You are much blamed for having asked him to ride a horse so much under his weight. All have refused to accept their bets but Kinshela the grocer. I have written to Sir H. Trafford, and I telegraphed to him Dr. Tobin's opinion, which is not favorable. I suppose you will come back at once; if not, telegraph what you advise to be done. Mr. Balfour is here still, but I do not find he is of much use. The veterinary decided Crescy should be shot, as the plate-bone, I think he called it, was fractured; and as he was in great pain, I consented. I hope I have done right.—Yours truly,

"Lucy Sewell."

"Here's a go! a horse I refused four hundred and fifty for on Tuesday last! I *am* a lucky dog, there 's no denying it. I did n't know there was a man in Europe could have made that horse balk his fence. What a rumpus to make about a fellow getting a 'cropper'! My share of the disaster is a deuced deal the worst. I 'll never chance on such a horse again. How am I to find either of these men?" muttered he, as he took up the telegram. He rang the bell violently, and scarcely ceased to pull at it till the servant entered.

"Where does Dr. Eccles live?"

"Sir Gilbert, sir?"

"Ay, if he be Sir Gilbert."

"Merrion Square, sir," said the man reproachfully, for he thought it rather hard to ignore one of the great celebrities of the land.

"Take this note to him, that I 'll write now, and if he be from home go to the other man,—what's his name?—Beattie."

"Dr. Beattie is coming to dinner to-day, sir," said the servant, thinking to facilitate matters.

"Just do as I tell you, my good fellow, and don't interrupt. If I am to take up my quarters here, you'll all of you have to change some of your present habits." As he spoke, he dashed off a few hasty lines, addressing them to Sir Gilbert Eccles or Dr. Beattie. "Ask if it's 'all right;' that will be sufficient reply; and now send me my bath." As he proceeded with his dressing,—a very lengthy affair it always was,—he canvassed with himself whether or not he ought to take the train and go down to the country with the doctor. Possibly few men in such circumstances would have given the matter a doubt. The poor fellow who had incurred the mishap had been, at his insistence, acting for him. Had it not been for Se well's pressing this task upon him, Trafford would at that moment have been hale and hearty. Sewell knew all this well; he read the event just as nineteen out of every twenty would have read it, but having done so, he proceeded to satisfy himself why all these reasonings should give way to weightier considerations.

First of all, it would not be quite convenient to let the old Judge know anything of these doings in the country. His strait-laced notions might revolt at races and betting-rings. It might not be perhaps decorous that a registrar of a high court should be the patron of such sports. These were prudential reasons, which he dilated on for some time. Then came some, others more sentimental. It was to a house of doctors and nurses and gloom and sorrow he should go back. All these were to him peculiarly distasteful. He should be tremendously "bored" by it all, and being "bored" was to him whatever was least tolerable in life. It was strange that there was one other reason stronger than all these,—a reason that really touched him in what was the nearest thing in his nature to heart. He couldn't go back and look at the empty loose-box where his favorite horse once stood, and where he was never to stand more. Cressy the animal he was so proud of,—the horse he counted on for who knows what future triumphs,—the first steeplechase horse, he felt convinced, in Ireland, if not in the kingdom,—such strength, such power in the loins, such square joints, such courage, should he ever see united again? If there was anything in that man's nature that represented affection, he had it for this horse. He knew well to what advantage he looked when on his back,—he knew what admiration and envy it drew upon him to see him thus mounted. He had won him at billiards from a man who was half broken-hearted at parting with him, and who offered immense terms rather than lose him.

"He said I'd have no luck with him," muttered Sewell, now in his misery,—"and, confound the fellow! he was right. No, I can't go back to look at his empty stall. It would half kill me."

It was very real grief, all this; he was as thoroughly heart-sore as it was possible for him to be. He sorrowed for what nothing in his future life could replace to him; and this is a very deep sorrow.

Trafford's misfortune was so much the origin and cause of his own disaster that he actually thought of him with bitterness. The man who could make Cressy balk! What fate could be too hard for him?

Nor was he quite easy in his mind about that passage in his wife's letter stating that men would not take their bets. Was this meant as reflecting upon him? Was it a censure on him for making Trafford ride a horse beneath his weight? "They get up some stupid cry of that sort," muttered he, "as if I am not the heaviest loser of all. I lost a horse that was worth a score of Traffords."

When dressed, Sewell went down to the garden and lit his cigar. His sorrow had grown calmer, and he began to think that in the new life before him he should have had to give up horses and sport of every kind. "I must make my book now on this old fellow, and get him to make me his heir. He cares little for his son, and he can be made to care just as little for his granddaughter. That's the only game open to me,—a dreary life it promises to be, but it's better than a jail."

The great large wilderness of a garden, stretching away into an orchard at the end, was in itself a place to suggest sombre thoughts,—so silent and forsaken did it all appear. The fruit lay thick on the ground uncared for; the artichokes, grown to the height of shrubs, looked monsters of uncouthness; and even in the alleys flower-seeds had fallen and given birth to flowers, which struggled up through the gravel and hung their bright petals over the footway. There was in the neglect, the silence, the un-cared-for luxuriance of the place, all that could make a moody man moodier; and as he knocked off the great heads of the tall hollyhocks, he thought, and even said aloud, "This is about as much amusement as such a spot offers."

"Oh no, not so bad as that," said a laughing voice; and Lucy peeped over a laurel-hedge with a rake in her hand, and seemed immensely amused at his discomfiture.

Lucy peeped over the hedge.

"Where are you?—I mean, how is one to come near you?" said he, trying to laugh, but not successfully.

"Go round yonder by the fish-pond, and you'll find a wicket. This is *my* garden, and I till it myself."

"So!" said he, entering a neat little enclosure, with beds of flowers and flowering shrubs, "this is your garden?"

"Yes,—what do you think of it?"

"It's very pretty,—it's very nice. I should like it larger, perhaps."

"So would I; but, being my own gardener, I find it quite big enough."

"Why doesn't the Chief give you a gardener?—he's rich enough, surely."

"He never cared for gardening himself. Indeed, I think it is the wild confusion of foliage here that he likes. He said to me one day, 'In *my* old garden a man loses himself in thought. In this trimly kept place one is ever occupied by the melon-frame or the forcing-house.'"

"That's the dreadful thing about old people; they are ever for making the whims and crotchets of age the rules of life to others. I wonder you bear this so well."

"I didn't know that I bore anything," said she, with a smile.

"That's true slave doctrine, I must say; and when one does not feel bondage, there's no more to be said."

"I suspect I have a great deal more freedom than most girls; my time is almost all my own, to dispose of as I will. I read, or play, or walk, or work, as I feel inclined. If I wish to occupy myself with household matters, I am the mistress here."

"In other words, you are free to do everything that is not worth doing,—you lead the life of a nun in a convent, only that you have not even a sister nun to talk to."

"And which are the things you say are worth doing?"

"Would you not care to go out into the world, to mix in society, to go to balls, theatres, fêtes, and such-like? Would you not like to ride? I don't mean it for flattery, but would you not, like the admiration you would be sure to meet,—the sort of homage people render to beauty, the only tribute the world ever paid freely,—are all these not worth something?"

"I am sure they are: they are worth a great deal to those who can enjoy them with a happy heart; but remember, Colonel Se well, I have a father living in exile, simply to earn a livelihood, and I have a brother toiling for his bread in a strange land: is it likely I could forget these, or is it likely that I could carry such cares about with me, and enjoy the pleasures you tell of?"

"Oh! as for that, I never met the man, nor woman either, that could bring into the world a mind unburdened by care. You must take life as it is. If I was to wait for a heart at ease before I went into society, I 'd have to decline a few dinner-parties. Your only chance of a little respite, besides, is at your age. The misfortunes of life begin as a little drizzle, but become a regular downpour when one gets to *my* time of life. Let me just tell you what this morning brought forth. A letter and then a telegram from my wife, to tell me that my favorite horse—an animal worth five hundred pounds if he was worth five shillings—the truest, bravest, best horse I ever backed— has just been killed by a stupid fellow I got to ride for me. What he did to make the horse refuse his leap, what magic he used, what conjuring trick he performed, I can't tell. With *me* it was enough to show him his fence, and if I wanted it I could n't have held him back. But this fellow—a dragoon, too, and the crack rider of his regiment—contrives to discourage my poor beast, then rushes him at the jump at half speed. I know it was a widish brook, and they tumbled in, and my horse smashed his blade bone,—of course there was nothing for it but to shoot him."

"How sad! I am really sorry for you."

"And all this came of the old Judge's message, the stupidity of sending me five words in a telegram, instead of writing a proper note, and saying what he wanted. But for that I 'd have stayed at home, ridden my horse, won my match, and spared myself the whole disaster."

"Grandpapa is often very hasty in his decisions, but I believe he seldom sees cause to revoke them."

"The old theory, 'The King can do no wrong,'" said Sewell, with a saucy laugh; "but remember he can often do a deal of mischief incidentally, as it were,—as on the present occasion."

"And the rider, what of him? Did he escape unhurt?" said she, eager to avoid unpleasant discussion.

"The rider! my dear young lady," said he, with affected slowness,—"the rider came to grief. What he did, or how he did it, to throw my poor horse down, is his own secret, and, from what I hear, he is likely to keep it. No, no, don't look so horrified,—he's not killed, but I don't suspect he's a long way off it. He got a smashing fall at a fence I 'd have backed myself to ride with my hands tied. Ay, and to have my good horse back again, I 'd ride in that fashion to-morrow."

"And the poor fellow, where is he now?"

"The poor fellow is receiving the very sweetest of Mrs. Sewell's attentions. He is at my house,—in all likelihood in my room,—not that he is very conscious of all the favors bestowed upon him."

"Oh, don't talk with that pretended indifference! You must be, you cannot help being, deeply sorry for what has happened."

"There can be very little doubt on that score. I've lost such a horse as I never shall own again."

"Pray think of something beside your horse. Who was he? What's his name?"

"A stranger,—an Englishman; you never heard of him; and I wish I had never heard of him!"

"What are you smiling at?" said she, after a pause, for he stood as though reflecting, and a very strange half-smile moved his mouth.

"I was just thinking," said he, gravely, "what his younger brother ought to give me; for this fellow was an elder son, and heir to a fine estate too."

She turned an indignant glance towards him, and moved away. He was quickly after her, however, and, laying his hand on her arm, said good-humoredly: "Come, don't be angry with me. I 'm sorry, if you like,—I 'm very sorry for this poor fellow. I won't say that my own loss does not dash my sorrow with a little anger,—he was such a horse! and the whole thing was such a blunder! as fair a brook,—with a high bank, it's true,—but as fair a fence as ever & man rode at, and ground like this we 're walking over to take off from."

"Is he in danger?"

"I believe so; here's what my wife says. Oh, I haven't got the letter about me, but it comes to this, I was to send down one of the best doctors by the first train, telling him it was a case of compression or concussion, which is it? And so I have despatched Beattie, your grandfather's man. I suppose there 's no better?"

"But why have you not gone back yourself? He was a friend, was he not?"

"Yes, he was what people would call a friend. I 'm like the hare in the fable, I have many friends; but if I must be confidential, I 'll tell you why I did not go. I had a notion, just as likely to be wrong as right, that the Chief would take offence at his Registrar being a sporting character, and that if I were to absent myself just now, he'd find out the reason, whereas by staying here I could keep all quiet, and when Beattie came back I could square him."

"You could what?"

"A thousand pardons for my bit of slang; but the fact is, just as one talks French when he wants to say nothings, one takes to slang when one requires to be shifty. I meant to say, I could manage to make the doctor hold his tongue."

"Not if grandpapa were to question him."

Sewell smiled, and shook his head in dissent.

"No, no. You're quite mistaken in Dr. Beattie; and what's more, you 're quite mistaken in grandpapa too, if you imagine that he 'll think the better of you for forgetting the claims of friendship."

"There was none."

"Well, of humanity, then! It was in *your* cause this man suffered, and it is in *your* house he lies ill. I think you ought to be there also."

"Do you think so?"

"I 'm sure of it. You know the world a great deal better than I do, and you can tell what people will say of your absence; but I think it requires no knowledge of more than one's own nature to feel what is right and proper here."

"Indeed!" said he, reflectingly.

"Don't you agree with me?"

"Perhaps,—that is, in part. I suppose what you mean about the world is, that there will be some scandal afloat, the 'young wife' story, and all that sort of balderdash?"

"I really do not understand you."

"You don't?"

"No. Certainly not. What do you mean?"

"Possibly you did not understand me. Well, if I am to go, there 's no time to be lost. It's four o'clock already, and the last train leaves at five-forty. I will go."

"You are quite right."

"You 'll make my excuses to the Chief. You 'll tell him that my wife's message was so alarming that I could not delay my departure. Beattie will probably be back tomorrow, and bring you news of us."

"Won't you write a few lines?"

"I 'm not sure,—I 'll not promise. I'm a bad penman, but my wife will write, I 've no doubt. Say all sorts of affectionate and dutiful things to the Chief for me; tell him I went away in despair at not being able to say good-bye; he likes that style of thing, does n't he?"

"I don't think he cares much for 'that style of thing,'" said she, with a saucy smile.

"What a capital mimic you are! Do you know I am just beginning to suspect that you are, for all your quiet simplicity of manner, a deuced deep one. Am I right?"

She shook her head, but made no reply.

"Not that I'd like you the less for it," said he, eagerly; "on the contrary, we'd understand each other all the better; there's nothing like people talking the same language, eh?"

"I hope you'll not lose your train," said she, looking at her watch; "I am half-past four."

"A broad hint," said he, laughing; "bye-bye,—*à bientôt.*"

CHAPTER XXXV
BEATTIE'S RETURN

The old Chief sat alone in his dining-room over his wine. If somewhat fatigued by the labors of the day,—for the Court had sat late,—he showed little of exhaustion; still less was he, as his years might have excused, drowsy or heavy. He sat bolt upright in his chair, and by an occasional gesture of his hand, or motion of his head, seemed as though he were giving assent to some statement he was listening to, or making his comments on it as it proceeded.

The post had brought a letter to Lucy just as dinner was over. It bore the post-mark "Cagliari," and was in her brother's hand; and the old man, with considerate kindness, told her to go to her room and read it. "No, my dear child," said he, as she arose to leave the room; "no! I shall not be lonely,—where there is memory there are troops of friends. Come back and tell me your news when you have read your letter."

More than an hour passed over, and he sat there heedless of time. A whole long life was passing in review before him, not connectedly, or in due sequence of events, but in detached scenes and incidents. Now it was some stormy night in the old Irish House, when Flood and Grattan exchanged their terrific denunciations and insults,—now it was a brilliant dinner at Ponsonby's, with all the wits of the day,—now he was leading the famous Kitty O'Dwyer, the beauty of the Irish Court, to her carriage, amid such a murmur of admiration as made the progress a triumph; or, again, it was a raw morning of November, and he was driving across the park to be present at Curran's meeting with Egan.

A violent ring of the hall bell startled him, and before he could inquire the cause a servant had announced Dr. Beattie.

"I thought I might be fortunate enough to catch you before bed-hour," said the doctor, "and I knew you would like to hear some tidings of my mission."

"You have been to—Where have you been?" said the old Judge, embarrassed between the late flood of his recollections and the sudden start of his arrival.

"To Killaloe, to see that poor fellow who had the severe fall in the hurdle-race."

"Ay—to be sure—yes. I remember all now. Give me a moment, however." He nodded his head twice or thrice, as if concurring with some statement, and then said, "Go on, sir; the Court is with you."

Beattie proceeded to detail the accident and the state of the sufferer,— of whom he pronounced favorably,—saying that there was no fracture, nor anything worse than severe concussion. "In fact," said he, "were it an hospital case, I'd say there was very little danger."

"And do you mean to tell me, sir," said the Judge, who had followed the narrative with extreme attention, "that the man of birth and blood must succumb in any conflict more readily than the low-born?"

"It's not the individual I was thinking of, so much as his belongings here. What I fear for in the present case is what the patient must confront every day of his convalescence."

Seeing that the Judge waited for some explanation, Beattie began to relate that, as he had started from Dublin the day before, he found himself in the same carriage with the young man's mother, who had been summoned by telegraph to her son's bedside.

"I have met," said he, "in my time, nearly all sorts and conditions of people. Indeed, a doctor's life brings him into contact with more maladies of nature and temperament than diseases of material origin; but anything like this woman I never saw before. To begin: she combined within herself two qualities that seem opposed to each other,—a most lavish candor on the score of herself and her family, and an intense distrust of all the rest of mankind. She told me she was a baronet's wife; how she had married him; where they lived; what his estate was worth; how this young fellow had become, by the death of a brother, the heir to the property; and how his father, indignant at his extravagance, had disentailed the estate, to leave it to a younger son if so disposed. She showed at times the very greatest anxiety about her son's state; but at other moments just as intense an eagerness to learn what schemes and intrigues were being formed against him,—who were the people in whose house he then was, what they were, and how he came there. To all my assurances that they were persons in every respect her son's equals, she answered by a toss of the head or a saucy half-laugh. 'Irish?' asked she. 'Yes, Irish.' 'I thought so,' rejoined she; 'I told Sir Hugh I was sure of it, though he said there were English Sewells.' From this instant her distrust broke forth. All Ireland had been in a conspiracy against her family for years. She had a brother, she said it with a shiver of horror, who was cruelly beaten by an attorney in Cork for a little passing pleasantry to the man's sister; he had kissed her, or something of the kind, in a railroad carriage; and her cousin,—poor dear Cornwall is Merivale,—it was in Ireland he found that creature that got the divorce against him two years since. She went on to say that there had been a plot against her son, in the very neighborhood where he now lay ill, only a year ago,—some intrigue to involve him in a marriage, the whole details of which she threatened me with the first time we should be alone.

"Though at some moments expressing herself in terms of real affection and anxiety about her poor son, she would suddenly break off to speculate on what might happen from his death. 'You know, doctor, there is only one more boy, and if his life lapsed, Holt and the Holt estate goes to the Carringtons.'"

"An odious woman, sir,—a most odious woman; I only wonder why you continued to travel in the same carriage with her."

"My profession teaches great tolerance," said the doctor, mildly.

"Don't call tolerance, sir, what there is a better word for,—subserviency. I am amazed how you endured this woman."

"Remember—it is to'be remembered—that in my version of her I have condensed the conversation of some hours, and given you, as it were, the substance of much talking; and also that I have not attempted to convey what certainly was a very perfect manner. She had no small share of good looks, a very sweet voice, and considerable attraction in point of breeding."

"I will accept none of these as alleviations, sir; her blandishments cannot blind the Court."

"I will not deny their influence upon myself," said Beattie, gently.

"I can understand you, sir," said the Judge, pompously. "The habits of your profession teach you to swallow so much that is nauseous in a sweet vehicle, that you carry the same custom into morals."

Beattie laughed so heartily at the analogy that the old man's good-humor returned to him, and he bade him continue his narrative.

"I have not much more to tell. We reached the house by about eleven o'clock at night, and my fellow-traveller sat in the carriage till I announced her to Mrs. Sewell. My own cares called me to the sick-room, and I saw no more of the ladies till this morning, just before I came away."

"She is, then, domesticated there? She has taken up her quarters at the Sewells' house?"

"Yes. I found her maid, too, had taken possession of Colonel Sewell's dressing-room, and dispossessed a number of his chattels to make room for her own."

"It is a happy thing, a very happy thing for me, that I have not been tried by these ordeals," said the Judge, with a long-drawn breath. "I wonder how Colonel Sewell will endure it."

"I have no means of knowing; he arrived late at night, and was still in bed and asleep when I left."

"You have not told me these people's name?"

"Trafford,—Sir Hugh Beecham Trafford, of Holt-Trafford, Staffordshire."

"I have met the man, or rather his father, for it was nigh fifty years ago,—an old family, and of Saxon origin; and his wife,—who was she?"

"Her name was Merivale. Her father, I think, was Governor of Madras."

"If so, sir, she has hereditary claims for impertinence and presumption. Sir Ulysses Merivale enjoyed the proud distinction of being the most insolent man in England. It is well that you have told me who she was, Beattie, for I might have made a very fatal blunder. I was going to write to Sewell to say, 'As this is a great issue, I would advise you to bring down your mother, "special,"' but I recall my intention. Lady Lendrick would have no chance against Lady Trafford. Irish insolence has not the finish of the English article, and we put an alloy of feeling in it that destroys it altogether. Will the young man recover?"

"He is going on favorably, and I see nothing to apprehend, except, indeed, that the indiscretions of his mother may prejudice his case. She is very likely to insist on removing him; she hinted it to me as I took my leave."

"I will write to the Sewells to come up here at once. They shall evacuate the territory, and leave her in possession. As persons closely connected with my family, they must not have this outrage put upon them." He rang the bell violently, and desired the servant to request Miss Lendrick to come to him.

"She is not very well, my Lord, and has gone to her room. She told Mrs. Beales to serve your Lordship's tea when you were ready for it."

"What is this? What does all this mean?" said the old Judge, eagerly; for the idea of any one presuming to be ill without duly apprising him— without the preliminary step of ascertaining that it could not inconvenience him—was more than he was fully prepared for.

"Tell Mrs. Beales I want her," said he, as he rose and left the room. Muttering angrily as he went, he ascended the stairs and traversed the long corridor which led to Lucy's room; but before he had reached the door the housekeeper was at his side.

"Miss Lucy said she 'd like to see your Lordship, if it was n't too much trouble, my Lord."

"I am going to see her. Ask her if I may come in."

"Yes, my Lord," said Mrs. Beales from the open door. "She is awake."

"My own dear grandpapa," said Lucy, stretching out her arms to him from her bed, "how good and kind of you to come here!"

"My dear, dear child," said he, fondly; "tell me you are not ill; tell me that it is a mere passing indisposition."

"Not even so much, grandpapa. It is simply a headache. I was crying, and I was ashamed that you should see it; and I walked out into the air; and I came back again, trying to look at ease; and my head began to throb and to pain me so that I thought it best to go to bed. It was a letter I got,—a letter from Cagliari. Poor Tom has had the terrible fever of the island. He said nothing about it at first, but now he has relapsed. There are only three lines in his own hand,—the rest is from his friend. You shall see what he says. It is very short, and not very hard to read."

The old man put on his spectacles and read:—

"'My very dear Lucy.'

"Who presumes to address you in this way? 'Brook Fossbrooke?' What! is this the man who is called Sir Brook Fossbrooke? By what means have you become so intimate with a person of his character?"

"I know nothing better, nothing more truly noble and generous, than his character," said she, holding her temples as she spoke, for the pain of' her head was almost agony. "Do read on,—read on, dearest grandpapa."

He turned again to the letter, and read it over in silence till he came to the few words in Tom's hand, which he read aloud: "Darling Lu—I shall be all right in a week. Don't fret, but write me a long—long"—he had forgotten the word "letter,"—"and love me always."

She burst into tears, as the old man read the words, for by some strange magic, the syllables of deep affection, uttered by one unmoved, smite the heart with a pang that is actual torture.

"I will take this letter down to Beattie, Lucy, and hear what he says of it," said the old man, and left the room.

"Read this, Beattie, and tell me what you say to it," said the Chief Baron, as he handed the doctor Sir Brook's letter; "I'll tell you of the writer when you have read it."

Beattie read the note in silence, and as he laid it on the table said, "I know the man, and his strange old-fashioned writing would have recalled him without his name."

"And what do you know of him, sir?" asked the Judge, sternly.

"I can tell you the story in three words: He came to consult me one morning, about six or eight months ago. It was about an insurance on his life,—a very small sum he wanted to raise, to go out to this very place he writes from. He got to talk about the project, and I don't exactly know how it came about,—I forget the details now,—but it ended by my lending him the money myself."

"What, sir! do you combine usury with physic?"

"On that occasion I appear to have done so," said Beattie, laughing.

"And you advanced a sum of money to a man whom you saw for the first time, simply on his showing that his life was too insecure to guarantee repayment?"

"That puts the matter a little too nakedly."

"It puts it truthfully, sir, I apprehend."

"If you mean that the man impressed me so favorably that I was disposed to do him a small service, you are right."

"You and I, Beattie, are too old for this impulsive generosity,—too old by thirty years! After forty philanthropy should take a chronic form, and never have paroxysms. I think I am correct in my medical language."

"Your medicine pleases me more than your morality," said Beattie, laughing; "but to come back to this Sir Brook, I wish you had seen him."

"Sir, I have seen him, and I have heard of him, and if not at liberty to say what I have heard of him, it is quite enough to state that *my* information cannot corroborate *your* opinion."

"Well, my Lord, the possibility of what I might hear will not shake the stability of what I have seen. Remember that we doctors imagine we read human nature by stronger spectacles than the laity generally."

"You imagine it, I am aware, sir; but I have met with no such instances of acuteness amongst your co-professionals as would sustain the claim; but why are we wandering from the record? I gave you that letter to read that you might tell me, is this boy's case a dangerous one?"

"It is a very grave case, no doubt; this is the malaria fever of Sardinia,— bad enough with the natives, but worse with strangers. He should be removed to better air at once if he could bear removal."

"So is it ever with your art," said the Judge, in a loud declamatory voice. "You know nothing in your difficulties but a piteous entreaty to the unknown resources of nature to assist you. No, sir; I will not hear your defence; there is no issue before the Court. What sort of practitioners have they in this island?"

"Rude enough, I can believe."

"Could a man of eminence be found to go out there and see him?"

"A man in large practice could not spare the time; but there are men of ability who are not yet in high repute: one of these might be possibly induced."

"And what might the expense be?"

"A couple of hundred—say three hundred pounds, would perhaps suffice."

"Go upstairs and see my granddaughter. She is very nervous and feverish; calm her mind so far as you are able; say that we are concerting measures for her brother's benefit; and by the time you shall come down again I will have made up my mind what to do."

Beattie was a valued friend of Lucy's, and she was glad to see him enter her room, but she would not suffer him to speak of herself; it was of poor Tom alone she would talk. She heard with delight the generous intentions of her grandfather, and exclaimed with rapture,—"This is his real nature, and yet it is only by the little foibles of his temper that the world knows him; but we, doctor,—we, who see him as he is, know how noble-hearted and affectionate he can be!"

"I must hasten back to him," said Beattie, after a short space; "for should he decide on sending out a doctor, I must lose no time, as I must return to see this young fellow at Killaloe to-morrow."

"Oh, in my greater anxieties I forgot him! How is he,—can he recover?"

"Yes, I regard him as out of danger,—that is, if Lady Trafford can be persuaded not to talk him into a relapse."

"Lady Trafford! who is she?"

"His mother; she arrived last night."

"And his name is Trafford, and his Christian name Lionel?"

"Lionel Wentworth Trafford. I took it from his dressing-case when I prescribed for him."

Lucy had been leaning on her arm as she spoke, but she now sank slowly backward and fainted.

It was a long time before consciousness came back, and even then she lay voiceless and motionless, and, though she heard what Beattie said to her, unable to speak to him, or intimate by a gesture that she heard him.

The doctor needed no confidences,—he read the whole story. There are expressions in the human face which have no reference to physical ills; nor are there any indications of bodily suffering. He who asked, "Canst thou minister to a mind diseased?" knew how hopeless was his question; and this very despair it is—this sense of an affliction beyond the reach of art—gives a character to the expression which the doctor's eye never fails to discriminate from the look worn by mere malady.

As she lay there motionless, her large eyes looking at him with that expression in which eagerness struggles against debility, he saw how he had become her confidant.

"Come, my dear child," said he, taking her hand between both his own, "you have no occasion for fears on this score,—so far I assure you on my honor."

She gave his hand a slight, a very slight pressure, and tried to say something, but could not. "I will go down now, and see what is to be done about your brother." She nodded, and he continued: "I will pay you another visit to-morrow early, before I leave town, and let me find you strong and hearty; and remember that though I force no confidences, Lucy, I will not refuse them if you offer."

"I have none, sir,—none," said she, in a voice of deep melancholy.

"So that I know all that is to be known?" asked he.

"All, sir," said she, with a trembling lip.

"Well, accept me as a friend whom you may trust, my dear Lucy. If you want me, I will not fail you; and if you have no need of me, there is nothing that has passed to-day between us ever to be remembered,—you understand me?"

"I do, sir. You will come to-morrow, won't you?"

He nodded assent, and left her.

CHAPTER XXXVI
AN EXIT

Colonel Sewell stood at the window of a small drawing-room he called "his own," watching the details of loading a very cumbrous travelling-carriage which was drawn up before the door. Though the postilions were in the saddle, and all ready for a start, the process of putting up the luggage went on but slowly,—now a heavy imperial would be carried out, and after a while taken in again; dressing-boxes carefully stowed away would be disinterred to be searched for some missing article; bags, baskets, and boxes of every shape and sort came and went and came again; and although the two footmen who assisted these operations showed in various ways what length of training had taught them to submit to in the way of worry and caprice, the smart "maid," who now and then appeared to give some order, displayed most unmistakable signs of ill-humor on her face. "Drat those dogs! I wish they were down the river!" cried she, of two yelping, barking Maltese terriers, which, with small bells jingling on their collars, made an uproar that was perfectly deafening.

"Well, Miss Morris, if it would oblige *you*—" said one of the tall footmen, as he caressed his whisker, and gave a very languishing look, more than enough, he thought, to supply the words wanting to his sentence.

"It would oblige *me* very much, Mr. George, to get away out of this horrid place. I never did—no, never—in all my life pass such a ten days."

"We ain't a-going just yet, after all," said footman number two, with a faint yawn.

"It's so like you, Mr. Breggis, to say something disagreeable," said she, with a toss of her head.

"It's because it's true I say it, not because it's onpleasant, Miss Caroline."

"I'm not Miss Caroline, at least from you, Mr. Breggis."

"Ain't she haughty,—ain't she fierce?" But his colleague would not assent to this judgment, and looked at her with a longing admiration.

"There's her bell again," cried the girl; "as sure as I live, she's rung forty times this morning;" and she hurried back to the house.

"Why do you think we're not off yet?" asked George.

"It's the way I heerd her talking that shows me," replied the other. "Whenever she 's really about to leave a place she goes into them fits of laughing and crying and screaming one minute, and a-whimpering the next; and then she tells the people—as it were, unknownst to her—how she hated them all,—how stingy they was,—the shameful way they starved the servants, and such-like. There's some as won't let her into their houses by reason of them fits, for she'll plump out everything she knows of a family,—who ran away with the Misses, and why the second daughter went over to France."

"You know her better than me, Breggis."

"I do think I does; it's eight years I 've had of it. Eh, what's that,—was n't that a screech?" and as he spoke a wild shrill scream resounded through the house, followed by a rapid succession of notes that might either have been laughter or crying.

Sewell drew the curtain; and wheeling an arm-chair to the fireside, lit his cigar, and began to smoke.

The house was so small that the noises could be heard easily in every part of it; and for a time the rapid passage of persons overhead, and the voices of many speaking together, could be detected, and, above these, a wild shriek would now and then rise above all, and ring through the house. Sewell smoked on undisturbed; it was not easy to say that he so much as heard these sounds. His indolent attitude, and his seeming enjoyment of his cigar, indicated perfect composure; nor even when the door opened, and his wife entered the room, did he turn his head to see who it was.

"Can William have the pony to go into town?" asked she, in a half-submissive voice.

"For what?"

"To tell Dr. Tobin to come out; Lady Trafford is taken ill."

"He can go on foot; I may want the pony."

"She is alarmingly ill, I fear,—very violent spasms; and I don't think there is any time to be lost."

"Nobody that makes such a row as that can be in any real danger."

"She is in great pain, at all events."

"Send one of her own people,—despatch one of the postboys,—do what you like, only don't bore *me*."

She was turning to leave the room, when he called out, "I say, when the attack came on did she take the opportunity to tell you any pleasant little facts about yourself or your family?" She smiled faintly, and moved towards the door. "Can't you tell me, ma'am? Has this woman been condoling with you over your hard fate and your bad husband? or has she discovered how that 'dear boy' upstairs broke his head as well as his heart in your service?"

"She did ask me certainly if there was n't a great friendship between you and her son," said she, with a tone of quiet disdain.

"And what did you reply?" said he, throwing one leg over the arm of the chair as he swung round to face her.

"I don't well remember. I may have said *you* liked *him*, or that *he* liked *you*. It was such a commonplace reply I made, I forget it."

"And was that all that passed on the subject?"

"I think I'd better send for the doctor," said she, and left the room before he could stop her, though that such was his intention was evident from the way he arose from his chair with a sudden spring.

"You shall hear more of this, Madam,—by Heaven, you shall!" muttered he, as he paced the room with rapid steps. "Who's that? Come in," cried he, as a knock came to the door. "Oh, Balfour! is it you?"

"Yes; what the deuce is going on upstairs? Lady Trafford appears to have gone mad."

"Indeed! how unpleasant!"

"Very unpleasant for your wife, I take it. She has been saying all sorts of unmannerly things to her this last hour,—things that, if she were n't out of her reason, she ought to be thrown out of the window for."

"And why didn't you do so?"

"It was a liberty I couldn't think of taking in another man's house."

"Lord love you, I'd have thought nothing of it! I'm the best-natured fellow breathing. What was it she said?"

"I don't know how I can repeat them."

"Oh, I see, they reflect on me. My dear young friend, when you live to my age you will learn that anything can be said to anybody, provided it only be done by 'the third party.' Whatever the law rejects as evidence, assumes in social life the value of friendly admonition. Go on, and tell me who it is is in love with my wife."

Cool as Mr. Cholmondely Balfour was, the tone of this demand staggered him.

"Art thou the man, Balfour?" said Sewell at last, staring at him with a mock frown.

"No, by Jove! I never presumed that far."

"It's the sick fellow, then, is the culprit?"

"So his mother opines. She is an awful woman! I was sitting with your wife in the small drawing-room when she burst into the room and cried out, 'Mrs. Sewell, is your name Lucy? for, if so, my son has been rambling on about you this last hour in a wonderful way: he has told me about fifty times that he wants to see you before he dies; and now that the doctor says he is out of danger he never ceases talking of dying. I suppose you have no objection to the interview; at least they tell me you were constantly in his room before my arrival.'"

"How did my wife take this?—what did she say?" asked Sewell, with an easy smile as he spoke.

"She said something about agitation or anxiety serving to excuse conduct which otherwise would be unpardonable; and she asked me to send her maid to her,—as I think, to get me away."

"Of course you rang the bell and sat down again."

"No; she gave me a look that said, I don't want you here, and I went; but the storm broke out again as I closed the door, and I heard Lady Trafford's voice raised to a scream as I came downstairs."

"It all shows what I have said over and over again," said Sewell, slowly, "that whenever a man has a grudge or a grievance against a woman, he ought always to get another woman to torture her. I'll lay you fifty pounds Lady Traf-ford cut deeper into my wife's flesh by her two or three impertinences than if I had stormed myself into an apoplexy."

"And don't you mean to turn her out of the house?"

"Turn whom out?"

"Lady Trafford, of course."

"It's not so easily done, I suspect. I'll take to the long-boat myself one of these days, and leave her in command of the ship."

"I tell you she's a dangerous, a very dangerous woman; she has been ransacking her son's desk, and has come upon all sorts of ugly memoranda,—sums lost at play, and reminders to meet bills, and such-like."

"Yes; he was very unlucky of late," said Sewell, coldly.

"And there was something like a will, too; at least there was a packet of trinkets tied up in a paper, which purported to be a will, but only bore the name Lucy."

"How delicate! there's something touching in that, Balfour; isn't there?" said Sewell, with a grin. "How wonderfully you seem to have got up the case! You know the whole story. How did you manage it?"

"My fellow Paxley had it from Lady Trafford's maid. She told him that her mistress was determined to show all her son's papers to the Chief Baron, and blow you sky high."

"That's awkward, certainly," said Sewell, in deep thought. "It would be a devil of a conflagration if two such combustibles came together. I 'd rather she 'd fight it out with my mother."

"Have you sent in your papers to the Horse Guards?"

"Yes; it's all finished. I am gazetted out, or I shall be on Tuesday."

"I'm sorry for it. Not that it signifies much as to this registrarship. We never intended to relinquish our right to it, we mean to throw the case into Chancery, and we have one issue already to submit to trial at bar."

"Who are *we* that are going to do all this?"

"The Crown," said Balfour, haughtily.

"*Ego et rex meus*; that's the style, is it? Come now, Balfy, if you 're for a bet, I 'll back my horse, the Chief Baron, against the field. Give me sporting odds, for he 's aged, and must run in bandages besides."

"That woman's coming here at this moment was most unlucky."

"Of course it was; it would n't be *my* lot if it were anything else. I say," cried he, starting up, and approaching the window, "what's up now?"

"She's going at last, I really believe."

The sound of many and heavy footsteps was now heard descending the stairs slowly, and immediately after two men issued from the door, carrying young Trafford on a chair; his arms hung listlessly at his side, and his head was supported by his servant.

"I wonder whose doing is this? Has the doctor given his concurrence to it? How are they to get him into the coach, and what are they to do with him when he is there?" Such was the running commentary Balfour kept up all the time they were engaged in depositing the sick man in the carriage.

Again a long pause of inaction ensued, and at last a tap came to the door of the room, and a servant inquired for Mr. Balfour.

"There!" cried Sewell, "it's *your* turn now. I only hope she 'll insist on your accompanying her to town."

Balfour hurried out, and was seen soon afterwards escorting Lady Trafford to the carriage. Whether it was that she was not yet decided as to her departure, or that she had so many injunctions to give before going, the eventful moment was long delayed. She twice tried the seat in the carriage, once with cushions and then without. She next made Balfour try whether it might not be possible to have a sort of inclined plane to lie upon. At length she seemed overcome with her exertions, sent for a chair, and had a glass of water given her, to which her maid added certain drops from a phial.

"You will tell Colonel Sewell all I have said, Mr. Balfour," said she, aloud, as she prepared to enter the carriage. "It would have been more agreeable to me had he given me the opportunity of saying it to himself, but his peculiar notions on the duties of a host have prevented this. As to Mrs. Sewell, I hope and believe I have sufficiently explained myself. She at least knows my sentiments as to what goes on in this house. Of course, sir, it is very agreeable to *you*. Men of pleasure are not persons to be overburdened with scruples,—least of all such scruples as interfere with self-indulgence. This sort of life is therefore charming; I leave you to all its delights, sir, and do not even warn you against its dangers. I will not promise the same discretion, however, when I go hence. I owe it to all mothers who have sons, Mr. Balfour,—I owe it to every family in which there is a name to be transmitted, and a fortune to be handed down, to declare what I have witnessed under this roof. No, Lionel,—no, my dear boy; nothing shall prevent my speaking out." This was addressed to her son, who by a deep sigh seemed to protest against the sentiments he was not able to oppose. "It may suit Mr. Balfour's habits, or his tastes, to remain here,—with these I have nothing to do. The Duke of Bayswater might possibly think his heir could keep better company,—with that I have no concern; though when the matter comes to be discussed before me,—as it one day will, I have no doubt,—I shall hold myself free to state my opinion. Good-bye, sir; you will, perhaps, do me the favor to call at the Bilton; I shall remain till Saturday there; I have resolved not to leave Ireland till I see the Viceroy; and also have a meeting with this Judge, I forget his name, Lam—Lena—what is it? He is the Chief something, and easily found."

A few very energetic words, uttered so low as to be inaudible to all but Balfour himself, closed this address.

"On my word of honor,—on my sacred word of honor,—Mr. Balfour," said she, aloud as she placed one foot on the step, "Caroline saw it,—saw it with her own eyes. Don't forget all I have said; don't drop that envelope; be sure you come to see me." And she was gone.

"Give me five minutes to recover myself," said Balfour, as he entered Sewell's room, and threw himself on a sofa; "such a 'breather' as that I have not had for many a day."

"I heard a good deal of it," said Sewell, coolly. "She screams, particularly when she means to be confidential; and all that about my wife must have reached the gardener in the shrubbery. Where is she off to?"

"To Dublin. She means to see his Excellency and the Chief Baron; she says she can't leave Ireland till she has unmasked all your wickedness."

"She had better take a house on a lease then; did you tell her so?"

"I did nothing but listen,—I never interposed a word. Indeed, she won't let one speak."

"I 'd give ten pounds to see her with the Chief Baron. It would be such a 'close thing.' All his neat sparring would go for nothing against her; for though she hits wide, she can stand a deal of punishment without feeling it."

"She 'll do you mischief there."

"She might," said he, more thoughtfully. "I think I 'll set my mother at her; not that she 'll have a chance, but just for the fun of the thing. What 's the letter in your hand?"

"Oh, a commission she gave me. I was to distribute this amongst your household;" and he drew forth a banknote. "Twenty pounds! you have no objection to it, have you?"

"I know nothing about it; of course you never hinted such a thing to me;" and with this he arose and left the room.

CHAPTER XXXVII
A STORMY MOMENT

Within a week after the first letter came a second from Cagliari. It was but half a dozen lines from Tom himself.

"They are sending me off to a place called Maddalena, dearest Lucy, for change of air The priest has given me his house, and I am to be Robinson Crusoe there, with an old hag for Friday,—how I wish for you! Sir Brook can only come over to me occasionally. Look out for three rocks—they call them islands—off the N. E. of Sardinia; one of them is mine.—Ever your own,

"Tom L."

Lucy hastened down with this letter in her hand to her grandfather's room, but met Mr. Haire on the stairs, who whispered in her ear, "Don't go in just yet, my dear; he is out of sorts this morning; Lady Lendrick has been here, and a number of unpleasant letters have arrived, and it is better not to disturb him further."

"Will you take this note," said she, "and give it to him at any fitting moment? I want to know what I shall reply,—I mean, I 'd like to hear if grandpapa has any kind message to send the poor fellow."

"Leave it with me. I 'll take charge of it, and come up to tell you when you can see the Judge." Thus saying, he passed on, and entered the room where the Chief Baron was sitting. The curtains were closely drawn, and in one of the windows the shutters were closed,—so sensitive to light was the old man in his periods of excitement. He lay back in a deep chair, his eyes closed, his face slightly flushed, breathing heavily, and the fingers of one hand twitching slightly at moments; the other was held by Beattie, as he counted the pulse. "Dip that handkerchief in the cold lotion, and lay it over his forehead," whispered Beattie to Haire.

"Speak out, sir; that muttering jars on my nerves, and irritates me," said the Judge, in a slow firm tone.

"Come," said Beattie, cheerfully, "you are better now; the weakness has passed off."

"There is no weakness in the case, sir," said the old man, sitting bolt upright in the chair, as he grasped and supported himself by the arms. "It is the ignoble feature of your art to be materialist. You can see nothing in humanity but a nervous cord and a circulation."

"The doctor's ministry goes no further," said Beattie, gently.

"Your art is then but left-handed, sir. Where 's Haire?"

"Here, at your side," replied Haire.

"I must finish my story, Haire. Where was it that I left off? Yes; to be sure,—I remember now. This boy of Sewell's—Reginald Victor Sewell—was, with my permission, to take the name of Lendrick, and be called Reginald Victor Sewell Lendrick."

"And become the head of your house?"

"The head of my house, and my heir. She did not say so, but she could not mean anything short of it."

"What has your son done to deserve this?" asked Haire, bluntly.

"My son's rights, sir, extend but to the modest fortune I inherited from my father. Whatever other property I possess has been acquired by my own ability and labor, and is mine to dispose of."

"I suppose there are other rights as well as those of the statute-book?"

"Listen to this, Beattie," cried the old Judge, with a sparkle of the eye,— "listen to this dialectician, who discourses to me on the import of a word. It is not generous I must say, to come down with all the vigor of his bright, unburdened faculties upon a poor, weak, and suffering object like myself. You might have waited, Haire, till I had at least the semblance of power to resist you."

"What answer did you give her?" asked Haire, bluntly.

"I said,—what it is always safe to say,—'Le roi s'avisera.' Eh, Beattie? this is the grand principle of your own craft. Medicine is very little else than 'the wisdom of waiting.' I told her," continued he, "I would think of it,—that I would see the child. 'He is here,' said she, rising and leaving the room, and in a few moments returned, leading a little boy by the hand,—a very noble-looking child, I will say, with a lofty head and a bold brow. He met me as might a prince, and gave his hand as though it were an honor he bestowed. What a conscious power there is in youth! Ay, sirs, that is the real source of all the much-boasted vigor and high-heartedness. Beattie will tell us some story of arterial action or nervous expansion; but the mystery lies deeper. The conscious force of a future development imparts a vigor that all the triumphs of after life pale before."

"'*Fiat justitia, ruât coelum,*'" said Haire,—"I'd not provide for people out of my own family."

"It is a very neat though literal translation, sir, and, like all that comes from you, pointed and forcible."

"I'd rather be fair and honest than either," said Haire, bluntly.

"I appeal to you, Beattie, and I ask if I have deserved this;" and the old Judge spoke with an air of such apparent sincerity as actually to impose upon the doctor. "The sarcasms of this man push my regard for him to the last intrenchment."

"Haire never meant it; he never intended to reflect upon you," said Beattie, in a low tone.

"He knows well enough that I did not," said Haire, half sulky; for he thought the Chief was pushing his raillery too far.

"I 'm satisfied," said the Judge, with a sigh. "I suppose he can't help it. There are fencers who never believe they have touched you till they see the blood. Be it so; and now to go back. She went away and left the child with me, promising to take him up after paying a visit she had to make in the neighborhood. I was not sorry to have the little fellow's company. He was most agreeable, and, unlike Haire, he never made me his butt. Well, I have done; I will say no more on that head. I was actually sorry when she came to fetch him, and I believe I said so. What does that grunt mean, Haire?"

"I did not speak."

"No, sir; but you uttered what implied an ironical assent,—a *nisi prius* trick,—like the leer I have seen you bestow upon the jury-box. How hard it is for the cunning man to divest himself of the subtlety of his calling!"

"I want to hear how it all ended," muttered Haire.

"You shall hear, sir, if you will vouchsafe me a little patience. When men are in the full vigor of their faculties, they should be tolerant to those footsore and weary travellers who, like myself, halt behind and delay the march. But bear in mind, Haire, I was not always thus. There was a time when I walked in the van. Ay, sir, and bore myself bravely too. I was talking with that child when they announced Mr. Balfour, the private secretary, a man most distasteful to me; but I told them to show him in, curious, indeed, to hear what new form of compromise they were about to propose to me. He had come with a secret and confidential message from the Viceroy, and really seemed distressed at having to speak before a child of six years old, so mysterious and reserved was he. He made a very long story of it,—full an hour; but the substance was this: The Crown had been advised to dispute my right of appointment to the registrarship, and to make a case for a jury; but—mark the 'but'—in consideration for my high name and great services, and in deference to what I might be supposed to feel from an open collision with the Government, they were still willing for an accommodation, and would consent to ratify any appointment I should make, other than that of the gentleman I had already named,—Colonel Sewell.

"Self-control is not exactly the quality for which my friends give me most credit. Haire, there, will tell you I am a man of ungovernable temper, and who never even tried to curb his passion; but I would hope there is some injustice in this award. I became a perfect dove in gentleness, as I asked Balfour for the reasons which compelled his Excellency to make my stepson's exclusion from office a condition. 'I am not at liberty to state them,' was the cool reply. 'They are personal, and, of course, delicate?' asked I, in a tone of submission, and he gave a half assent in silence. I concurred,—that is, I yielded the point. I went even further. I hinted, vaguely of course, at the courteous reserve by which his Excellency was willing to spare me such pain as an unpleasant disclosure—if there were such—might occasion me. I added, that old men are not good subjects for shocks; and I will say, sirs, that he looked at me as I spoke with a compassionate pity which won all my gratitude! Ay, Beattie, and though my veins swelled at the temples, and I felt a strange rushing sound in my ears, I had no fit, and in a moment or two was as calm as I am this instant.

"'Let me be clear upon this point,' said I to him. 'I am to nominate to the office any one except Sewell, and you will confirm such nomination?' 'Precisely,' replied he. 'Such act on my part in no way to prejudice whatever claim I lay to the appointment in perpetuity, or jeopardize any rights I now assert?' 'Certainly not,' said he. 'Write it,' said I, pushing towards him a pen and paper; and so overjoyed was he with his victorious negotiation that he wrote word for word as I dictated. When I came to the name Sewell, I added, 'To whose nomination his Excellency demurs, on grounds of character and conduct sufficient in his Excellency's estimation to warrant such exclusion; but which, out of deference to the Chief Baron's feelings, are not set forth in this negotiation.' 'Is this necessary?' asked he, as he finished writing. 'It is,' was my reply; 'put your name at foot, and the date;' and he did so.

"I now read over the whole aloud; he winced at the concluding lines, and said, 'I had rather, with your permission, erase these last words; for though I know the whole story, and believe it too, there 's no occasion for entering upon it here.'

"As he spoke, I folded the paper and placed it in my pocket. 'Now, sir,' said I, 'let *me* hear the story you speak of.' 'I cannot. I told you before I was not at liberty to repeat it.' I insisted, and he refused. There was a positive altercation between us and he raised his voice in anger, and demanded back from me the paper which he said I had tricked him into writing. I will not say that he meant to use force, but he sprang from his chair and came towards me with such an air of menace that the boy, who was playing in the corner, rushed at him and struck him with his drumstick, saying, 'You sha'n't beat grandpapa!' I believe I rang the bell; yes, I rang the bell sharply. The child was crying when they came. I was confused and flurried. Balfour was gone."

"And the paper?" asked Haire.

"The paper is here, sir," said he, touching his breastpocket. "The country shall ring with it, or such submission shall I exact as will bring that Viceroy and his minions to my feet in abject contrition. Were you to ask me now, I know not what terms I would accept of."

"I would rather you said no more at present," said Beattie. "You need rest and quietness."

"I need reparation and satisfaction, sir; that is what I need."

"Of course—of course; but you must be strong and well to enforce it," said Beattie.

"I told Lady Lendrick to leave the child with me. She said she would bring him back to-morrow. I like the boy. What does my pulse say, Beattie?"

"It says that all this talking and agitation are injurious to you,—that you must be left alone."

The old man sighed faintly, but did not speak.

"Haire and I will take a turn in the garden, and be within call if you want us," said Beattie.

"Wait a moment,—what was it I had to say? You are too abrupt, Beattie; you snap the cords of thought by such rough handling, and we old men lose our dexterous knack of catching the loose ends, as we once did. There, there—leave me now; the skein is all tangled in hopeless confusion." He waved his hand in farewell, and they left him.

CHAPTER XXXVIII
A LADY'S LETTER

"Lucy asked me to show him this note from her brother," said Haire, as he strolled with Beattie down the lawn. "It was no time to do so. Look over it and say what you advise."

"The boy wants a nurse, not a doctor," said Beattie. "A little care and generous diet would soon bring him round; but they are a strange race, these Lendricks. They have all the stern qualities that brave danger, and they are terribly sensitive to some small wound to their self-love. Let that young fellow, for instance, only begin to feel that he is forgotten or an outcast, and he 'll droop at once. A few kind words, and a voice he loved, *now*, will do more than all my art could replace a little later."

"You mean that we ought to have him back here?" asked Haire, bluntly.

"I mean that he ought to be where he can be carefully and kindly treated."

"I 'll tell the Chief you think so. I 'll say that you dropped the remark to myself, of course,—never meaning to dictate anything to *him*."

Beattie shook his head in sign of doubt.

"I know him well, better perhaps than any one, and I know there's no more generous man breathing; but he must not be coerced,—he must not be even influenced, where the question be one for a decision. As he said to me one day, 'I want the evidence, sir, I don't want your speech to it.'"

"There 's the evidence, then," said Beattie,—"that note with its wavering letters, weak and uncertain as the fingers that traced them,—show him that. Say, if you like, that *I* read it and thought the lad's case critical. If, after that, he wishes to talk to me on the subject, I 'm ready to state my opinion. If the boy be like his father, a few tender words and a little show of interest for him will be worth all the tonics that ever were brewed."

"It's the grandfather's nature too; but the world has never known it,— probably never will know it," said Haire.

"In that I agree with you," said Beattie, dryly.

"He regards it as a sort of weakness when people discover any act of generosity or any trait of kindliness about him; and do you know," added he, confidentially, "I have often thought that what the world regarded as irritability and sharpness was nothing more nor less than shyness,—just shyness."

"I certainly never suspected that he was the victim of that quality."

"No, I imagine not. A man must know him as I do to-understand it. I remember one day, long, long ago, I went so far as to throw out a half hint that I thought he labored under this defect; he only smiled and said, 'You suspect me of diffidence. I am diffident,—no man more so, sir; but it is of the good or great qualities in other men.' Was n't that a strange reply? I never very clearly understood it,—do you?"

"I suspect I do; but here comes a message to us."

Haire spoke a word with the servant, and then, turning: to Beattie, said: "He wants to see me. I 'll just step in, and be back in a moment."

Beattie promised not to leave till he returned, and strolled along by the side of a little brook which meandered tastefully through the greensward. He had fallen into a revery,—a curious inquiry within himself whether it were a boon or an evil for a man to have acquired that sort of influence over another mind which makes his every act and word seem praiseworthy and excellent. "I wonder is the Chief the better or the worse for this indiscriminating attachment? Does it suggest a standard to attain to, or does it merely minister to self-love and conceit? Which is it? which is it?" cried he, aloud, as he stood and gazed on the rippling rivulet beside him.

"Shall I tell you?" said a low, sweet voice; and Lucy Lendrick slipped her arm within his as she spoke,—"shall I tell you, doctor?"

"Do, by all means."

"A little of both, I opine. Mind," said she, laughing, "I have not the vaguest notion of what you were balancing in your mind, but somehow I suspect unmixed good or evil is very rare, and I take my stand on a compromise. Am I right?"

"I scarcely know, but I can't submit the case to you. I have an old-fashioned prejudice against letting young people judge their seniors. Let us talk of something else. What shall it be?"

"I want to talk to you of Tom."

"I have just been speaking to Haire about him. We must get him back here, Lucy,—we really must."

"Do you mean here, in this house, doctor?"

"Here, in this house. Come, don't shake your head, Lucy. I see the necessity for it on grounds you know nothing of. Lady Lendrick is surrounding your grandfather with her family, and I want Tom back here just that the Chief should see what a thorough Lendrick he is. If your grandfather only knew the stuff that's in him, he 'd be prouder of him than of all his own successes."

"No, no, no,—a thousand times no, doctor! It would never do,—believe me, it would never do. There are things which a girl may submit to in quiet obedience, which in a man would require subserviency. The Sewells, too, are to be here on Saturday, and who is to say what that may bring forth?"

"She wrote to you," said the doctor, with a peculiar significance in his voice.

"Yes, a strange sort of note too; I almost wish I could show it to you,—I 'd so like to hear what you 'd say of the spirit of the writer."

"She told me she would write," said he again, with a more marked meaning in his manner.

"You shall see it," said she, resolutely; "here it is;" and she drew forth the letter and handed it to him. For an instant she seemed as if about to speak, but suddenly, as if changing her mind, she merely murmured, "Read it, and tell me what you think of it." The note ran thus:—

"My dearest Lucy,—We are to meet to-morrow, and I hope and trust to meet like sisters who love each other. Let me make one brief explanation before that moment arrives. I cannot tell what rumors may have reached you of all that has happened here. I know nothing of what people say, nor have I the faintest idea how our life may have been represented. If you knew me longer and better, you would know that I neither make this ignorance matter of complaint nor regret. I have lived about long enough to take the world at its just value, and not to make its judgments of such importance as can impair my self-esteem and my comfort. It would, however, have been agreeable to me to have known what you may have heard of me—of us— as it is not impossible I might have felt the necessity to add something,— to correct something,—perhaps to deny something. I am now in the dark, and pray forgive me if I stumble rudely against you, where I only meant to salute you courteously.

"You at least know the great disaster which befell here. Dr. Beattie has told you the story,—what more he may have said I cannot guess. If I were to wait for our meeting, I should not have to ask you. I should read it in your face, and hear it in every accent of your voice; but I write these few lines that you may know me at once in all frankness and openness, and know that if *you* be innocent of *my* secret, *I* at least have *yours* in my keeping. Yes, Lucy, I know all; and when I say all, I mean far more than you yourself know.

"If I were treacherous, I would not make this avowal to you. I should be satisfied with the advantage I possessed, and employ it to my benefit. Perhaps with any other woman than yourself I should play this part,—with you I neither can nor will. I will declare to you frankly and at once, you have lost the game and I have won it. That I say this thus briefly, is because in amplifying I should seem to be attempting to explain what there is no explaining. That I say it in no triumph, my own conscious inferiority to you is the best guarantee. I never would have dreamed of a rivalry had I been a girl. It is because I cannot claim the prize I have won it. It is because my victory is my misery I have gained it. I think I know your nature well enough to know that you will bear me no ill-will. I even go so far as to believe I shall have your compassion and your sympathy. I need them more, far more, than you know of. I could tell you that had matters fallen out differently it would not have been to *your* advantage, for there were obstacles—family obstacles—perfectly insurmountable. This is no pretence: on my honor I pledge to the truth of what I say. So long as I believed they might be overcome, I was in *your* interest, Lucy. You will not believe me, will you, if I swear it? Will you if I declare it on my knees before you?

"If I have not waited till we met to say these things, it is that we may meet with open hearts, in sorrow, but in sincerity. When I have told you everything, you will see that I have not been to blame. There may be much to grieve over, but there is nothing to reprehend—anywhere. And now, how is our future to be? It is for you to decide. I have not wronged you, and yet I am asking for forgiveness. Can you give me your love, and what I need as much, your pity? Can you forget your smaller affliction for the sake of my heavier one, for it is heavier?

"I plead guilty to one only treachery; and this I stooped to, to avoid the shame and disgrace of an open scandal. I told his mother that, though Lucy was my name, it was yours also; and that you were the Lucy of all his feverish wanderings. Your woman's heart will pardon me this one perfidy.

"She is a very dangerous woman in one sense. She has a certain position in the world, from which she could and would open a fire of slander on any one. She desires to injure me. She has already threatened, and she is capable of more than threatening. She says she will see Sir William. This she may not be able to do; but she can write to him. You know better than I do what might ensue from two such tempers meeting; for myself I cannot think of it.

"I have written you a long letter, dear Lucy, when I only meant to have written five or six lines. I have not courage to read it over; were I to do so, I am sure I would never send it. Perhaps you will not thank me for my candor. Perhaps you will laugh at all my scrupulous honesty. Perhaps you will—no, that you never will—I mean, employ my trustfulness against myself.

"Who knows if I have not given to this incident an importance which you will only smile at? There are people so rich that they never are aware if they be robbed. Are you one of these, Lucy? and, if so, will you forgive the thief who signs herself your ever-loving sister,

"Lucy Skwell.

"I have told Dr. Beattie I would write to you; he looked as if he knew that I might, or that I ought,—which is it? Doctors see a great deal more than they ought to see. The great security against them is, that they acquire an indifference to the sight of suffering, which, in rendering them callous, destroys curiosity, and then all ills that can neither be bled nor blistered they treat as trifles, and end by ignoring altogether. Were it otherwise,—that is, had they any touch of humanity in their nature,—they would be charming confidants, for they know everything and can go everywhere. If Beattie should be one of your pets, I ask pardon for this impertinence; but don't forget it altogether, as, one day or other, you will be certain to acknowledge its truth.

"We arrive by the 4.40 train on Saturday afternoon. If I see you at the door when we drive up, I shall take it as a sign I am forgiven."

Beattie folded the letter slowly, and handed it to Lucy without a word. "Tell me," said he, after they had walked on several seconds in silence,—"tell me, do you mean to-be at the door as she arrives?"

"I think not," said she, in a very low voice.

"She has a humble estimate of doctors; but there is one touch of nature she must not deny them,—they are very sensitive about contagion. Now, Lucy, I wish with all my heart that you were not to be the intimate associate of this woman."

"So do I, doctor; but how is it to be helped?"

He walked along silent and in deep thought.

"Shall I tell you, doctor, how it can be managed, but only by your help and assistance? I must leave this."

"Leave the Priory! but for where?"

"I shall go and nurse Tom: he needs *me*, doctor, and I believe I need *him*; that is, I yearn after that old companionship which made all my life till I came here—Come now, don't oppose this plan; it is only by your hearty aid it can ever be carried out. When you have told grandpapa that the thought is a good one, the battle will be more than half won. You see yourself I ought not to be here."

"Certainly not here with Mrs. Sewell; but there comes the grave difficulty of how you are to be lodged and cared for in that wild country where your brother lives?"

"My dear doctor, I have never known pampering till I came here. Our life at home—and was it not happy!—was of the very simplest. To go back again to the same humble ways will be like a renewal of the happy past; and then Tom and I suit each other so well,—our very caprices are kindred. Do say you like this notion, and tell me you will forward it."

"The very journey is an immense difficulty."

"Not a bit, doctor; I have planned it all. From this to Marseilles is easy enough,—only forty hours; once there, I either go direct to Cagliari, or catch the Sardinian steamer at Genoa—"

"You talk of these places as if they were all old acquaintances; but, my dear child, only fancy yourself alone in a foreign city. I don't speak of the difficulties of a new language."

"You might, though, my dear doctor. My French and Italian, which carry me on pleasantly enough with Racine and Ariosto, will expose me sadly with my 'commissionnaire.'"

"But quite alone you cannot go,—that's certain."

"I must not take a maid, that's as certain; Tom would only send us both back again. If you insist, and if grandpapa insists upon it, I will take old Nicholas. He thinks it a great hardship that he has not been carried away over seas to see the great world; and all his whims and tempers that tortured us as children will only amuse us now; his very tyranny will be good fun."

"I declare frankly," said the doctor, laughing, "I do not see how the difficulties of foreign travel are to be lessened by the presence of old Nicholas; but are you serious in all this?"

"Perfectly serious, and fully determined on it, if I be permitted."

"When would you go?"

"At once! I mean as soon as possible. The Sewells are to be here on Saturday. I would leave on Friday evening by the mail-train from London. I would telegraph to Tom to say on what day he might expect me."

"To-day is Tuesday; is it possible you could be ready?"

"I would start to-night, doctor, if you only obtain my leave."

"It is all a matter of the merest chance how your grandfather will take it," said Beattie, musing.

"But *you* approve? tell me you approve of it."

"There is certainly much in the project that I like. I cannot bear to think of your living here with the Sewells; my experience of them is very brief, but it has taught me to know there could be no worse companionship for you; but as these are things that cannot be spoken of to the Chief, let us see by what arguments we should approach him. I will go at once. Haire is with him, and he is sure to see that what I suggest has come from you. If it should be the difficulty of the journey your grandfather objects to, Lucy, I will go as far as Marseilles with you myself, and see you safely embarked before I leave you."

She took his hand and kissed it twice, but was not able to utter a word.

"There, now, my dear child, don't agitate yourself; you need all your calm and all your courage. Loiter about here till I come to you, and it shall not be long."

"What a true, kind friend you are!" said she, as her eyes grew dim with tears. "I am more anxious about this than I like to own, perhaps. Will you, if you bring me good tidings, make me a signal with your handkerchief?"

He promised this, and left her.

Lucy sat down under a large elm-tree, resolving to wait there patiently for his return; but her fevered anxiety was such that she could not rest in one place, and was forced to rise and walk rapidly up and down. She imagined to herself the interview, and fancied she heard her grandfather's stern question,—whether she were not satisfied with her home? What could he do more for her comfort or happiness than he had done? Oh, if he were to accuse her of ingratitude, how should she bear it? Whatever irritability he might display towards others, to herself he had always been kind and thoughtful and courteous.

She really loved him, and liked his companionship, and she felt that if in leaving him she should consign him to solitude and loneliness, she could scarcely bring herself to go; but he was now to be surrounded with others, and if they were not altogether suited to him by taste or habit, they would, even for their own sakes, try to conform to his ways and likings.

Once more she bethought her of the discussion, and how it was faring. Had her grandfather suffered Beattie to state the case fully, and say all that he might in its favor? or had he, as was sometimes his wont, stopped him short with a peremptory command to desist? And then what part had Haire taken? Haire, for whose intelligence the old Judge entertained the lowest possible estimate, had somehow an immense influence over him, just as instincts are seen too strong for reason. Some traces of boyish intercourse yet survived and swayed his mind with his consciousness of its power.

"How long it seems!" murmured she. "Does this delay augur ill for success, or is it that they are talking over the details of the plan? Oh, if I could be sure of that! My poor dear Tom, how I long to be near you—to care for you—and watch you!" and as she said this, a cold sickness came over her, and she muttered aloud: "What perfidy it all is! As if I was not thinking of myself, and my own sorrows, while I try to believe I am but thinking of my brother." And now her tears streamed fast down her cheeks, and her heart felt as if it would burst. "It must be an hour since he left this," said she, looking towards the house, where all was still and motionless. "It is not possible that they are yet deliberating. Grandpapa is never long in coming to a decision. Surely all has been determined on before this, and why does he not come and relieve me from my miserable uncertainty?"

At last the hall door opened, and Haire appeared; he beckoned to her with his hand to come, and then re-entered the house. Lucy knew not what to think of this, and she could scarcely drag her steps along as she tried to hasten back. As she entered the hall, Haire met her, and, taking her hand cordially, said, "It is all right; only be calm, and don't agitate him. Come in now;" and with this she found herself in the room where the old Judge was sitting, his eyes closed and his whole attitude betokening sleep. Beattie sat at his side, and held one hand in his own. Lucy knelt down and pressed her lips to the other hand, which hung over the arm of the chair. Gently drawing away the hand, the old man laid it on her head, and in a low faint voice said: "I must not look at you, Lucy, or I shall recall my pledge. You are going away!"

The young girl turned her tearful eyes towards him, and held her lips firmly closed to repress a sob, while her cheeks trembled with emotion.

"Beattie tells me you are right," continued he, with a sigh; and then, with a sort of aroused energy, he added; "But old age, amongst its other infirmities, fancies that right should yield to years. '*Ce sont les droits de la decrepitude,*' as La Rochefoucauld calls them. I will not insist upon my 'royalties,' Lucy, this time. You shall go to your brother." His hand trembled as it lay on her head, and then fell heavily to his side. Lucy clasped it eagerly, and pressed it to her cheek, and all was silent for some seconds in the room.

At last the old man spoke, and it was now in a clear distinct voice, though weak. "Beattie will tell you everything, Lucy; he has all my instructions. Let him now have yours. To-morrow we shall, both of us, be calmer, and can talk over all together. To-morrow will be Thursday?"

"Wednesday, grandpapa."

"Wednesday,—all the better, my dear child; another day gained. I say, Beattie," cried he in a louder tone, "I cannot have fallen into the pitiable condition the newspapers describe, or I could never have gained this victory over my selfishness. Come, sir, be frank enough to own that where a man combats himself, he asserts his identity. Haire will go out and give that as his own," muttered he; and as he smiled, he lay back, his breathing grew heavier and longer, and he sank into a quiet sleep.

CHAPTER XXXIX
SOME CONJUGAL COURTESIES

"You have not told me what she wrote to you," said Sewell to his wife, as he smoked his cigar at one side of the fire while she read a novel at the other. It was to be their last evening at the Nest; on the morrow they were to leave it for the Priory. "Were there any secrets in it, or were there allusions that I ought not to see?"

"Not that I remember," said she, carelessly.

"What about our coming? Does the old man seem to wish for it?—how does she herself take it?"

"She says nothing on the subject, beyond her regret at not being there to meet us."

"And why can't she?—where will she be?"

"At sea, probably, by that time. She goes off to Sardinia to her brother."

"What! do you mean to that fellow who is living with Fossbrooke? Why did n't you tell me this before?"

"I don't think I remembered it; or, if I did, it's possible I thought it could not have much interest for you."

"Indeed, Madam! do you imagine that the only things I care for are the movements of *your* admirers? Where 's this letter? I 'd like to see it."

"I tore it up. She begged me to do so when I had read it."

"How honorable! I declare you ladies conduct your intercourse with an integrity that would be positively charming to think of if only your male friends were admitted to any share of the fair dealing. Tell me so much as you can remember of this letter."

"She spoke of her brother having had a fever, and being now better, but so weak and reduced as to require great care and attention, and obliged to remove for change of air to a small island off the coast."

"And Fossbrooke,—does she mention *him?*"

"Only that he is not with her brother, except occasionally: his business detains him near Cagliari."

"I hope it may continue to detain him there! Has this-young woman gone off all alone on this journey?"

"She has taken no maid. She said it might prove inconvenient to her brother; and has only an old family servant she calls Nicholas with her."

"So, then, we have the house to ourselves so far. She 'll not be in a hurry back, I take it. Anything would be better than the life she led with her grandfather."

"She seems sorry to part with him, and recurs three or four times to his kindness and affection."

"His kindness and affection! His vanity and self-love are nearer the mark. I thought I had seen something of conceit and affectation, but that old fellow leaves everything in that line miles behind. He is, without exception, the greatest bore and the most insupportable bully I ever encountered."

"Lucy liked him."

"She did not,—she could not. It suits you women to say these things, because you cultivate hypocrisy so carefully that you carry on the game with each other! How could any one, let her be ever so abject, like that incessant homage this old man exacted,—to be obliged to be alive to his vapid jokes and his dreary stories, to his twaddling reminiscences of college success or House of Commons—Irish House too—triumphs? Do you think if I wasn't a beggar I 'd go and submit myself to such a discipline?"

To this she made no reply, and for a while there was a silence in the room. At last he said, "*You'll* have to take up that line of character that *she* acted. *You'll* have to 'swing the incense' now. I'll be shot if *I* do."

She gave no answer, and he went on: "You 'll have to train the brats too to salute him, and kiss his hand and call him—what are they to call him—grandpapa? Yes, they must say grandpapa. How I wish I had not sent in my papers! If I had only imagined I could have planted you all here, I could have gone back to my regiment and served out my time."

"It might have been better," said she, in a low voice.

"Of course it would have been better; each of us would have been free, and there are few people, be it said, take more out of their freedom,—eh, Madam?"

She shrugged her shoulders carelessly, but a slight, a very slight, flush colored her cheek.

"By the way, now we're on that subject, have you answered Lady Trafford's letter?"

"Yes," said she; and now her cheek grew crimson.

"And what answer did you send?"

"I sent back everything."

"What do you mean?—your rings and trinkets, the bracelet with the hair—mine, of course,—it could be no one's but mine."

"All, everything," said she, with a gulp.

"I must read the old woman's letter over again. You have n't burnt *that*, I hope?"

"No; it's upstairs in my writing-desk."

"I declare," said he, rising and standing with his back to the fire, "you women, and especially fine ladies, say things to each other that men never would dare to utter to other men. That old dame, for instance, charged you with what we male creatures have no equivalent for,—cheating at play would be mild in comparison."

"I don't think that *you* escaped scot-free," said she, with an intense bitterness, though her tone was studiously subdued and low.

"No," said he, with a jeering laugh. "I figured as the accessory or accomplice, or whatever the law calls it. I was what polite French ladies call *le mari complaisant,*—a part I am so perfect in, Madam, that I almost think I ought to play it for my Benefit.' What do you say?"

"Oh, sir, it is not for me to pass an opinion on your abilities."

"I have less bashfulness," said he, fiercely. "I 'll venture to say a word on *yours.* I 've told you scores of times—I told you in India, I told you at the Cape, I told you when we were quarantined at Trieste, and I tell you now— that you never really captivated any man much under seventy. When they are tottering on to the grave, bald, blear-eyed, and deaf, you are perfectly irresistible; and I wish—really I say it in all good faith—you would limit the sphere of your fascinations to such very frail humanities. Trafford only became spooney after that smash on the skull; as he grew better, he threw off his delusions,—did n't he?"

"So he told me," said she, with perfect calm.

"By Jove! that was a great fluke of mine," cried he, aloud. "That was a hazard I never so much as tried. So that this fellow had made some sort of a declaration to you?"

"I never said so."

"What was it then that you *did* say, Madam? Let us understand each other clearly."

"Oh, I am sure we need no explanations for that," said she, rising, and moving towards the door.

"I want to hear about this before you go," said he, standing between her and the door.

"You are not going to pretend jealousy, are you?" said she, with an easy laugh.

"I should think not," said he, insolently. "That is about one of the last cares will ever rob me of my rest at night. I'd like to know, however, what pretext I have to send a ball through your young friend."

"Oh, as to that peril, it will not rob *me* of a night's rest," said she, with such a look of scorn and contempt as seemed actually to sicken him, for he staggered back as though about to fall and she passed out ere he could recover himself.

"It is to be no quarter between us then! Well, be it so," cried he, as he sank heavily into a seat. "She's playing a bold game when she goes thus far." He leaned his head on the table, and sat thus so long that he appeared to have fallen asleep; indeed, the servant who came to tell him that tea was served, feared to disturb him, and retired without speaking. Far from sleeping, however, his head was racked with a maddening pain, and he kept on muttering to himself, "This is the second time—the second time she has taunted me with cowardice. Let her beware! Is there no one will warn her against what she is doing?"

"Missis says, please, sir, won't you have a cup of tea?" said the maid timidly at the door.

"No; I'll not take any."

"Missis says too, sir, that Miss Blanche is tuk poorly, and has a shiverin' over her, and a bad headache, and she hopes you 'll send in for Dr. Tobin."

"Is she in bed?"

"Yes, sir, please."

"I'll go up and see her;" and with this he arose and passed up the little stair that led to the nursery. In one bed a little dark-haired girl of about three years old lay fast asleep; in the adjoining bed a bright blue-eyed child of two years or less lay wide awake, her cheeks crimson, and the expression of her features anxious and excited. Her mother was bathing her temples with cold water as Sewell entered, and was talking in a voice of kind and gentle meaning to the child.

"That stupid woman of yours said it was Blanche," said Sewell, pettishly, as he gazed at the little girl.

"I told her it was Cary; she has been heavy all day, and eaten nothing. No, pet,—no, darling," said she, stooping over the sick child, "pa is not angry; he is only sorry that little Cary is ill."

"I suppose you'd better have Tobin to see her," said he, coldly. "I 'll tell George to take the tax-cart and fetch him out. It's well it was n't Blanche," muttered he, as he sauntered out of the room. His wife's eyes followed him as he went, and never did a human face exhibit a stronger show of repressed passion than hers, as, with closely compressed lips and staring eyes, she watched him as he passed out.

"The fool frightened me,—she said it was Blanche," were the words he continued to mutter as he went down the stairs.

Tobin arrived in due time, and pronounced the case not serious,—a mere feverish attack that only required a day or two of care and treatment.

"Have you seen Colonel Sewell?" said Mrs. Sewell, as she accompanied the doctor downstairs.

"Yes; I told him just what I 've said to you."

"And what reply did he make?"

"He said, 'All right! I have business in town, and must start to-morrow. My wife and the chicks can follow by the end of the week.'"

"It's so like him!—so like him!" said she, as though the pent-up passion could no longer be restrained.

CHAPTER XL
MR. BALFOUR'S OFFICE

On arriving in Dublin, Sewell repaired at once to Balfour's office in the Castle yard; he wanted to "hear the news," and it was here that every one went who wanted to "hear the news." There are in all cities, but more especially in cities of the second order, certain haunts where the men about town repair; where, like the changing-houses of bankers, people exchange their "credits,"—take up their own notes, and give up those of their neighbors.

Sewell arrived before the usual time when people dropped in, and found Balfour alone and at breakfast. The Under-Secretary's manner was dry, so much Sewell saw as he entered; he met him as though he had seen him the day before, and this, when men have not seen each other for some time, has a certain significance. Nor did he ask when he had come up, nor in any way recognize that his appearance was matter of surprise or pleasure.

"Well, what's going on here?" said Sewell, as he flung himself into an easy-chair, and turned towards the fire. "Anything new?"

"Nothing particular. I don't suppose you care for the Cattle Show or the Royal Irish Academy?"

"Not much,—at least, I can postpone my inquiries about them. How about my place here? Are you going to give me trouble about it?"

"Your place,—your place?" muttered the other, once or twice; and then, standing up with his back to the fire, and his skirts over his arms, he went on. "Do you want to hear the truth about this affair, or are we only to go on sparring with the gloves, eh?"

"The truth, of course, if such a novel proceeding should not be too much of a shock to you."

"No, I suspect not. I do a little of everything every day just to keep my hand in."

"Well, go on now, out with this truth."

"Well, the truth is,—I am now speaking confidentially,—if I were you I 'd not press my claim to that appointment,—do you perceive?"

"I do not; but perhaps I may when you have explained yourself a little more fully."

"And," continued he, in the same tone, and as though no interruption had occurred, "that's the opinion of Halkett, and Doyle, and Jocelyn, and the rest."

"Confidentially, of course," said Sewell, with a sneer so slight as not to be detected.

"I may say confidentially, because it was at dinner we talked it over, and we were only the household,—no guests but Byam Herries and Barrington."

"And you all agreed?"

"Yes, there was not a dissentient voice but Jocelyn's, who said, if he were in your place, he'd insist on having all the papers and letters given up to him. His view is this: 'What security have I that the same charges are not to be renewed again and again? I submit now, but am I always to submit? Are my Indian'—(what shall I call them? I forget what he called them; I believe it was escapades)—'my Indian escapades to declare me unfit to hold anything under the Crown?' He said a good deal in that strain, but we did not see it. It was hard, to be sure, but we did not see it. As Halkett said, 'Sewell has had his innings already in India. If, with a pretty wife and a neat turn for billiards, he did not lay by enough to make his declining years comfortable, I must say that he was not provident.' Doyle, however, remarked that after that affair with Loftus up at Agra—wasn't it Agra?"—Sewell nodded—"it was n't so easy for you to get along as many might think, and that you were a devilish clever fellow to do what you had done. Doyle likes you, I think." Sewell nodded again, and, after a slight pause, Balfour proceeded: "And it was Doyle, too, said, 'Why not try for something in the colonies? There are lots of places a man can go and nothing be ever heard of him. If I was Sewell, I 'd say, Make me a barrackmaster in the Sandwich Islands, or a consul in the Caraccas.'

"They all concurred in one thing, that you never did so weak a thing in your whole life as to have any dealings with Trafford. It was his mother went to the Duke—ay, into the private office at the Horse Guards—and got Clifford's appointment cancelled, just for a miserable five hundred pounds Jack won off the elder brother,—that fellow who died last year at Madeira. She's the most dangerous woman in Europe. She does not care what she says, nor to whom she says it. She 'd go up to the Queen at a drawing-room and make a complaint as soon as she 'd speak to you or me. As it is, she told their Excellencies here all that went on in your house, and I suppose scores of things that did not go on either, and said, 'And are you going to permit this man to be'—she did not remember what, but she said—'a high official under the Crown? and are you going to receive his wife amongst your intimates?' What a woman she is! To hear her you 'd think her 'dear child,' instead of being a strapping fellow of six feet two, was a brat in knickerbockers, with a hat and feather. The fellow himself must be a consummate muff to be bullied by her; but then the estate is not entailed, they say, and there's a younger brother may come into it all. His chances look well just now, for Lionel has got a relapse, and the doctors think very ill of him."

"I had not heard that," said Sewell, calmly.

"Oh, he was getting on most favorably,—was able to sit up at the window, and move a little about the room,—when, one morning Lady Trafford had driven over to the Lodge to luncheon, he stepped downstairs in his dressing-gown as he was, got into a cab, and drove off into the country. All the cabman could tell was that he ordered him to take the road to Rathfarnham, and said, 'I 'll tell you by and by where to;' and at last he said, 'Where does Sir William Lendrick live?' and though the man knew the Priory, he had taken a wrong turn and got down to ask the road. Just at this moment a carriage drove by with two grays and a postilion—A young lady was inside with an elderly gentleman, and the moment Trafford saw her he cried out, 'There she is,—that is she!' As hard as they could they hastened after; but they smashed a trace, and lost several minutes in repairing it, and as many more in finding out which way the carriage had taken. It was to Kingstown, and, as the cabman suspected, to catch the packet for Holyhead; for just as they drove up, the steamer edged away from the pier, and the carriage with the grays drove off with only the old man, Trafford fell back in a faint, and appeared to have continued so, for when they took him out of the cab at Bilton's he was insensible.

"Beattie says he'll come through it, but Maclin thinks he 'll never be the same man again; he 'll have a hardening or a softening—which is it?—of the brain, and that he'll be fit for nothing."

"Except a place in the viceregal household, perhaps. I don't imagine you want gold-medallists for your gentlemen-in-waiting?"

"We have some monstrous clever fellows, let me tell you. Halkett made a famous examination at Sandhurst, and Jocelyn wrote that article in 'Bell's Life,' 'The Badger Drawn at Last.'"

"To come back to where we were, how are you to square matters with the Chief Baron? Are you going to law with him about this appointment, or are you about to say that I am the objection? Let me have a definite answer to this question."

"We have not fully decided; we think of doing either, and we sometimes incline to do both. At all events, we are not to have it; that's the only thing certain."

"Have you got a cigar? No, not these things; I mean something that can be smoked."

"Try this," said Balfour, offering his case.

"They 're the same as those on the chimney. I must say, Balfour, the traditional hospitalities of the Castle are suffering in their present hands. When I dined here the last time I was in town, they gave me two glasses of bad sherry and one glass of a corked Gladstone; and I came to dinner that day after reading in Barrington all about the glorious festivities of the Irish Court in the olden days of Richmond and Bedford."

"Lady Trafford insists that your names—your wife's as well as your own—are to be scratched from the dinner-list. Sir Hugh has three votes in the House, and she bullies us to some purpose, I can tell you. I can't think how you could have made this woman so much your enemy. It is not dislike,—it is hatred."

"Bad luck, I suppose," said Sewell, carelessly.

"She seems so inveterate too; she'll not give you up, very probably."

"Women generally don't weary in this sort of pursuit."

"Couldn't you come to some kind of terms? Couldn't you contrive to let her know that you have no designs on her boy? You've won money of him, have n't you?"

"I have some bills of his,—not for a very large amount, though; you shall have them a bargain."

"I seldom speculate," was the dry rejoinder.

"You are right; nor is this the case to tempt you."

"They 'll be paid, I take it?"

"Paid! I'll swear they shall!" said Sewell, fiercely. "I'll stand a deal of humbug about dinner invitations, and cold salutations, and such-like; but none, sir, not one, about what touches a material interest."

"It's not worth being angry about," said Balfour, who was really glad to see the other's imperturbability give way.

"I'm not angry. I was only a little impatient, as a man may be when he hears a fellow utter a truism as a measure of encouragement. Tell your friends—I suppose I must call them your friends—that they make an egregious mistake when they push a man like me to the wall. It is intelligible enough in a woman to do it; women don't measure their malignity, nor their means of gratifying it; but *men* ought to know better."

"I incline to think I'll tell my 'friends' nothing whatever on the subject."

"That's as you please; but remember this,—if the day should come that I need any of these, details you have given me this morning, I'll quote them, and you too, as their author; and if I bring an old house about your ears, look out sharp for a falling chimney-pot! You gave me a piece of advice awhile ago," continued he, as he put on his hat before the glass, and arranged his necktie. "Let me repay you with two, which you will find useful in their several ways: Don't show your hand when you play with as shrewd men as myself; and, Don't offer a friend such execrable tobacco as that on the chimney;" and with this he nodded and strolled out, humming an air as he crossed the Castle yard and entered the city.

CHAPTER XLI
THE PRIORY IN ITS DESERTION

The old Judge was very sad after Lucy's departure from the Priory. While she lived there they had not seen much of each other, it is true. They met at meal-times, and now and then Sir William would send up the housekeeper to announce a visit from him; but there is a sense of companionship in the consciousness that under the same roof with you dwells one upon whose affection you can draw, whose sympathy will be with you in your hour of need; and this the old man now felt to be waiting; and he wandered restlessly about the house and the garden, tenacious to see that nothing she liked or loved was threatened with any change, and repeating to all that she must find everything as she left it when she came back again.

Sewell had been recalled to the country by the illness of his child, and they were not expected at the Priory for at least a week or two longer. Haire had gone on circuit, and even Beattie the Judge only saw hurriedly and at long intervals. With Lady Lendrick he had just had a most angry correspondence, ending in one of those estrangements which, had they been nations instead of individuals, would have been marked by the recall of their several envoys, but which they were satisfied to signalize by an order at the Priory gate-lodge not to admit her Ladyship's carriage, and an equally determined command at Merrion Square for the porter to take in no letters that came from the Chief Baron.

Lest the world should connect this breach with any interest in my story, I may as well declare at once the incident had no possible bearing upon it. It was a little episode entirely self-contained, and consisted in Lady Lendrick having taken advantage of Sir William's illness and confinement to house to send for and use his carriage-horses,—a liberty which he resented by a most furious letter, to which the rejoinder begot another infinitely more sarcastic,—the correspondence ending by a printed notice which her Ladyship received in an envelope, that the Chief Baron's horses would be sold on the ensuing Saturday at Dycer's to the highest bidder, his Lordship having no further use for them.

Let me own that the old Judge was sincerely sorry when this incident was concluded. So long as the contest lasted, while he was penning his epistle or waiting for the reply, his excitement rallied and sustained him. He used to sit after the despatch of one of his cutting letters calculating with himself the terror and consternation it produced, just as the captain of a frigate might have waited with eager expectancy that the smoke might drift away and show him the shattered spars or the yawning bulwarks of his enemy. But when his last missive was returned unopened, and the messenger reported that the doctor's carriage was at her Ladyship's door as he came away, the Judge collapsed at once, and all the dreariness of his deserted condition closed in upon him.

Till Sewell returned to-town, Sir William resolved not to proceed farther with respect to the registrarship. His plan, long determined upon, was to induct him into the office, administer the oaths, and leave him to the discharge of the duties. The scandal of displacing an official would, he deemed, be too great a hazard for any government to risk. At all events, if such a conflict came, it would be a great battle, and with the nation for spectators.

"The country shall ring with it," was the phrase he kept repeating over and over as he strolled through his neglected garden or his leafy shrubberies; but as he plodded along, alone and in silence, the dreary conviction would sometimes shoot across his mind that he had run his race, and that the world had wellnigh forgotten him. "In a few days more," sighed he out, "it will be over, and I shall be chronicled as the last of them." And for a moment it would rally him to recall the glorious names with which he claimed companionship, and compare them—with what disparagement!—with the celebrities of the time.

It was strange how bright the lamp of intellect would shine out as the wick was fast sinking in the socket. His memory would revive some stormy scene in the House, some violent altercation at the Bar, and all the fiery eloquence of passion would recur to him, stirring his heart and warming his blood, till he half forgot his years, and stood forth, with head erect and swelling chest, strong with a sense of power and a whole soul full of ambition.

"Beattie would not let me take my Circuit," would he say. "I wish he saw me to-day. Decaying powers! I would tell them that the Coliseum is grander in its ruin than all their stuccoed plastering in its trim propriety. Had he suffered me to go, the grand jury would have heard a charge such as men's ears have not listened to since Avonmore! Avon-more! what am I saying?—Yelverton had not half my law, nor a tenth part of my eloquence."

In his self-exaltation he began to investigate whether he was greater as an advocate or as prosecutor. How difficult to decide! After all, it was in the balance of the powers thus displayed that he was great as a judge. He recalled the opinions of the press when he was raised to the bench, and triumphantly asked aloud, had he not justified every hope and contradicted every fear that was entertained of him? "Has my learning made me intolerant, or my brilliancy led me into impatience? Has the sense of superiority that I possess rendered me less conciliatory? Has my 'impetuous genius'—how fond they were of that phrase!—carried me away into boundless indiscretions? and have I, as one critic said, so concentrated the attention of the jury on myself that the evidence went for nothing and the charge was everything?"

It was strange how these bursts of inordinate vanity and self-esteem appeared to rally and invigorate the old man, redressing, as it were, the balance of the world's injustice—such he felt it—towards him. They were like a miser's hoard, to be counted and re-counted in secret with that abiding assurance that he had wealth and riches, however others might deem him poor.

It was out of these promptings of self-love that he drew the energetic powers that sustained him, broken and failing and old as he was.

Carried on by his excited thoughts, he strayed away to a little mound, on which, under a large weeping-ash, a small bench was placed, from which a wide view extended over the surrounding country. There was a tradition of a summer-house on the spot in Curran's day, and it was referred to more than once in the diaries and letters of his friends; and the old Chief loved the place, as sacred to great memories.

He had just toiled up the ascent, and gained the top, when a servant came to present him with a card and a letter, saying that the gentleman who gave them was then at the house. The card bore the name, "Captain Trafford,—th Regiment." The letter was of a few lines, and ran thus:—

"My dear Sir William,—I had promised my friend and late patient Captain Trafford to take him over to the Priory this morning and present him to you. A sudden call has, however, frustrated the arrangement; and as his time is very brief, I have given him this as a credential to your acquaintance, and I hope you will permit him to stroll through the garden and the shrubberies, which he will accept as a great favor. I especially beg that you will lay no burden on your own strength to become his entertainer: he will be amply gratified by a sight of your belongings, of which he desires to carry the memory beyond seas.—Believe me very sincerely yours,

"J. Beattie."

"If the gentleman who brought this will do me the favor to come up here, say I shall be happy to see him."

As the servant went on his message, the old man lay back on his seat, and, closing his eyes, muttered some few dropping words, implying his satisfaction at this act of reverential homage. "A young soldier too; it speaks well for the service when the men of action revere the men of thought. I am glad it is a good day with me; he shall carry away other memories than of woods and streams. Ah! here he comes."

Slowly, and somewhat feebly, Trafford ascended the hill, and with a most respectful greeting approached the Judge.

"I thank you for your courtesy in coming here, sir," said the Chief; "and when we have rested a little, I will be your *Cicerone* back to the house." The conversation flowed on pleasantly between them, Sir William asking where Traflford had served, and what length of time he had been in Ireland,—his inquiries evidently indicating that he had not heard of him before, or, if he had, had forgotten him.

"And now you are going to Malta?"

"Yes, my Lord; we sail on the 12th."

"Well, sir, Valetta has no view to rival that. See what a noble sweep the bay takes here, and mark how well the bold headlands define the limits! Look at that stretch of yellow beach, like a golden fillet round the sea; and then mark the rich woods waving in leafy luxuriance to the shore! Those massive shadows are to landscape what times of silent thought are to our moral natures. Do you like your service, sir?"

"Yes, my Lord; there is much in it that I like. I would like it all if it were in 'activity.'"

"I have much of the soldier in myself, and the qualities by which I have gained any distinction I have won are such as make generals,—quick decision, rapid intelligence, prompt action."

Traflford bowed to this pretentions summary, but did not speak.

The old Judge went on to describe what he called the military mind, reviewing in turn the generals of note from Hannibal down to Marlborough. "What have they left us by way of legacy, sir? The game, lost or won, teaches us as much! Is not a letter of Cicero, is not an ode of Horace worth it all? And as for battle-fields, it is the painter, not the warrior, has made them celebrated. Wouvermans has done more for war than Turenne!"

"But, my Lord, there must be a large number of men like myself who make very tolerable soldiers, but who would turn out sorry poets or poor advocates."

"Give me your arm now, and I will take you round by the fish-pond and show you where the 'Monks of the Screw' held their first meeting. You have heard of that convivial club?" Trafiford bowed; and the Judge went on to tell of the strange doings of those grave and thoughtful men, who-deemed no absurdity too great in their hours of distraction and levity. When they reached the house, the old man was so fatigued that he had to sit down in the porch to rest. "You have seen all, sir; all I have of memorable. You say you 'd like to see the garden, but there is not a memory connected with it. See it, however, by all means; saunter about till I have rallied a little, and then join me at my early dinner. I 'll send to tell you when it is ready. I am sorry it will be such a lonely meal; but she who could have thrown sunshine over it is gone—gone!" And he held his hands over his face, and said no more. Trafiford moved silently away, and went in search of the garden. He soon found the little wicket, and ere many minutes was deep in the leafy solitude of the neglected spot. At last he came upon the small gate in the laurel hedge, passing through which he entered the little flower-garden. Yes, yes; there was no doubting it! This was hers! Here were the flowers she tended; here the heavy bells from which she emptied the rain-drops; here the tendrils her own hands had trained! Oh, force of love, that makes the very ground holy, and gives to every leaf and bud an abiding value! He threw himself upon the sward and kissed it. There was a little seat under a large ilex—how often had she sat there thinking!—could it be thinking over the days beside the Shannon,—that delicious night they came back from Holy Island, the happiest of all his life? Oh, if he could but believe that she loved him! if he could only know that she did not think of him with anger and resentment!—for she might! Who could tell what might have been said of his life at the Sewells'? He had made a confidante of one who assumed to misunderstand him, and who overwhelmed him with a confession of her own misery, and declared she loved him; and this while he lay in a burning fever, his head racked with pain, and his mind on the verge of wandering. Was there-ever a harder fate than his? That he had forfeited the affection of his family, that he had wrecked his worldly fortunes, seemed little in his eyes to the danger of being thought ill of by her he loved.

His father's last letter to him had been a command to leave the army and return home, to live there as became the expectant head of the house. "I will have your word of honor to abandon this ignoble passion"—so he called his love; "and in addition, your solemn pledge never to marry an Irishwoman." These words were, he well knew, supplied by his mother. It had been the incessant burden of her harangues to him during the tedious days of his recovery; and even when, on the morning of this very day, she had been suddenly recalled to England by a severe attack of illness of her husband, her last act before departure was to write a brief note to Lionel, declaring that if he should not follow her within a week, she would no longer conceive herself bound to maintain his interests against those of his more obedient and more affectionate brother.

"Won't that help my recovery, doctor?" said he, showing the kind and generous epistle to Beattie. "Are not these the sort of tonic stimulants your art envies?"

Beattie shook his head in silence, and after a long pause said, "Well, what was your reply to this?"

"Can you doubt it? Don't you know it; or don't you know *me?*"

"Perhaps I guess."

"No, but you are certain of it, doctor. The regiment is ordered to Malta, and sails on the 12th. I go with them! Holt is a grand old place, and the estate is a fine one; I wish my brother every luck with both. Will you do me a favor,—a great favor?"

"If in my power, you may be certain I will. What is it?"

"Take me over to the Priory; I want to see it. You can find some pretext to present me to the Chief Baron, and obtain his leave to wander through the grounds."

"I perceive—I apprehend," said Beattie, slyly. "There is no difficulty in this. The old Judge cherishes the belief that the spot is little short of sacred; he only wonders why men do not come as pilgrims to visit it. There is a tradition of Addison having lived there, while secretary in Ireland; Curran certainly did; and a greater than either now illustrates the locality."

It was thus that Trafford came to be there; with what veneration for the haunts of genius let the reader picture to himself!

"His Lordship is waiting dinner, sir," said a servant, abruptly, as he sat there—thinking, thinking; and he arose and followed the man to the house.

The Chief Baron had spent the interval since they parted in preparing for the evening's display. To have for his guest a youth so imbued with reverence for Irish genius and ability, was no common event. Young Englishmen and soldiers, too, were not usually of this stuff; and the occasion to make a favorable impression was not to be lost.

When he entered the dinner-room, Trafford was struck by seeing that the table was laid for three, though they were but two; and that on the napkin opposite to where he sat a small bouquet of fresh flowers was placed.

"My granddaughter's place, sir," said the old Judge, as he caught his eye. "It is reserved for her return. May it be soon!"

How gentle the old man's voice sounded as he said this, and how kindly his eyes beamed! Trafford thought there was something actually attractive in his features, and wondered he had not remarked it before.

Perhaps on that day when the old Judge well knew how agreeable he was, what stores of wit and pleasantry he was pouring forth, his convictions assured him that his guest was charmed. It was a very pardonable delusion,—he talked with great brilliancy and vigor. He possessed the gift—which would really seem to be the especial gift of Irishmen of that day—to be a perfect relater. To a story he imparted that slight dash of dramatic situation and dialogue that made it lifelike, and yet never retarded the interest nor prolonged the catastrophe. Acute as was his wit, his taste was fully as conspicuous, never betraying him for an instant, so long as his personal vanity could be kept out of view.

Trafford's eager and animated attention showed with what pleasure he listened; and the Chief, like all men who love to talk and know they talk well, talked all the better for the success vouchsafed to him. He even arrived at that stage of triumph in which he felt that his guest was no common man, and wondered if England really turned out many young fellows of this stamp,—so well read, so just, so sensible, so keenly alive to nice distinction, and so unerring in matters of taste.

"You were schooled at Rugby, sir, you told me; and Rugby has reason to be proud if she can turn out such young men. I am only sorry Oxford should not have put the fine edge on so keen an intellect."

Trafford blushed at a compliment he felt to be so unmerited, but the old man saw nothing of his confusion,—he was once again amongst the great scenes and actors of his early memories.

"I hope you will spare me another day before you leave Ireland. Do you think you could give me Saturday?" said the Chief, as his guest arose to take leave.

"I am afraid not, my Lord; we shall be on the march by that day."

"Old men have no claim to use the future tense, or I should ask you to come and see me when you come back again."

"Indeed will I. I cannot thank you enough for having asked me."

"Why are there not more young men of that stamp?" said the old Judge, as he looked after him as he went. "Why are they not more generally cultivated and endowed as he is? It is long since I have found one more congenial to me in every way. I must tell Beattie I like his friend. I regret not to see more of him."

It was in this strain Sir William ruminated and reflected; pretty much like many of us, who never think our critics so just or so appreciative as when they applaud ourselves.

CHAPTER XLII
NECESSITIES OP STATE

It is, as regards views of life and the world, a somewhat narrowing process to live amongst sympathizers; and it may be assumed as an axiom, that no people so much minister to a man's littleness as those who pity him.

Now, when Lady Lendrick separated from Sir William, she carried away with her a large following of sympathizers. The Chief Baron was well known; his haughty overbearing temper at the bar, his assuming attitude in public life, his turn for sarcasm and epigram, had all contributed to raise up for him a crowd of enemies; and these, if not individually well disposed to Lady Lendrick, could at least look compassionately on one whose conjugal fate had been so unfortunate. All *her* shortcomings were lost sight of in presence of *his* enormities, for the Chief Baron's temper was an Aaron's rod of irascibility, which devoured every other; and when the verdict was once passed, that "no woman could live with him," very few women offered a word in his defence.

It is just possible that if it had not been for this weight in the opposite scale, Lady Lendrick herself would not have stood so high. Sir William's faults, however, were accounted to her for righteousness, and she traded on a very pretty capital in consequence. Surrounded by a large circle of female friends, she lived in a round of those charitable dissipations by which some people amuse themselves; and just as dull children learn their English history through a game, and acquire their geography through a puzzle, these grown-up children take in their Christianity by means of deaf and dumb bazaars, balls for blind institutions, and private theatricals for an orphan asylum. This devotion, made easy to the lightest disposition, is not, perhaps, a bad theory,—at least, it does not come amiss to an age which likes to attack its gravest ills in a playful spirit, to treat consumption with cough lozenges, and even moderate the excesses of insanity by soft music. There is another good feature, too, in the practice: it furnishes occupation and employment to a large floating class which,' for the interest and comfort of society, it is far better should be engaged in some pursuit, than left free to the indulgence of censorious tastes and critical habits. Lady Lendrick lived a sort of monarch amongst these. She was the patroness of this, the secretary of that, and the corresponding member of some other society. Never was an active intelligence more actively occupied; but she liked it all, for she liked power, and, strange as it may seem, there is in a small way an exercise of power even in these petty administrations. Loud, bustling, overbearing, and meddlesome, she went everywhere, and did everything. The only sustaining hope of those she interfered with was that she was too capricious to persist in any system of annoyance, and was prone to forget to-day the eternal truths she had propounded for reverence yesterday.

I am not sure that she conciliated—I am not sure that she would have cared for—much personal attachment; but she had what certainly she did like, a large following of very devoted supporters. All her little social triumphs—and occasionally she had such—were blazoned abroad by those people who loved to dwell on the courtly attentions bestowed upon their favorite, what distinguished person had taken her "down" to dinner, and the neat compliment that the Viceroy paid her on the taste of her "tabinet."

It need scarcely be remarked that the backwater of all this admiration for Lady Lendrick was a swamping tide of ill-favor for her husband. It would have been hard to deny him ability and talent. But what had he made of his ability and talent? The best lawyer of the bar was not even Chief-Justice of the Queen's Bench. The greatest speaker and scholar of his day was unknown, except in the reminiscences of a few men almost as old as himself. Was the fault in himself, or was the disqualifying element of his nature the fact of being an Irishman? For a number of years the former theory satisfied all the phenomena of the case, and the restless, impatient disposition— irritable, uncertain, and almost irresponsible—seemed reason enough to deter the various English officials who came over from either seeking the counsels or following the suggestions of the bold Baron of the Exchequer. A change, however, had come, in pail; induced by certain disparaging articles of the English press as to the comparative ability of the two countries; and now it became the fashion to say that had Sir William been born on the sunnier side of St. George's Channel, and had his triumphs been displayed at Westminster instead of the Four Courts, there would have been no limit to the praise of his ability as a lawyer, nor any delay in according him the highest honors the Crown could bestow.

Men shook their heads, recalled the memorable "curse" recorded by Swift, and said, "Of course there is no favor for an Irishman." It is not the place nor the time to discuss this matter here. I would only say that a good deal of the misconception which prevails upon it is owing to the fact that the qualities which win all the suffrages of one country are held cheaply enough in the other. Plodding unadorned ability, even of a high order, meets little favor in Ireland, while on the other side of the Channel Irish quickness is accounted as levity, and the rapid appreciation of a question without the detail of long labor and thought, is set down as the lucky hit of a lively but very idle intelligence. I will not let myself wander away further in this digression, but come back to my story. Connected with this theory of Irish depreciation, was the position that but for the land of his birth Sir William would have been elevated to the peerage.

Of course it was a subject to admit of various modes of telling, according to the tastes, the opportunities, and the prejudices of the tellers. The popular version of the story, however, was this: that Sir William declined to press a claim that could not have been resisted, on account of the peculiarly retiring, unambitious character of him who should be his immediate successor. His very profession—adopted and persisted in, in despite of his father's wish—was a palpable renunciation of all desire for hereditary honor. As the old Judge said, "The *Libro d, Oro* of nobility is not the Pharmacopoeia;" and the thought of a doctor in the peerage might have cost "Garter" a fit of apoplexy.

Sir William knew this well,—no man better; but the very difficulties gave all the zest and all the flavor to the pursuit. He lived, too, in the hope that some Government official might have bethought him of this objection, that he might spring on him, tiger-like, and tear him in fragments.

"Let them but tell me this," muttered he, "and I will rip up the whole woof, thread by thread, and trace them! The noble duke whose ancestor was a Dutch pedler, the illustrious marquess whose great-grandfather was a smuggler, will have to look to it. Before this cause be called on I would say to them, better to retain me for the Crown! Ay, sirs, such is my advice to you."

While these thoughts agitated Sir William's mind, the matter of them was giving grave and deep preoccupation to the Viceroy. The Cabinet had repeatedly pressed upon him the necessity of obtaining the Chief Baron's retirement from the bench,—a measure the more imperative that while they wanted to provide for an old adherent, they were equally anxious to replace him in the House by an abler and readier debater; for so is it, when dulness stops the way, dulness must be promoted,—just as the most tumble-down old hackney-coach must pass on before my Lord's carriage can draw up.

"Pemberton must go up," said the Viceroy. "He made a horrid mess of that explanation t' other night in the House. His law was laughed at, and his logic was worse; he really must go on the bench. Can't you hit upon something, Balfour? Can you devise nothing respecting the Chief Baron?"

"He 'll take nothing but what you won't give him; I hear he insists on the peerage."

"I'd give it, I declare,—I 'd give it to-morrow. As I told the Premier t' other day, Providence always takes care that these law lords have rarely successors. They are life peerages and no more; besides, what does it matter a man more or less in 'the Lords'? The peer without hereditary rank and fortune is like the officer who has been raised from the ranks,—he does not dine at mess oftener than he can help it."

Balfour applauded the illustration, and resolved to use it as his own.

"I say again," continued his Excellency, "I'd give it, but they won't agree with me; they are afraid of the English bar,—they dread what the benchers of Lincoln's Inn would say."

"They'd only say it for a week or two," mumbled Balfour.

"So I remarked: you'll have discontent, but it will be passing. Some newspaper letters will appear, but Themis and Aristides will soon tire, and if they should not, the world who reads them will tire; and probably the only man who will remember the event three months after will be the silversmith who is cresting the covered dishes of the new creation. You think you can't go and see him, Balfour?"

"Impossible, my Lord, after what occurred between us the last time."

"I don't take it in that way. I suspect he 'll not bear any malice. Lawyers are not thin-skinned people; they give and take such hard knocks that they lose that nice sense of injury other folks are endowed with. I think you might go."

"I 'd rather not, my Lord," said he, shaking his head.

"Try his wife, then."

"They don't live together. I don't know if they're on speaking terms."

"So much the better,—she'll know every chink of his armor, and perhaps tell us where he is vulnerable. Wait a moment. There has been some talk of a picnic on Dalkey Island. It was to be a mere household affair. What if you were to invite her?—making of course the explanation that it was a family party, that no cards had been sent out; in fact, that it was to be so close a thing the world was never to hear of it."

"I think the bait would be irresistible, particularly when she found out that all her own set and dear friends had been passed over."

"Charge her to secrecy,—of course she'll not keep her word."

"May I say we 'll come for her? The great mystery will be so perfectly in keeping with one of the household carriages and your Excellency's liveries."

"Won't that be too strong, Balfour?" said the Viceroy, laughing.

"Nothing is too strong, my Lord, in this country. They take their blunders neat as they do their sherry, and I'm sure that this part of the arrangement will, in the gossip it will give rise to, be about the best of the whole exploit."

"Take your own way, then; only make no such mistake as you made with the husband. No documents, Balfour,—no documents, I beg;" and with this warning laughingly given, but by no means so pleasantly taken, his Excellency went off and left him.

CHAPTER XLIII
MR. BALFOUR'S MISSION

Lady Lendrick was dictating to her secretary, Miss Morse, the Annual Report of the "Benevolent Ballad-Singers' Aid Society," when her servant announced the arrival of Mr. Cholmondely Balfour. She stopped abruptly short at a pathetic bit of description,—"The aged minstrel, too old for erotic poetry, and yet debarred by the stern rules of a repressive policy from the strains of patriotic song,"—for, be it said parenthetically, Lady Lendrick affected "Irishry" to a large extent,—and, dismissing Miss Morse to an adjoining room, she desired the servant to introduce Mr. Balfour.

Is it fancy, or am I right in supposing that English officials have a manner specially assumed for Ireland and the Irish,—a thing like the fur cloak a man wears in Russia, or the snowshoes he puts on in Lapland, not intended for other latitudes, but admirably adapted for the locality it is made for? I will not insist that this theory of mine is faultless, but I appeal to a candid public of my own countrmen if they have not in their experience seen what may support it. I do not say it is a bad manner,—a presuming manner,—a manner of depreciation towards these it is used to, or a manner indicative of indifference in him who uses it. I simply say that they who employ it keep it as especially for Ireland as they keep their macintosh capes for wet weather, and would no more think of displaying it in England than they would go to her Majesty's levee in a shooting-jacket. Mr. Balfour was not wanting in this manner. Indeed, the Administration of which he formed a humble part were all proficients in it. It was a something between a mock homage and a very jocular familiarity, so that when he arose after a bow, deep and reverential enough for the presence of majesty, he lounged over to a chair and threw himself down with the ease and unconcern of one perfectly at home.

"And how is my Lady? and how are the fourscore and one associations for turnkeys' widows and dog-stealers' orphans doing? What's the last new thing in benevolence? Do tell me, for I've won five shillings at loo, and want to invest it."

"You mean you have drawn your quarter's salary, Mr. Balfour."

"No, by Jove; they don't pay us so liberally. We have the run of our teeth and no more."

"You forget your tongue, sir; you are unjust."

"Why, my Lady, you are as quick as Sir William himself; living with that great wit has made you positively dangerous."

"I have not enjoyed over-much of the opportunity you speak of."

"Yes, I know that; no fault of yours, though. The world is agreed on that point. I take it he's about the most impossible man to live with the age has yet produced. Sewell has told me such things of him!—things that would be incredible if I had not seen him."

"I beg pardon for interrupting, but of course you have not come to dilate on the Chief Baron's defects of temper to his wife."

"No, only incidentally,—parenthetically, as one may say,—just as one knocks over a hare when he's out partridge-shooting."

"Never mind the hare, then, sir; keep to your partridges."

"My partridges! my partridges! which are my partridges? Oh, to be sure! I want to talk to you about Sewell. He has told you perhaps how ill we have behaved to him,—grossly, shamefully ill, I call it."

"He has told me that the Government object to his having this appointment, but he has not explained on what ground."

"Neither can I. Official life has its mysteries, and, hate them as one may, they must be respected; he ought n't to have sold out,—it was rank folly to sell out. What could he have in the world better than a continued succession of young fellows fresh from home, and knowing positively nothing of horse-flesh or billiards?"

"I don't understand you, sir,—that is, I hope I misunderstand you," said she, haughtily.

"I mean simply this, that I'd rather be a lieutenant-colonel with such opportunities than I 'd be Chairman of the Great Overland."

"Opportunities—and for what?"

"For everything,—for everything; for game off the balls, on every race in the kingdom, and as snug a thing every night over a devilled kidney as any man could wish for. Don't look shocked,—it's all on the square; that old hag that was here last week would have given her diamond ear-rings to find out something against Sewell, and she could n't."

"You mean Lady Trafford?"

"I do. She stayed a week here just to blacken his character, and she never could get beyond that story of her son and Mrs. Sewell."

"What story? I never heard of it."

"A lie, of course, from beginning to end; and it's hard to imagine that she herself believed it."

"But what was it?"

"Oh, a trumpery tale of young Trafford having made love to Mrs. Sewell, and proposed to run off with her, and Sewell having played a game at écarté on it, and lost,—the whole thing being knocked up by Trafford's fall. But you must have heard it! The town talked of nothing else for a fortnight."

"The town never had the insolence to talk of it to *me*."

"What a stupid town! If there be anything really that can be said to be established in the code of society, it is that you may say anything to anybody about their relations. But for such a rule how could conversation go on?—who travels about with his friend's family-tree in his pocket? And as to Sewell,—I suppose I may say it,—he has not a truer friend in the world than myself."

She bowed a very stiff acknowledgment of the speech, and he went on: "I 'm not going to say he gets on well with his wife,—but who does? Did you ever hear of him who did? The fact I take to be this, that every one has a certain capital of good-nature and kindliness to trade on, and he who expends this abroad can't have so much of it for home consumption; that's how your insufferable husbands are such charming fellows for the world! Don't you agree with me?"

A very chilling smile, that might mean anything, was all her reply.

"I was there all the time," continued he, with unabated fluency. "I saw everything that went on: Sewell's policy was what our people call non-intervention; he saw nothing, heard nothing, believed nothing; and I will say there 's a great deal of dignity in that line; and when your servant comes to wake you in the morning, with the tidings that your wife has run away, you have established a right before the world to be distracted, injured, overwhelmed, and outraged to any extent you may feel disposed to appear."

"Your thoughts upon morals are, I must say, very edifying, sir."

"They 're always practical, so much I will say. This world is a composite sort of thing, with such currents of mixed motives running through it, if a man tries to be logical he is sure to make an ass of himself, and one learns at last to become as flexible in his opinions and as elastic as the great British constitution.

"I am delighted with your liberality, sir, and charmed with your candor; and as you have expressed your opinion so freely upon my husband and my son, would it appear too great a favor if I were to ask what you would say of myself?"

"That you are charming, Lady Lendrick, —positively charming," replied he, rapturously. "That there is not a grace of manner, nor a captivation, of which you are not mistress; that you possess that attraction which excels all others in its influence; you render all who come within the sphere of your fascination so much your slaves that the cold grow enthusiastic, the distrustful become credulous, and even the cautious reserve of office gives way, and the well-trained private secretary of a Viceroy betrays himself into indiscretions that would half ruin an aide-de-camp."

"I assure you, sir, I never so much as suspected my own powers."

"True as I am here; the simple fact is, I have come to say so."

"You have come to say so! What do you mean?"

With this he proceeded to explain that her Excellency had deputed him to invite Lady Lendrick to join the picnic on the island. "It was so completely a home party, that, except himself and a few of the household, none had even heard of it. None but those really intimate will be there," said he; "and for once in our lives we shall be able to discuss our absent friends with that charming candor that gives conversation its salt. When we had written down all the names, it was her Excellency said, 'I 'd call this perfect if I could add one more to the list.' 'I'll swear I know whom you mean,' said his Excellency; and he took his pencil and wrote a line on a card. 'Am I right?' asked he. She nodded, and said, 'Balfour, go and ask her to come. Be sure you explain what the whole thing is, how it was got up, and that it must not be talked of.' Of course, do what one will, these things do get about. Servants will talk of them, and tradespeople talk of them, and we must expect a fair share of ill-nature and malice from that outer world which was not included in the civility; but it can't be helped. I believe it's one of the conditions of humanity, that to make one man happy you may always calculate on making ten others miserable."

This time Lady Lendrick had something else to think of besides Mr. Balfour's ethics, and so she only smiled and said nothing.

"I hope I 'm to bring back a favorable answer," said he, rising to take leave. "Won't you let me say that we 're to call for you?"

"I really am much flattered. I don't know how to express my grateful sense of their Excellencies' recollection of me. It is for Wednesday, you say?"

"Yes, Wednesday. We mean to leave town by two o'clock, and there will be a carriage here for you by that hour. Will that suit you?"

"Perfectly."

"I am overjoyed at my success. Good-bye till Wednesday, then." He moved towards the door, and then stopped. "What was it? I surely had something else to say. Oh, to be sure, I remember. Tell me, if you can, what are Sir William's views about retirement: he is not quite pleased with us just now, and we can't well approach him; but we really would wish to meet his wishes, if we could manage to come at them." All this he said in a sort of careless, easy way, as though it were a matter of little moment, or one calling for very slight exercise of skill to set right.

"And do you imagine he has taken me into his confidence, Mr. Balfour?" asked she, with a smile.

"Not formally, perhaps,—not what we call officially; but he may have done so in that more effective way termed 'officiously.'"

"Not even that. I could probably make as good a guess about your own future intentions as those of the Chief Baron."

"You have heard him talk of them?"

"Scores of times."

"And in what tone,—with what drift?"

"Always as that of one very ill-used, hardly treated, undervalued, and the like."

"And the remedy? What was the remedy?"

"To make him a peer,—at least, so his friends say."

"But taking that to be impossible, what next?"

"He becomes 'impossible' also," said she, laughing.

"Are we to imagine that a man of such intelligence as he possesses cannot concede something to circumstances,—cannot make allowances for the exigencies of 'party,'—cannot, in fact, take any other view of a difficulty but the one that must respond to his own will?"

"Yes; I think that is exactly what you are called on to imagine. You are to persuade yourself to regard this earth as inhabited by the Chief Baron, and some other people not mentioned specifically in the census."

"He is most unreasonable, then."

"Of course he is; but I wouldn't have you tell him so. You see, Mr. Balfour, the Chief imagines all this while that he is maintaining and upholding the privileges of the Irish Bar. The burden of his song is, 'There would have been no objection to my claim had I been the Chief Baron of the English Court.'"

"Possibly," murmured Balfour; and then, lower again, "Fleas are not—"

"Quite true," said she, for her quick ear caught his words,—"quite true. Fleas are not lobsters,—bless their souls! But, as I said before, I'd not remind them of that fact. 'The Fleas' are just sore enough upon it already."

Balfour for once felt some confusion. He saw what a slip he had made, and now it had damaged his whole negotiation. Nothing but boldness would avail now, and he resolved to be bold.

"There is a thing has been done in England, and I don't see why we might not attempt it in the present case. A great lawyer there obtained a peerage for his wife—"

She burst out into a fit of laughter at this, at once so hearty and so natural that at last he could not help joining, and laughing too.

"I must say, Mr. Balfour," said she, as soon as she could speak,—"I must say there is ingenuity in your suggestion. The relations that subsist between Sir William and myself are precisely such as to recommend your project."

"I am not so sure that they are obstacles to it. I have always heard that he had a poor opinion of his son, who was a common-place sort of man that studied medicine. It could be no part of the Chief Baron's plan to make such a person the head of a house. Now, he likes Sewell, and he dotes on that boy,—the little fellow I saw at the Priory. These are all elements in the scheme. Don't you think so?"

"Let me ask you one question before I answer yours: Does this thought come from yourself alone, or has it any origin in another quarter?"

"Am I to be candid?"

"You are."

"And are *you* to be confidential?"

"Certainly."

"In that case," said he, drawing a long breath, as though about to remove a perilous weight off his mind, "I will tell you frankly, it comes from authority. Now, don't ask me more,—not another question. I have already avowed what my instructions most imperatively forbid me to own,— what, in fact, would be ruin to me if it were known that I revealed. What his Excellency—I mean, what the other person said was, 'Ascertain Lady Lendrick's wishes on this subject; learn, if you can,—but, above all, without compromising yourself,—whether she really cares for a step in rank; find out, if so, what aid she can or will lend us.' But what am I saying? Here am I entering upon the whole detail? What would become of me if I did not know I might rely upon you?"

"It's worth thinking over," said she, after a pause.

"I should think it is. It is not every day of our lives such a brilliant offer presents itself. All I ask, all I stipulate for, is that you make no confidences, ask no advice from any quarter. Think it well over in your own mind, but impart it to none, least of all to Sewell."

"Of course not to *him*," said she, resolutely, for she knew well to what purposes he would apply the knowledge.

"Remember that we want to have the resignation before Parliament meets,—bear that in mind. Time is all-important with us; the rest will follow in due course." With this he said "Good-bye," and was gone.

"The rest will follow in due course," said she to herself, repeating his last words as he went. "With your good leave, Mr. Balfour, the 'rest' shall precede the beginning."

Was n't it Bolingbroke that said constitutional government never could go on without lying,—audacious lying too? If the old Judge will only consent to go, her Ladyship's peerage will admit of a compromise. Such was Mr. Balfour's meditation as he stepped into his cab.

CHAPTER XLIV
AFTER-DINNER THOUGHTS

Her Majesty's—th had got their orders for Malta, and some surmised for India, though it was not yet known; but all agreed it was hard,—"confoundedly hard," they called it. "Had n't they had their turn of Inidan service?—how many years had that grim old major passed in the Deccan,—what weary winters had the bronzed bald captain there spent at Rangoon!"

How they inveighed against the national niggardliness that insisted on making a small army do the work of a large one! How they scouted the popular idea that regiments were treated alike and without favoritism! *They* knew better. They knew that if they had been the Nine Hundred and Ninth, or Three Thousand and First, there would have been no thought of sending them back to cholera and jungle fever. Some, with a little sly flattery, ascribed the order to their efficiency, and declared that they had done their work so well at Gonurshabad, the Government selected them at once when fresh troubles were threatening; and a few old grumblers, tired of service, sick of the Horse Guards,—not over-enamored of even life,—agreed that it was rank folly to join a regiment where the Lieutenant-Colonel was not a man of high connections; as they said, "If old Cave there had been a Lord George or even an Honorable, we 'd have had ten years more of home service."

With the exception of two or three raw subalterns who had never been out of England, and who wanted the glory of pig-sticking and the brevet to tell tiger stories, there were gloom and depression everywhere. The financially gifted complained that as they had all or nearly all bought their commissions, there was no comparison between the treatment administered to them and to officers in any foreign army; and such as knew geography asked triumphantly whether a Frenchman, who could be only sent to Africa, or an Austrian, whose most remote banishment was the "Banat," was in the same position as an unfortunate Briton, who could be despatched to patrol the North Pole to-day, and to-morrow relieve guard at New Zealand? By a unanimous vote it was carried that the English army was the worst paid, hardest worked, and most ill-treated service in Europe; but the roast-beef played just at the moment, and they went in to dinner.

As the last bars of that prandial melody were dying away, two men crossed the barrack-yard towards the mess-house. They were in close confabulation, and although evidently on their way to dinner, showed by their loitering pace how much more engrossed they were by the subject that engaged them than by any desire for the pleasures of the table. They were Colonel Cave and Sewell.

"I can scarcely picture to my mind as great a fool as that," said Sewell, angrily. "Can you?"

"I don't know," said Cave, slowly and doubtingly. "First of all, I never was heir to a large estate; and, secondly, I was never, that I remember, in love."

"In love! in fiddlestick. Why, he has not seen the girl this year and half; he scarcely knows her. I doubt greatly if she cares a straw for him; and for a caprice—a mere caprice—to surrender his right to a fine fortune and a good position is absolute idiocy; but I tell you more, Cave, though worse—far worse." Here his voice grew harsh and grating, as he continued: "When I and other men like me played with Trafford, we betted with the man who was to inherit Holt. When I asked the fellow to my house, and suffered a certain intimacy—for I never liked him—it was because he represented twelve thousand a year in broad acres. I 'd stand a good deal from a man like that, that I 'd soon pull another up for,—eh?"

The interrogative here puzzled Cave, who certainly was not a concurring party to the sentiment, and yet did not want to make it matter of discussion.

"We shall be late,—we've lost our soup already," said he, moving more briskly forward.

"I 'd no more have let that fellow take on him, as he did under my roof, than I 'd suffer him to kennel his dogs in my dressing-room. You don't know—you can't know—how he behaved." These words were spoken in passionate warmth, and still there was that in the speaker's manner that showed a want of real earnestness; so it certainly seemed to Cave, who secretly determined to give no encouragement to further disclosures.

"There are things," resumed Sewell, "that a man can't speak on,—at least, he can only speak of them when they become the talk of the town."

"Come along, I want my dinner. I'm not sure I have not a guest, besides, who does not know any of our fellows. I only remembered him this instant. Is n't this Saturday?"

"One thing I 'll swear,—he shall pay me every shilling he owes me, or he does not sail with the regiment. I 'll stand no nonsense of renewals; if he has to sell out for it, he shall book up. You have told him, I hope, he has nothing to expect from my forbearance?"

"We can talk this all over another time. Come along now,—we 're very late."

"Go on, then, and eat your dinner; leave me to my cigar—I 've no appetite. I 'll drop in when you have dined."

"No, no; you shall come too,—your absence will only make fellows talk; they are talking already."

"Are they? and in what way?" asked he, sternly.

"Nothing seriously, of course," mumbled Cave, for he saw how he had fallen into an indiscretion; "but you must come, and you must be yourself too. It's the only way to meet flying rumors."

"Come along, then," said Sewell, passing his arm within the other's; and they hurried forward without another word being spoken by either.

It was evident that Sewell's appearance caused some surprise. There was a certain awkward significance in the way men looked at him and at each other that implied astonishment at his presence.

"I didn't know you were down here," said the old Major, making an involuntary explanation of his look of wonderment.

"Nothing very remarkable, I take it, that a man is stopping at his own house," said Se well, testily. "No—no fish. Get me some mutton," added he to the mess-waiter.

"You have heard that we 've got our orders," said a captain opposite him.

"Yes; Cave told me."

"I rather like it,—that is, if it means India," said a very young-looking ensign.

Sewell put up his eye-glass and looked at the speaker, and then, letting it drop, went on with his dinner without a word.

"There 's no man can tell you more about Bengal than Colonel Sewell there," said Cave, to some one near him. "He served on the staff there, and knows every corner of it."

"I wish I did n't, with all my heart. It's a sort of knowledge that costs a man pretty dearly."

"I 've always been told India was a capital place," said a gay, frank-looking young lieutenant, "and that if a man did n't drink, or take to high play, he could get on admirably."

"Nor entangle himself with a pretty woman," added another.

"Nor raise a smashing loan from the Agra Bank," cried a third.

"You are the very wisest young gentlemen it has ever been my privilege to sit down with," said Sewell, with a grin. "Whence could you have gleaned all these prudent maxims?"

"I got mine," said the Lieutenant, "from a cousin. Such a good fellow as he was! He always tipped me when I was at Sandhurst, but he's past tipping any one now."

"Dead?"

"No; I believe it would be better he were; but he was ruined in India,—'let in' on a race, and lost everything, even to his commission."

"Was his name Stanley?"

"No, Stapyleton,—Frank Stapyleton,—he was in the Grays."

"Sewell, what are you drinking?" cried Cave, with a loudness that overbore the talk around him. "I can't see you down there. You 've got amongst the youngsters."

"I am in the midst of all that is agreeable and entertaining," said Sewell, with a smile of most malicious meaning. "Talk of youngsters, indeed! I'd like to hear where you could match them for knowledge of life and mankind."

There was certainly nothing in his look or manner as he spoke these words that suggested distrust or suspicion to those around him, for they seemed overjoyed at his praise, and delighted to hear themselves called men of the world. The grim old Major at the opposite side of the table shook his head thoughtfully, and muttered some words to himself.

"They 're a shady lot, I take it," said a young captain to his neighbor, "those fellows who remain in India, and never come home; either they have done something they can't meet in England, or they want to do things in India they couldn't do here."

"There's great truth in that remark," said Sewell. "Captain Neeves, let us have a glass of wine together. I have myself seen a great deal to bear out your observation."

Neeves colored with pleasure at this approval, and went on: "I heard of one fellow—I forget his name—I never remember names; but he had a very pretty wife, and all the fellows used to make up to her, and pay her immense attention, and the husband rooked them all at écarté, every man of them."

"What a scoundrel!" said Sewell, with energy. "You ought to have preserved the name, if only for a warning."

"I think I can get it, Colonel. I'll try and obtain it for you."

"Was it Moorcroft?" cried one.

"Or Massingbred?" asked another.

"I'll wager a sovereign it was Dudgeon; wasn't it Dudgeon?"

But no; it was none of the three. Still, the suggestions opened a whole chapter of biographical details, in which each of these worthies vied with the other. No man ever listened to the various anecdotes narrated with a more eager interest than Sewell. Now and then, indeed, a slight incredulity—a sort of puzzled astonishment that the world could be so very wicked, that there really were such fellows—would seem to distract him; but he listened on, and even occasionally asked an explanation of this or of that, to show the extreme attention he vouchsafed to the theme.

To be sure, their attempts to describe the way some trick was played with the cards or the dice, how the horse was "nobbled" or the match "squared," were neither very remarkable for accuracy nor clearness. They had not been well "briefed," as lawyers say, or they had not mastered their instructions. Sewell, however, was no captious critic; he took what he got, and was thankful.

When they arose from the table, the old Major, dropping behind the line of those who lounged into the adjoining room, caught a young officer by the arm, and whispered some few words in his ear.

"What a scrape I'm in!" cried the young fellow as he listened.

"I think not, this time; but let it be a caution to you how you talk of rumors in presence of men who are strangers to you."

"I say, Major," asked a young captain, coming up hurriedly, "isn't that Sewell the man of the Agra affair?"

"I don't think I'd ask him about it, that's all," said the Major, slyly, and moved away.

"I got amongst a capital lot of young fellows at my end of the table—second battalion men, I think,—who were all new to me, but very agreeable," said Sewell to Cave, as he sipped his coffee.

"You'd like your rubber, Sewell, I know," said Cave; "let us see if we haven't got some good players."

"Not to-night,—thanks,—I promised my wife to be home early; one of the chicks is poorly."

"I want so much to have a game with Colonel Sewell," said a young fellow. "They told me up at Delhi that you hadn't your equal at whist or billiards."

Sewell's pale face grew flushed; but though he smiled and bowed, it was not difficult to see that his manner evinced more irritation than pleasure.

"I say," said another, who sat shuffling the cards by himself at a table, "who knows that trick about the double ace in picquet? That was the way Beresford was rooked at Madras."

"I must say good-night," said Sewell; "it's a long drive to the Nest You 'll come over to breakfast some morning before you leave, won't you?"

"I 'll do my best. At all events, I 'll pay my respects to Mrs. Sewell;" and with a good deal of hand-shaking and some cordial speeches Sewell took his leave and retired.

Had any one marked the pace at which Sewell drove home that night, black and dark as it was, he would have said, "There goes one on some errand of life or death." There was something of recklessness in the way he pushed his strong-boned thoroughbred, urging him up hill and down without check or relief, nor slackening rein till he drew up at his own door, the panting beast making the buggy tremble with the violent action of his respiration. Low muttering to himself, the groom led the beast to the stable, and Sewell passed up the stairs to the small drawing-room where his wife usually sat.

She was reading as he entered; a little table with a tea equipage at her side. She did not raise her eyes from her book when he came in; but whether his footstep on the stair had its meaning to her quick ears or not, a slight flush quivered on her cheek, and her mouth trembled faintly.

"Shall I give you some tea?" asked she, as he threw himself into a seat. He made no answer, and she laid down her book, and sat still and silent.

"Was your dinner pleasant?" said she, after a pause.

"How could it be other than pleasant, Madam," said he, fiercely, "when they talked so much of *you?*"

"Of *me?* — talked of *me?*"

"Just so; there were a set of young fellows who had just joined from another battalion, and who discoursed of you, of your life in India, of your voyage home, and lastly of some incidents that were attributed to your sojourn here. To me it was perfectly delightful. I had my opinion asked over and over again, if I thought that such a levity was so perfectly harmless, and such another liberty was the soul of innocence? In a word, Madam, I enjoyed the privilege, very rarely accorded to a husband, I fancy, to sit in judgment over his own wife, and say what he thought of her conduct."

"Was there no one to tell these gentlemen to whom they were speaking?" said she, with a subdued, quiet tone.

"No; I came in late and took my place amongst men all strangers to me. I assure you I profited largely by the incident. It is so seldom one gets public opinion in its undiluted form, it 's quite refreshing to taste it neat. Of course they were not always correct. I could have set them right on many points. They had got a totally wrong version of what they called the 'Agra row,' though one of the party said he was Beresford's cousin."

She grasped the table convulsively to steady herself, and in so doing threw it down, and the whole tea equipage with it.

"Yes," continued he, as though responding to this evidence of emotion on her part,—"yes; it pushed one's patience pretty hard to be obliged to sit under such criticism."

"And what obliged you, sir? was it fear?"

"Yes, Madam, you have guessed it. I was afraid—terribly afraid to own I was your husband."

A low faint groan was all she uttered, as she covered her face with her hands. "I had next," continued he, "to listen to a dispute as to whether Trafford had ever seriously offered to run away with you or not. It was almost put to the vote. Faith, I believe my casting voice might have carried the thing either way if I had only known how to give it." She murmured something too low to be heard correctly, but he caught at part of it, and said: "Well, that was pretty much what I suspected. The debate was, however, adjourned; and as Cave called me by my name at the moment, the confidences came to an abrupt conclusion. As I foresaw that these youngsters, ignorant of life and manners as they were, would be at once for making apologetic speeches and such-like, I stole away and came home, *more domestico*, to ruminate over my enjoyments at my own fireside."

"I trust, sir, they were strangers to your own delinquencies. I hope they had no unpleasant reminders to give you of yourself."

"Pardon, Madam. They related several of what you pleasantly call my delinquencies, but they only came in as the by-play of the scene where you were the great character. We figured as brigands. It was *you* always who stunned the victim; *I* only rifled his pockets—fact, I assure you. I'm sorry that china is smashed. It was Saxe,—wasn't it?"

She nodded.

"And a present of Trafford's too! What a pity! I declare I believe we shall not have a single relic of the dear fellow, except it be a protested bill or two." He paused a moment or so, and then said, "Do you know, it just strikes me that if they saw how ill—how shamefully you played your cards in this Trafford affair, they 'd actually absolve you of all the Circe gifts the world ascribes to you."

She fixed her eyes steadfastly on him, and as her clasped hands dropped on her knees, she leaned forward and said: "What do you mean by it? What do you want by this? If these men, whose insolent taunts you had not courage to arrest or to resent, say truly, whose the fault? Ay, sir, whose the fault? Answer me, if you dare, and say, was not my shame incurred to cover and conceal *yours?*"

"Your tragedy-queen airs have no effect upon me. I 've been too long behind the scenes to be frightened by stage thunder. What is past is past. You married a gambler; and if you shared his good luck, you oughtn't to grumble at partaking his bad fortune. If you had been tired of the yoke, I take it you 'd have thrown it behind you many a day ago."

"If I had not done so, you know well why," said she, fiercely.

"The old story, I suppose,—the dear darlings upstairs. Well, I can't discuss what I know nothing about. I can only promise you that such ties would never bind *me*."

"I ask you once again what you mean by this?" cried she, as her lips trembled and her pale cheeks shook with agitation. "What does it point to? What am I to do? What am I to be?"

"That's the puzzle," said he, with an insolent levity; "and I 'll be shot if I can solve it! Sometimes I think we 'd do better to renounce the partnership, and try what we could do alone; and sometimes I suspect—it sounds odd, does n't it?—but I suspect that we need each other."

She had by this time buried her face between her hands, and by the convulsive motion of her shoulders, showed she was weeping bitterly.

"One thing is certainly clear," said he, rising, and standing with his back to the fire,—"if we decide to part company, we have n't the means. If either of us would desert the ship, there 's no boat left to do it with."

She arose feebly from her chair, but sank down again, weak and overcome.

"Shall I give you my arm?" asked he.

"No; send Jane to me," said she, in a voice barely above a whisper.

He rang the bell, and said, "Tell Jane her mistress wants her;" and with this he searched for a book on the table, found it, and strolled off to his room, humming an air as he went.

CHAPTER XLV
THE TIDELESS SHORES

They who only know the shores of the Mediterranean in the winter months, and have but enjoyed the contrast—and what a contrast!—between our inky skies and rain-charged atmosphere with that glorious expanse of blue heaven and that air of exciting elasticity,—they, I say, can still have no conception of the real ecstasy of life in a southern climate till they have experienced a summer beside the tideless sea.

Nothing is more striking in these regions than the completeness of the change from day to night. It is not alone the rapidity with which darkness succeeds,—and in this our delicious twilight is ever to be regretted; what I speak of is the marvellous transition from the world of sights and sounds to the world of unbroken silence and dimness. In the day the whole air rings with life. The flowers flaunt out their gorgeous petals, not timidly or reluctantly, but with the bold confidence of admitted beauty. The buds unfold beneath your very eyes, the rivulets sing in the clear air, and myriads of insects chirp till the atmosphere seems to be charged with vitality. This intense vitality is the striking characteristic of the scene; and it is to this that night succeeds, grand, solemn, and silent, at first to all seeming in unrelieved blackness, but soon to be displayed in a glorious expanse of darkest, deepest blue, with stars of surpassing size. To make this change more effective, too, it is instantaneous. It was but a moment back, and you were gazing on the mountain peaks bathed in an opal lustre, the cicala making the air vibrate with his song; a soft sea-breeze was blowing, and stirring the oranges amongst the leaves; and now all is dim and silent and breathless, as suddenly as though an enchanter's wand had waved and worked the miracle.

In a little bay—rather a cleft in the shore than a bay—bounded by rocks and backed by a steep mountain overgrown with stunted olives, stood a small cottage,—so very small that it looked rather like a toy house than a human dwelling, a resemblance added to now as the windows lay wide open, and all the interior was a blaze of light from two lamps. All was still and silent within; no human being was to be seen, nor was there a sign of life about the place; for it was the only dwelling on the eastern shore of the island, and that island was Maddalena, off Sardinia.

In a little nook among the rocks, close to the sea, sat Tom and Lucy Lendrick. They held hands, but were silent; for they had come down into the darkness to muse and ponder, and drink in the delicious tranquillity of that calm hour. Lucy had now been above a week on the island, and every day Tom made progress towards recovery. She knew exactly, and as none other knew, what amount of care and nursing he would accept of without resistance,—where companionship would gratify and where oppress him; she knew, besides, when to leave him to the full swing of his own wild discursive talk, and never to break in upon his moods of silent reflection.

For upwards of half an hour they had sat thus without a word, when Tom, suddenly turning round, and looking towards the cottage, said, "Is n't this the very sort of thing we used to imagine and wish for long ago, Lucy?"

"It was just what was passing through my mind. I was thinking how often we longed to have one of the islands on Lough Derg, and to go and live there all by ourselves."

"We never dreamed of anything so luxurious as this, though. We knew nothing of limes and oranges, Lucy. We never fancied such a starry sky, or an air so loaded with perfume. I declare," cried he, with more energy, "it repays one for all the disappointment, to come and taste the luxury of such a night as this."

"And what is the disappointment you speak of, Tom?"

"I mean about our project-that blessed mine, by which we were to have amassed a fortune, and which has only yielded lead enough to shoot ourselves with."

"I never suspected that," said she, with a sigh.

"Of course you never did; nor am I in a great hurry to tell it even now. I'd not whisper it if Sir Brook were on the same island with us. Do you know, girl, that he resents a word against the mine as if it was a stain upon his own honour. For a while I used to catch up his enthusiasm, and think if we only go on steadily, if we simply persist, we are sure to succeed in the end. But when week after week rolled over, and not a trace of a mineral appeared when the very workmen said we were toiling in vain when I felt half-ashamed to meet the jeering questions of the neighbours, and used to skulk up to the shaft by the back way,—he remarked it, and said to me one morning, 'I am afraid, Tom, it is your sense of loyalty to me that keeps you here, and not your hope of success. Be frank, and tell me if this be so.' I blundered out something about my determination to share his fate, whatever it might be, and it would have been lucky if I had stopped there; but I went on to say that I thought the mine was an arrant delusion, and that the sooner we turned our backs on it, and addressed our energies to another quarter, the better. 'You think so?' said he, looking almost fiercely at me. 'I am certain of it,' said I, decisively; for I thought the moment had come when a word of truth could do him good service. He went out without speaking, and instead of going to Lavanna, where the mine is, he went over to Cagliari, and only came home late at night. The next morning, while we were taking our coffee before 'setting out, he said to me, 'Don't strap on your knapsack to-day. I don't mean you should come down into the shaft again.' 'How so?' asked I; 'what have I said or done that could offend you?' 'Nothing, my dear boy,' said he, laying his hand on my shoulder; 'but I cannot bear you should meet this dreary life of toil without the one thing that can lighten its gloom—Hope. I have managed, therefore, to raise a small sum on the mine; for,' said he, with a sly laugh, 'there are men in Cagliari who don't take the despondent view you have taken of it; and I have written to my old friend at the Horse Guards to give you a commission, and you shall go and be a soldier.' And leave you here, sir, all alone?' 'Far from alone, lad. I have that companion which you tell me never joined *you*. I have Hope with *me*.'

"'Then I'll stay too, sir, and try if he'll not give me his company yet. At all events, I shall have *yours*; and there is nothing I know that could recompense me for the loss of it.' It was not very easy to turn him from his plan, but I insisted so heartily-for I'd have stayed on now, if it were to have entailed a whole life of poverty-that he gave in at last; and from that hour to this, not a word of other than agreement has passed between us. For my own part, I began to work with a will, and a determination that I never felt before; and perhaps I overtaxed my strength, for I caught this fever by remaining till the heavy dews began to fall, and in this climate it is always a danger."

"And the mine, Tom—did it grow better?" "Not a bit. I verily believe we never saw ore from that day. We got upon yellow clay, and lower down upon limestone rock, and then upon water; and we are pumping away yet, and old Sir Brook is just as much interested by the decrease of the water as if he saw a silver floor beneath it. 'We've got eight inches less this morning, Tom; we are doing famously now.' I declare to you, Lucy, when I saw his fine cheery look and bright honest eye, I thought how far better this man's fancies are than the hard facts of other people; and I'd rather have his great nature than all the wealth success could bring us."

"My own dear brother!" was all she could say, as she grasped his hand, and held it with both her own.

"The worst of all is, that in the infatuation he feels about this mining project he forgets everything else. Letters come to him from agents and men of business asking for speedy answers; some occasionally come to tell that funds upon which he had reckoned to meet certain payments had been withdrawn from his banker long sinca When he reads these, he ponders a moment, and mutters, 'The old story, I suppose. It is so easy to write Brook Fossbrooke;' and then the whole seems to pass out of his mind, and he'll say, 'Come along, Tom; we must push matters a little; I'll want some coin by the end of the month.'

"When I grew so weak that I could n't go to the mine, the accounts he used to give me daily made me think we must be prospering. He would come back every night so cheery and so hopeful, and his eyes would sparkle as he 'd tell of a bright vein that they 'd just 'struck.' He owned that the men were less sanguine, but what could they know? They had no other teaching than the poor experiences of daily labor. If they saw lead or silver, they believed in it. To him, however, the signs of the coming ore were enough; and then he would open a paper full of dark earth in which a few shining particles might be detected, and point them out to me as the germs of untold riches. 'These are silver, Tom, every one of them; they are oxidized, but still perfectly pure. I 've seen the natives in Ceylon washing earth not richer than this;' and the poor fellow would make this hopeful tidings the reason for treating me to champagne, which in an unlucky moment the doctor said would be good for me, and which Sir Brook declared always disagreed with him. But I don't believe it, Lucy,—I don't believe it! I am certain that he suffered many a privation to give me luxuries that he would n't share. Shall I tell you the breakfast I saw him eating one morning? I had gone to his room to speak to him before he started to the mine, and, opening the door gently, I surprised him at his breakfast,—a piece of brown bread and a cup of coffee without milk was his meal, to support him till he came home at nightfall. I knew if he were aware that I had seen him that it would have given him great distress, so I crept quietly back to my bed, and lay down to think of this once pampered, flattered gentleman, and how grand the nature must be that could hold up uncomplaining and unshaken under such poverty as this. Nor is it that he ignores the past, Lucy, or strives to forget it,—far from that. He is full of memories of bygone events and people, but he talks of his own part in the grand world he once lived in as one might talk of another individual; nor is there the semblance of a regret that all this splendor has passed away never to return. He will be here on Sunday to pay us a visit, Lucy; and though perhaps you 'll find him sadly changed in appearance, you 'll see that his fine nature is the same as ever."

"And will he persist in this project, Tom, in spite of all failure and in defiance of hope?"

"That's the very point I 'm puzzled about. If he decide to go on, so must I. I 'll not leave him, whatever come of it."

"No, no, Tom; that I know you will not do."

"His confidence of success is unshaken. It was only t' other night, as we sat at a very frugal supper, he said, 'You 'll remember all this, Tom, one of these days; and as you sip your Burgundy, you 'll tell your friends how jolly we thought ourselves over our little acid wine and an onion.' I did not dare to say what was uppermost in my thoughts, that I disbelieved in the Burgundy era."

"It would have been cruel to have done it."

"He had the habit, he tells me, in his days of palmiest prosperity, of going off by himself on foot, and wandering about for weeks, roughing it amongst all sorts of people,—-gypsies, miners, charcoal-burners in the German forests, and such-like. He said, without something of this sort, he would have grown to believe that all the luxuries he lived amongst were *bona fide* necessities of life. He was afraid too, he said, they would become part of him; for his theory is, never let your belongings master your own nature."

"There is great romance in such a man."

"Ah! there you have it, Lucy; that's the key to his whole temperament; and I 'd not be surprised if he had been crossed in some early love."

"Would that account for all his capricious ways?" said she, smiling.

"My own experiences can tell me nothing; but I have a sister who could perhaps help me to an explanation. Eh, Lucy? What think you?"

She tried to laugh off the theme, but the attempt only half succeeded, and she turned away her head to hide her confusion.

Tom took her hand between his own, and patted it affectionately.

"I want no confessions, my own dear Lucy," said he, gently; "but if there is anything which, for your own happiness or for my honor, I ought to know, you will tell me of it, I am certain."

"There is nothing," said she, with a faint gasp.

"And you would tell me if there had been?"

She nodded her head, but did not trust herself to speak.

"And grandpapa, Lucy?" said he, trying to divert her thoughts from what he saw was oppressing her; "has he forgiven me yet, or does he still harp on about my presumption and self-sufficiency?"

"He is more forgiving than you think, Tom," said she, smiling.

"I am not so sure of that. He wrote me a long letter some time back,—a sort of lecture on the faults and shortcomings of my disposition, in which he clearly showed that if I had all the gifts which my own self-confidence ascribed to me, and a score more that I never dreamed of, they would go for nothing,—absolutely nothing, so long as they were allied with my unparalleled—no, he did n't call it impudence, but something very near it. He told me that men of my stamp were like the people who traded on credit, and always cut a sorry figure when their accounts came to be audited; and, perhaps to stave off the hour of my bankruptcy, he enclosed me fifty pounds."

"So like him!" said she, proudly.

"I suppose it was. Indeed, as I read his note, I thought I heard him talking it. There was an acrid flippancy about it that smacked of his very voice."

"Oh, Tom, I will not let you say that."

"I 'll think it all the same, Lucy. His letter brought him back to my mind so palpably that I thought I stood there before him on that morning when he delivered that memorable discourse on my character after luncheon."

"Did you reply to him?"

"Yes, I replied," said he, with a dry sententiousness that sounded as though he wished the subject to drop.

"Do tell me what you said. I hope you took it in good part. I am sure you could not have shown any resentment at his remarks."

"No; I rather think I showed great forbearance. I simply said, 'My dear Lord Chief Baron, I have to acknowledge the receipt of your letter, of which I accept everything but the enclosure.—I am, faithfully yours.'"

"And refused his gift?"

"Of course I did. The good counsel without the money, or the last without the counsel, would have beeu all very well; but coming together, in what a false position the offer placed me! I remember that same day we happened to have an unusually meagre dinner, but I drank the old man's health after it in some precious bad wine; and Sir Brook, who knew nothing about the letter, joined in the toast, and pronounced a very pretty little eulogium on his vigor and energy; and thus ended the whole incident."

"If you only knew him better, Tom! if you knew him as I know him!"

Tom shrugged his shoulders, and merely said, "It was nicely done, though, not to tell *you* about this. There was delicacy in *that*."

Lucy went on now to relate all his kind intentions towards Tom when the news of his illness arrived,—how he had conferred with Beattie about sending out a doctor, and how, at such a sacrifice to his own daily habits, he had agreed that she should come out to Cagliari. "And you don't know how much this cost him, Master Tom," said she, laughing; "for however little store you may lay by my company, he prizes it, and prizes it highly too, I promise you; and then there was another reason which weighed against his letting me come out here,—he has got some absurd prejudice against Sir Brook. I call it absurd, because I have tried to find out to what to trace it, and could not; but a chance expression or two that fell from Mrs. Sewell leads me to suppose the impression was derived from them."

"I don't believe he knows the Sewells. I never heard him speak of them. I 'll ask when he comes over here. By the way, how do you like them yourself?"

"I scarcely know. I liked her at first,—that is, I thought I should like her; and I fancied, too, it was her wish that I might—but—"

"But what? What does this 'but' mean?"

"It means that she has puzzled me, and my hope of liking her depends on my discovering that I have misunderstood her."

"That's a riddle, if ever there was one! but I suppose it comes to this, that if you have read her aright you do not like her."

"I wish I could show you a letter she wrote me."

"And why can't you?"

"I don't think I can tell you even that, Tom."

"What a mysterious damsel you have grown! Does this come of your living with that great law lord, Lucy? If so, tell him from me he has spoiled you sadly. How frank you were long ago!"

"That is true," said she, sighing.

"How I wish we could go back to that time, with all its dreaminess and all its castle-building. Do you remember, Lu, when we used to set off of a morning in the boat on a voyage of discovery, as we called it, and find out new islands and new creeks, and give them names?"

"Do I not? Oh, Tom, were we not a thousand times happier then than we knew we were?"

"That's a bit of a bull, Lucy, but it's true all the same. I know all you mean, and I agree with you."

"If we had troubles, what light ones they were!"

"Ay, that's true. We were not grubbing for lead in those days, and finding only quartz; and our poor hearts, Lucy, were whole enough then." He gave a half malicious laugh as he said this; but, correcting himself quickly, he drew her towards him and said, "Don't be angry with me, dear Lu; you know of old what a reckless tongue I 've got."

"Was that thunder, Tom? There it is again. What is it?"

"That's a storm getting up. It's coming from the south'ard. See how the drift is flying overhead, and all the while the sea beneath is like a mill-pond! Watch the stars now, and you 'll see how, one by one, they will drop out, as if extinguished; and mark the little plash—it is barely audible—that begins upon the beach. There! did you hear that,—that rushing sound like wind through the trees? That's the sea getting up. How I wish I was strong enough to stay out here. I 'd like to show you a 'Levanter,' girl,—a regular bit of Southern passion, not increasing slowly, like a Northern wrath, but bursting out in its full fury in an instant. Here it comes!" and as he spoke two claps of thunder shook the air, followed by a long clattering roll like musketry, and the sea, upheaving, surged heavily hither and thither, while the air was still and calm; and then, as though let loose from their caverns, the winds swept past with a wild shrill whistle that swelled into a perfect roar. The whole surface of the sea became at once white, and the wind, sweeping across the crests of the waves, carried away a blinding drift that added to the darkness. The thunder, too, rolled on unceasingly, and great flashes of lightning broke through the blackness, and displayed tall masts and spars of ships far out to sea, rocking fearfully, and in the next instant lost to sight in the dense darkness.

"Here comes the rain, and we must run for it," said Tom, as a few heavy drops fell. A solemn pause in the storm ensued, and then, as though the very sky was rent, the water poured down in cataracts. Laughing merrily, they made for the cottage, and though but a few yards off, were drenched thoroughly ere they reached it.

"It's going to be a terrific night," said Tom, as he passed from window to window, looking to the bars and fastenings. "The great heat always brings one of the Levant storms, and the fishermen here know it so well that on seeing certain signs at sunset they draw up all their boats on shore, and even secure the roofs of their cabins with strong spars and stones."

"I hope poor old Nicholas is safe by this time. Could he have reached Cagliari by this?" said Lucy.

"Yes, he is snug enough. The old rogue is sitting at his supper this minute, cursing the climate and the wine and the place, and the day he came to it."

"Come, Tom! I think he bears everything better than I expected."

"Bears everything better! Why, child, what has he to bear that you and I have not to bear? Is there one privation here that falls to his share without coming to us?"

"And what would be the value of that good blood you are so proud of, Tom, if it would not make us as proof against petty annoyances as against big dangers?"

"I declare time and place make no change on you. You are the same disputatious damsel here that you used to be beside the Shannon. Have I not told you scores of times you must never quote what one has once said, when it comes in opposition to a present opinion?"

"But if I cease to quote you, Tom, whence am I to derive those maxims of wisdom I rely upon so implicitly?"

"Take care, young lady,—take care," said he, shaking his finger at her. "Every fort has its weak side. If you assail me by the brain, I may attack you at the heart! How will it be then, eh?" Coloring till her face and neck were crimson, she tried to laugh; but though her lips parted, no sound came forth, and after a second or two of struggle, she said, "Good-night," and rushed away.

"Good-night, Lu," cried he after her. "Look well to your window-fastenings, or you will be blown away before morning."